HAMMON FALLS

Dave Hoing & Roger Hileman

ALL THINGS THAT MATTER PRESS

Ta se ag cuir baisteach,
Cora,
Ach ta tu go halainn

(It is raining,
Cora,
But you are beautiful)

NOW AND THEN

WILL
Waterton, Iowa
May 2008

The day after a monster tornado leveled half of Parkersburg, a small town west of Waterton, ninety-four-year-old Will Hammon relaxed in the walk-in Jacuzzi his daughter Katie had insisted he install. He resented the necessity of the thing at first, but the jets of water did feel good against his joints, and the whir of the motor was soothing.

From where he reclined he could see out the east window. It was Memorial Day. The sun splintered through the elms and maples that edged his property line. A warm breeze carried in the smell of lilac blossoms. It was such a beautiful spring morning, in contrast to yesterday's horrific storms. If that twister had veered just a few degrees south instead of moving straight east, it would have gone through Will's living room.

But it hadn't, and Waterton had only gotten some false-alarm sirens and a good drenching. Still, the devastation looked like a war zone. It was all over the news, and would be for weeks.

After a rain like that, the grass would sprout up like crazy. It'd need to be cut today, once it dried out. Will still did his own lawn work, although his Landon riding mower was half as old as he and nearly as decrepit. He did all the repairs himself, too. His muscles might not work like they used to, but his hands had never lost their magic with engines. Any engine, any time. He could wear a blindfold and his hands would remember.

Will loved the smell and feel of grease, loved the *idea* of it. With any luck the mower would need tinkering first.

The telephone rang.

"Shut up," he said. Probably a neighbor, checking on him again. Katie always had people spying on him, when she wasn't doing it herself. The phone was across the hall in his bedroom. Too much bother to get out of the tub. That's what answering machines were for.

After the machine's canned greeting he made out Katie's voice over the jet's motor. "Dad, come on, pick up. I know you're there. I need to talk to you. You on the john? Dad?"

Click.

She'd call back. That tone of voice? Wouldn't be long, either.

Might as well face the inevitable. Muttering to himself, Will pulled the plug and waited for the water to drain enough to open the door. The slip-free rubber mat on the floor reminded him once more of the necessary indignities of longevity.

The phone rang again, right on schedule.

Still wet, Will walked naked across to his bedroom to pick up the receiver.

Rows of photographs lined the hallway walls, pictures of Will and Elaine, of Katie and her son Charlie, of fishing excursions on the Oak River and vacations to mountains and beaches, and of backyard croquet games where Will would rather whack someone else's ball onto the neighbor's lawn than hit his own through the hoops. He lost Elaine to emphysema in '89. Katie's husband abandoned her in '91, and now she and Charlie didn't visit as often as they used to. Nevertheless, life was okay for him, for all of them. It was okay.

He picked up the receiver. "What?"

"Dad," Katie said, "you never told me there was a gas station under the construction site. *Your* gas station, Will's Standard, from the 1930s. Matthews checked the city records."

Will's Standard? Will thought. Those were the days. "I sold that place back in '42, '43," he said. "Sometime during the war, anyway. Gas rationing was killing me. I thought they tore it down."

"They *did* tear it down, Dad, but, dammit, there's an old tank buried there."

"That's where I used to keep the gas."

Katie had always shown annoyance with silence. After several seconds she said, "We'll have to test the goddamn thing before we can dig any further. If it takes a spark…"

"After over 60 years? What could be left?"

"Has to be tested anyway. It'll cost me at least three days and a couple thousand bucks to get the EPA people here. This project's going to make or break my company, Dad."

To Katie *every* inconvenience was an emergency that would make or break her company. Will sighed. "That was some storm yesterday," he said. "I ever tell you how your great grandma Margaret survived the Pomeroy cyclone in '93? That'd be *eighteen* ninety-three."

"Probably since I was in Mom's womb. Dad, I don't care about the tornado. I mean, it's too bad, but I've got my own problems."

Eight people dead, and she had her own problems. "Just thought you might be interested," Will said. "That much damage, they'll need a lot of construction."

"I have a project, Dad. I can't take on any more right now."

"Why are you at work on a holiday?"

"I stopped in to read last week's reports."

"Well, I was in your damned Jacuzzi. Anything else you want?"

After another long pause Katie said, "We unearthed a wooden box. It had a silver cross in it. Pretty big one, with a circle behind the cross. The silver's tarnished, but it looks like it might've been worth something once. Maybe could be again if it was cleaned up. The box has some initials on it. Can't make them all out, but it looks like there's an H and two M's. Like in Hammon."

Not just a cross, a Celtic cross. My God. Will's father George left it for him at the station in '37. Will never brought it home, never even took it out of the box. He'd simply pushed it under the counter and forgotten about it.

Will lay back on his bed and looked up at the only photograph to adorn his bedroom wall. Not Elaine's, not Katie's, not Charlie's. Just this one. His grandmother had given it to him. Yellowed and tattered behind the glass, the picture had hung in the bedroom of every house he had ever owned. In it a teenaged boy wearing the uniform of the British infantry stood alone on a vast scarred plain, layers of clouds stopped mid-swirl by the camera's lens. The boy's clothes rippled in long-silent wind. He carried an army pack on his back and a bayoneted rifle in his right hand. The thumb and index finger of his left hand grasped the visor of his dress cap. His face was slightly out of focus, as if a sudden small movement blurred the image. Only one eye, the right one, was clearly defined. Even squinting against the wind, it captured light in a way that made the whole photograph revolve around it, a whirlpool of gray spiraling into, or out of, a single bright point. In that eye Will saw the sum of the teenager's life. Although there was much more to come, his tale was already one of surprise, and sadness, and fear.

Handwritten on the bottom of the picture were the words, "Ypres, 1915," the year Will turned one.

For the thousandth time, the ten-thousandth, the millionth, Will studied the soldier in the photograph. It was his father George at nineteen.

The cross had a different provenance, but its story was the same.

"Dad?" Katie said. "You there?"

"Yeah," he said.

Christ, George, what do you want?

LUKA
Waterton, Iowa
March 1914

"There's nothing I can do," Officer Barrows said the morning after Orville "Luka" Curtis's daughter Cora had run away from home. Barrows was sipping coffee from a glass mug and trying to read Sunday's *Waterton Record*.

"Wrong answer," Luka said. Cora was seventeen and in the ninth month of pregnancy. She had snuck out of church right under the maid's nose and vanished into thin air. Since the father of her child, George Hammon, was also missing, it wasn't hard to figure out who'd made off with her.

"They're married, right?" Barrows said.

"On paper," Luka said.

"Then they're legal adults. They can go where they please, when they please."

"So you're just going to sit there?"

Barrows shrugged. "Where's the crime?"

"George Hammon kidnapped my little girl!"

"A man can't kidnap his own wife." He held up his mug. "Pour you a cup?"

Luka ran a beer distribution warehouse, but his influence and financial interests went deeper than that. "Goddamn it, I *own* this city," he said. "I could have your job—"

"I'm not one of your lackeys, Curtis. Save that shit for someone who's impressed by it. No law has been broken. Now get out of here and quit wasting my time."

***

That afternoon Luka retained a man named Greene from the William Burns Detective Agency. Luka paced and drank and smoked cigars and paced and drank some more as Greene grilled the Finnish maid, Birgitta, in the parlor. Birgitta had accompanied Cora to church yesterday with explicit instructions to keep an eye on her.

"She needed to use the toilet," Birgitta said quietly, repeating what she'd told Luka yesterday. "Pregnant girls must go often. The baby pushes on their bladder." She drew out her vowels and ended each sentence in a rising tone that made statements sound like questions.

"Why didn't you go with her?" Greene said. He wrote something on a note pad.

"Miss Cora is seventeen. She does not require my assistance in the toilet!"

"She couldn't have done this alone, Missus—?"

"*Miss*. Auf Ursin."

"This was obviously planned. Someone had to help her. Someone had to be waiting for her outside. A pregnant girl couldn't have just walked away unseen on a Sunday morning. Who helped her, Miss auf Ursin? Was it you?"

Birgitta looked at Luka, then back at the detective. "She said she was going to the toilet, that is all. I did not leave my pew."

"Any thoughts on who it might have been?"

"Her husband, George Hammon. No other."

"If I understand Mr. Curtis, his daughter and Hammon were not allowed to communicate. How could Hammon have gotten word to her?"

"I do not know."

"See any strange people lurking about?"

"People do not *lurk* at church."

The detective wrote on his pad again. Luka had paced close enough to see the word, *Lying*? "All right," Greene said. "You can go for now."

After Birgitta left Luka said, "She didn't like George, either. I don't think she was involved. She's just stupid and careless."

"You weren't in church?"

"I've had late shipments, and some ass to chew."

"You talked to the pastor? The congregation?"

"Pastor was busy singing hymns. A couple of people saw Cora get up but didn't pay attention where she went."

"I'll interview them all again, of course. What about Margaret Hammon?"

"Maggie thought her son was too good for Cora. She opposed the marriage, never mind my daughter's reputation. But she's as anxious to find George as I am Cora. She's hired a Pinkerton's."

"Hmmph," Greene said. "Fat lot of good *that* will do her." He stood up and stuffed the notepad into his back pocket. "You'll be hearing from me."

***

By Wednesday morning, Luka was still waiting. He hadn't slept more than an hour or two at a stretch since Sunday, hadn't eaten or bathed at all. He looked and felt like shit.

He lived in a prestigious home on Middlesex Boulevard, the second-best neighborhood in Waterton, behind Gloire de Matin Island, where the city's old money families gravitated. Luka was new money. After his wife Emma succumbed to cancer of the womb in 1907, Cora was all he had left, the only person he cared about. Without her, the house seemed cavernous and empty. Every creak and moan of the frame, every rustling of wind, was magnified a thousand times, crying out, *She's gone, she's gone, she's gone.*

And behind the cacophony of the house, his conscience whispered, *You did this to yourself.*

Luka was stretched out on his bed, wide awake, when Greene returned that afternoon.

Nobody knew a thing, the detective claimed. He'd even talked to some of Cora and George's friends. "Want worse news?" he said, standing stiffly before Luka.

"No." Luka lit a cigar, if for no other reason than to mask his own stink. "I want Cora."

"I tracked down a passenger at the Illinois Central who said they saw a white girl kiss an old black man. The passenger was so shocked she didn't notice if the girl was pregnant or who else she might have been with—"

"No daughter of mine would kiss a nigger," Luka said.

"Even if it was her, she didn't board the train. The depots keep carbons of every ticket sold. Your daughter and Hammon probably wouldn't have traveled under their own names, but I checked all the carbons at every station in town and accounted for the names on them. All real people. Nothing from the cabbing services, either."

"Including Kline's?" Luka said. "George used to work there."

"Including Kline's. Hammon doesn't own a motor car. One of his mother's servants does, but the vehicle isn't missing. According to police, not a single horse, carriage, or automobile has been stolen from anywhere in northeast Iowa in the past two weeks."

"Jesus Christ," Luka said. "Did she just step out that door and *evaporate?*"

"They probably never left town. My guess is someone's hiding them until it's safe to get away."

Luka hadn't thought of that. "Or until the baby is born. Get out of here," he said to Greene. "Don't come back without Cora or an address I can find her at. We clear?"

"Crystal," the detective said as he walked out the door.

Nobody, nothing, none.

She's gone, she's gone, she's gone.

You did this to yourself.

Luka stubbed out his cigar and opened another expensive bottle of wine.

***

The sun still rose, the world still turned, and business went on. Although he would never give up on Cora, ordinary things demanded Luka's attention: a delivery here, a bill there, rats in the warehouse, cracks in the casks, water in the beer.

Twelve days after Cora's disappearance he was on the phone with Chicago when someone knocked on his door. Birgitta was in her room, fretting over some letter she received from her cousin out east, so she didn't hear the pounding. Luka slammed the phone down in mid-sentence, hoping Greene had finally earned his money.

He was surprised to find Margaret Hammon and her young attorney, Arlen Kelper, standing on his stoop.

What the hell? Maggie would never lower herself to visiting him. She considered him white trash, despite his home in the second-best neighborhood in Waterton.

"May we come in?" she said. She was dressed in a navy winter coat, too heavy for the weather. Her hair was pulled back in a bun as always, and rigid as glass.

"What's this about?"

"You know what it's about," Kelper said.

"You've found Cora!"

"Yes," Maggie said, not meeting his eyes. At forty-one, she was two years older than Luka. She was a handsome woman, but she looked fifty. She had always looked fifty. She was probably born looking fifty. "I received news from Buffalo," she said.

"Buffalo, New York?"

"From a doctor in Buffalo. I felt I should come in person. Orville...," she said.

Oh, no.

"Is Cora all right?" he said.

Margaret looked at him, then away.

Kelper cleared his throat. "Mr. Curtis, your daughter died in childbirth."

Although Luka heard the words, it was as if the lawyer had spoken in tongues. "In Buffalo, New York?" he said stupidly. "They ran away to *Buffalo*?"

A single tear cut a line through Margaret's rouge. "Yes, Orville," she said, "they went to Buffalo. I don't know how or why."

"The child survived," Kelper said. "A boy."

"My maid and I will be traveling to New York to get him," Maggie said.

The child survived. Luka still wasn't grasping what they were telling him. "Where's George?" he said. "Is he coming home?"

"Nobody knows where George is," Maggie said.

GEORGE
Ypres, Belgium
May 1915

The pop of the guns came later, after the bullets had already whisked by. The bullets themselves made the same sound whether they struck trench walls or a man's chest: *plock, plock. Plock. Plock plock plock.* In his short time with the Dorset Regiment, George Hammon had lost several boys he'd come to think of as friends. All had been within arm's reach, having a smoke, praying, telling a joke. One was rereading a letter from his sweetheart. A high-pitched sizzle preceded the *plock,* then came the grunt, the look of surprise, the distant pop, the blood, the collapse. Sometimes the bodies simply fell down dead. Other times they twitched and thrashed a bit. Those with a final breath left to them inevitably gasped out for their mothers or wives, but for most the last word spoken before the *plock* became their last word ever.

Gerry's aim was always a few feet left, right, or above George. So far the only blood he'd gotten on himself was from his fellow troops. He crouched in the trench as he sloshed behind Mick O'Leary, the genial Irish corporal who was unreeling telephone wire from a spool. The spool's clanking seemed loud enough to attract every gunner in the enemy's arsenal.

"Don't let it tangle," Mick said.

A cannon shell burst in the plain behind them, spraying water and mud. At least the Germans weren't using gas in this attack. The regiment had been promised masks, but none had arrived. Soldiers had been forced to use urine-soaked kerchiefs for protection. The gas stank less but hurt more.

George peered over the lip of the trench. "That was close."

"Get your head down!" Mick said.

George was nineteen, and didn't much care if he ever saw twenty, but when another shell exploded nearby, he ducked. Mick stumbled in a rut on the trench floor. The spool banged his knee as he fell into the muck. In helping him up, George noticed how raw and blistered the man's hands were. "You okay?"

Filth dripped from Mick's face. A spot of mud was wedged in the gap between his two front teeth. He loosened it with his tongue and spit it out. "Can life be better than this?"

"I could carry the spool."

"How about you just order me a wireless? There's a good fellow." He shook water from his uniform jacket, then tested his weight on his bruised knee. The shelling continued. "Got a smoke?"

"Matches are drenched."

"Like everything else," Mick said. He picked up the spool. "Well, come on, then."

The sky opened up with wind and rain just as they arrived at a T in the trench.

"Which way?" George said.

Sizzle, *plock*, pop. Booming of artillery, rumbles of thunder. Gunpowder and decay wafted through the rain.

"Hell if I remember. One slop hole's the same as the next." Mick nodded to the right. "I think they're over there."

The trench was shallower once they turned the corner, and they had to crawl to avoid exposing themselves to the gunfire. Travel was slow and tedious. They were already on their elbows and knees in mud, and the weight of the pack and rifle on their backs pushed them down farther. With rain filling the trench at an alarming rate, the telephone wire was under water most of the time. Twice it looped around Mick's shoes. Mick's hands were too battered to extricate himself. George did it for him, although the incessant wetness was starting to affect him, too. His own fingers were wrinkled and aching and pale as dead flesh.

Freed of the wire the second time, Mick slumped against the trench wall to catch his breath. "Jesus and Mary," he said, "but that smoke would taste good about now."

"Yeah," George said.

They forced themselves to move. The rain and the shelling did not abate. The bullets were *splatting* rather than *plocking* as the ground became saturated. Finally, after a few hundred yards they heard voices. Mick stopped so abruptly that George nearly rammed his helmet into his companion's backside.

"Give me some warning!" George said.

"Just wanted to be sure they're not speaking German, lad."

***

That night in a bunker carved into the plains of Belgium, a medic taped Mick's hands. The shelling had let up for the moment. George huddled in a blanket on a bench, trying to doze. His uniform was still wet.

Many of the men of the Dorset Regiment were asleep around him, but just as many were awake, too nervous or exhausted for sleep.

"Not so tight," Mick said to the medic. He drew a long puff from the cigarette clenched between his teeth, then exhaled the smoke through his nose. Ashes drooped from the end of the cigarette. "Flick my butt, will you?"

The medic grunted indifferently and continued to wrap the Irishman's hands. "Flick your own fagg, Paddy." He spoke in a nearly indecipherable geordie dialect.

Mick jerked his head, and the ashes dropped onto the medic's boot. "So, Georgie, tell me a story."

George pulled the blanket around his ears. He liked being called Georgie. His best friend Lewis, back home, used to call him that. "Not now, Mick."

"Why's it always 'Not now, Mick?' What's a Yank doing in a British regiment?"

"What's an Irishman?"

"Home Rule, lad. We help them now, they keep their promise after the war."

"You might all be ruled from Berlin by then."

The medic secured the last piece of tape to Mick's hand. "Enough of that kind of talk, Private," he said to George, or at least that was what it sounded like. "We'll salute the Kaiser's ass with English boots, no thanks to the colonies."

"Can't feel my fingers," Mick said.

"Won't hurt when you pick potatoes, then." The medic stood and snapped his bag shut. "Didn't ask for either of you."

"Piss off," Mick said, and the medic moved on to the other side of the bunker where a man lay wheezing for breath. Mick smiled his gap-toothed smile at George. "He's on our side, right?"

"Makes me feel warm inside."

"Now, about that story. You underage?"

"I'm old enough."

"What makes a Yank leave the green fields of America and run away to war? I'm thinking it must be a lass, eh? There's always a lass."

George slumped sideways onto the bench and closed his eyes. "Not now, Mick."

MARGARET
Hammon Falls, Iowa
November 1915

George's son suffered from nightmares. He'd wake screaming at some bad dream or imaginary apparition, and wouldn't quiet down until one of Margaret's servants, Ed or Estella, rocked him back to sleep.

Margaret had named the boy William, after her father. She and Estella had traveled all the way to Buffalo, New York, to retrieve him. George was long gone by then, leaving behind no trace. All that was ever found was the Curtis girl's suitcase in a boarding house near the train station. Although the little slut was technically married to George, Margaret refused to call her Hammon.

George didn't know his son had survived, and so had no reason to come looking for him. William was crying now, accompanied by the creaking of the rocker.

Margaret looked out her bedroom window at the woods on the north end of Gloire de Matin Island. The season's first snow had fallen, dusting the trees with a beautiful patina of white. A blustery wind was blowing, though, rattling the windows, coming in through unseen gaps in the house. Margaret pulled her housecoat tighter. She could tolerate cold and ice, but she hated the wind, *hated* it. She drew the drapes closed and sat on her bed. The room was dark. She removed the pins from her hair, letting it fall down over her shoulders. She used to have lovely hair.

A second Thanksgiving had come and gone without George. Estella had prepared an excellent feast and set a fine table: candles, lace, the best china and silverware. Margaret sat by herself at the head of her formal dining table. Ed brought out the various courses. The food was superb, but she ate little, just enough to keep from hurting Estella's feelings. The servants, as was their custom, took their meal in the kitchen.

William's highchair was also in the kitchen, where Estella fed him strained fruit and warmed milk from a bottle. Alone at her table, Margaret had heard the boy gurgling happily.

Holidays were the worst, holidays and George's birthday. He'd be nineteen now, wherever he was.

Margaret slowly brushed her hair, one stroke, two, three, four, five. The clock on the mantle ticked, measuring out the long moments of her solitude. George couldn't spare a few words for his mother to say he was all right? A letter, a telegram, a telephone call? *Hello, Mother, don't worry about me, I'm fine.* Was that too much to ask?

She understood, now, how furious he must have been after the debacle at the courthouse. The marriage had been Orville's doing.

Margaret had acquiesced only under irresistible pressure. They'd both agreed their children would not live together afterward. George was only a teenager. Every emotion was heightened in young people, their anger more righteous, their passion more melodramatic. He probably thought he loved this Cora creature. Perhaps he did.

All right, so he was hurt, he felt betrayed. But was that any reason to lash out with his silence *forever*? Margaret hadn't taken a pregnant girl on a journey halfway across the continent. She hadn't caused Cora's complications, and she wasn't responsible for her death. That was God's doing.

Margaret had experience dealing with God's wrath.

She brought up the flame on the oil lamp on her desk. It threw off harsh shadows that merged into the darkness of the room. The little flame mocked her mood with its twinkling.

When troubled she usually calmed her mind by reading passages from *Ecclesiastes*, her favorite book from the Bible. *A time for every purpose under heaven.* Tonight, however, she couldn't concentrate. Instead, she thought about Orville Curtis. He had lost his daughter, and yet in all this time he had never seen, nor asked to see, the only part of Cora that still remained, her son. Margaret had often thought of contacting him. She never had, not once.

William's crying had subsided, although the rocker still creaked. Ed or Estella, probably Estella, was still comforting him, stroking his hair, making little cooing noises.

Margaret turned back the covers on the bed. She used to do that for George when he was young. She could still picture his sweet face looking up at her as she tucked him in.

A face that had grown so hateful after the sham wedding.

He must have been heartbroken when the girl died. Of course he was. She had felt the same when her husband G.W. had been killed in the Spanish-American War in '98. But she had soldiered through her pain, stuck it out, made another new life for herself. Even with all her travails, she realized, as George did not, that she possessed no monopoly on misfortune. Self-pity was a sin, or should be, and running away solved nothing.

Margaret rose and peered anxiously out the window again, as if George might emerge from the trees. With the oil lamp at her back and the night in front of her, she could see her reflection in the glass, transparent and wraithlike, her image superimposed upon the view of the snowy woods.

What a sight. A woman her age, looking like this, raising a child? Lord, she was tired.

The wind spit sleet at the window. Margaret shivered. She dimmed the oil lamp and lay down. The pillow was cold against her cheek.

Where are you, George?

Come home, son.

Just come home.

GEORGE
Picardy, France
June 30-July 1, 1916

It had been raining for weeks, but by the end of June 1916 the weather finally dried out. The upcoming battle promised to be a bloody one. Thirteen British divisions would lead an attack near the River Somme, hoping to draw enemy forces away from Verdun. Although the Royal Flying Corps had achieved air supremacy over the region, nobody was optimistic. A week of artillery bombardment failed to soften the German lines, partly because a third of the American-made shells failed to explode. The mood was so bleak that even the normally stoic Captain Cornish seemed morose. His customary pep speech to the troops the night before sounded more like a farewell than a rallying cry.

George and Mick had served together for nearly eighteen months and become great friends. George finally told his story, and Mick told his. In a tent full of men and murmurs, Mick lay bare-chested on his bunk, absently stroking the silver cross he always wore around his neck. The cross's flared tines were backed with a circle engraved with intricate rune-like markings.

"So," Mick said, cigarette dangling from his lips, "what about it, Georgie-boy? Time you wrote your Mum, eh?"

"You aren't falling for Corny's doom and gloom?" George said, folding clothes and arranging them in his duffle.

Mick put out the cigarette. When he smiled, the gap between his teeth lightened the darkness. It was hard to be afraid in the presence of that silly grin. "I plan to live forever, lad. I was more worried about you."

"Gerry couldn't hit me in an outhouse with two guns and dynamite. I'll be okay."

"Gerry, hell." Mick sat up and took his pistol from beneath the bunk. "You don't put pen to paper this very minute, I'll shoot you myself."

"She's better off not knowing."

"That's it, then." Mick launched himself from his bunk, minus the pistol, and tackled George. The two wrestled on the ground while their comrades gathered round, egging them on with taunts of "Kill the Yank!" and "Kill Paddy!"

George clapped a headlock on Mick, who pretended to gurgle and choke. The crowd applauded, but stopped when Mick easily broke the hold and kissed George on the neck.

"Jesus!" George sputtered, jumping to his feet. "I didn't know you were a fairy boy!"

Mick panted and grinned. "Sorry, Georgie, been meaning to tell you."

"No, I liked it."

There was a silent but ominous pause until George broke the tension by winking. Everybody laughed, and the men went back to their writing and praying. George helped Mick up. They sat next to each other on George's bunk.

"Brit bastards," Mick whispered, without much malice. He wasn't good at malice. He had a thin trickle of blood on his chest where one of the tines of his cross had scratched him while they wrestled. He dipped his finger in the blood, then touched the finger to his tongue. "Hmm," he said. "Blood on silver."

"Blood on the cross," George said.

"It's a bad sign."

"You're going to live forever, remember?"

"This is *how* we live forever, lad. Never forget that."

George reached out his hand. "May I?"

Mick removed the chain and cross from his neck, wiped the blood from it with a piece of gauze, and placed it in George's palm. "It goes to my eldest son Tommy."

George examined the beautifully engraved surface and the circular motif behind the cross. "Never seen one like this. What's the circle for?"

"It's Celtic. Goes back to the Druids, but the priests'll tell you it's a halo representing God's eternal love." Mick pressed the gauze against the small cut on his chest. "And being a good Catholic, well, I guess it *is* a halo. Been in my family since before America *had* families."

"I'm not Catholic, and I don't have family anymore."

"You got your Mum. Someday you'll find another lass and make wee Georgies."

"I'm done with children," George said. He gave the cross back. "Sure is pretty."

Mick hung it around his neck. "That it is."

***

The assault began at 7:30 the next morning, preceded ten minutes before by the detonation of mines under bridges and near the enemy lines. By sundown almost twenty thousand English troops lay dead, with another thirty-seven thousand injured, missing, or captured. It was the bloodiest day in the history of the British army.

George and Mick were assigned to an offensive north of the Albert-Bapaume Road, near a stream that fed into the River Ancre. The objective was to break through the first German line and regain a precious few meters of French soil. The same men who had called George "Yank" and Mick "Paddy" in the tent fought and died bravely at their side on the field—and died, and died, and died. The cacophony of artillery, not-so-distant pops, and *plocks* drowned out the officers' commands. Smoke from their own guns obscured their vision. In a few hours the dead outnumbered the living, and still the troops had made no progress. The carnage in the morning so overwhelmed George that he spent as much time on his knees vomiting as on his feet fighting. The wind was against the Germans, so they didn't use gas, but the stench of released bowels and exposed guts forced George to put on his mask. Others did the same. It didn't help.

By afternoon George had become inured to death. The bodies of his comrades were no more startling than driftwood on a beach, their blood simply wet spots in the dirt. Hard to believe it was only four years ago he'd seen his first dead person, the shrouded corpse of his mother's stepmother, Clara. Then, being in the same coach with her had nearly unnerved him. After today he could lie in a coffin next to her remains and not lose a moment's sleep.

Captain Cornish fell just as the sun dipped below the horizon. By dark only a few of George's regiment remained alive, he and Mick and a handful of others. They crouched in the shelter of some trees near the stream. Nobody spoke. They had all taken their masks off. Bodies bobbed in the water, their uniforms billowing like great gelatinous lumps, but even the miasma of bloated flesh was preferable to the hot stale air they drew in through the filters.

The stars were unusually bright and distinct, swathed by the Milky Way. And still the Germans kept firing. Bullets striking trees had a sound all their own, a dull thump followed by the tiny spray of bark shards raining down.

Take away the bodies and the stink, George thought, and this river, these trees, could pass for the little cove on Red Hawk Creek where he and Cora used to swim. He looked at his dead comrades in the water. In the moonlight the rounded bits of clothing protruding above the surface could pass for the turtles that had sunned themselves on the toppled cottonwood log in the Red Hawk.

After a lull in the shooting, footsteps approached. "Stay down," a sergeant ordered, but Mick rose to have a better look.

"Georgie," he whispered, and *plock*. He tumbled sideways into the stream. Without thinking George plunged in after him. He heard panicked voices and a few more gunshots. Then someone said, "*Seht zu, daß sie alle tot sind.*" George thought there was regret in the voice. Germans waded into the stream and started bayoneting every body that wasn't obviously dead. George slipped beneath Mick, finding a gap at his friend's armpit just large enough for his nose. He felt a sickening thud as an enemy blade penetrated Mick's breastbone and came out his back. The force of the thrust pushed them under, and the removal of the bayonet pulled them back up. George wasn't harmed.

There could be no tears under water. As soon as the Germans had moved away, George reached around Mick and searched beneath his shirt for the Celtic cross. Finding it, he snapped the chain and slipped the cross into his own breast pocket. There was no speaking under water, either, but George spoke anyway, and the name "Tommy" floated to the surface in the form of a bubble.

***

George had no sense of time. He must have stayed in the stream for hours, freezing, making his way from corpse to corpse until the corpses ran out. Eventually the sound of voices and gunfire faded, and he came ashore. He crept stealthily through the darkness, taking cover in bushes and behind barns. Avoiding both enemy and friend, he was soon warming himself in the morning sun, alone in the French countryside. He had no intention of going back.

George Hammon, who had run away to war, now ran away from it.

LUKA
Hammon Falls, Iowa
July 1916

The area that would become Electrical Park was purchased by the Waterton Park Commission in 1893 from the unincorporated township known in those days as Johnson's Landing. The land was situated in the clearing of a wooded glade on the west side of the Oak River. Gloire de Matin Island lay just to the northeast between the convergence of the Oak, some of its channels, and Red Hawk Creek. Just across the river was Chautauqua Park, where visiting preachers on the Circuit Chautauqua shouted the word of the Lord to the faithful. William Jennings Bryan lectured there several times, including in 1903 when he repeated his famous "Cross of Gold" speech.

In the first years of the new century the City of Waterton built amusement rides, a funhouse, and a new ballroom equipped with electric lights and lavatories with flush toilets. There was also an electric trolley service to bring revelers in from all parts of the city. On Saturday nights an orchestra would play while young people danced until midnight. Beer was sold for a nickel a glass to anyone who could pass for twenty-one.

The fairgrounds east of the ballroom boasted carnival rides such as the Spiral Terror rollercoaster, a Ferris wheel, and a spider-cabled contraption called Aero-Thrill, with hanging chairs made up to look like biplanes. From the top of the wheel one could see for miles, from Cedar Crossing to the northwest to downtown Waterton to the southeast. The impressive new Block's Department Store and Waterton Building, eight- and ten-stories tall, jutted into the skyline across the Oak River from one another.

In defiance of the county's ban on professional boxing, the grounds also maintained an outdoor arena. Matches were held every Tuesday and Friday from March through October, weather permitting. To get around the law, promoters charged extra admission into the park rather than to the fights themselves, and billed the events as sideshow attractions.

Orville Curtis was a beer distributor, but at Electrical Park he'd gained a popular following as a fighter. Although he was never more than a brawling middleweight, he took on all comers. One day he knocked out four different farm boys who, for two bits apiece, had hoped to win a twenty-five dollar prize by going three rounds. They didn't make it out of the first. That feat had earned Orville the nickname he so relished, Luka, short for palooka.

At forty-one, his boxing career would be over if he'd been in the big-time. As it was, he probably had another ten years in him. He didn't need to fight—always looking to expand his business opportunities beyond beer, he had his fingers in enough pies to set him up for decades—but he still thrilled at the feeling of beating a man, *beating* him, *winning*.

***

Luka stood on the bridge that connected Gloire de Matin Island with the Electrical Park grounds. Children laughed and screamed as the Aero-Thrill and Spiral Terror rides spun round and round in their circles. Carnies called out sales pitches for food and games. Verdant summer smells mixed with those of cotton candy, cooked sausages, gasoline exhaust, horse manure, and fish. A young couple with three toddlers passed by. The kids were slurping ice cream in cones, getting as much on their faces as in their mouths.

The sun was shining, the sky clear. Luka scanned the faces of the crowd. Everyone smiling, everyone laughing, and all he could think about was Cora, who should have been here, should have been enjoying the festivities like any other young person.

Unbelievably, she'd been gone two years already. Her baby had survived, apparently with a disfigurement of some sort. Margaret Hammon was raising the boy. Without consulting Luka, she had named him William. Will Hammon.

The kid was his reason for coming here today. He hadn't seen Maggie since the night she and her lawyer broke the news of Cora's death. In all that time, she had kept young Will away from him, never once offering to let him see his own grandson.

Not that he'd wanted to. Until recently, it was still too painful to him to face the child who had, through no fault of its own, caused the death of Luka's daughter.

His feelings had changed. He was ready. In fact, he had plans. He was tired of being called white trash.

When Maggie arrived, she was regally overdressed as always. She descended the Gloire de Matin Bridge as if she expected onlookers to bow as she passed.

"Ah, Maggie," Luka said. He offered his hand, but she ignored it.

"Margaret," she corrected him, and the breeze tossed her perfectly coiffed hair. "You wanted to talk."

Luka's thin black mustache lined his upper lip like an oiled centipede. His nose had been broken several times, and now angled crookedly toward his left cheek. Still, dressed as he was in a finely starched white shirt and scarlet necktie, he considered himself a dashing figure of a man. He lit a cigar, drew in a puff, and said, "Do you mind?"

Maggie shook her head.

Luka led her to a picnic area next to the Oak River, away from the noise of the Electrical Park fairgrounds. They sat across from each other in the shade of a little gazebo. Maggie kept her eyes fixed on her hands, which she folded together in front of her. Luka noticed she was still wearing the wedding ring her late husband had given her. In 1898 G.W. Hammon had become Johnson's Landing's only casualty of the Spanish-American War. His status as war hero prompted local officials to change the township's name to Hammon Falls—that, and the impressive fortune he left his wife in local banks.

"This is a mistake," Margaret said, never looking up. "I shouldn't be meeting with you without Mr. Kelper."

"And yet here we are."

After a long pause she said, "You'll send me a statement for the expenses, won't you? Not just the arrangements, but whatever it cost you to bring her home."

"That was two years ago, Maggie. I don't need your money," he said, although he very much *wanted* her money.

"*Margaret.* I know you don't, but I thought… George was— "

"Have you heard from the little bastard?"

"I would have told you."

A steam-powered paddle boat brought more park visitors up the Oak River from Waterton. The people exited the boat with big smiles, anticipating a carefree afternoon of fun and relaxation. A frog splashed into the river nearby, a blue jay squawked in the trees. Youngsters of all ages laughed with horrified glee as the Aero-Thrill flung them out over the water and then pulled them back again with its shiny metal cables.

"So you agree George is not a factor?" Luka said.

"I suppose not."

"Then you know what I want. Under the circumstances, I'd say it's my right."

"*I* went to get William," Maggie said. "*I* paid his medical bills. *I've* raised him. It's *my* right, too."   This last was whispered, almost like a plea, and Luka knew he had her.

He grinned and blew cigar smoke up and over his head. "Oh? You don't really want the courts to settle this, do you? You know how that worked out before."

"Why now? You've never taken the slightest interest in William."

"He's my grandson, and you've kept him from me."

"I haven't *kept* him from you. You never asked."

"You've had him for two years. It's my turn."

"And you think I'm just going to give him to you?"

"I think we need to make a new arrangement."

"I really should discuss this with Mr. Kelper—"

"Forget Seaweed! Don't let him do your thinking for you."

"He's my attorney."

Luka ground his cigar out on the table. "And a damn poor one, if you ask me. Pardon my French."

Now forty-three years old, Margaret Hammon had been a widow for eighteen. "I don't have anyone else," she said.

WILL
Watertown, Iowa
July 2008

After the winds in May, the rains came in June, and kept coming, causing catastrophic flooding throughout eastern Iowa that hadn't been seen since—well, ever. The weather guy said it was a once-in-500-year event. Downstream, Cedar Rapids and Iowa City took the worst of it, but it was bad enough in Waterton. Gloire de Matin Island had been virtually submerged, including Will's old home.

Will sat in the plush upholstered seat of his grandson Charlie's 1967 Austin Healy convertible. They were on the way home from the doctor. Will didn't drive anymore, but he still loved cars. He'd bought the junked-out Healy in 1986 when Charlie was born, restored it to mint condition, and saved it for the boy's sixteenth birthday. He was pleased that now, six years later, Charlie was still driving it.

"Been taking your pills?" Charlie said. He was starting law school at the University of Iowa in the fall—that is, if there was anything left of Iowa City after the floods. His hair was neat and black and too long. He wore prescription sunglasses.

"Most the time."

"Grandpa—"

Will touched a finger to Charlie's lips. "Don't start."

"I'm just worried about you."

"Then visit more often," Will muttered low so Charlie wouldn't hear.

"What?"

"I said, 'don't be.'"

He looked out the window at the bridge on Caladonia Street. Old Oakfront Stadium was off to the left, its field still muddy. He recalled many an afternoon there in the mid-'40's, attending baseball games with Elaine and their friends and, later, little Katie. He'd always preferred cars to sports, but looking back, he was surprised how pleasant those memories were, the cheers of the crowd, the hot dogs, the beer, the Crackerjacks and the crack of the bat, the hot sweat and the cool breezes, the bingo between innings. He saw an unassisted triple play once. Didn't mean much to him, but his friends said it was really something.

Will chuckled. Reminiscing about baseball!

"What's funny?" Charlie said.

"We always remember life better than we lived it."

"I know what you mean," he said, but he didn't.

They drove onto the just-reopened bridge next to Gloire de Matin Island. White foam thick as meringue washed up on the banks with each new wave. Flood debris was everywhere, branches, old tires, broken glass, shingles, planks from ruined houses. A car had been swept up into the nook of a tree. Christ, the whole island looked like it had been spray painted with mud. The river had receded, but the damage it left behind was appalling. Sludge from the water line reached the second floor on the homes.

"Lot a million dollar houses," Will said.

"Not anymore," Charlie said, with the insouciance of a youth who didn't know what it meant to lose something.

"Probably gonna have to bulldoze my old place," Will said. He couldn't bring himself to look up the lane to where the mansion stood. "Cat fishing used to be good here, back when the island was still part of Hammon Falls."

"Mom's pretty mad at you about that gas tank," Charlie said, crossing over the bridge. They passed Electrical Park. What was once a simple country road was now a conglomeration of streets and onramps leading to the new divided six-lane Highway 212. The new highway was about a half-mile north of the old one, which was now called, depending where you were on it, University Ave. and Washington Street and Andale Road, and who the hell knew what else.

"Why would she be?" Will said. "How was I supposed to know it was still buried there? I sold the place and walked away."

"She says you don't take her seriously, her being a woman in the construction business."

"That's got nothing to do with anything."

"She thinks it does." Charlie cut over to Hansbro to 212 to Green Park to Prism. He turned off Prism onto a narrow lane called Carlyle Street and pulled into Will's driveway.

"Hmmph," Will said. "Tell her she can go play a swinette, for all I care."

"Do I want to know?"

"Musical instrument. Stretch a rubber band across a pig's ass and pluck it with your teeth."

"Maybe I won't tell her that," Charlie said, but he was smiling. "Your limo has arrived."

Will climbed out of the Austin Healy. Five-speed on the dash, black exterior, red leather interior with black trim, spoke wheels... Damn, what a fine-looking automobile! Will did good fixing this one up. His grandson was no great lover of cars, but at least he kept it clean inside and out. "Starter sounded a little weak back there," Will said.

Charlie shrugged. "You'd know better than me."

"Probably nothing, just need to re-gap your plugs."

"Thanks, Grandpa, I'll look into it." He kept his foot on the brake as he shifted into reverse.

"You're not coming in?" Will said. "Pepsi and beer in the fridge."

"I'm due back at work in twenty minutes. Your doctor lets you drink that stuff?"

Will pushed the car door shut. "Tell your mother to stop her pouting and get over here. She's got something of mine."

LUKA
Waterton, Iowa
December 1916

Riding his horse Bonnie home from downtown Waterton, Luka got caught in a hell of a winter storm. The wind was wicked cold. Snow buffeted him, froze in his eyelashes, on his mustache, on his cheeks. Despite gloves and a scarf, his fingers and ears felt as if they were going to fall off.

City lights illuminated low-hanging clouds, transforming the night sky to ash and silhouetting buildings and trees in black. The normally busy West Fourth Street was virtually deserted. It was like riding through a ghost town.

Luka turned onto Middlesex Boulevard and then up his lane. His stable wasn't heated, but compared to outside it was positively balmy. Bonnie went straight to her stall. Luka dismounted and removed his gloves. His fingers felt stiff as gun barrels as he fumbled to light the kerosene lamp. He cupped his hands around the lamp, letting its flame slowly draw out the cold. Once the blood was flowing again he unhooked the saddle and draped it over the railing between stalls. Then he brushed and oated Bonnie, extinguished the lamp, and headed for the house.

Blessedly hot air greeted him inside the front door. Birgitta took his coat and scarf. He had never forgotten, nor let her forget, her negligence in allowing Cora to escape, but she was a hard worker who suited most of his needs perfectly. Most, because in all their years together her stout form had never attracted his wandering eye, one of the few women in Red Hawk County who hadn't.

"You will catch your death," she said as she hung his snow-covered coat on the rack next to the steam pipes. "You should buy a motor car. It would keep you dry."

"Don't want one," Luka said. "Half the time the damn things won't start, and the other half they either get stuck in a drift or slide off the road into a ditch. A man could get killed. Horses do just fine."

Birgitta shook her head. "Margaret Hammon telephoned," she said. "I just left a meeting with her."

Maggie had forced him to take her to court over custody of their grandson Will. The case, wallowing since summer, was finally starting to move forward. Judge Hauken had been assigned to hear the arguments.

"She wants to speak to you again."

Luka loosened his tie and kicked off his boots, all the while watching himself in the floor-to-ceiling mirror across from the door. Even with his left-leaning nose, he liked looking at his own image, whether in photographs or mirrors. Hanging above the mantle was his most prized picture, him shaking hands with William Jennings Bryan in 1903. Luka was just twenty-eight then, and already important enough to merit an introduction to the great man. Bryan had signed it, *To my young friend Orville. God Bless. Wm J Bryan.*

Luka smiled, but it wasn't for Bryan. Maggie had telephoned. Good.

In custody cases the sympathy of most judges lay with the natural mother. However, things were more complicated here. Cora was dead. George—well, who cared where the little shit had run off to? The point was, he was out of the picture. Without the mother or father, the grandparents were the closest blood relatives. Both Luka and Maggie had lost spouses, so neither could provide the boy with a two-parent family. Money was not an issue. Luka had plenty, and what Maggie didn't own of Hammon Falls was either a park or a church. There weren't all that many parks or churches in the little township.

At their meeting this afternoon Maggie's attorney Arlen Kelper had in effect tried to bribe Luka. *If you will drop your claim, Mrs. Hammon is prepared to offer you substantial financial considerations.*

Judge Hauken had definitely not been impressed. "Mrs. Hammon," he said, "are you trying to *buy* the child from Mr. Curtis?"

"No, Your Honor. The child is not his to sell."

"That's good, madam, because in these parts we don't buy or sell human beings."

Kelper had beaten a hasty retreat in withdrawing the proposal. But the damage had been done. Before adjourning, Hauken had scheduled another hearing in a week, just before Christmas. It was becoming evident which way he was leaning.

Maggie knew it, too. Why else would she be telephoning so soon after their meeting? This was working out perfectly.

Birgitta had set a copy of today's *Record* on Luka's favorite chair. Luka switched on his electric lamp. His house was one of the first private residences in Waterton to be wired for electricity. He opened the paper to peruse the holiday ads.

"Shall I get her on the line for you?" Birgitta said impatiently.

"That won't be necessary. She needs time to think things over."

"Time to squirm, you mean."

"You have such a way with words."

"Sometimes," Birgitta said, "I do not like you so much."

He had never approved of women speaking their minds, but Birgitta's Finnish accent made every comment sound harmless and cute.

"What's for supper?" he said.

MARGARET
Pomeroy, Iowa
July 1893

On Thursday, July 6, 1893, Independence Day decorations were still in place throughout the small village of Pomeroy, Iowa, out west of Fort Dodge. The celebration of the country's 117th birthday had Pomeroy's citizens in high spirits. Even Margaret's normally dour father, Bill Morrissey, basked in the afterglow of the festivities. Profits from his general store had allowed him to contribute to the big fireworks display. And what a show it had been! Few could remember such a grand spectacle, with dazzling rockets and streamers of light brightening the sky until almost eleven p.m. The smell of gunpowder floated through the streets like fog. Not even the centennial jubilee of '76 could match the splendor of this evening.

July 4 had been a typically hot summer day in Iowa, followed by a beautiful, starry night.

Two days later the weather hadn't changed much, although the humidity was higher and the air had a strange calmness to it.

Bill and Clara, Margaret's stepmother, were closing up the general store just before seven, as usual. And, as usual, Margaret had come into town to help with the receipts, as she had the best ciphering skills in the family. Her buggy was parked out front next to theirs. The horses were stomping their hooves and whinnying loudly.

"What's the matter with them?" Bill said, peering toward the window.

"I don't know," Margaret said. She was twenty, unmarried, and still living with Bill and Clara, despite the snickering of the townspeople and their taunts of "old maid."

Clara went to the door. "Getting awful dark to the northwest," she said.

Margaret set her pencil down on the desk and checked over her figures. "We did real well today, Papa," she said, closing the ledger book.

Bill joined his wife at the door. Looking at the sky, he said, "Best be getting on home now, all of us."

"What's wrong?" Margaret said.

"The horses are nervous. You go on ahead, leave the ledger by the register. We'll be right behind you. Hurry."

Margaret frowned. Bill Morrissey was a deliberate man, not at all given to panic or haste. After a typhoid outbreak in '81 had carried away Margaret's mother, two sisters, and brother, almost nothing could break through his staid demeanor. "Okay, Papa," she said. She went out and climbed onto her buggy. There was no rain, but the clouds had assumed a sickly green color, churning, nearly scraping their bellies on the lush cornfields outside of Pomeroy.

What looked like a column of smoke stitched the sky to the ground. The sound of wind washed over the town, although there wasn't any wind yet, not the slightest breeze.

"Son of a bitch," Bill said. "Son of a bitch! Go!" He untied Margaret's horse Silas from the post and slapped him on the rear flanks. Happy to comply, the animal bolted to a gallop, veering away from the approaching storm.

Margaret clutched her bonnet as they raced south toward the town limit. She heard Bill and Clara's buggy right behind hers, their horse's breath coming in great bellowing snorts. The church bell struck seven. She sneaked a peek over her shoulder. Behind Bill and Clara, the column of smoke had split into four smaller columns, all rotating around each other.

"Don't look back!" her father cried. "It's a cyclone! Goddamn it, ride!"

Margaret's heart pounded, sweat drenched her corset. Hard as she panted, she couldn't pull enough air into her lungs. This was Iowa, twisters were common enough, but she'd never had one bearing down on her like this.

Suddenly all of Pomeroy was frantic with activity. Other people had seen the mass of swirling death descending upon them and were trying to get out of its path. Several men on horses passed her buggy. "Papa!" she yelled, but a strong straight wind had come up at her back, blowing her voice ahead of her.

The two tall wooden poles that served as the gateway to Pomeroy still had Independence Day banners strung between them, although the cord on one side had snapped and the banner was flapping noisily. An American flag arced fiercely against its moorings on the pole to the right.

Margaret fled the city limits of Pomeroy. Their farm was less than a quarter mile away. The storm, moving toward the southeast, entered the west edge of town. She dared not look again, but she could hear ghastly roar of exploding buildings. Debris was already raining down ahead of the cyclone, and she was pelted with splinters and gravel and whatever else the storm chose to spit out of its whirling maw.

Old Silas was desperate with terror. The horse hauled her wildly up their lane and, without being guided, headed immediately for the barn. Bill and Clara's buggy flew in behind her. Margaret jumped down and started to unhook Silas, but rough hands grabbed her from behind and dragged her toward their storm cellar. "No time!" her father said.

He flung open the cellar door and the three of them hurdled down the stairs, Bill pulling the door shut on top of them and latching it. With shaking hands he lit a match and touched it to a small kerosene lantern hanging from a rafter in the ceiling.

Margaret was crying. Clara huddled into a corner, canned peaches and potatoes on shelves above her head. When Margaret came to her for comfort, the woman pushed her away. Bill shoved her to the ground and protected her with his body.

The lantern swayed ominously. The wind howled on different levels, deeper than a hundred trains, shriller than a thousand women shrieking. Clara covered her ears. Bill, his weight pressing down on Margaret, prayed under his breath, reciting some Old Testament verse. "Please, Lord," he said, "not again."

Margaret knew he was talking about the typhoid that had taken most of his first family. Only she and her father had survived, and she just barely. Then Clara came along. Clara might have been a decent woman, but her constitution wasn't made for producing babies, and she resented both Margaret and her dead mother with a bitterness that was frightening.

The ground trembled, first a small vibration and then a violent rumble, as if some gargantuan plow were gashing and scouring the earth above them.

In her vilest nightmares Margaret could not have conceived such an evil sound. It was indescribable, this voice out of the whirlwind, this lathe ripping and clawing at the things of her world. Two explosions that could only signify the destruction of their house and barn followed in rapid succession. The cellar door strained against its hinges and latch. Something heavy crashed against it, a tree, a buggy, a horse. The wood creaked and cracked, but whatever the weight had been was quickly lifted again and flung elsewhere.

The canned goods on the shelves above Clara rattled but somehow did not fall. Then the lantern was extinguished as air seemed to be sucked out of the cellar through the gaps between planks of the door.

All three of them were screaming. A few moments later the hundred trains moved away, the thousand women stopped shrieking, and a gentle rained tapped at the cellar door. Clara calmed from screams to sobs. Bill rolled off Margaret. He stood up and relit the lantern. "You all right?" he asked them both. They nodded. He looked up the steps.

"Don't go," Clara said.

Bill went anyway. He ascended the stairs, unlatched the door, and forced it open. Margaret couldn't imagine what must be going through his mind, or maybe she could. He kept his eyes on his feet as he climbed into the light. Then he gazed out over his property.

"Oh, no," he said softly.

***

The life they knew was gone. Their house, their livestock, their store, their neighbors. Eighty percent of Pomeroy had been obliterated. Only thirty houses in the entire town still stood, and most of them were damaged. More than seventy people were dead, including entire families.

Many of the residents who made it through vowed to rebuild, start anew. But Bill Morrissey was devastated in ways that couldn't be measured by financial loss alone. He gave up his dreams that day, his hope, his spirit. He gave up God.

All the cash he had left was what was in his pocket when the twister hit. He'd never trusted banks, so most of his money was kept in a safe in the parlor. The safe was lifted into the sky and deposited elsewhere— Missouri or Timbuktu, for all anyone knew, because it was never found. A loan from his brother in Fort Dodge bought a wagon and two horses. Bill loaded his family and the few possessions they could salvage from the ruins and left Pomeroy forever.

They came to rest in Waterton, more than a hundred miles to the east.

Bill never recovered from the trauma. Before finding a house or employment, he simply willed the life right out of his body, leaving Margaret and Clara with nothing.

Clara sold the wagon and horses, keeping the money rather than repaying her brother-in-law. She found domestic work and a room in an old hotel. She chose not to share that room, or her earnings, with Margaret.

GEORGE
Bayonne, France
December 1916

George loved the sea. In Iowa there were no coasts, no mountains, just vast rolling plains of farmland and prairie. Oh, the state was beautiful enough with its myriad shades of green, but it couldn't express George's moods the way the roiling sea did. He felt most at peace sitting on a rocky shoreline as the sun set over the Atlantic, the tops of the waves turned amber in the dying light.

On the beach in a tiny fishing settlement near Bayonne, France, he waded barefoot in the surf and thought about his father. G.W. Hammon had died when George was almost two. He didn't remember G.W., but he knew everything about him. His photographs showed a bearded, stern-looking fellow with spectacles and a full head of unkempt hair. George's mother Margaret spoke incessantly of his kindness, his generosity, and, of course, his status as a war hero. By virtue of walking into somebody's bullet, he'd been bestowed with a medal, a statue, and an entire township named in his honor.

George wondered: was that in his mind when he fled to Canada and then England to join the British infantry? It wasn't *why* he ran, but if his father was a war hero, maybe he could redeem himself by becoming one, too.

The sea swished in over his feet, over the sand. The sun colored sky and water in fiery orange. Here on this beach in France George could admit that it wasn't the concept of heroism that appealed to him as much as the manner by which one achieved it. He'd just turned twenty, with an entire life ahead of him. He'd briefly been a husband and nearly a father, and now was neither. In the luscious rays of the French sunset all he yearned for, all he desired, was the comforting embrace of *nothingness*. The void had taken G.W., it had taken Cora and the child, it had taken Mick O'Leary. It could have him, too. He welcomed an ending, any ending, and forget the statues, the medals, and the place names.

And yet he'd run away from death as well. In the Battle of the Somme, when all he had to do was stand up and say, "Here I am, you Hun bastards, come get me!" he'd instead dived into the water and used the body of his friend to save his own skin.

Not only that, but then he'd chosen to hide out in southwestern France, close to the safety of neutral Spain.

Christ, what a pathetic creature he was, an American scrabbling out an existence in French coastal villages. He'd learned to speak the language, more or less. He fished, he harvested, he hired on for construction projects. He was breathing the bitter fumes of a life that had lost its energy, but he couldn't bring himself to die.

The sun dropped beneath the Atlantic, and the sky completed its fade to black.

MARGARET
Hammon Falls, Iowa
August 1893 - December 1916

Typhoid had taken Margaret's mother, brother, and two sisters. A cyclone had taken her home and livelihood. Despair had taken her father. Bitterness had taken her stepmother's reason, causing the woman to abandon her in Waterton.

But Margaret was twenty, resilient and strong. She'd seen tragedy before and come out whole. After a period of aimlessness and the good will of others, she met the man who would change her life for the better. G.W. Hammon, twenty-six years her senior, took her into his home as a laundress. He was a childless widower who had never remarried. As a teenager he'd served briefly in the Civil War, although he never saw combat. Following Appomattox, he returned to Iowa. Through family connections, smart real estate investments, and an abundance of luck, he made his fortune. By the time Margaret arrived on the scene he owned most of the little village of Johnson's Landing, near Gloire de Matin Island.

Through normal means Margaret and G.W. fell in love, and in September 1894 they married. G.W.'s union with a young servant loosened many a salacious tongue in conservative Waterton, Iowa, but G.W. didn't care, because he owned a substantial chunk of that city as well. Wealth conveyed eccentricity, and none dare call it anything more, at least to his face.

Margaret was happy. She'd lost all the keepsakes of her previous life and loves, and now she'd been delivered from her pain. She had a loving husband—who also, if truth be told, served very nicely as a surrogate father—a large house, money, and two kindly servants, Ed and Estella, to see to her needs. Two years later when she bore G.W.'s only child, a son they named George, all the dreams and hopes and faith Bill Morrissey had abandoned after the twister had been restored to her, with interest. Everything was perfect.

But, as she'd learned many times before, perfection was a transitory state. On February 15, 1898, in Havana Harbor, Cuba, an explosion aboard the U.S.S. Maine killed two hundred and sixty American sailors. The government blamed Spain, and war was afoot. G.W., nearly fifty-one years old and still bemoaning his exclusion from the battlefields of the Civil War, enlisted as an officer for what promised to be, and was, a very short affair.

Sadly, not short enough for G.W. An accidental bullet from one of his own comrades ended his military adventure and, soon, his life. He held on long enough to be shipped back to the mainland, but a particularly nasty infection set in on the train to Iowa. He expired somewhere in Illinois, never seeing his home or family again and missing the rechristening, in posthumous glory, of Johnson's Landing to Hammon Falls.

Margaret refused to let this new tragedy break her. God was testing her, but she was determined to do His will and accept what came. She missed her husband desperately, loved her son fiercely, and got on with life.

***

That was eighteen years ago. Her one consolation was that at least G.W. didn't have to endure the shame George had brought on the family because of that little Curtis whore.

A blizzard howled outside. The creaking timbers of her home recalled the Pomeroy horror. Although cyclones did not occur in Iowa in December, wind still terrified Margaret.

William, perhaps startled awake by the storm, perhaps by his nightmares, was crying.

Margaret had named the child after her father, not out of respect, but out of hope for redemption. Bill Morrissey had lost himself to a whim of nature. Little William Hammon, with so much of nature against him already, would not. His poor face would always be scarred, but there was nothing wrong with his lungs! The two-year-old was howling in his crib upstairs. Ed or Estella would see to his needs.

Margaret tried telephoning Orville again. She refused to call him by that barbaric nickname, Luka. The Finnish woman still claimed he wasn't home. How could that be? They had left the courthouse at the same time. He was playing games with her now. She was in no position to do anything about it. After she'd consented to Kelper's ridiculous plan to pay Orville off, Judge Hauken's attitude toward her had definitely turned icy. If Iowa law didn't absolutely require him to give her legal custody of Will, he wouldn't. And she couldn't bear that, not this time, not after having lost everybody she loved again. God could stop with the tests now.

"It's important," she said to Orville's housekeeper. Bridget, was it? Birgitta. Didn't matter. "You will tell him I telephoned?"

"Of course I will, Mrs. Hammon. I have told you this. I am sure he will contact you as soon as he arrives. Or if it is too late tonight, perhaps tomorrow?"

Margaret thanked her and signed off. The scoundrel was there, he was home! She could almost hear him snickering in the background.

"Scoundrel" was too nice a word, but she didn't use the kind of language Orville deserved. She sat down on the davenport in her library, lit her lamp, and opened a book she'd been reading. *1914 and Other Poems* was a sad, idealistic volume written by the young Englishman Rupert Brooke, made sadder by Brooke's recent death in the Great War currently raging in Europe.

***

If I should die, think only this of me:
That there's some corner of a foreign field
That is for ever England.

***

G.W. had left no corner of Iowa in a foreign field. Every part of him that made him him, except *him*, now lay beneath an elaborate marble monument in Memorial Cemetery. Margaret closed Brooke's book, unable to go on. So, so much pain in the world.

The weather was worsening by the minute. Wind rattled the windows. Frost encroached across the glass toward a shrinking hole in the center. Through that hole she could see snow drifting chest deep against the barn. It plastered the north sides of the maples in white, leaving the back half black and invisible in the night, half-trees bending in the storm. Branches strained and popped. The *house* strained and popped. Maybe Orville really wasn't home yet. Maybe his horse had succumbed to the cold, and him with it. Margaret feared and hoped it might be true.

No! No. While the man's demise would surely be a simple solution to a complex problem, the thought was unworthy of her. This trial would just have to be faced like all the others, with courage and faith.

She tried, and failed, again to read. She paced, she sat. She stared at the telephone, as if the act of observing would cause it to ring.

She couldn't give up Will, she *couldn't*. The only reason Orville wanted him was because Margaret had him. Until recently, Orville was quite content to let the boy die or live or never to have existed at all.

Something small snapped and crashed against the house. Margaret cringed. She couldn't help it. She wasn't a defeatist like her father, but the incessant wind was driving her mad. It wailed like a ghost trapped in ethereal vapors. Like memory blown out of the past.

Feeling chilled, she rang the bell for Ed to come add wood to the fireplace. In the spring she intended to convert to coal, but that wouldn't warm her now.

She should just retire for the night, but Orville might return her call any moment.

LUKA
Waterton, Iowa
December 1916

Luka had built a small gymnasium in his house. In it he had a sauna, a punching bag to practice for next summer's fights in Electrical Park, and a rowing machine to strengthen his limbs and increase his endurance. He was troubled. The custody hearing was tomorrow, but Judge Hauken's ruling was in the bag, and Luka barely gave it a thought.

He stretched before beginning his workout. Business occupied his mind. He owned the beer distributing rights for a roadhouse across from Electrical Park called Stanley's Parkside Amusements, as well as many of the east-side taverns in Waterton. Distribution brought in good money, but what he really wanted was the lease on Stanley's itself. That was owned, like most everything else, by Maggie. She was a teetotaler, a card-carrying member of the Anti-Saloon League currently pestering towns all across America. The accountants she employed to manage her investments had created holding companies and other diversions for the roadhouse, not to hide the income from the authorities but from Maggie's conscience. They told her, and she let herself believe, that Stanley's was a roller skating arena. She had never set foot in the place, of course. If Luka were the kind to worry about hypocrisy, he might have accused her of it.

Leaving his boxing gloves untied, he warmed up by tapping the bag softly, just enough to get it swinging on its chain.

He didn't foresee any lasting effects from the Anti-Saloon League, but he could foresee Maggie succumbing to her own scruples and converting Stanley's into a real skating rink, or a museum or a dry cleaners or God knew what else. What a perfectly good waste of her property and his profits. Iowans were a beer-drinking lot, and Luka didn't intend to lose their business because of Maggie's outdated morality. Besides, he had bigger plans for the place. Owning it would open up whole new avenues of business for him. He could run numbers games in the back, maybe some girls upstairs… Why not? Big Jim Colosimo over in Chicago was getting fat doing just that.

Luka hit the bag harder and faster, like a flurry of jabs to the gut.

He'd rename it Curtis's Garden. That had a nice ring to it. If he could just get his hands on that lease—better still, on *all* of Maggie's real estate holdings…There was a way.

There was a way.

Breathing heavily now, he gave the punching bag his best one-two uppercut. Sweat dripped from his forehead and stung his eyes, poured down his chest, sluiced along the small of his back, into his cotton drawers and between the cheeks of his buttocks. He kept slugging away. It was no longer a canvas surface he was attacking but an image of Maggie.

Slam!

He wondered what was fueling so much fury all of a sudden?

I *went to get the child*, she'd said. I *paid his medical bills*. I've *raised him. It's* my *right, too*.

Slam!

If you will drop your claim, Mrs. Hammon is prepared to offer you substantial financial considerations.

Slam!

Goddamn it, he would *not* drop his claim! His only daughter had died giving life to that kid. Of *course* Luka wanted him, although custody was less an end than a means. He would have Will *and* the financial considerations. Everything, everything Maggie ever had or would have. She was going to pay, and pay hard, for what her son had done, for what she had done. He'd make her swallow that bitter pill whole and love him for it afterward.

There was a way. If he'd ever had scruples, they were buried with Cora.

Slam!

And then he saw George Hammon's smug face looking back at him. His thoughts always returned to George. George the rapist, slam! George the murderer, slam! George the coward, slam! *Where are you, you gutless piece of shit*?

Slam slam slam!

Luka tore into the bag until the chain suspending it from the ceiling beam snapped. Finally spent, he shook off his gloves and dropped to his knees in a pool of his own sweat.

He smiled with grim satisfaction. His knuckles weren't even bruised.

WILL
Waterton, Iowa
July 2008

"The tank was bone dry," Katie said, sipping a beer and perching on the edge of Will's couch, never quite relaxing.

"What'd you expect after sixty-odd years?" Will said.

"We still have to haul it out of there. Takes time and money. Not to mention the paperwork with the EPA."

Will got himself a Pepsi One from the fridge, popped the top and took a long drink. "Hate this diet crap," he said. "Doc won't let me drink the hard stuff."

"I just wish you'd told me," Katie said.

"Why? Would you have built somewhere else?"

"No."

"Then you'd've had to test it and take it out anyway."

Katie had nothing to say to that. She'd always looked for someone else to blame for her anger, and she always seemed to be angry. Probably why her husband left her in '91, why no other man had stuck around since. She removed a small wooden box from her purse. "Well," she said. "This is what we dug up."

The box was once enameled and varnished, but most of that had worn off. An H and two M's adorned the lid in bas relief. There was a space between the H and M's where an A used to be, and deep scratches where the letters ON were.

Will was embarrassed by his trembling hands as he reached for it.

"What's wrong, Dad?"

"Nothing," he said irritably. "This belonged to your grandfather George. Got it in Dubya Dubya One. All these years, I thought it was lost." Actually, he'd never thought about it at all. "I guess it was."

"But now it's found."

Will lifted the cross from the box. He breathed hard on the tarnished silver surface, then rubbed it on his sleeve. "Now it's found," he said.

***

Will slouched on his bed, a low-watt lamp on his end table spilling small light against the shade in the otherwise dark room. He cradled the Celtic cross in his hands, caressing it like a rosary, and gazed up at the 1915 photograph of the soldierboy in Ypres. George. His father. Dad. One eye in shadow, one in sun. Down through the years, across the chasm that separated them, George was looking at Will in the here-and-now, looking directly *at* him. All the light in the picture swirled into that eye, or maybe out of it. There was something in his mind, words on the verge of being spoken, things he wanted to tell Will: a teenager trying to counsel an old, old man.

"You left me for dead," Will said. "Did you love her that much?"

The boy, frozen in the act of almost-speech, almost-revelation, said nothing.

Will curled his fingers around the cross and chuckled. "Katie'd put me in a home, she knew I was talking to you."

MARGARET
Hammon Falls, Iowa
December 1916

The letter arrived several months late, accompanied by a large boxed package.

It was nearly dark on the evening before the custody hearing with Judge Hauken. Margaret was so sick with worry that she hadn't read her mail in a week, hadn't slept, hadn't eaten, hadn't done much of anything. A dozen envelopes lay unopened on the small highboy inside the front door. The package sat on the floor. Ed dutifully collected the mail every day from the mailbox at the end of the lane and deposited it there, neatly stacked according to postmark date.

Mr. Kelper telephoned her every other hour to reassure her that their chances were good. Hauken was a reasonable man. Legal bias nearly always favored the woman. In any case, tradition was on her side. Blah blah blah.

Margaret knew better.

She opened her front door, as if expecting someone, some thing, some miracle to save her. After last week's storm, the weather had warmed dramatically. Hammon Falls was having its January thaw in December. The sky was overcast, as it usually was this time of year, making dusk even gloomier. Melted snow drained into the hollows of her lawn, forming pools of black liquid in the gray-white drifts. Icicles dripped from her window panes, her eaves, her door frame.

Another whoosh of air rustled the letters on the table, blowing some off the top of the stack and onto the floor. Margaret closed the door and stooped to retrieve them. She glanced through them cursorily, until one on formal stationary gave her pause.

It was stamped the British Ministry of War and addressed to Mrs. G.W. Hammon.

The British Ministry of War?

She held the letter with an overwhelming sense of dread. Her nerves tingled as if the envelope were electrified. There was an opener in the top drawer of the highboy, but her hands were fumbling so badly she couldn't grip it. Eventually she ripped the end off the envelope and pulled the paper through the hole.

She only needed to read the first few lines of the typed message:

***

Dear Mrs. Hammon,

His Majesty King George V regrets to inform you that your son, Private George P. Hammon, is missing in action and presumed dead. On or about July 1, 1916, his regiment was engaged by a superior enemy force near the River Ancre in France. We have sent his personal effects....

***

There was more, but Margaret didn't finish. She dropped the letter, then folded herself to the floor and sat on the welcome mat, which was still wet with Ed's footprints.

George didn't go to war.

George couldn't go to war.

George *wouldn't* go to war.

George was here, somewhere, in the States, not in France. He was in hiding, perhaps out of shame, perhaps grief, perhaps fear, confusion, or even youthful defiance. But he didn't go to war.

He wouldn't do that, not after all she'd told him about G.W. The family didn't need another dead war hero.

He didn't, he couldn't, he wouldn't.

He did.

She opened the package, which had the same postmark. Inside were clothes, shoes, knick-knacks, and a wallet, all belonging to George. At the very bottom of the box, as if to provide final proof, was a photograph of a young man in uniform, with the words "Ypres, 1915" scrawled on the bottom. George.

"No," Margaret said. Her body shook, but the screams were a long time in coming. When they did, her servants Ed and Estella rushed to her aid, and little William, playing in his room upstairs, added his voice to hers.

LUKA
Waterton, Iowa
December 1916

News traveled through channels only servants knew. One of Maggie's people, Ed or Estella, must have told someone's maid, who told someone's cook, who told Birgitta, who told Luka. He'd just stepped out of the bath after his workout with the punching bag.

George Hammon was dead, Birgitta said in an accent that made even the dreariest news sound cheery. Killed in the European war.

In the *war*?

Another Hammon hero, just what this town needed. Maybe one of George's own men shot him, too, just like old G.W.

No matter. What an *astonishing* turn of events. The little bastard was dead, his Cora avenged at last. This was even better than what Luka had been planning. He laughed out loud. Things just seemed to fall in place for him.

"You are happy now?" Birgitta said, not bothering to hide her disgust.

"I don't wish for any man's death," Luka said.

"You are…how is it in English? Full of shit?"

"Remember yourself, Birgitta."

She nodded stiffly once, and went up the stairs to her room.

Luka immediately telephoned his lawyer, an ex-Chicagoan named Weinshank. He instructed him to contact Judge Hauken and ask for a continuance of the custody hearing until March. What were a few extra months now? He was going to win anyway. He could afford to be generous.

Less than half an hour later Weinshank reported that Hauken had agreed to delay his ruling. Luka then called Maggie to offer his condolences. It was a terrible tragedy, he said, a terrible tragedy.

Maggie was too devastated to question his sincerity, because all she did was blubber.

He told her about the continuance. "In view of the circumstances," he said. "Take all the time you need."

"Thank you, Orville. That's very decent of you."

Yeah, Luka smiled. Surprisingly decent.

MARGARET
Waterton, Iowa
March 1917

George Hammon's body had never been found. Apparently the British had erected a marker for him somewhere in France, but Margaret refused to stage a formal funeral service for him at home "until he could rest in peace at his father's side."

She sat quietly on a wooden bench in courtroom 329-B, located on the third floor of the Red Hawk County Courthouse. Still grieving for George, she nevertheless had insisted on hearing Judge Hauken's ruling, despite Orville's offer of another extension. Kelper had convinced her that not only was legal bias on her side, now human sympathy would be as well. If she couldn't have George, at least she would keep George's son.

Or so her lawyer had claimed.

In reality, the judge had been swayed by neither bias nor sympathy. "In the best interests of the child William Hammon," he'd announced, "custody is hereby granted to Mr. Orville Curtis of Waterton, effective as soon as reasonable arrangements for transference can be made. Mrs. Hammon is to be allowed unsupervised visits on weekends."

He did not explain his decision.

Margaret gasped. Suddenly the room was spinning, its electric bulbs spewing not light but bile. The contents of her stomach churned toward her throat. She clasped her hand over her mouth. "No," she said, and that was all.

It was a high-profile case. Her servants, Ed and Estella, shouted their outrage from the spectators' gallery. Everyone in the audience reacted noisily, for or against. Reporters scribbled and, contrary to the judge's orders, photographers took pictures. Hauken pounded his gavel.

Kelper shot to his feet. "Notice of intent to appeal," he said.

The judge nodded. "So noted."

In God We Trust, it said above the courthouse door. Margaret folded her hands together.

***

As the mountain falls and crumbles away,
and the rock is removed from its place;
the waters wear away the stones;
the torrents wash away the soil of the earth;
so you destroy the hope of mortals.

***

Why *must* He keep testing her? Hadn't He already spoken to her out of the whirlwind that leveled Pomeroy? Hadn't she given her answers, time and again? "Lord," she said.

"Next case," Hauken announced with another slam of his gavel, and then Kelper was helping Margaret up and leading her toward the aisle.

"We'll fight this," he assured her.

"Didn't we just do that?" she said.

Orville and his lawyer, some awful man out of Chicago with a Jewish name, sat on the opposite side of the bench, conferring. Both looked up at her as she passed. The lawyer sneered triumphantly, but Orville, who should have been rejoicing, smiled sadly, almost compassionately.

"Maggie," he said.

"Margaret," she said.

"Margaret," he said.

"Mrs. Hammon!" the reporters shouted. The courtroom roared and flashed like a thunderstorm, a sound and light show that echoed Margaret's feelings.

Kelper tried to push her toward the door.

"There's another way," Orville said, and she stopped.

"You don't have to talk to him," Kelper said.

"What other way?" Margaret said.

"A way for us *both* to keep custody of Will."

"I don't understand."

"Can we talk privately?"

GEORGE
Bayonne-Paris, France
April 1917 - February 1920

In April 1917 George was drinking ale in a bistro in Bayonne when he heard that America had entered the war at last. Despite President Wilson's warnings, German U-boats refused to stop sinking U.S. merchant ships, thus ending America's isolationism.

George experienced a brief patriotic surge at the thought of joining his countrymen in battle, but the ale was very good and the bistro comfortable, and by Armistice Day a year and a half later he had worked his way northeast to the front, not as a soldier but as one of thousands of men assembled to fill in the trenches that scarred the land and psyche of France.

"La grippe" caught up with him in December 1918. By then the dreadful influenza pandemic known as the Spanish Flu had already claimed more than twice the number of victims worldwide as the Great War had. One snowy morning a hundred and sixty kilometers east of Paris he noted a slight headache and general muscle stiffness. By that night his face had turned blue, and by morning he was coughing up blood. A long period of haze, darkness, and women in white followed. When he woke he was in a hospital bed, clutching Mick's Celtic cross. Trees were budding outside his window, flowers pushing sunward through the soil. Beyond fenced grounds he could see the medieval skyline of Rheims. It was March 1919.

A pretty nurse smiled and said in French, "Hello, my friend. Are you feeling better?"

"Yes, thank you. Where am I?"

She patted him on the hand. "Back from the dead."

***

It goes to my eldest son Tommy, Mick had said.

After being discharged from the hospital, George recalled the vow he'd made as he cowered in the stream beneath his friend's body: to deliver the cross to Mick's son in Ireland. Snatching the thing had been reflex, but purpose must have guided his hand. Later it became the justification he used for having run away from Somme, and for continuing to survive now—now, when death called to him, seduced him with a promise of release.

Mick would have said the cross was the reason George hadn't died, then or since. George wasn't so sure. It certainly hadn't protected Mick.

The Great War was over. The Treaty of Versailles had put the Kaiser in his place and restored order in Europe. Travel was again possible. But there were problems getting to Ireland. In the aftermath of the war and the influenza epidemic, both of which had claimed primarily young adults, laborers were in high demand. Thousands of kilometers of trenches had to be filled in, the slashed countryside healed. George needed money if he expected to go anywhere.

He spent the rest of 1919 engaged in a massive land beautification project, toiling in heat, rain, mud and, later, snow. In a trench near the River Ancre in Picardy, not far from where Mick must lie buried, his coworker Jean reported rumors he'd heard about *Cogadh na Saoirse*, the Irish War of Independence. It seems the British had stepped out of one conflict and right into another. Much of southern Ireland was demanding home rule, and its people were taking up arms in order to get it. Bills passed by Parliament before the war were slow to be enacted afterward, so the revolutionary Sinn Fein and IRB were forcing London's hand. How ironic would Mick have found *that*? He and other Irishmen had offered their lives to England's war effort for the express purpose of achieving self-government, only to have England renege.

"Why would you want to go to Ireland?" Jean asked George in French.

"To help a friend."

"The *dead* friend you told me about?"

"Yes."

"Then what's the hurry, eh? The dead can wait."

No hurry at all, he thought.

Except that Tommy wasn't dead.

But he was still a boy. There was time.

George, who had no great love of life, was nevertheless thoroughly sick of war. Even if he could get to Ireland, he had no desire to find himself caught between the militant home-rulers and the British—or, for that matter, between the Irish Catholics and Protestants.

He went to Paris instead.

Not being a French citizen, he wasn't eligible for a conventional passport, and he'd abandoned all his military papers at the River Ancre—not that he could use those anyway. If the British authorities discovered he was alive, they'd probably have him extradited and shot for desertion. Therefore, if he wanted to leave the country, he'd need travel documents. Jean told him about people in Paris who could, for a price and not entirely legally, make some for him.

He'd always wanted to visit the Eiffel Tower anyway.

***

He never did. As the tallest structure in Paris, the monument was visible from nearly every vantage point, but George didn't go to the Champ de Mars to see it up close. Thirty years after its construction, most Parisians still considered it an eyesore. The writer Guy de Maupassant was said to have hated it so much that he ate in its restaurant every day, because that was the only place in the city where one *couldn't* see the Tower. George thought it was quite pretty from a distance.

He'd acquired a taste for ale during the two and a half years he lived in Bayonne, and in Paris he found he liked the wine even better. In his first two months he squandered the francs he'd earned at the trenches on alcohol, cheap flats, and an occasional streetwalker. The rooms stank and the sticky fumblings with whores conjured only a perverted iteration of what he'd lost—but the wine, the wine was good.

On a cold morning in February he was sleeping one off under a bench by the Seine when he was awakened by a woman with bobbed hair and the Dorelia look that was all the rage in Paris—full, flowing skirt and blouse bright with reds and yellows. She was around twenty-five, blondish, with the round face of an angel or a gypsy.

"Are you all right?" she said. "Who are you?"

George sat up, blinking into the slanting sun. Snow dusted his clothing. Across the Seine on the Île de la Cité the spires of Notre Dame were black monoliths against the bright blue sky. The river's current sounded like a train in George's ears. He was freezing. He told her his name.

"I'm Suzanne," she said, shaking his hand. "Are you sure you're all right?"

"Hello, Suzanne. I'm fine, thanks."

"You smell bad."

"Sorry. Long night."

He rose to his feet, then thought better of it and fell back onto the bench. French wine wasn't so good the next day. The inside of his head felt like shattered glass.

"You'll catch your death," she said. "The flu is killing everyone." She brushed the snow from his coat, tried to warm him by rubbing his arms.

Surprised by her forwardness, George nudged her hands away. "The flu has already killed me. My body just doesn't know yet. I'm working on it."

"I see that. So young, so sad."

Mick's cross hung like a weight around George's neck. He touched his hand to his chest, traced its mystical outline with his fingers. "Your accent doesn't sound French," he said.

"Neither does yours. Are you British?"

"American."

Suzanne seemed delighted. "Me, too!" she said in English. "Helena, Montana. Where did you learn French? You don't talk like the Americans I know here."

English! George hadn't heard or spoken English aloud since the Battle of the Somme, nearly four years ago. "What other Americans?"

"In Saint-Germain-des-Prés. Writers, painters, philosophers, radicals, free thinkers, suffragettes. The Parisians call us bohemian. I think that's their word for vagrant."

"Which one are you?"

"All of them. Did you know there's an amendment in the States to give women the vote?"

George shook his head. "I haven't been home since before the war."

"Do you have a place to stay?"

"Sometimes. I didn't make it there last night."

"Obviously. You're blue."

"Try sleeping under a bench sometime."

"I have. Would you like to meet my friends? We can find a bed for you."

"Just like that? You don't know me. What if I'm a sex fiend?"

Suzanne smiled coyly and helped him up. That little turn of the lip reminded him of Cora, although the two didn't look anything alike. "What if *I* am?" she said.

GEORGE AND CORA

CORA
Waterton, Iowa
October 1909

Cora Curtis got her first period two days after her thirteenth birthday. She lay in bed, cramping and pressing a rag between her legs while her father was downstairs telephoning the doctor.

Birgitta rolled her eyes. "Oh, for heaven's sake," she said, "it is only your courses. Your mother, God rest her soul, should have told you."

"Is it supposed to hurt?" Cora whimpered.

"For some girls it does." After heating a towel on the radiator, the maid placed it across Cora's abdomen. "This will help with the cramps."

Footsteps on the stairs, knocking at the door. "Cora?" Luka said. "Are you decent?"

Birgitta covered her with a blanket. "Come in."

His concerned expression was so comical that Cora almost laughed despite the pain.

"The doctor will be here in an hour," he said

Birgitta tut-tutted. "She does not need a doctor."

"Emma's problem started with bleeding," he said.

"Mrs. Curtis had a cancer. Your Cora does not. She is becoming a woman. That is all." Birgitta shook a finger at him. "Go away now. This is not for you. Tell Doctor to stay home."

***

The next day Cora sat on the floor of the gym, arms wrapped around her knees, and watched her father practice bare-fisted on the punching bag. His name was Orville, but even she thought of him by his silly nickname, Luka, because he seemed to like it. She would never call him that to his face.

"Why do you fight, Daddy?" she said.

"For the exercise," he said. "For the competition. There's nothing like a good match to stir the blood. Got a big one coming up tomorrow in Electrical Park." He aimed a right jab at the top of the bag. "Boom!" he said. "I just knocked a couple of the other guy's teeth out."

"Aren't you afraid you'll get hurt?"

Luka stopped hitting the bag, smiled, and tousled her hair. Sweat darkened his shirt, and he smelled awful. His knuckles oozed blood. "Who told you pain is a bad thing? You've got to beat it if you want to succeed. I don't know how many times my nose has been busted, but here I am, a stronger and better man for it. You learn from pain."

"What about the men you fight?"

"They learn a lot from me!" He winked at her. "Seriously, if they can whip me, more power to them. But they never do."

"I bet I could take you." Cora rose and put up her dukes, bouncing on the balls of her feet like a jumping jack and flailing wildly. She playfully clipped him on the ear.

"You'll have to do better than that," he said, laughing. He pointed her toward the bag and told her to swing away. "Put some muscle into it."

Unlike human tissue, the sand-filled bag had no give in it. Her first punch wrenched her wrist sharply, and she cried out.

Luka, so shrewd and hard with others, had always doted on her. He apologized repeatedly as he led her to a chair and sat her down.

"I'll be all right," she said.

"Can you bend your wrist?"

She moved it back and forth. "It hurts, but yes."

"At least it's not broken." He kissed the injury, as if that would make it better.

"Oh, Daddy, I'm not a little girl anymore."

"Yeah, so Birgitta tells me," he said.

Cora blushed.

Luka wiped the blood from his knuckles, then wrapped her wrist with the same roll of gauze he used to pad his gloves. "What's a young lady need with a good right jab, anyway?" he said.

"It's more fun than cooking and cleaning and stuff girls usually get stuck with."

"When you're married, you'll have to do all that."

"Why can't my husband do it?"

He tenderly cupped her chin. "Because it's woman's work."

Cora stood up defiantly. "Did Momma do woman's work?"

"Your mother was sick a long time, honey. A long time. You saw her. That's why I hired Birgitta. But you can't depend on someone else to carry the load for you. A man expects certain things from his wife."

"What about what *I* expect?"

***

Waterton was an industrial town, a mechanized town. Some twenty manufacturers occupied the Westland Addition area near Hammon Falls, including the J.P. Kelly Mfg. Co., the Waterton Threshing Machine Co., Heiland Brothers Foundry, Waterton Motor Works, the Waterton Gasoline Engine Company, Sims Manufacturing, and the city's biggest employer, Landon & Co, which made farm implements. There were dozens of others on both sides of the river. Seventy-five trains a day clattered into the city, disgorging their cargo at the Illinois Central or Northern Line depots, raw material to feed the factories' insatiable appetites. Except Sundays and holidays smoke and steam spewed into the sky day and night. Cora could see the pollution from their house on Middlesex several miles away. The whole town seemed to be engulfed in a stinky black haze.

And Roth's Packing Company, clear over on the northeast side of town, smelled worse than all of the factories combined. On hot, still summer afternoons when Roth's was running its hog kill operations, the reek of death was so thick it made the eyes water and crawled right into the skin and hair.

If it weren't for its industries, Waterton would be such a pretty place, with its rolling hills and greenbelts, the Oak River and Red Hawk Creek.

The sky was overcast but there was no rain yet. After school Cora rode the Hartland trolley into downtown Waterton, then switched to the Gloire de Matin line to take her to Electrical Park. She got off at her stop and crossed the bridge from Gloire de Matin Island to Electrical Park. Luka would lock her in the house forever if he ever found out what she was doing. He forbade her to attend his matches.

Admission to the park was usually two bits, but on Tuesdays and Fridays during the hours fights were staged, the price went up to two dollars. The arena was set down in a natural depression in the ground, like the Greek amphitheatres Cora had read about in history class. The bleachers abutting two sides of the ring were filled to capacity, with another throng of people jostling for position on the hills of the other two sides. Minors weren't allowed to watch the fights, but there was only one man at the gate, and with all the confusion Cora slipped in easily, without paying the two dollars. Although she saw several other young faces, none of them were female. If cooking and cleaning were women's work, then watching people get the hell beat out of them must be men's work.

The whole thing had a carnival atmosphere, with a lot of cheering and yelling. Vendors pushed through the crowd selling hot dogs and Dr. Pepper. The air was heavy with the smells of cotton candy and body odor and barbecued sausages. A "pre-fight" fight was going on at the moment between two skinny black men. This was just to tease the crowd's taste for blood while they awaited the main event. The main event, whenever he chose to strap on his gloves, was Luka.

One of the black men caught the other on the chin with a big uppercut, knocking him to the canvas. He didn't get up. Nobody applauded as the winner pranced around the ring with his arms in the air. Generally, native citizens of Waterton resented blacks, who were viewed as invaders. The Illinois Central had recently been troubled by a workers' strike, so the railroad had paid to transport Mississippi Negroes north as strikebreakers in the shops. Once the strike ended, the blacks stayed, settling in the squalid area of the east side known as Smoky Row, which was the only place local ordinance would allow them to live. Most would work for less money than whites demanded, which worsened already existing racial prejudices.

None of that mattered much to Cora, who was insulated from life's unpleasantness by her father's money and protective nature. Two park employees came to carry the fallen boxer away. The winner exited right behind. A custodian dry-mopped the sweat from the canvas, and then an expectant hush fell over the audience.

A little man next to Cora pushed her aside to get a better look. She jammed her injured wrist against someone in front of her. "Ow!" she howled.

"Hey," the man said, "you're underage."

"I'm old enough," she said, and prudently went somewhere else.

A chorus of catcalls and hissing rose as a big white fellow lumbered through the crowd and climbed into the ring. He had immense slabs of muscle on his arms and rolls of flab hanging over his boxing trunks. His hairy chest and back made him look like a bald-headed bear. He was *huge*!

The taunts quickly turned to cheers as Luka appeared. The crowd parted for him like the Red Sea before Moses. He was clad in black short pants, leather athletic boots, and nothing else. His sinewy muscles and bare chest were already sweaty. In her whole life she had never, ever, seen him without a shirt, not close up, not from a distance, not through an open window shade or door left carelessly ajar. Although the other boxers were half naked, too, this was different, almost indecent.

After ascending the platform and squeezing between the ropes, Luka made a slow circle of the ring, ignoring his opponent while he exhorted his fans. They called his name and cheered even louder. All this adulation was for her father!

A referee brought Luka and the bear-man together to shake hands. He explained something Cora couldn't hear. Then he signaled for them to return to their respective corners, where they sat on little stools until a bell rang.

The match was underway.

Luka stood up gracefully, as if preparing to leave for the opera. Without warning the brute charged ahead, more like a bull moose than a bear. Luka sidestepped him easily and jabbed him in the ribs as he passed. The man's flab jiggled, but he seemed unfazed. He turned and swung his gigantic gloves in ponderously slow motion. Luka ducked this way and that, never suffering the slightest touch. He winked at the audience, flashing a playful smile.

Enraged, bear-man roared and lunged.

And in an instant the fight was over.

Luka slammed a thunderous wheelhouse into the man's nose. Even from where she stood Cora could hear the nauseating crunch of shattered cartilage. Blood poured from his nostrils like water from a well pump. He staggered, tried to steady himself on the rope, missed, and toppled over.

The crowd was ecstatic as the referee counted out ten and then raised Luka's hand. Her father acknowledged the ovation with an exaggerated bow.

And then bear-man sat up. Legs splayed, elbows on the canvas, face in his gloves, he did the most amazing thing. He wept. He *wept*. Loudly, abjectly, and Cora had no idea why. Was his family starving? Did so much depend on the money from one fight?

The spectators hushed, uncertain what to make of this. For a moment the only sound was the bear-man's noisy, bloody sobs. Luka broke the silence when he scornfully slapped him on the back of the head. "Oh, boo hoo," he said, and the crowd erupted in laughter.

Luka encouraged them, gesturing like a conductor in front of an orchestra. His adversary looked up, wiped his eyes on his great hairy arms, and pushed himself off the mat. Large amounts of his blood stained the canvas, his chest, his face. Head bowed, he ducked between the ropes and slunk away. The spectators continued to mock him as he shoved through them. Some threw objects at him: apple cores, half-filled soda cups, and the uneaten remnants of hot dogs.

"Boo hoo," they called, "boo hoo."

Cora couldn't believe it. Luka had already beaten the poor fellow. What was the point of hurting him like this, too? Just shake his hand and wish him better luck next time.

"Daddy," she whispered. Then she fled the arena, the people, the park, and crossed Gloire de Matin Bridge to await the trolley. The overcast sky darkened, more toward rain than sunset. A northerly breeze stung her with little pinpricks of drizzle. She paced frantically, not bothering to excuse herself when she bumped into other commuters. By the time the trolley arrived her skin was moist and her breathing rapid, almost panicked. Cora couldn't put a name to her feelings. Anger, disappointment, pity, but that wasn't it, not all of it. As she stepped into the car, she knew she would go home tonight and shut herself into her room. She would cry herself hoarse, and maybe her father would ask her what was wrong, but even if she told him, he wouldn't understand.

GEORGE
Hammon Falls, Iowa
March - June 1912

Over his mother's objections, sixteen-year-old George Hammon took a job at Kline's Livery on West Park Avenue and Jefferson Street in Waterton, two miles from his home on Gloire de Matin Island.

"You don't need the money," his mother said.

"I want to work," George said.

"At a livery stable?"

"Why not?"

"It's filthy."

"You've been rich too long, Mother. Your father started small."

"And ended a failure."

"Well, I won't."

On his first day on the job Mr. Kline made it clear that the Hammon name didn't cut much with him. During the week he'd be expected to report in immediately after school and stay until closing time at 10:00 p.m. On Saturdays it would be 7:00 a.m. sharp until 10:00 p.m., and if didn't like the hours, by God, he could just find employment elsewhere. "And, in case you didn't know, Hammon, we *work* around here," Kline said. "*Real* work. We got no servants to wipe your ass and blow your nose for you. You can start by mucking out the stables."

He thrust a shovel into George's hands, and with that, George became a laborer.

***

His relationship with the horses was tenuous. He was tall but skinny with undeveloped muscles. At home Ed handled all the horse duties, which was one of the reasons George wanted to work here, to learn how to do something useful. Somehow spending money he hadn't earned and basking in the glory of a heroically dead father just didn't seem like a worthwhile life's pursuit. Still, these horses were intimidating beasts. Big and powerful, they immediately sensed he wasn't comfortable around them. Old Brownie, a palomino mare, took particular delight in rearing and skittering away while he tried to brush her down. She also insisted on soiling her stall the moment he'd finished cleaning it. He knew it would be messy again the next day anyway, they all would, but he couldn't stand to leave at night with dirty stalls.

"Can't you hold your shit for once?" he complained to Brownie one Thursday night in April. *Shit* was a term his mother would not approve of, but in the livery business you quickly learned to call a thing what it was.

Brownie whinnied as if pleased with herself. A bag of oats, which is what she'd wanted all along, calmed her enough for George to finish brushing and oiling her. As he retrieved the shovel, he heard a coach pull up outside. That would be Lewis, a middle-aged Negro who'd come north as a railroad strikebreaker. When the strike ended and the white employees returned to their jobs, Lewis had not been able to find other work at first because, unlike many blacks, he refused to accept lower pay. Mr. Kline had been impressed by the man's spirit, and hired him as a driver.

A few minutes later Lewis brought his team in and led them into their stalls. "The hell you still doing here, Georgie?" he said. "You got school in the morning."

"Brownie's up to her tricks again."

Lewis laughed. His eyes glowed yellow in the lantern light. "Come on over here," he said. His two bays were sweaty and smelly in ways only horses could be. Their muscles twitched as if electrical currents were running through them. "You can't be scared of them," Lewis said. "They big, but dumb. Soon as you show 'em you ain't gonna take no nonsense, they settle right down." He nodded toward Susie, a dappled white and brown mare. "Watch."

Even in his driver's uniform, Lewis was a large, rough man, but he placed his massive hands against Susie's neck with incredible gentleness. She nickered her approval. "Sometimes a little loving work, too," he said. "Now you try."

George caressed the mare as Lewis had. She didn't flinch.

"Right," Lewis said. "But when you brush her, brush hard. That how horses like it. Get down deep in the coat, right to the skin. Then when you oil them, go back to loving, nice slow circles."

George brushed and oiled Susie, but when he started toward her partner, Bucktooth, Lewis stopped him. "No, I'll get him. You go on home now. Long walk over to the Island."

"You think Mr. Kline'll ever let me pick up fares?"

"Whatcha wanna do that for? All it is is driving a bunch of spoiled white girls round to do whatever-it-is-white-girls-do in their white-girl social clubs."

"I don't really *mind* white girls…"

Lewis grinned and clapped him on the back. "You all right, son. Work good in the stables, boss'll let you drive. But not tonight. Tonight you need to get your ass on home to bed."

"Thanks, Lewis."

"And, Georgie? Next time Brownie shit in her stall after you already muck it, she can just stand in her own filth all night. Serve the old girl right."

***

The trolleys didn't run after six p.m, and George's mother wouldn't let him take one of their horses. She claimed it was because she didn't want the animal out all day. There was probably something to that, because he did leave early in the morning for school and come home late at night from work. Still, he suspected she did it more out of spite.

The night was especially warm for April, with humidity like summer. But the stars were out and the breeze was pleasant, so he didn't mind walking. During the day he preferred paralleling the Oak River because of the view, but at night he kept to the main roads. He took Jefferson west to Westland Avenue, past the succession of factories. Even at this hour they belched foul-smelling vapors into the sky. Industry was the lifeblood of Waterton, but the buildings blighted the beautiful landscape where Red Hawk Creek emptied into the Oak. The only time George went this way was at night, when darkness concealed their dreary façades.

He turned onto Caladonia, passing Electrical Park and crossing over to Gloire de Matin Island. A warm bath would be awaiting him, as Ed or Estella drew one for him every evening at this time. His mother couldn't bear the stink of manure that permeated his clothes—the stink of manual labor, really—and she wouldn't talk to him until he'd cleaned up.

She was in the library reading the family Bible when he came through the door. He waved at her and headed for the tub.

After his bath and a change into his pajamas, he glanced through the *Waterton Record*. Last Sunday the ocean liner *Titanic* had struck an iceberg and sunk. The horrifying casualty figures were just starting to trickle in. The story was too depressing, and he couldn't finish it. Instead, he joined his mother in the library.

"Lewis said Kline might let me drive some day," he said.

"Lewis is the colored man?" she said.

"What difference does that make?"

"I wouldn't trust what one of them tells you."

"Lewis is okay."

She carefully marked her place in the bible and closed the book. "You want to drive people around like a common servant? I'm so glad your father didn't live to see this."

"My father," George said, "would have been proud."

***

In May a driver quit and, much to his mother's embarrassment, George got his chance. When he came in to work Kline sent him to talk to Lewis about the etiquette of cabbing.

He found his friend smoking a cigarette in the alley behind the livery. Startled, Lewis dropped the cigarette and crushed it with his shoe. "Damn, son, don't sneak up on me like that. You scare the bejesus outta me. Kline boot me out for sure, he catch me smoking."

"He doesn't like people smoking?"

"He don't like fire. He tell me some boys set hay alight in this very alley back in '06, burned down the livery."

"I remember it. Thurman's Opera House and a couple of churches burned, too."

"I don't know nothing 'bout no opera house and churches. Old man's favorite horse died, stallion called Prince. Kline still grouches 'bout that. You was probably one of them hooligans playing with matches." Lewis lit up another cigarette. "Our secret, right?"

"Give me one, too."

"I got a boy your age. I ever find him smoking, I'd beat his ass."

"*You* smoke."

"Do I look like I'm sixteen years old?"

"Well, I smoke all the time."

"Hell you do. You do, your Momma put you in *jail*. So. You come back here for a reason, or just to annoy me?"

"Yeah, Samuels quit. Kline wants you to teach me cabbing."

"Just like that? Like cabbing *easy*?" Lewis took a few more puffs, then extinguished the cigarette against the brick wall and put the butt in his pocket. "Well, come on, then."

George followed him inside. The livery had a variety of carriages, broughams and landaus, ambulances and hearses. Before letting him near one, Lewis made him study a map of Waterton. "You got to memorize every street in town," he said, "from Cedar Crossing to Andale. And know both the shortest and the easiest way to get to a place, which ain't always the same."

George had driven the family wagon on occasion, so handling a horse and carriage wasn't a big adjustment. It was mostly getting used to the difference in weight between a wagon and a carriage, and learning to control the horses so the customer had a smooth ride.

One rainy night when testing George in both horsemanship and directions, Lewis instructed him to take a brougham to an obscure address in southern Waterton. The route wound through some of the richer neighborhoods on the west side.

"These places," Lewis said with pride, "they don't let niggers come 'round, but I do. 'Course, you won't have to worry 'bout that, being a rich white boy yourself."

"My mother's rich, I'm not."

"I know where your house be. Don't tell me no sad stories. I used to live in a boxcar over by Smoky Row."

The rain slanted down on a strong breeze. George grabbed onto his hat. "You lived in a *train*?"

"Hell, yes. Illinois Central pay a bunch of us to come up from Biloxi, but they got no place for us to live. So a train pull in, they take off cars they ain't using and put us in 'em."

"That's not right."

Lewis lowered his cap over his eyes. Rain water on his skin reflected in the electric street lamps like shiny scars. "White man's world, Georgie. Least they don't lynch us up here."

George didn't know what to say to that.

"Turn left," Lewis said. "Hope that long face ain't for me, son. Got my wife and boys with me now, and we bought us a real house over in Smoky Row. I'm fine. Most folks don't mean to be hurtful, they just don't know no better."

***

In June George was ready. He started off taking short fares to familiar places, but increased his range as his knowledge of Waterton's nooks and crannies grew. At the end of the month Kline pulled him aside and said, "I need you to pick up a girl over on Middlesex Boulevard. Her father's an important man, so don't muck it up."

CORA
Waterton, Iowa
May - June 1912

In May 1912, a week before school dismissed for the summer, Cora and her best friends Millie, Lizzie, and Jean huddled together in the high school's chorus room. School was out for the day, and the room was empty save for the four tenth-graders. Lizzie had stolen a pamphlet from her parents' dresser, written by that Sanger woman, the famous troublemaker from out east. The pamphlet discussed the almost incomprehensible subject of birth control. Most of the article was boring, philosophical stuff about family planning, but it got more entertaining when it came to the drawings of the actual birth control *devices*. For women, there were diaphrams, cups, sponges, suppositories, pessaries, chemical concoctions...

"And these go *where*?" Cora said.

Lizzie told them in an exaggerated stage whisper, and all the girls squealed, "Eew!"

For men there was the condom. It was once fashioned from sheep intestines, the article said, but was now made of modern Vulcanized rubber. A funny-looking balloon, a condom was strong, sturdy, and reusable. It not only would prevent pregnancy but also protect against disease. Men were supposed to wear it over their...thing.

Cora was having trouble visualizing the concept from the pamphlet's two-dimensional picture—mostly because she'd never seen a penis, and had no clear idea what one looked like.

"Look what else I found!" Lizzie said suddenly, and pulled a real condom from her blouse pocket. There was a seam down its thin rubber surface. "It was in my brother's bedroom!"

Now the girls really screamed. Lizzie chased them around the room with it, brandishing it like a worm. They were carrying on in mock horror and real squeamishness when the door flew open and their music teacher, Miss Volmensky, barged in. "What are you children doing?"

Lizzie quickly hid the condom in her blouse, but the pamphlet was lying open on a desk, now on the other side of the room from the girls. Cora tried to get to it, but the teacher intercepted her. "What's this?" the woman said. She picked up the pamphlet and glanced at the pictures. "Where did you get this *filth*?"

"We found it," Lizzie said.

"Be quiet. You'll only lie anyway." Miss Volmensky held the pamphlet by one corner, exactly as if it were a dead rat. "Margaret Sanger. Hmmph. The woman's a pornographer and an insult to decent society. You're all coming with me to the principal's office. We'll see how funny it is when he telephones your parents. This means expulsion for the lot of you."

***

Cora had been banished to her room. She curled up on her bed with her favorite Teddy bear and stared at her ugly yellow wallpaper with its black patterns that looked like women's faces. Years ago, after Uncle Carlin had died in a fire, they'd taken in his dog Hannah, a blue heeler mix. Cora wished she were here now. The dog's slimy tongue and boundless energy would cheer her up better than any stuffed bear. But Hannah wasn't here. Luka had sent her away to live on a farm when Momma got sick. She'd be old for a dog now, maybe fifteen. She was probably dead.

Downstairs her father railed to Birgitta about the ingratitude of children. Most of his venom was reserved for her friends. He considered them the instigators who involved his innocent daughter. Still, he made sure to yell loud enough for Cora to hear. No matter who was ultimately to blame, he did not appreciate the shame she'd brought on his name. Everything was always about him.

Poor Birgitta. She just had to stand there and take the brunt of his wrath. Her voice was inaudible, but she must have said something, because there'd be a lull in Luka's shouting, followed by a new verbal barrage. After a few minutes of silence, she heard footsteps on the stairs. *Here it comes*, she thought. She squeezed her bear tighter.

Luka entered without being invited. He stood over her bed, so angry his little black mustache trembled. When he finally spoke, though, it was in a gentle, almost plaintive, voice. "What have I done to you, Cora? Why do you treat me like this?"

"We were curious, Daddy," she said, "that's all."

"It's not just the pamphlet. You used to be such a sweet little girl, but lately you've fought me over everything. I tell you to sit and you stand. I ask you to do chores and you go back to bed. I don't understand."

Boo hoo, he'd taunted the big bear-man in the ring. *Boo hoo*. If she lived forever she'd never forget. That's what's wrong, Daddy. You're not nice.

"Why don't you have any photographs of Momma?" Cora said.

"What?"

"You've got photographs all over this house. You and Mr. Bryan. You and me. You at work. You, you, you, but none of Momma."

"Don't change the subject."

"I want to know!"

"Well, if it's any of your business, your mother didn't like having photographs made of herself. There was only one time. And I do have it, I have it right here."

He removed his pocket watch and opened it. Inside was a small oval picture of his wife, her mother, as a young woman. Actually, Emma Curtis never got to be anything *but* a young woman. Cancer took her before she was thirty. Cora stared at the photograph, savoring the image, memorizing it, *loving* it. All the emotions of the past five years surged inside her, and she cried. "Oh, Momma."

Even Luka seemed to be fighting tears. "I keep her picture with me always," he said.

"I didn't know."

He sat down on the edge of her bed. "Is that what this is all about, sweetie? You miss your mother?"

"No, Daddy. I mean, I do, but it's just...maybe I don't want to be somebody's good little wife and do woman's work."

Luka stroked her hair. "What makes you think people get a choice? We do what's expected of us. I have to, and so will you."

"When women get to vote, things'll be different—"

Suddenly angry—and nobody got angry as fast or as completely as Luka did—he slapped the mattress, hard, like he was attacking an opponent. "This is what reading that *shit* does to you! Women will never get the vote. Their purpose is to be mothers and homemakers. It's a *good* purpose. It's in the Bible. You have to accept that. I'm only trying to prepare you."

Cora threw her bear on the floor. "I don't want to be *prepared*."

Luka stood up and loomed over her. "That's too bad, little girl. You will obey me. You will do your housework. You will be respectful. And if I *ever* hear of you reading that Sanger woman's trash again, well, you don't want to know."

***

Cora didn't return to school that spring, but Luka did pull some strings to allow her to pass her sophomore year. Over her teachers' protests, the principal agreed to accept her marks up to the point of her expulsion as her final grades.

Birgitta instructed her in the fine art of woman's work. Cora hated it, but she made the effort, not to please the housekeeper but to avoid her father's admonitions. Unfortunately, Birgitta wasn't a tolerant teacher. She had little patience for Cora's "rich-girl laziness."

"The sooner you learn how to work," she said, "the sooner you will be happy."

"That's not happiness," Cora said. They were standing in the kitchen over a tub of dirty plates and silverware.

"It is all you will ever get. Happiness comes in the fulfillment of your duties."

Washing dishes, laundry, windows, and floors was *not* fulfilling, and never would be. But Cora muddled through her chores, and in June Birgitta decided it was time for her to do the grocery shopping alone. She made a list and thrust it into Cora's hand.

"Am I supposed to carry them home on the trolley?" Cora said.

"I do."

"Well, I won't. You can't order me around."

"No?" Birgitta said. "Suit yourself. I will fetch your father."

Furious, Cora rushed upstairs to her room. She slammed her door, then opened it and slammed it again for effect. She flung herself onto her bed.

Predictably, Birgitta followed soon after, and Luka was with her.

"I need the wagon today," her father said, "but you *will* buy the groceries. Put them on my account." He turned to Birgitta. "Telephone Kline's. Have him send a carriage and driver over to take my little princess shopping. And tell him I don't want that buck nigger he employs."

Before Cora could protest, Luka stopped her. "Not a word from you," he said.

GEORGE
Waterton, Iowa
June 1912

If George Hammon wasn't who he was, if he didn't live where he did, the Curtis home on Middlesex would have been truly impressive. Built in the Queen Anne Victorian style of the 1870's, the house sat on a spacious well-manicured lot bordered on the north and west by elm and red spruce trees planted to protect against Iowa's wicked winter winds. It boasted over a dozen rooms. An outdoor porch wrapped around the south and east sides, supported by narrow white pillars. The irregularly-shaped roof was sharply pitched, with a dominant gable to the west and a conical turret on the east. Textured triangular shingles adorned the entire façade of the house, while larger, more conventional shingles covered the roof. The walls were bluish-gray, the roof a darker gray.

It was a beautiful house, and the stable behind it was nearly the size of Kline's.

All very nice, but not quite up to the standards of the dwellings on Gloire de Matin.

George fidgeted in the driver's seat of a brougham. Wearing his best three-piece suit, a black tie, and a brand new derby hat, he considered himself quite dashing. The gold chain attached to the pocket watch in his vest was an especially attractive touch, he thought. Lewis had teased him, saying he looked like a little monkey-boy who'd gotten into his daddy's finery. "Maybe you grow yourself some whiskers," he'd laughed, "you be more like a proper driver."

He'd announced his arrival to a servant woman with a foreign accent, but the girl he was supposed to pick up had not yet emerged from the house. George didn't mind the wait, but the horses, Brownie and Bucktooth, demonstrated their impatience by stomping their hooves.

A light breeze rustled in the treetops, but the air at ground level was calm. For late June the humidity was surprisingly low. After several minutes in the sun, though, George's starched collar started to chafe. Clammy beads of sweat moistened his undershirt. He was about to go ring the bell again when the front door flew open and a teenaged girl stormed out. "I *hate* you!" she shrieked at someone inside before kicking the door shut. George pretended not to notice her tantrum. "You're late," she said to him as she approached the brougham.

Actually, he'd been punctual: 4:00 p.m. sharp. But the girl, who appeared to be about his age, had fashionably bobbed hair, green eyes, and the most adorable pouty lips. "I'm sorry, Miss," he said. "It won't happen again."

"Hmmph." She climbed in the carriage, her red dress swishing against the cushions.

"My name is George."

"I don't care who you are."

Sometimes it was difficult to remain polite. "Mr. Kline has us introduce ourselves," George said, "in case the customer wants to ask for us by name next time."

"There better not *be* a next time."

He'd been instructed never to turn and look directly at his fares. "Where to, then?"

"Dale's Grocery. You know where that is?"

"Yes, Miss. All of the Kline drivers are fully trained."

The girl flopped against the back of the seat hard enough that George could feel the vibration. She sighed and muttered, "Daddy thinks I'm a common scullery maid."

George knew she was just thinking out loud, but he responded anyway. "Your father's that fighter at Electrical Park?"

"My father is a beer distributor. I don't know who that beast at Electrical Park is."

There could only be one Orville "Luka" Curtis, but George didn't argue. "Must be a different Curtis."

"Did I say I wanted a conversation with you?"

George's mother would be outraged to hear anyone address her son so rudely, even if that person's father was almost as rich as she was. "Sorry, Miss," he said.

He shook the reins and the brougham jerked gently forward. At the end of her lane he turned right onto Middlesex and right again two blocks later onto Fourth Street. Several other carriages cluttered the road, and a few motor cars. They were nearing the busiest time of the day, when first shift at the local businesses let out.

George saw a pothole on the street too late to avoid it, and the brougham's front left wheel clanked into it, causing a nasty bump.

"Watch where you're going," the girl said.

"Sorry."

"You're just a boy. Why didn't they send an experienced driver?"

"I'm old enough, Miss, and I know my way around."

"I doubt that."

George turned left onto Locus Street. Dale's Grocery was straight ahead. He pulled in behind the store, and the girl stepped out of the brougham. "Shall I wait here?" he said.

"No, you idiot, I thought I'd carry the groceries home on my back."

"I don't mean to make you angry," he said.

70

She walked up next to him. He could feel her glaring at him, but he didn't look down. "Hey," she said, and "Hey" again when he didn't answer.

He sneaked a peek out of the corner of his eyes.

The girl's expression had softened. "It's not you I'm mad at," she said finally. "Will you come in and help me with the groceries?"

"Sure," he said.

"Thank you," she said. "My name is Cora."

***

George relaxed in the bathtub as he read the paper. In April a U.S. Senate subcommittee headed by Ohio Senator William Alden Smith had concluded that the *Titanic* disaster had been caused by the ship's excessive speed at the time it hit the iceberg. In May the British Board of Trade had begun its own inquiry, which was just now wrapping up. The British conclusion? That the *Titanic* disaster had been caused by the ship's excessive speed at the time it hit the iceberg.

George folded the paper and tossed it onto the sink. The water in the tub was hot, just the way he liked it. He slid his head under and held his breath for a few moments. It felt good to wash the sweat from his skin.

My name is Cora, she'd said.

Cora Curtis.

George blew a bubble, then raised his face above the surface. His entire body was immersed in water except his nose, mouth and eyes. The warmth engulfing him, coupled with thoughts of Cora, gave him a tingling sensation that was alarmingly pleasant.

The ride back to Middlesex had gone better than the trip out. He'd listened to her complaints about the unfair way her sex was expected to behave in the world. She had a notion that women would get the vote some day, and when they did, watch out, men! Her tirade was a monologue, broken only by an occasional *yes-I'm-still-interested* "Uh-huh" from him whenever she paused for a breath. All her venom was directed at her father, which meant she wasn't yelling at George, which was fine with him. After a while he quit paying attention to what she was saying and just savored the rhythm of her voice.

It wasn't a high-pitched girly voice, like most of the teenagers he knew, but the deeper, more mature tones of someone older.

At her house the foreign maid came out to pay him. Cora, who until then had shown little inclination toward friendliness, smiled sweetly and said, "Thank you *so* much, George."

She brushed her fingertips against his cheek, flipped her hair flirtatiously, and then strolled inside without once looking at the servant.

71

George knew it had only been a performance for the woman to pass on to Cora's father, but he enjoyed her touch anyway.

"Do you want me to help with the groceries?" he'd said to the woman.

"I will carry them," she said. She handed him a twenty dollar bill and told him to keep the change. Even for someone as accustomed to money as George was, twenty dollars was a huge tip for a fifty cent fare.

He barely remembered the ride back to Kline's or the customers he picked up afterwards.

My name is Cora.

The bath water was starting to cool, but his teenaged body wasn't. He got out of the tub and slowly toweled himself off, continuing to rub even after he was dry. The *Record's* story about the *Titanic* lay face up on the sink. The disaster had been caused by the ship's excessive speed when it hit the iceberg.

Should have slowed down, he thought, rubbing furiously.

CORA
Waterton, Iowa
July 1912

"Goddamn it, Weinshank," her father screamed into the telephone, "I don't want excuses. *Find* a way to make her sell!"

He disconnected, then pounded his right fist into the palm of his left hand.

As Cora descended the stairs she noticed a woman making herself comfortable on their plush davenport in the parlor. Informally attired, she was several years too young for Luka, but she was pretty and had the curly blond hair he favored in his whores. Sipping brandy from a crystal wineglass, the woman smiled and said hello.

She sounded nice. Cora returned the smile. In her best little girl voice she said, "Are you the same one who was here last night?"

The woman's expression turned icy. "Why, yes, dear, I am."

Cora shook her head in mock surprise. "That's unusual."

"*Cora Jean Curtis!*" Luka said. "That will be *enough*."

He apologized to the woman, but the damage had been done. She rearranged her clothing, made her excuses, and left. Luka offered to call a carriage, but she was already out the door. She'd spilled brandy on their expensive Persian rug.

Cora went to make a sandwich in the kitchen, then slipped up the back stairs to her room. She lay on her bed, eating her snack and waiting for her father's angry footsteps. Well, what did he expect? She'd always known he had an eye for ladies, but he'd never been quite so blatant about his indiscretions before. For two months he'd been bringing home as many as four women a week, all too young for him and all blonds. Her mother's hair had been blond.

Did he think Cora wouldn't notice? Did he think she couldn't hear the sounds coming from his bedroom? It was right under hers, for God's sake! She knew what was happening, even if she couldn't quite grasp the mechanics yet.

"A man has needs," Birgitta had explained one night as Cora cried into her pillow. A man has needs. Ah.

"And what do women need?" Cora said.

"Women need men," Birgitta said with something very like disgust in her voice.

Cora swallowed the last of her sandwich. Luka carried a small photograph of her mother in his pocket watch. As his footsteps thundered toward her room, as she knew they would, she wondered:

Does he wear his watch when he's with his women, or hide it away in a drawer out of respect for the dead?

***

When she was told to do the shopping the next day, she insisted on telephoning Kline's herself. Luka's wagon was available, but that boy cabbie had been polite and willing to listen—qualities her father lacked—and she wanted to talk to him again. She'd behaved abominably toward him the first time. Perhaps she would apologize.

The man who answered at Kline's, however, replied that there were three drivers called George. What was his last name?

"I don't know," she said. "He's young, a teenager."

"That would be George Hammon."

Hammon? *Hammon*? She knew of only one Hammon family in town. The widow of the war hero was even richer than her father. She did have a boy, although Cora couldn't remember his name. Why on earth would the son of Margaret Hammon be working at a livery stable? "Of the Hammon Falls Hammons?" she said.

"There is no other."

"This is Orville Curtis's daughter. Is he available?"

"Nope. Out on a hospital run. Would you like to request another driver, Miss Curtis?"

"No, I'll try back later," Cora said, and disconnected.

How do you like that? she thought. Here she was all ready to say she was sorry, and the lout didn't even have the grace to be there.

Still, a *Hammon*! What would her father think of that?

GEORGE
Waterton and Hammon Falls, Iowa
July 1912

George had been on hospital runs before. Sometimes he served as an ambulance driver, transporting sick or injured people to the hospital. Sometimes he took recovered patients home from the hospital. This one was different, though. The call had come from Gindt's Funeral Services. They wanted Kline's to pick up a body from the Presbyterian Hospital on Levi Street and bring it in for embalming.

George had never seen a dead person. Worse, this wasn't just any dead person, it was Clara Morrissey, the woman who'd married his grandfather Bill after Bill's first wife died back in the '80's. She was the only human being George's mother truly hated.

Clara's name was not spoken at home. George didn't know she was still in the area. Hell, he didn't know she was still *alive*.

Only now she wasn't.

He wasn't looking forward to this.

"Don't you fret none," Lewis said en route to the hospital, "the dead ain't people any more. Nothing they did or didn't do matter now. Whatever they got coming to 'em in the everlasting already been done. By the time we get 'em, they only slabs of meat."

Lewis clicked his tongue and the horses surged out onto West Park Street. The afternoon was warm and muggy, with an overcast sky that did not threaten rain.

"She was my grandmother, sort of." George said. "My mother's stepmother."

"Ever meet the lady?"

"No."

"Then she weren't no kin of yours."

As the hearse clattered toward the Presbyterian Hospital, George told Lewis Clara's story as his mother had told it to him. When he was done Lewis said, "Well, I guess that's sad, all right. But, you know, down in Mississippi that kind of thing happen all the time. *All* the time. Only white man *took* our families from us, sold us like cattle."

George didn't know exactly how old Lewis was, but surely he'd been born after the Emancipation Proclamation. "Slavery ended fifty years ago," he said.

"Slavery ain't never ended," Lewis said as they arrived at the hospital. "Don't you know that?" He took the carriage around back to the loading dock.

"This is creepy," George said.

"Wait here while I ring the bell," Lewis said. "They'll bring her out and put her in the coach. You don't even gotta see her face, you don't want to. She be under a sheet."

"I always wondered what Clara looked like."

Lewis hopped down. "She never look dead before, that for sure. Just let her be, son."

Moments later two attendants emerged from the hospital pushing a gurney bearing the shrouded lump that had once been Clara Morrissey. Lewis helped them lift her into the hearse. He whispered to one of the attendants, who whispered back.

On the way to Gindt's Funeral Services, George said, "What was that all about?"

"'Case your Momma ever wanna know, I ask him what the lady die of."

"And?"

"He say her liver 'bout the size of a watermelon and all pocked up like the moon. Had a hard life, Georgie. Drink herself to death."

George glanced over his shoulder. The hearse was covered, so he couldn't see anything, but just the idea of the corpse's head lying a few inches away gave him the shivers. "Do you believe in ghosts, Lewis?"

"Shit, son, I got enough problems in this world already to be worrying 'bout spooks from the next."

***

Back at Kline's they put away the hearse and tended the horses. While in the office turning in the payment from the hospital, George learned that the Curtis girl had requested his services, asked for him by name. She would call back. Until then, Kline had instructed him not to accept other fares. That set his stomach all aflutter again. Cora Curtis. Last time she'd acted like she hated him.

"Did you hear that, Lewis? She wants me to drive her again!"

"A lady's man at sixteen, my, my."

"What should I do?"

"What should you *do*? When she call, pick her up. What happen after, well, you can work that out for your own self." Lewis broke into a big grin. His teeth were crooked and yellow, but his smile glowed like the sun. "Just one thing. Her daddy one mean sumbitch. You be careful of that man. He a fighter over at Electrical Park, you know."

The call came.

George went.

He tried not to think about anything on the way to Middlesex. Clara Morrissey's dead body was too sad, Luka Curtis's fists too intimidating,

Cora's pouty lips too exciting. The clouds kept the temperature from getting oppressive, but the humidity felt thick enough to douse a match. The smells of the city, the horse droppings and factory smoke and motor car exhaust, hung motionless in the air. It was almost too heavy to breathe.

Or maybe the tightness in his chest was nerves.

At the Curtis house, Cora rushed to greet him. "Hello, George Hammon!" she said.

The foreign woman was nowhere to be seen, but George noticed the curtains in one of the windows pull back. The shadowy figure of a man was watching them. Had Cora said something to her father?

"You know my last name?" he said.

She stepped up into the brougham. "You didn't tell me Kline's had *three* Georges. I had to ask which one you were."

"Sorry. Dale's Groceries?"

"You apologize a lot."

"Sorry," he said, and they both laughed.

"Dale's," she said. "But first, take me to Electrical Park. I hear the aero-plane ride is scary. You can come with and hold my hand when I scream."

"I can't. I work until ten." He shook the reins and thought about what an idiot he was.

He'd dreamed of Cora Curtis many nights in his bath, in his bed. More than dreamed. Now the best he could manage was *I can't. I work until ten*?

"Dale's, then." After that she was silent for a while. As they turned onto Third Street she finally said, "It's hot and the air smells and why does a Hammon have to drive a carriage, anyway?"

He pulled to a stop behind Dale's. "I don't have to, I want to."

"What for? Your mother is rich."

"I want to earn my own money."

Cora got out of the brougham and climbed up next to him in the second driver's seat. She leaned in uncomfortably close when spoke. He felt his face flushing. "Is this allowed?" she said.

"No, I mean, yes. Whatever the customer wants, I guess."

"Good. So. I say it's stupid to work when you don't need the money."

"Your father gets paid to fight. He doesn't need the money."

She turned a shoulder to him. "My father is a brute. I don't want to talk about him. And don't you dare say you're sorry!"

George kept his eyes on his feet. "I'll help you with the groceries."

She hopped down. Her brown hair had curled and frayed in the humidity. "You are *so* infuriating, George Hammon."

George decided to take a chance. "I'm not infuriating when I'm off duty."

Cora's face lit up. "Oh?" she said.

***

Before he dropped her off they agreed to meet at Electrical Park on George's next full day off, the first Sunday in August. Walking home from work that night, the only thing that kept his giddiness in check was the knowledge that he'd have to tell his mother about Clara Morrissey. He didn't want her to read it in the paper first.

He took his bath, then found her, as always, in the library. She wasn't studying her Bible this time. She seemed to be waiting for him.

"Mother," he said, "something happened today. I know you don't like anyone mentioning her name, but—"

"Clara is dead. I know."

"You know?"

His mother patted the chair next to hers. She looked somber, almost angry. "Sit down."

George sat. "She drank herself to death."

"I'm not surprised. I've had people watching her. She had a dreadful existence. What a sad, wasted life."

"If you knew, why didn't you help her?"

"She made her choices."

"Mother, whatever you thought of her, she was your father's wife."

"She didn't come to me, she didn't ask. She knew who I'd married and where I lived, and she *didn't ask.*"

"*Would* you have helped?"

She lifted the family Bible from the reading table and opened it at random. She pretended to read, but she was just staring at pages. Her eyes didn't move. "She didn't ask," she said.

George didn't know what else to say.

She slammed the Bible shut and stood up. "We will not be attending the funeral." Her jaw was set, her teeth clenched, her eyes hard. She was *daring* him to argue.

Instead, he said softly, "I met a girl today."

"How nice," she said, and stormed off to her bedroom.

George just gawked at her. He'd never dreamed his mother capable of such vehemence, and her a Christian woman.

Later that night, though, in his room next to hers, he heard her weeping.

CORA
Hammon Falls, Iowa
August 1912

Cora flew out over the Oak River, screaming and laughing. She dug the fingernails of both hands into George's right bicep. The Aero-Thrill was the most popular attraction at Electrical Park. It always had the longest waiting lines. Its metal cables whipped biplane-shaped chairs around with impossible speed, dipping down to ten or fifteen feet above the ground and then soaring upward into the dome of the great blue sky.

From her little plane Cora could see for miles. In quick succession the river rose up and dwindled, then the grounds, the woods, the ballroom, the trees, the train depot, the hated boxing arena. She never really came near to any of these landmarks, but at this speed they seemed close enough to touch—or rather, to crash into.

"I want to fly in a real aero-plane someday," she said.

George looked thoroughly pale. "I think I might throw up," he said.

"You better not," she said.

He didn't, but when the Aero-Thrill ride was over, Cora insisted on trying the Spiral Terror rollercoaster, then the Ferris wheel. Then she needed a hot dog and cotton candy. Then to "freshen herself." When she came out of the ballroom's toilet, she caught George counting his money. "Don't tell me it's gone already," she said.

"That was a whole week's wages," he said. Color had returned to his face.

"Well, if you can't *afford* me...."

"No, it's okay. Can we just walk?"

Cora played coy. "All right, but I have to be home by six-thirty. No funny business."

She still wasn't sure exactly what "funny business" entailed, but her friends used the phrase all the time. She thought about the pamphlets that had gotten her expelled from school, and especially about the sounds coming out of her father's room when he was with his whores.

"Word of honor," George said.

His tone of voice made her wonder if *he* knew what funny business was.

They exited Electrical Park and turned right onto Caladonia, which soon merged into the North Waterton-Cedar Crossing Road. From here Waterton's many factories were only a short distance to the south and east, but to the west stood a beautiful expanse of woods that had survived the early settlers' axes.

"I used to play out this way all the time when I was a kid," George said.

She shushed him. "Just enjoy the sunshine," she said.

Neither spoke as the city gave way to wilderness. For the first time since she had witnessed her father fight, Cora was at peace. She'd had a wonderful time today. She didn't need George's voice right now, only the quiet and the shared closeness she felt with him—although she did rather hope he would hold her hand.

He didn't.

After half an hour, a series of widely-spaced mounds rose up on the north side of the road, between the asphalt and the trees. Not quite as tall as a man, the mounds resembled the spiny ridges on the backs of dragons.

"Look," she said, and turned toward the closest one.

"Don't," George said. "Indians are buried there."

Cora stopped. "What?"

"When a warrior died in battle, his tribe sat him up with his weapons and beads and stuff around him and covered him with dirt. That's what those mounds are. They go on for miles."

"There's *skeletons* in those little hills?" she said.

"Probably all that's left by now is the dirt."

"I don't want to find out. Can we go back? The last trolley's at six."

George shrugged, as if to say, *If that's what you want.* Cora was mildly annoyed he gave in so easily. He'd done whatever she asked all afternoon. Didn't *he* ever want anything? On the other hand, they were only a few feet away from a graveyard full of dead Indians—dead Indians who were sitting up, watching the road, watching *them.*

"I'm scared," she said. "Put your arm around me?"

"There's nothing to be scared of—"

"Put your arm around me anyway."

He did. His hand was trembling. On the way to the trolley he told her about his Negro friend Lewis. Cora's father despised colored people, but she had no experience with them and so had no opinion. The way she felt about Luka, though, anything he hated was bound to be good.

They passed Electrical Park, which had closed at five, and crossed the bridge onto Gloire de Matin Island. George's home was nearby, although she didn't know which one it was.

"I'll stay 'til the trolley comes," he said. Only a few people were waiting for the last run of the day. Cora and George sat at the end of a bench, away from the others. He kept his arm around her, and she let him, although propriety frowned upon such familiarity in public.

George was flexing the muscles in his right arm and opening and closing his fist.

"What's wrong?" she said.

He smiled. "You squeezed me so hard on the aero-plane ride that I'm just now getting feeling back."

She shoved him playfully and said, "Did not."

"No, really, I'm fine. I'll probably be able to use my arm again in a week or two."

They laughed, and for a moment she thought he might kiss her, but he backed away. "Are you ever going to invite me to your house?" she said.

He looked over his shoulder and pointed to a palatial home nestled in a cul-de-sac at the end of a private lane.

"Oh, my," she said.

"Yeah," he said.

"I've heard a lot about your mother and your late father."

"She's been out of sorts," he said. "Her stepmother Clara just died."

"My mother died, too. I was ten and a half. She had a cancer. I miss her so much."

George stood up and jammed his hands into his pockets. He didn't say anything.

"What?" Cora said. "I didn't mean to make you sad."

"It's not that. My mother *hated* Clara."

"I don't understand."

"I do."

A dinging bell signaled the approach of the electric trolley. George helped Cora up. They were standing almost chest to chest.

He was breathing rapidly through his nose, as if he were nervous.

She was nervous, too. As the trolley rattled to a stop, George looked at her expectantly, and she at him. "Have you ever kissed a girl before?" she said.

He leaned forward and smooched her right on the lips. "I have now," he said.

GEORGE
Hammon Falls & Waterton, Iowa
September - October 1912

Ed and Estella were in their seventies, married to each other, with something like ten grown children. They had been employed in the Hammon household since the late '60's, but only moved in once their kids had left the nest. George thought of them almost as grandparents.

He sat with his mother at the dining table as Ed set a luscious poultry dish before them.

"It's duck something-or-other," the servant said, his eyes twinkling, "something Essie threw together." He scooped portions onto each of their plates, then withdrew to the kitchen.

George dug right in. The duck was delicious. He finished before his mother even took a bite. "What's wrong?" he said, sipping his milk. "Why aren't you eating?"

She turned her eyes toward him. Her expression was unreadable. She didn't speak. The ticking of the antique grandfather clock in the library filled the silence.

"*What?*" George said.

"Cora Curtis," she said.

"Cora Curtis?" he said.

"You didn't tell me *that* was the girl you've taken up with."

"You didn't ask. I haven't *taken up* with her."

"Need I remind you that you're sixteen years old?"

"What's wrong with Cora? I thought you'd approve. Her father is rich."

She pushed her plate away. "I don't care how rich he is. Orville Curtis is trash. He's trying to buy this town, and he doesn't care how he gets it. For God's sake, George, he's a *boxer*. He prances around half naked in public while a mob drools for blood."

"I've never met him."

"And you never will. You're done seeing his daughter."

George rose and glared down at her. "No," he said, "I'm not."

"There will be repercussions," she said.

His mother often huffed and puffed, but she never blew the house down. Her lawyer, Arlen Kelper, handled all her dirty work—and what was Kelper going to do? Take him to court?

George continued to see Cora when he could, but those times became less frequent once school started in the fall. He was in class all day during the week, then at Kline's until ten. He also worked on Saturdays. The only times they could meet was on Sundays or the occasional trip to

Dale's. His mother made a half-hearted attempt to interfere by increasing his chores and insisting that he attend church every week.

But he figured her resolve would crumble, and it did. She wasn't good at saying no to him.

"It's Cora's birthday tomorrow," he told her on the first Sunday in October. "We're going to Electrical Park." The rides were innocent fun, he claimed, remembering how her breasts had pressed against him as she'd dug her fingernails into his arm.

"Oh, do what you want," his mother said, waving her hand dismissively, as if it were all so tiresome.

***

Soon he was experiencing the most startling feelings for Cora. They were wonderful and agonizing at the same time, and he knew that once a week wasn't enough anymore. He wanted to see her every day, every minute.

He couldn't drop out of school. But he could quit Kline's to free up his evenings.

"Am I doing the right thing?" he said to Lewis. They sat together on the fence that separated the stalls of Brownie and Bucktooth. The autumn air was pungent with the smells of horse droppings and hay.

"Folks do foolish things and call it love," Lewis said. "My Freddie, he got a girl. Hell, he light his own hair on fire, she ask him to. See, he 'bout your age, and sometimes young boys, they don't think things through like they should."

"I've thought and *thought* about it."

"You sixteen, Georgie, you got time. Working keep you an honest man."

"You just don't want me to leave."

Lewis smiled sadly. "Can't say that ain't true. You and Mr. Kline probably the finest white people I ever know. Treat me the same as you do your own. That mean something to me." One of the horses neighed in its sleep, responding to some horse-dream. Outside, the last of the season's crickets sang into the night. George hopped down from the fence, and Lewis followed. "Shake an old nigger's hand before you go?"

George looked at his friend, his dark face, his teeth and eyes yellow in the lanterns' glow. "I don't like that word."

"Me neither."

George took Lewis' hand, savoring the rough texture of the man's skin, the strength of his fingers. "This isn't enough," he said.

"Nope," Lewis said, and swept George up in a big bear hug.

"I'll visit you, I promise," George said.

"You better. You don't, I'll come looking for a ass to kick."

CORA
Waterton, Iowa
October 1912 - March 1913

"George *Hammon*?" Luka said.

"Yes," Cora said. She'd never told her father who she saw on Sunday afternoons. His lawyer Weinshank probably ratted them out. That horrible man was always snooping around.

"That's the boy been driving you to Dale's all this time? Maggie Hammon's son?"

"So?"

"And he's working for Kline?"

"Not any more, he quit last week. Anyway, he just worked there because he wanted to."

"I hear he's going with you to Electrical Park on Sunday? Birgitta had a birthday dinner planned for you."

"My birthday's not 'til Monday. Have her fix it then."

"Or we could have George over. Don't you think you ought to introduce him?"

This was not the reaction she'd expected. She assumed when her father learned about George he'd forbid her to have anything to do with him. Instead, he invited him to dinner. Okay, so he wanted something. Not from George, obviously, so it must be Mrs. Hammon. "I don't think he'll come," she said. "He's pretty shy."

Luka smiled. "Well, he'll have to get over that. No man ever gets anywhere in life by being timid. He's got to *take* what he wants."

Including me? Cora thought. "I'll ask him," she said.

"George Hammon," her father said. "I'll be damned."

***

After Electrical Park Cora felt different. She was happy, but underneath there was something else. Unease, maybe, restlessness, anticipation. Although she was no longer frightened by the rides, she continued to dig her fingers into George's arm and pull herself close. She wondered if he noticed how her breasts pressed against his body or how her heart beat faster when he kissed her goodbye at the trolley.

After serving her expulsion for the pamphlet incident in May, she had been reinstated in school this fall, and was now a junior. She'd been on her best behavior for weeks, but the next day, her sixteenth birthday, she couldn't concentrate on her lessons because she was thinking about George. He made her distinctly *tingly*.

"Miss Curtis," said Miss Volmensky, the music teacher who'd gotten her kicked out of school, "would you like to join the class today?"

"Sorry, Ma'am."

"E flat above middle C. Pay attention, please. On the upbeat."

Cora sang and went to her other classes and, when the bell rang, left for home.

George didn't join them for supper that night, but he did for Thanksgiving, and by Christmas he was a regular visitor. He seemed intimidated by Luka but came anyway.

George's mother never reciprocated the invitation.

Cora didn't mind the snub. Margaret Hammon had developed an aura about her, a mystique that was only intensified by her social reclusiveness. Luka was brutish and bombastic but approachable. Mrs. Hammon was impenetrable. George had brought Cora into his home, but his mother refused to be introduced. She moved wraithlike through other rooms, at the top of the stairs, a barely-seen presence who cast a shadowy pall over the entire house.

Ed and Estella were nice, though.

Electrical Park had closed for the season in the middle of October, and a typically frigid Iowa winter followed. Instead of aero-plane amusements and rollercoasters, Cora and George delighted at the moving picture shows at the *Majestic* and the *Lyric* theatres or ice skated on the frozen Oak River near George's house.

They kissed a lot more now, and that was all right with Cora. She learned to look forward to those strange underlying feelings he inspired in her.

***

At supper in February her father triumphantly thrust a copy of the *Waterton Record* at Cora. "I knew the Germans were a sensible people," he said. "The Berlin Reichstag just rejected a petition for suffrage. I told you women would never get the vote!"

"This isn't Germany," Cora said.

"Germany, America, it doesn't matter. They said no and so will we, if it comes to that."

Cora hated the way his thin little mustache wiggled when he spoke, especially when he was being smug. She tapped a napkin at the corner of her mouth and stood up. "May I be excused?" she said.

As she headed for the stairs he said, "Are you seeing George tomorrow?"

"We're going to a flicker at the *Majestic*."

"Does he ever try anything with you in the dark?"

She knew what he was getting at. "*Try* anything? Like what?"

"You're not being stupid, are you?"

"Like you are when you're with your girlfriends?" she said, and skipped up the steps to her room. She lay on her stomach on the bed and flipped open the February *Harper's Magazine* to a short story called "Vivia Climbs the Heights," by Louise Closser Hale. The story didn't hold her interest, but the notion of George "trying" in the dark did. She tried to visualize what went on in her father's room, which triggered memories of the Sanger birth control pamphlet and the rubbery condom, which led her to speculate, again, about penises.

She knew it was indecent for a girl to think about such things, but her friend Lizzie talked of nothing else, and even claimed to have *touched* one. She described it in some detail. Unlikely as her depiction seemed, well, that *was* how the condom had been shaped.

But was it true what Lizzie said men did with them? Is that what Luka did to his women? Is that what George might do to *her* someday?

Shocked by her own depraved imagination, she turned off her lamp, covered her head with a pillow, and tried to sing the desire right out of her mind.

***

By the end of March the ice on the Oak River had melted, except for brittle shelves clinging to the banks. The sky was clear blue, the temperature close to fifty degrees. Spring's first buds were starting to poke through the ground. George had telephoned to tell Cora to bundle up, he had a surprise for her. He took her to the water's edge near the Sixth Street Bridge, where he had a rowboat waiting.

"What on earth are you doing?" she said.

He pointed to a tiny islet in the middle of the river "forested" with a dozen or so elm trees. "Come on," he said. "That's Lover's Island. Half the babies in town were created right there."

Cora slapped his shoulder playfully. "You're awful," she said.

George helped her into the boat, then stepped in behind her. Part of the ice shelf broke away under his feet. "I'll row," he said.

The current was slow for this time of year. Melting snows in Minnesota usually swelled the streams to near flood stage, but a cold snap up north had delayed the thaw there, and today the river moved peacefully in its course. George pulled on the oars, and the boat glided easily out onto the water. Despite the warmth, Cora could see her breath. "I want to row, too," she said.

"I can do it," George said.

"You don't have to show off for me."

"I'm not showing off."

"Then let me row. It's only a little ways." She scrambled up next to him and took an oar.

"In rhythm," he said. "One, two, one, two."

On the island he secured the boat, then led her to a spot in the midst of the trees. By June there'd be enough greenery to shield them from passersby on the shores or the bridge above, but in March the defoliated elms offered little shelter.

"What are your intentions, sir?" Cora said, feeling a little naughty. There was that tingly sensation again.

"Just talk," he said. The ground was still wet from recent snows, but the bark on a fallen trunk had warmed enough in the sun to make for a dry seat. "Any other time there'd be a lot of couples here, kissing or, well, you know. But we've got it all to ourselves now. I thought it would be nice to go somewhere where there weren't all those people. You know, Electrical Park, school, the flickers, your house, they're all fun, but we never get to be alone."

She sat next to him and folded her arms around her knees. Maybe he expected something, or maybe she did, but neither made a move. A slight breeze from the west carried a reminder of winter and a hint of spring.

"Indians used to come to this island," George said abruptly. "The Sac or Fox tribe, I don't remember which. When I was a kid, there was this story about an Indian maiden who used to meet her white lover here. It was the only place they could find peace. The Indians hated him and the whites hated her. So they came here where they could love each other in their own little world."

"Romantic," Cora said.

"Yeah, but one day, an Indian from her tribe saw them. He shot at the man, but the maiden threw herself in front of him. The arrow went through her heart. She died in her lover's arms."

Cora looked up. "Then the Indian shot the white man, too, right? So they both died. Thanks for telling me *that* story. I love happy endings."

"It's like Romeo and Juliet."

"'Wherefore art thou, Romeo?'" she said in a fake British accent. It was the only line she memorized from the play. "Are you ever going to kiss me again?"

"I thought I would," he said, and did.

Alone on their island, unhidden by the leafless trees, they kissed, enthusiastically and for a long time, and Cora realized her tingling was what Lizzie called *passion*. Passion was very nice.

She lifted George's hand and cupped it over her breast. Neither of them would feel much through her winter coat, but it didn't matter. She knew now that this is what she'd been dreaming about since the Aero-Thrill ride in Electrical Park.

"Are you sure?" he said.

"I want you to," she said.

She wanted to do more, too—whatever *more* was—but on that spring day on Lover's Island, they didn't.

GEORGE
Waterton, Iowa
April 1913

More finally happened on April 29, 1913, on a rainy night in the loft of Luka Curtis's stable. George was seventeen, Cora sixteen. It took them three tries on three different nights. The first time George was so terrified of being caught that they never even got undressed. He was still afraid of her father, although the man was friendly enough and always made him feel welcome. Still, he was a *boxer*. George never forgot what Lewis had said: *Her daddy one mean sumbitch. You be careful of that man.*

The second time Cora giggled when she saw him naked, not derisively but out of nervousness and surprise. Her laughter had a decidedly deflating effect on the ardor her nudity had inspired, and no amount of coaxing or apologizing could rekindle his interest that night.

The third time, the success, was a blur. He remembered that the smell of horses and hay in the stable made him think of Kline's at a time he was fairly certain he shouldn't be thinking of Kline's. He remembered the rain on the shingles and the wind spinning the weather vane on the roof. He remembered an anxiety so intense he nearly puked. He remembered some ups and downs, and ups, and then having difficulty in placement. When he finally got where he wanted to be, where they both wanted him to be, the fit was tight and the chafing it caused would ache for days afterward. But then a little spurt of Cora's blood made things slipperier and more pleasant.

It ended very quickly with both of them crying and thunder building in the west.

CORA
Waterton, Iowa
April 1913

She didn't mean to giggle, but the silly thing looked *exactly* like Lizzie said it would. It started off rigid and upright, but when she laughed it went soft and small in a hurry. She hoped she didn't hurt George's feelings too badly, but she was new at this, too. It didn't take them long to figure out that nothing much could happen with him in *that* condition. And so they held each other, and that was nice.

The night they succeeded was rainy and a little too cold to be naked in a stable. The horses stank. The hay was damp and smelled of mildew. The roof leaked in one corner, where it always did, drip drip drip. She was anxious and wanted to throw up. George went up and down and up again like a jumping jack. When he was finally ready, he had problems finding the bull's eye.

"Are you *sure* this is how it's supposed to work?" she said. She felt chilly, but his skin was hot and sweaty.

"Pretty sure," he said.

The hay was pointy and itchy on her back as he tried again. The penetration, when it came, was surprisingly painful, not at all what she imagined it might be. By the look on George's face, it wasn't altogether comfortable for him, either. Was this the need Birgitta said men have? Why, if it hurt so much?

But then the blood came, not the blood of her period but the blood of her first time, and the lubrication it provided hinted, briefly, at the potential of this strange activity called sex.

George suddenly made an alarming series of funny sounds, shuddered two or three times, and then it was over.

The physical experience hadn't impressed her much—she was sure it would improve with time and practice—but her emotional response was overwhelming. This was a gift they'd given to each other, and if it wasn't perfect, so what? Love made it beautiful.

"Thank you," he said, and they both cried. Thunder announced that the storm had turned bumpy, but she would always remember April 29 as a clear and starry night.

PROHIBITION AND DEPRESSION

MARGARET
Hammon Falls, Iowa
May 1920

Wednesday, May 12, 1920, was the third anniversary of their wedding. Margaret sat alone in the house, as she had for her first and second anniversaries. Orville was speaking at a meeting of Electrical Park's board of directors, of which he was now chair. Margaret had declined to attend. She didn't approve of the way he'd wrested control of the park from the previous managers. But then, she didn't approve of much of anything Orville did.

He needed Electrical Park, he claimed, since passage of the Volstead Act in January—Prohibition—had shut down his beer warehouse. If he'd owned a distillery, he could have converted his operation to the manufacture of ice cream, as many breweries had. But he was only the middle-man, and both ends had dried up on him.

Margaret sat in the library, reading her Bible. William was playing with his toy automobiles at her feet. A gentle rain fell outside, tapping on the windows with a lovely, lulling sound. All in all, the night was rather pleasant. She didn't mind Orville's absence. That's when she disliked him least.

"Grandma," William said, "can I read with you?"

Now six, he was too big to fit comfortably in her lap anymore, especially since her lap, like William, was expanding with the years.

"Not now, dear," she said. "Why don't you lie down?"

"I'm not tired," he said.

"You don't have to go to your room, just here on the sofa."

"Okay, Grandma."

Despite his protestations, he was asleep almost as soon as his head hit the cushion. He was such a good little fellow. Everything she'd done, she'd done for him.

Margaret watched him adoringly. His poor face, his poor eye. Even at his age he had to wear glasses with a frosted lens to hide the effects of a prenatal infection. Despite the disfigurement, he was a beautiful child. She had to admit, he favored his mother more than his father. But he was all Margaret had left of George, and she was determined to hold onto him at all costs.

At *all* costs.

Once Judge Hauken had ruled against her in the custody case, her options had dwindled to two: take the boy and run, or accept Orville's marriage proposal. Running was out of the question —she would not stoop to George's level—so only marriage remained. She wasn't a fool.

She knew Orville didn't love her. He did seem to have feelings for William, but he didn't let sentiment prevent him from using his own grandson to get what he wanted from Margaret.

And he got it, most of it anyway. Their entire relationship had been one of accommodation. *Quid pro quo* was the Latin term, or so Mr. Kelper said. Over time, the negotiations amounted to something like this:

Orville: Marry me and share custody of Will.

Margaret: You can't adopt the boy. He'll keep George's last name.

Orville: But you'll take mine.

Margaret: I won't sell my home.

Orville: I'll sell mine.

Margaret: Separate bedrooms.

Orville: Transfer the Stanley's lease to me.

Margaret: What do you want with a roller skating rink?

Orville: It's a saloon, Maggie.

Margaret: Don't be ridiculous.

Orville: Don't play dumb.

Margaret: Ed and Estella stay.

Orville: Birgitta's coming, too.

It was supposed to be fair to each of them, but the more Margaret thought about it, the more she realized how unilateral the agreement had actually been. Orville had gotten everything he wanted—her house, access to her fortune, Stanley's Parkside Amusement's, William—while all she'd gained was a superfluous husband.

She turned to Matthew 19:4-6, where Jesus said:

***

Have you not read…that at the beginning the Creator "made them male and female," and said, "For this reason a man will leave his father and mother and be united to his wife, and the two will become one flesh?" So they are no longer two, but one. Therefore what God has joined together, let man not separate.

***

The two will become one flesh. Margaret smiled wryly. That's a good one, Lord. You have a sense of humor.

The merging of their flesh had been a hurry-up affair performed by a justice of the peace Orville knew in Chicago. Margaret and Orville were high society here, but in a city the size of Chicago they were just two faces in the crowd. They hoped their anonymity would keep the press away, and in Chicago it did. The ceremony had lasted all of fifteen minutes, and was witnessed by exactly three people other than the participants and the judge. Birgitta had attended under protest, and Ed and Estella out of outrage.

And of course, the press was waiting for them anyway when they returned to Hammon Falls, taking unwelcome photographs and writing scandalous stories.

It was hardly what Jesus had in mind when he spoke of marriage. In fact, if there was any otherworldly involvement, it had not come from above. But what could she do? She and Orville had battled it out in court twice now, over Will in 1917, and over Orville's precious little whore-daughter in 1913. Orville had won both times.

The most galling thing of all was that Margaret had had to transfer G.W.'s wedding ring from her left hand to her right to make room for Orville's. Oh, to have her beloved G.W. relegated to second place behind Orville Curtis! Three years later, it still felt wrong, blasphemously wrong.

She had her house on Gloire de Matin, but her last human connection to her old life with G.W. ended when the Spanish flu reaped its horrendous harvest, rising out of Kansas and crossing the ocean and back again. Only one person Margaret knew intimately was claimed by it, but that person was Estella. She didn't even have time to put up a brave fight. The symptoms started before dawn, and by sunset she was gone. Although untouched by the disease, Ed's spirit was crushed by her death. Inconsolable, he resigned to move in with an unmarried daughter in Ohio.

That left only the Finnish woman for a servant. Margaret didn't care for Birgitta, but she had to give the lady credit: she was not afraid to tell Orville what she thought.

Margaret was not able to do that.

The rain came down harder. William stirred on the sofa. Margaret set the Bible aside and scooped her grandson into her arms to carry him upstairs to his room.

She had never approved of Orville Curtis, the man with the barbaric nickname of "Luka," and now she was married to him. But of all the things of hers he coveted, Margaret herself was not among them. Brutish as he was, not once had he tried to force marital relations on her.

LUKA

"This is the place I have in mind," Luka said, checking a set of blueprints he'd drawn himself. Although the day was clear and warm, it was windy. He had trouble holding onto the papers. He'd retained Mueller's Development Company for the project. Mueller and several of his men had met Luka in a clearing of the woods north of Gloire de Matin Island.

"The ground's pretty uneven," Mueller said. "Take a lot of leveling."

"I'm just looking to put trailers in here," Luka said. "The land doesn't have to be perfect."

"Trailer parks are illegal in Waterton," Mueller said. "You'll never get a permit."

"This isn't Waterton, it's Hammon Falls. Waterton's got nothing to do with it."

"You own the land?"

"Financing just came through."

"Why trailers?"

Luka put his arm around Mueller's shoulder and walked him away from his men. They stood in the shadows of the trees. "Immigrants," he whispered. "They're cheaper than local labor, but they need a place to live away from decent folk. That's what the Illinois Central did when they brought the niggers in after the strike. Set them up in boxcars. I figure used trailers can be bought for next to nothing."

Mueller glanced back at his employees. "Wish I could do that. These guys' wages are bankrupting me."

"Which is why I need this trailer park."

"What's happened with your warehouse?" Mueller said. "You must've lost your ass."

"You'd be surprised." True, Prohibition had ended legal distribution of beer. But, like Johnny Torrio in Chicago, he'd found that dealing in bootleg liquor was more rewarding than selling it legitimately. In fact, most of the booze he handled now was imported from Torrio via late-night trucks equipped with extra gas tanks to hide the hooch. Since acquiring Stanley's from Margaret, refurbishing it, and renaming it Curtis's Garden, he was making more money than he had ever dreamed possible. From one roadhouse. Amazing.

"I hear you're running Electrical Park," Mueller said

And turning a nice profit there, as well. "Yeah," Luka said, "fifty-one percent of the stock. I got a few board members to vote my way."

Mueller stepped out of the shadows and into the sun. "Well, this is a pretty enough location. Long as we don't have to fight Waterton, I don't see a problem."

"That's what I like to hear," Luka said. "Come on, I want to show you something. Bring your men, too."

At Margaret's urging, Luka had given in and purchased his first automobile earlier in the year, a bright yellow 1919 Franklin Model 9-B Touring. He'd once vowed he would never own a motor car, but times were changing, with or without him. The days of horse and wagon were ending, so it might as well be with him. He led Mueller to the car. After stuffing the blueprints in the front seat, he detached the tonneau in the back of the Touring to reveal a tub filled with ice and a couple of dozen corked brown bottles.

"What the hell?" Mueller said.

His men nodded appreciatively.

"I was hoping we'd have reason to celebrate," Luka said. "Help yourself, boys."

The next hour was spent getting pleasantly tipsy in the afternoon sun, although an argument erupted when somebody mentioned suffrage. The Nineteenth Amendment had just passed in August, giving women the vote. While that wouldn't affect Luka financially, he vehemently opposed it on principle. "Never been more ashamed of my country," he said.

"Long as they vote like we tell 'em to, eh?" Mueller said.

"When's the last time your wife did what you told her to?" Luka said. "Listen, they can *cancel out* our votes. Maggie would do it just to spite me. Do you really want to let them decide?"

"Well, I'm sick of the whole thing," one of the workers said. "Everywhere you go, yak yak yak. The papers, city hall, even in church. I don't care one way or the other, just shut *up* about it."

Luka turned his back on the discussion, let the wind on his face calm him. The subject was dredging up memories of Cora. She had insisted this day would come, and now it had.

But she didn't live to see it.

Goddamn it, he missed his little girl. She would have been twenty-four next month. He hated suffrage, but he'd escort her to the polls if he could have her back.

Luka gulped down the rest of his beer, spilling foam on his suit coat.

"What's wrong?" Mueller said.

"Thinking about my daughter," Luka said.

Mueller sympathetically patted him on the back. Everyone in town had heard her story. "How's the little boy?"

"Spitting image of Cora, except, you know, for the eye. And smart? Shit, the kid's six years old and he can take apart any machine and put it back together better than it was before."

Mueller smiled. He was a grandfather, too. "We should be getting back," he said. "Been letting these bums slack long enough."

"We got a deal?" Luka said.

"We got a deal."

Luka re-attached the tonneau to the Touring as Mueller and his men drove off. Thinking about Cora reminded him of George, and that always got his blood boiling. The bastard had corrupted his little girl, then run off to war and gotten himself killed. Just like old G.W.

War hero, my ass.

He was a coward.

Luka blamed Will's deformity on George. It was a punishment from God, if there still was a God.

***

The thing about automobiles was they were fast, clean – no scooping horse shit – didn't need to be fed or groomed, and offered a sense of personal independence that no other form of transportation could. Best of all, they ran on gasoline. More and more people owned cars, and every one of them needed to buy fuel. Luka had converted some of his properties into filling stations, which were proving lucrative—not to mention being perfect cover for the trucks importing hooch from Chicago.

It was well past dark as he pulled the Touring into his Standard station on East Fourth. Two trucks had parked in the bays in the back, and the drivers were siphoning the liquor into wooden casks by the light of a single bulb that hung from the ceiling. The bulb swung back and forth in a slight breeze, throwing weird shadows. Luka stopped behind the trucks and got out to inspect the goods.

The drivers were rough-looking hoodlums. Luka wondered what they'd be like in the ring. He was sure he could whip them, but then he thought he could whip anybody.

One had cauliflower ears and the other a crooked nose. Both looked like they had already lost too many fights, although Bent Nose was too slight to ever have been much of a boxer. He must be the brains. "Price has gone up," he said.

"Jesus Christ," Luka said, "you're killing me. People are already buying up all the malt in town and brewing their own. The only reason they still buy from me is I can provide it cheaper than they can make it."

"Yeah," said Cauliflower, lighting a cigarette, "that, and Torrio's is top-of-the-line stuff. Ain't that rotgut shit folks stew in their basement."

"Are you a complete idiot?" Luka said. "Put that out. You want to blow us all up?"

Cauliflower looked around stupidly. Gasoline. Alcohol. Flames. It finally sank in. "Oh," he said, and extinguished the cigarette between his bare fingers.

"You ever read the Volstead Act?" Bent Nose said, speaking in a New York accent. Bronx, Brooklyn, Queens, they all sounded alike to Luka. Wasn't that where Torrio imported most of his thugs from? Before Luka could answer, Bent Nose went on, ticking the verbs off on his fingers as he spoke. "Says that 'No person shall manufacture, sell, barter, transport, import, export, deliver, furnish, or possess any intoxicating liquor.'"

"You've got the thing memorized?"

"Long as you don't stop him in the middle," Cauliflower said. "Then he's gotta start over again."

"What's that got to do with raising your prices?" Luka said.

"You know what it don't say?" Bent Nose said. "It don't say you can't *drink* booze."

"So?"

"So you take all the risks. Cops find someone with a bottle in their medicine cabinet, they might rap some knuckles, but that's a hell of a lot better than what happens when they're caught making their own. Whatever you charge for it, they'll pay."

Luka lifted the trap door hidden in the service bay's work area. It opened onto a crawlspace big enough for twenty casks. He and the men lowered the contraband into the hole.

"Anyway," Cauliflower said, "you get too many 'independent businessmen,' you just hire some fellas to have a discussion with them. You know, 'Buy mine or I'll bomb your house.' Be surprised how many people see the light after that."

They finished packing the casks. Luka closed the trap door and removed a wad of bills from his suit coat. "Tell Torrio I don't appreciate this."

Both men laughed as Bent Nose wrote out a receipt. "*You* tell Torrio."

WILL
Waterton, Iowa
August 2008

Will held George's Celtic cross in the palm of his hand, where it left smudges on already mottled skin. He'd have to have it professionally cleaned. The silver was stained beyond anything soap and water could fix. Still, the black patina in the grooves of the engravings added legitimacy to the thing, placed it in time, made it real. This was not some shiny showroom collectible. It was an artifact that wore its history proudly. It had been prayed over and handed down and looked to for comfort and love. Dammit, that *meant* something.

It meant something.

And yet when his father left it for him at the station back in '37, Will hadn't even taken it out of the box. Youth could be so stupid. He draped the chain over the frame of the photograph of George in Ypres. "Sorry, Dad," he said.

Dad? A little late for that, isn't it?

The front door opened and closed, and then Katie was standing in the doorway to his bedroom. "I brought you some groceries. Who are you talking to?"

"No one," he said.

Katie looked at the photograph. "I see you found a place for the cross. Nice."

Will brushed past her. She'd set two plastic bags on his kitchen counter containing bananas, little tubs of sugar-free Jello, oatmeal, milk, bread, a box of Depends and, from the pharmacy, two of his prescriptions. "Thanks," he said. "What do I owe you?"

"You don't owe me anything."

His knees ached as he put the groceries away. Jesus, now his daughter was buying Depends for him.

He heard her moving. "I'm in the living room," she said. "Let's talk."

Will got a glass of water and took his arthritis pill. "What's there to talk about?"

As always, she was seated right on the edge of the couch. Couldn't that woman ever just lay back and *relax*? She sipped from a bottle of Evian water. A dollar and a half for a bottle of water? It was crazy, when she could get it from the tap for free.

"Come on, Dad," she said. "Just for a minute. Please?"

He hobbled into the living room and sat in his favorite recliner. "Is this going to be another I'm-worried-about-you-living-alone-in-this-big-house conversation?"

She twisted the cap back onto her water. "Well, I am."

"I can take care of myself."

Katie leaned forward and touched her hand to his. "Dad, I just heard you talking to a photograph in your room."

"I was thinking out loud. Don't you ever think out loud?"

"Of course I do, but—"

"Then what of it? I was just looking at a picture of my father."

Katie bit her lip like she used to when she was a little girl about to cry. She wouldn't cry now. She never cried anymore, not since her husband walked out on her. "I'm looking at my Dad, too," she said tenderly, "and I'm scared."

GEORGE
Saint-Germain-des-Prés, Paris, France
April 1921

"I can't understand what you're saying, ma'am!" George yelled into the telephone. Long distance connections were always unreliable from their little flat in Saint-Germain-des-Prés, Paris, and the woman's all-but-indecipherable Irish accent only made things worse. "I'm looking for a Mrs. Mary O'Leary, whose husband Mick—Michael—was killed in the Great War. He had a son named Tommy."

"Don't know no Mick O'Leary," the woman might have said, breaking the connection.

George slammed the phone down. "Damn it," he said. He should just go to Ireland. They got their home rule, it ought to be safe by now.

His rescuer, Suzanne Josephson from Helena, Montana, sat at the kitchen table and read literature from whatever radical movement had captured her attention this week. Anarchy, Marxism, Freudian and/or Jungian psychology, existentialism, free-thinking suffragettes advocating birth control and sexual equality for women....

"Those calls are costing us a fortune," she said.

George poured a glass of wine. He did not pour her one. "I made a promise," he said.

"To who? Mick? He was already dead, so who did you promise? What do you owe him?"

George emptied his glass in one swig. "It's called loyalty," he said. The Celtic cross felt heavy around his neck.

"You drink too much."

"I pay for everything, so what's it to you?"

Since the night Suzanne had pulled him from a drunken stupor by the Seine and brought him to her flat in the Rue de Verneuil, George had basked in intellectual life among the Americans in Saint-Germain-des-Prés. Paris was a vibrant, whirling dervish of a city—boisterous, cluttered, confusing, smelly, sacred, vile and, when morning fog gilded its geometry in sepia tones, breathtakingly beautiful. He'd enjoyed Suzanne's liberated views of sex, both of them doing whatever they wanted with whomever they wanted. But in the end they grew weary of nomadic morality. Free love transformed itself into a monogamous, but unmarried, relationship. George took a job as an apprentice electrician. Suzanne stayed home or went to cafes with her friends.

They'd become French citizens and settled into middle-class Parisian life.

And, goddamn, it was boring. He was restless, she was restless, they both wanted change, or out, or something.

"I thought I had a say in things," she said.

"You do," he said.

"Then stop wasting *our* money on useless telephone calls."

"I don't call that often."

Most of his inquiries had been via mail to various agencies in Dublin. The trouble was, there were hundreds of O'Learys in and around Dublin. George found several Michael O'Learys, but they were either still alive, had died too old or too young, weren't married, or didn't have a son named Thomas. The logical place to check was the British Infantry, Dorset Regiment, in which both he and Mick served, but he still feared repercussions from his desertion.

"Mick would want you to get on with your life. Anyway, you know you want to keep it for yourself."

When he was sober the cross had always comforted him. Mick could have told him it would. *This is* how *we live forever, lad. Never forget that.* As George wrapped his fingers around the outline of its silver tines, he had to concede there might be some truth to what she said.

LUKA
Waterton, Iowa
October 1922

"Wait a minute," Luka said. He was sitting in Arlen Kelper's office on the west side of Waterton. "You want me to invest in Landon and Company stock? *Landon?*"

Arlen Kelper sighed. "That's what I'm saying, yes."

"Jesus, they got nothing. The strike nearly wiped them out them three years ago."

"But didn't."

"Ford makes a better and cheaper tractor—"

"Cheaper, not better. Next year Landon is dropping the Waterton Boy tractors and coming out with a new line, the Model D. It'll have a better design than the Fordson, and won't cost that much more. Their stock's going to take off."

"Agriculture is dead."

Kelper glared at him. "Curtis, I don't like you. I never have. You're bottom-feeding scum who poisons everything you touch. But Margaret is my client, and I happen to like her very much. Your concerns, unfortunately, are now her concerns. Before you siphon all her resources into your accounts, I'm going to make sure she has long-term financial stability. Goddamn it, you *will* invest in this stock for her sake."

Luka leaned back in the chair, put his feet on Kelper's desk. "I don't remember giving you power of attorney."

Kelper shoved Luka's feet off his desk. "She's your *wife*, you son-of-a-bitch."

"That's right, *my* wife. I've got my own lawyers, my own accountants, my own advisors. The only reason you're still around is because Maggie wants you. If it were up to me, I would've fired you before we finished saying 'I do.'"

Kelper dangled an unlit cigarette between his lips. "Waterton is going to annex your little hamlet, and then who will protect you? Once you're under the city's jurisdiction, all your illegal income will go away. *You'll* go away."

"Didn't know you smoked, Seaweed. I'm a cigar man myself." Luka took an expensive Havana from his suit pocket and struck a match. After two puffs he changed his mind and went to the sink in the corner of Kelper's office. He turned on the tap to extinguish the cigar, then cut off the end with a pen knife. The clippings swirled down Kelper's drain. "No sense wasting good tobacco on you," Luka said.

"Get out," Kelper said.

"Waterton will never annex Hammon Falls. It has no right."

"It has every right. It provides your electricity, sewer, water. The State says it can take Hammon Falls anytime it wants to. It'll just be another subdivision."

Luka laughed. "Somehow I don't think it's that easy, Kelper. And just for the record, I am not involved in illegal activities."

"You mean other than the liquor and immigrants and gambling and whores—"

"Bullshit," Luka said. He returned the shortened cigar to his coat pocket and walked toward the door, then tossed a silver dollar toward Kelper. The coin hit his desk and clanked to the floor. "There. Invest in Landon for Maggie."

"Do you have a soul at all?" Kelper said.

"None that I'm aware of. I lost it when her son killed my little girl."

MARGARET
Hammon Falls, Iowa
June 1923

The man who came to get Margaret was driving a Ford automobile. It was raining as she climbed into the back seat. Even with her husband at the wheel she preferred the back to the front, like in the old days when Kline still offered his cabbing service.

"What's happened?" she said to the man. He was a good-sized fellow, about thirty, with red hair and surprisingly delicate features. Nice looking, but he smelled bad. Sweaty and bruised, he wore athletic clothes, as if he'd come straight from the gym.

"Mr. Curtis is in the hospital, ma'am." Before she could react he said, "Nothing serious, just a broken jaw and a little dizziness."

"A broken jaw isn't serious?"

"Doctors say it was a clean break, the kind that heals quick."

Margaret sighed with disgust. "He was fighting at Electrical Park again, wasn't he? He's forty-eight years old, for God's sake."

"Luka's a tough man, ma'am, but no one goes on forever."

"*Orville.* Not Luka. I hate that name." Margaret removed a small mirror from her handbag and watched herself as she combed her hair. The engine made a terrible racket, drowning out the rain on the roof. Motor cars were so loud. "He lost?"

"'Fraid so."

Armageddon must be at hand, because Orville never lost fights. He never lost at anything. She noticed in her mirror that she was smiling oh so slightly. "Who beat him?"

"I did, ma'am. Didn't mean to hurt him, though."

"What's your name? Have I heard of you?"

"James Henry Fisher. Folks call me Red. It's the hair."

Too many nicknames. Luka, Red. And Orville never got over his annoying habit of calling her Maggie. Maggie was a whore's name, like the girl in that Stephen Crane novel. "I don't know much about his friends or his business associates. Which are you?"

"I hope to be both, Ma'am, but tonight I was simply his opponent."

***

It was jarring to see Orville in a hospital bed, his jaw wired shut, his front teeth surgically removed so he could sip nutrition through a straw. His chin and left cheekbone sported ugly purple and yellow bruises, and the doctors had had to shave off his oily little mustache. Margaret had never cared much for the thing, but he looked almost childlike without it, despite his graying and, though he would never admit it, thinning hair.

Orville was certainly not lonely. His fleshy Jewish attorney Weinshank was with him, along with a nurse, a Waterton councilman, three men in suits, and a big-breasted woman Margaret didn't know. When Orville saw her and Fisher come in, he motioned for the sea of people to let them through.

"Maggie," he said, only his lips moving. "I guess you're pretty mad at me, huh?" He glanced around at the others in the room. "She doesn't approve of boxing."

"*Margaret*," she said. "Are you all right?"

"Well, I'm not as devilishly handsome as I used to be, thanks to Mr. Fisher here."

Fisher nodded in respect. "I only hope I'm as tough as you are when I'm your age."

Orville smiled, and Margaret could see the effort hurt him. "You beat me and insult my age on the same night. Touché, sir."

"How long will you be here?" Margaret said.

Orville looked at the nurse, who shrugged. "A day or two," she said.

"I'll need a bridge to replace my front teeth," he said.

"Who are these people?" Margaret said. "Shouldn't you be resting?"

"Business doesn't stop because of a broken jaw."

"The mayor is interested in learning more about your husband's operations," the councilman said. "This seemed like a good time to talk to him. He's a difficult man to corner."

Orville laughed, which was painful enough to moisten his eyes. "The mayor's looking for a piece of the hooch action."

"I don't want to know anything about that," Margaret said.

The councilman shook a finger at Orville. "Watch yourself, Curtis."

Weinshank, who rarely smiled, said, "Waterton's got no jurisdiction over Hammon Falls."

"Give us time," the councilman said.

"Your wife is right," the nurse said. "You should rest, Mr. Curtis."

Orville spread his hands in a what-can-I-do? gesture. "You heard the lady. Out."

"We'll talk again," the councilman said. He and the three men in suits left.

"In a pig's eye," Orville said after they were out the door.

Weinshank tipped his hat and shuffled out of the room. Margaret was sure he trailed slime behind him. God, how she disliked that man!

Next to leave was the woman, a bobbed blond no more than twenty-five. She leaned her big breasts over Orville and touched his hand in a way that seemed entirely too familiar. "See you later, Luka," she said.

Although the words were spoken without inflection, coming from her they sounded sleazy.

"Five minutes," the nurse said to Margaret, and followed the woman out.

Fisher turned to leave as well, but Orville stopped him. "Take Maggie home, will you, Red? Then come on back. We've got things to discuss."

"Who was that woman?" Margaret said.

"I don't know, somebody's secretary."

"She called you Luka."

"Most people do."

Margaret wasn't convinced, but badgering Orville did no good.

"Red?" Luka said.

Fisher nodded. He took Margaret by the elbow and led her toward the door.

"You could have just telephoned," she said to the man who had defeated her husband in the ring.

"He wanted you to see for yourself he was okay," Fisher said.

"How thoughtful," she said.

LUKA
Hammon Falls, Iowa
January 26, 1925

Luka sat behind the large mahogany desk he'd bought for the library. The temperature outside was nasty cold, but in here the radiator spewed hot air. The lights were off. A fire burned in the hearth. He'd installed a Philco radio set next to his desk, which as usual was tuned to WGN. The Austin High Gang was playing its version of "Craving." That Bud Freeman kid could really blow sax! Luka wasn't a romantic, but the atmosphere today was perfect for his mood.

Red Fisher sat on the other side of the desk from him.

"You heard the news yesterday?" Fisher said.

"The solar eclipse?" Luka said.

"The *other* news."

"Which is?"

"Torrio was gunned down in Chicago. Moran and a couple of his boys."

WGN was a Chicago station. If they had mentioned Torrio, Luka wasn't paying attention. He only listened to music. He turned the radio off. "Dead?"

"In surgery last I heard, but that was yesterday."

"Who's his number two?"

"Another Italian, what else? Capone, Caponi, something. Just a kid."

"Long as I get my shipments, I don't care."

"Torrio's organization is strong. You'll get it."

Luka shuddered.

"You okay?" Fisher said.

"Yeah. Our business here done?"

"I'll keep you posted."

After Fisher was gone, a young brunette crawled out from under the desk. "Well, *are* you okay?" she said with a naughty smile.

"Oh, yeah," Luka said.

***

That evening Luka was in the bath when Maggie barged in without invitation. She wouldn't look at him, although he was submerged to the neck in bubbles.

"William is crying," she said. "He needs you to talk to him."

"What this time?"

"Just come."

Luka sighed. The things he did for these people. As he stood up soapy water sluiced down his body. He thought he looked pretty good for a man of fifty, but Maggie turned her face away. "For Christ's sake, Maggie, we're *married*."

"Margaret," she said, closing the door behind her on her way out.

Luka toweled himself dry and donned his favorite red bathrobe. Maggie was waiting in Will's room when he arrived. Will lay face down with a pillow over his head. Luka didn't like it when he cried. The boy was almost eleven, after all.

He sat on the bed next to Will. "Hey, big guy," Luka said. "The kids at school again?"

Will rolled over and reached for his glasses. He seemed more comfortable, even among family, when the frosted left lens covered his deformity. His brown hair hung down over his forehead. "They called me Cyclops," he said, a tear on his right cheek.

"I hope you knocked them right on their ass."

"Language, Orville," Maggie said. "And don't encourage him to fight."

"There were three of them," Will said. "They were bigger than me."

"Margaret," Luka said, using her full name for effect, "give us a minute."

"*No* talk of fighting," she said, and left.

Will pulled his knees up under his chin.

"No," Luka said, patting his thighs, "come here. It's just you and me now, your Grandma won't see. You're not too big to sit on ol' Luka's lap."

Maggie had long ago told Will the truth of his parentage. She was adamant that he never mistake Luka for his father, heaven forbid. It was always George, George, George. Well, Cora was involved, too, and Will favored her more than George. As the boy climbed onto his lap, Luka caught a scent of his hair. Christ, he even *smelled* like Cora.

Will leaned his head into Luka's shoulder.

"Your Grandma's right," Luka said, looking at the goddamned soldier photo above Will's bed, "fighting usually doesn't solve anything. But sometimes you've got to take a punch, get up and show 'em you can take another. They might not like you, but they'll respect you."

"I don't like getting hit," Will said. "It hurts."

"Sure does," Luka said. His jaw still ached occasionally from Red Fisher's KO nearly two years ago, and the bridge to replace his two front teeth chafed, which gave him canker sores. But then, he'd thrown that match on purpose. Yeah, he got a busted jawbone and a couple of fake teeth out of the deal, but he sweetened his connections in Chicago by fawning over Fisher. Quickest way to befriend a man was to lose a fight to him—much as that stung the ego.

"Sometimes," he said, kissing Will's brow, "pain is the only way we know we're alive."

MARGARET
Waterton, Iowa
March 1925

As always the Reverend Clayton Andrews began his sermon with, "On this day that the Lord has made." His announced topic this morning was the evils of the "flapper generation," those licentious youngsters who flout God's law with their dancing, smoking, and consumption of illegal alcohol. The minister was a Methodist, but he spoke with the fire and passion of a Southern Baptist. Margaret found him mesmerizing. It was miserably cold and sleeting outside, but Andrews could warm a body with his oratory alone. He'd have been a natural for the old Chautauqua lectures, had he been old enough when the Circuit was in its heyday.

She sat in her usual pew in the front row of the United Methodist Church in Waterton. William was to her left, fidgeting the same way George did when he was that age. To her right was Orville, and to his right James Fisher, of all people. Margaret didn't like Fisher, didn't trust him, didn't approve of him. He had connections to the hoodlums in Chicago, connections he was using to drag Orville further down the path of wickedness. She doubted if any words from the Good Book could reach that man's tarnished soul.

"Sit still," she said to William.

The boy managed to remain motionless for a few moments before he was back to rustling and humming and picking at his nose. "This is so *boring*," he said. He'd brought along one of his toy automobiles he was always playing with, running it along the back of the pew and making revving sounds.

"These women with their short skirts and their gy-rat-ing hips," Andrews said, exaggerating each syllable and pounding the podium with his fist, "are a scourge—"

Orville and Fisher were talking quietly between themselves—a fine example they were setting for William!—but they paused at Andrews' statement. Fisher laughed and said, too loudly, "I don't know, sounds pretty good to me."

Orville laughed, too, trying to stifle his mirth with his hand over his mouth.

Margaret glared at them both. "Enough!"

Orville winked at her, then leaned his head toward Fisher and whispered something. Fisher looked at her and shrugged his shoulders innocently. "I'm Catholic," he mouthed.

Margaret knew some Catholics. Most of them were nice enough people, but Fisher wasn't one of them. He was about as religious as a ferret, and wouldn't know Jesus if he met Him on the street. In associating with Fisher and his cronies, Orville invited ridicule upon the Hammon household, although her name was no longer Hammon.

On the other hand, he had agreed to address the charity ball tomorrow night in her stead. By accepting her engagements he rescued her from becoming even more of a laughing stock in the community. She'd always been socially reticent, and the whole George/Cora fiasco, and all that ensued from it, had driven her further into seclusion. Her husband, it seemed, was immune to rumor, gossip, and shame.

"The Volstead Act," Andrews thundered, and his eyes lingered ever so briefly on Orville, "was intended to stop the pernicious use of alcohol, and yet it is smuggled into our community by unscrupulous men, where it falls into the hands of our precious youth."

When the Reverend looked away, Orville and Fisher did a mock toast to each other. "Long live Prohibition," Fisher said. Andrews didn't see or hear, but Margaret did, and so did William, who was still zooming his toy automobile along the pew.

LUKA
Hammon Falls, Iowa
May 1926

Luka, Maggie, and Will strolled through Electrical Park on a Sunday afternoon in May. There was a decent crowd, but not nearly as many as in years past. The amusements were being displaced by other diversions, such as moving pictures, illegal speakeasies, and the growing popularity of town baseball. The Aero-Thrill ride had broken down a few years back, and no one had bothered to fix it. Once Luka retired from boxing, the fights drew fewer and fewer fans, and eventually ceased altogether.

Luka's immigrant carnies ran the amusements and sold concessions. Business wasn't what it used to be, but the immigrants worked cheap, so he was still turning a nice profit.

Will wanted to try the Spiral Terror rollercoaster. He tugged on Maggie's hand. "Come *on*," he said. "I can't go alone."

"Good heavens, no," Maggie said. "Orville, you take him."

"He always goes with me," Will said. "I want you to. You never do anything fun."

The boy was right. As far as Luka could tell, Maggie wouldn't know fun if it bit her in the ass. If anything, she had become more of a recluse since they'd gotten married. She was perfectly content to read her Bible all day long. Luka tried to loosen her up by telling jokes, but the crude ones only annoyed her and the clean ones had no effect. She held onto her laughter as if Christ himself would strike her dead for cracking a smile.

"Try it," Luka said. "You might actually enjoy it."

"Ple-e-e-e-ease?" Will said, tugging harder.

"Don't do this to me," Maggie said.

"What are you afraid of?" Luka said.

"I'm fifty-three years old. How would it look for me to ride on that contraption with a mob of howling children?"

"It'd look like you were having fun," Will said.

"Yeah," Luka said.

"No," Maggie said.

"Jesus, Maggie," Luka said. "Come on, Will, I'll ride with you."

Luka and Will got in line with ten or fifteen kids and a couple sets of parents. One of them was a man Luka had met, although he couldn't remember his name. Some functionary from the city of Waterton. "Lining your own pocket, Curtis?" the man said as Luka bought two tickets.

"No, but you are."

"Cyclops," the man's son said in a loud stage whisper to Will.

The other kids in line took up the chant. "Cyclops! Cyclops! Little Willie One-Eye!"

"See?" Will said.

"What'd I tell you?" Luka said. "Knock him on his ass."

"That won't be necessary," the man said, and he slapped his son's face. "I didn't raise you like that. We don't mock people for something they can't help."

His son wailed and ran off into the sparse crowd, forgetting all about the Spiral Terror. The other children stopped chanting. The man handed his tickets to Luka. "Guess we won't need these after all," he said, and stormed off after his son.

"Thanks," Luka called, and he didn't mean the tickets.

The ride was far from full, and none of the other children chose to share the same car with Luka and Will.

"This isn't going to be fun anymore," Will said.

"Hold your head up like you're proud," Luka said, "and forget those jerks."

"Can we listen to *Sam 'N' Henry* on the radio when we get home?" Will said.

Luka hated that program, two white men pretending to be black. "Let's get through this first," he said.

The rollercoaster lurched slowly into motion. As it picked up speed, Luka's stomach didn't keep pace. By the time they rounded the highest curve and headed down the big descent, he was sure his noon meal would end up on his trousers.

On the second pass, though, he began to feel some of the exhilaration Cora must have experienced all those years ago. Will was certainly enjoying it. The boy's mouth gaped open with delight. He squealed like a fire engine siren. The sights of Electrical Park whisked by below and beside and below again.

The thought of Cora sobered Luka, and suddenly he wanted the ride to be over. At the top of the curve he looked down at the people. He caught a glimpse of Maggie standing among them but very much alone, right where they'd left her. In that moment he felt a capacity for pity for her, for she had lost someone, too.

GEORGE
Paris, France
May 22, 1927

The crowd surrounding the American Embassy stretched all along the Avenue Gabriel, hollering and jostling and cheering. The object of their desire, Charles Lindbergh, appeared at the balcony window and waved or bowed, then went back in, only to have his admirers cry out for him. He'd come out, go in, come out, go in. This went on for hours.

The noise was giving George a headache. He and Suzanne's friends had used Lindbergh's achievement as an excuse to celebrate last night, raising their glasses first with used-to-be and soon-to-be bohemian luminaries in Les Café Flore, then in any bistro throughout Saint-Germain-des-Prés that had space for them. It was well near dawn before he finally stumbled down the Rue de Verneuil to the apartment they shared.

George woke less than two hours later with a screaming hangover, but he couldn't afford to miss work again. Since receiving his EDF— Électricité de France—certifcation three years ago, he'd phoned in sick several times because of his drinking, and while his boss Paul was as tolerant a man as ever walked the planet, even his patience wasn't limitless.

George's assignment took him to an apartment near the embassy. But the people! Thousands and thousands of crazed fans clogged the Avenue Gabriel, lined every street and alley that fed into the Avenue, hung out of every open window, occupied every fire escape, and stood on every stopped vehicle, hoping to get a glimpse of their hero. Luckily George hadn't tried to drive, but the trolley only took him so far before the congested streets forced it to turn back. He walked the rest of the way burdened with his electrician's toolbox. He had to elbow through the mob to get to the apartment. It was a warm spring day, and with that many bodies in a relatively confined area, the air smelled like an open sewer. It was a madhouse. George rolled his ankles several times between the bricks of the cobbled streets trying to fight his way through. He arrived an hour late, but it didn't matter because his client had been swallowed up by the mass of humanity, too. At least he'd left his door unlocked.

The job was simple enough. The apartment was wired with the usual K & T system—knobs and tubes. The owner had already exposed the problem area by cutting a hole in the wall in the southwest corner. Apparently the building had settled, pulling the wires tight enough to break one of the ceramic knobs. This in turned had cracked a wire, causing shorts. After disconnecting the fuse to that circuit, George plugged an extension cord into a working outlet and soldered a new piece of wire to the old, adding more slack. Then he wrapped the spliced wire in cloth tape and replaced the knob with a new one. Since the owner himself had opened the hole in the wall, George did not patch it up. He reconnected the fuse and wrote out the bill, which he left on the kitchen table. The whole process had taken less than forty minutes.

But he still had to get home. The streets were just as chaotic when he left the apartment. The idiots were still out in force, but now they were sweatier and more ill-tempered. They were not pleased that Lindbergh had stopped acknowledging them. Once the dignitaries began arriving at the embassy, their hero had ducked back inside to receive private congratulations. He was also probably getting hundreds of telephone messages from famous people the world over. George wondered if Calvin Coolidge had called. Of course he had.

What a silly fuss. Sure, George had toasted Lindbergh's success, but that was more for the drinking than for the man. Lindbergh wasn't the first to cross the Atlantic in an airplane—not by a long shot. Something like eighty people had already managed it in stages. Lindbergh wasn't even the first to do it nonstop. He was just the first to do it solo.

George was probably a half mile from the Embassy before the crowd finally thinned. Exhausted, he stopped into a pub that was tucked away in an alley. A communist in a red beret was berating some hapless businessman about capitalism. Two gendarmes were swapping stories in the corner. A group of students was arguing about the latest trends in literature. A streetwalker leaned back in her chair with her feet splayed out on a table and her dress hiked halfway up her thighs. She wasn't soliciting, just weary. Her legs were especially hairy, even for a Parisian woman. She smiled at George as if to say, *What a day.*

Oui, George mouthed.

He ordered the cheapest wine on the menu. It wasn't even mid-afternoon, so technically he was still at work, but surely Paul wouldn't mind. His boss hadn't had to face this ridiculous mob today.

He kept drinking. One bottle, then two. From the customers who came and went he learned that Lindbergh had won a big cash prize for completing his flight. He was to receive the French Legion of Honor medal, or whatever they called it. There was to be a ticker-tape parade in New York City. Overnight he'd become the most famous man in the world.

George chuckled. Now that he'd rested his sore ankles and calmed his mind with wine, he found the whole thing amusing.

By dusk the crowds had dispersed completely. The gendarmes ended up arresting the communist, who was quickly replaced by an anarchist, pretty much the same thing. The students left, but artists came in to argue about the latest trends in painting. The streetwalker had gone back out to ply her trade. Others came in. There were always others.

George was stinking drunk.

Time to go home to Suzanne. Suzanne, his rescuer. Suzanne, the free spirit who did little these days but eat and listen to the radio and read magazines. Suzanne, the once pretty maid who, at thirty-two, was already middle-aged and fat.

George pushed himself up from his table. His tools clinked in the metal box. His legs wobbled, his head spun. He'd witnessed history today.

Someday he'd have to tell somebody all about it, embellishing the story until he was practically at Lindbergh's side in the balcony of the American Embassy. Then again, he'd need to have someone to tell.

Right now he had Suzanne. It should have been so exciting.

But his life was dull, dull, dull, and Suzanne wouldn't be impressed. Declaring Lindbergh a puppet of the bourgeoisie, she had refused to celebrate with George and her friends last night. When he told her he'd seen the American hero today, she'd simply shrug and ask if he'd remembered to buy her the latest issue of *L'Amour de L'Art*.

YOUNG WILL
Waterton, Iowa
February 1929

"What happened to your left eye, kid?" Red Fisher said. He was driving a sporty white 1928 Stutz Bearcat, a big step up from the Ford he used to have.

Will wiped the car's windshield with a dry rag. Almost a year ago, when he turned fourteen, Luka had gotten him this job at Bob's Standard on Franklin Street. Bob had needed help on weekends. His regular boy, Jack, frequently called in sick—as he did again today—and Will was eager to put his mechanical aptitude to work.

It was a cold and snowy Saturday morning, and the customers just kept coming. Red was the tenth one in the last hour. Will's fingers were going numb even through his gloves. He'd probably get frostbite. "Never had a left eye," he said, his breath freezing on the glass.

"You were born without it?" Red said.

"I guess. You want me to fill her up? Check your oil?"

"Yeah, give me the works." Red hung his elbow out the window. Roth's Packing Company was doing business today, and the odor of hog kill was in the air. It only happened on certain days when the wind was from the east, but when it did the reek was something awful. If it had been Will in the car, he'd have had the window up. "How do you focus?" Red said. "I mean, don't people need two eyes to lock in? When I close one I can't get any depth perception out of the other."

"I just look at things. I never had two, so I don't know the difference." He folded the hood back and pulled out the dipstick. The car didn't need oil.

"Well, don't let anybody give you shit about it. Bob tells me you'll end up being the best mechanic he's ever had."

Will dropped the hood and smiled. "I like working on engines," he said. "I even like the smell of grease."

"Good thing there's people like you in the world to take care of people like me," Red said. "I don't know a piston from a horse's ass."

Like many station owners, Bob had installed a Tokheim pump, which was shaped like a miniature lighthouse. It was an old-fashioned one in which the gasoline was visible in a glass tank on top so customers could see that the gas was clean and pure. Will inserted the hose's nozzle into Red's Bearcat. The meter rolled around to a $1.23, 12.3 gallons. "A horse's ass," Will said with a smile, "is the one with the tail. That'll be two pennies short of a buck and a quarter."

Red laughed as he handed Will a ten dollar bill. "You're all right, kid. Buy yourself some ear muffs with the change."

Will watched him turn onto Franklin and drive off. A crow flapped down and pecked at some dead thing on the road.

An $8.77 tip. Nice.

***

Jack Reece wasn't really sick, he just didn't feel like working. Two years older than Will, he had a mischievous streak that prompted him to do things Will would never consider on his own. Tonight he wanted to sneak into Curtis's Garden, the roadhouse—speakeasy—Luka had set up in Hammon Falls after prying the property out of Margaret's possession. It had always been a tavern, despite Margaret's accountants' attempts to hide its assets in holding companies to appease her teetotaler views. Now that alcohol was illegal, the Garden was even more of a tavern, and it offered other services as well upstairs and in back rooms. High rollers could always find card or wheel games to lose their dollars on, or slot machines to lose them in, and female solace afterward to ease the sting of the losses.

"Are you crazy?" Will said. They were parked in Jack's 1924 Durant Star alongside a curb on Caladonia Street. The snow had stopped and sky cleared, but the wind was up, driving the temperature below zero. To the southwest the factories on Westland Avenue billowed ghosts of white smoke across the face of a half-moon. "Do you know what my grandfather will do if he finds out? We're underage."

Jack laughed and slapped him on the back. "Underage? Hell, Will, the whole place is illegal! What's he gonna do, call the cops on us?"

"If we're lucky he'll call the cops. You don't want to piss him off."

"How'll he know?" Jack said. "It's dark. We go, we blend in, we have a couple of beers, we get out. I've been there before. They don't check your driver's license."

"I don't have a driver's license," Will said, his breath glowing in the headlights of an oncoming car. He tapped the frosted lens of his glasses. "Anyway, I'm pretty hard to miss."

The only heat in the car was generated by the boys' bodies. Jack hugged his arms to his chest for warmth. "You're such a Nancy boy," he said.

"Don't call me that!"

"Then don't act like one. Come on, it'll be fun."

When Jack said "fun," he usually meant stupid or dangerous, but Will felt he owed his friend a debt of gratitude. Two years ago, when Will was in seventh grade and Jack in ninth, Jack had defended Will against a bully who was tormenting him because of his eye. Even then Jack was on his way to becoming a popular athlete, tearing up junior high football fields as a fullback and linebacker. This particular bully, Eric Maxwell, was trying to impress some girls at Will's expense. In the hallway before class one morning, Maxwell had taunted him, saying, "Hey, Hammon, I hear they invented the word 'blind-sided' just for you." The girls giggled. Jack happened to be passing by at the time. For reasons Will still didn't understand, Jack heard Maxwell's comment and threw a forearm into the boy's jaw, knocking him down. "Hmm," Jack had said, "even with two eyes, guess you didn't see that one coming, did you, Maxwell?"

He and Will had been friends ever since, and when Jack Reece was your friend, lots of people were.

Only problem was, being his friend wasn't always the easiest thing in the world. Will sighed. "You're going to get me killed some day," he said. "Let's go."

"Now you're talking," Jack said. He shifted the car into gear and pulled away from the curb. The roadhouse was just over the Gloire de Matin Bridge, across from the Electrical Park ballroom, but Jack turned the Star around and drove farther into east Waterton.

"Where we going?" Will said.

"I need gas. I thought we could stop at Bob's first."

"You mean the filling station you work at?" Will said. "The place you called in sick to this morning? *That* Bob's?"

"Yikes," Jack said. "Maybe a different station?"

"Yeah," Will said. "Smells like you're burning oil, too."

"What, you got two noses to make up for your one eye?"

"You got a brain in your pecker to make up for none in your head?"

"At least I got a pecker."

"So do I. It's only got one eye, too."

The image must have struck Jack as especially funny, because he laughed so hard he cut the corner of Franklin too close, scraping the Star's front tire against the curb. "Who's gonna get who killed?" he said. He pulled over for a moment to wipe his eyes.

"You started it," Will said. The stench of oil baking on metal was strong. "You can't smell that? You're a *mechanic*, for chrissakes."

"Yeah, I know. Been meaning to check the seals."

"*Before* your engine burns up?"

"Wiseguy," he said. He ducked his head as he drove past Bob's Standard on Franklin. A few blocks later he turned right past Roosevelt Park onto East Fourth, where ice packed the grooves of the old trolley tracks that still traversed the street. Light from electric streetlamps glinted off parallel rows of metal running from Franklin southwest to the bridge at Water Street. There were no pedestrians and few other cars out on such a bitterly cold night.

Waterton was a growing city. Here in the downtown, every street was lined with two- and three-story brick structures, although Block's Department Store had eight floors and, across the river, the Waterton Building had ten. The WCC&N railroad terminal on East Fourth was still going strong, while down the road Kresge's and Block's vied for customers each year with fancy window displays and endless sales. The new Riviera Theatre, just on the east end of the bridge, drew theatrical actors from all over the region, as well as the dwindling troupes of vaudeville performers, all of whom had to shout to be heard over the clatter of trains.

The Oak River was frozen solid. In the moonlight it looked like an uneven mass of gray concrete, shadows striping the troughs of its immobile waves. The surface was too rough for skating, but people did anyway on Saturday afternoons and Sunday mornings after church. As Will and Jack crossed the bridge Will remembered that a little girl had fallen through the ice and drowned a few years back. That hadn't stopped anyone from skating.

"This is where they're going to build the new Y," Jack said, crossing the bridge to where East Fourth became West Fourth. "All the homos'll want a room."

"Better book yours early, then," Will said.

Jack turned left onto Commercial. "You're a funny guy," he said.

"Do you have any idea where you're going? The Garden's the other way."

"Just driving. Still need gas—"

"And oil."

"—and oil, and anyway, it's too early for the Garden. Won't be enough people there yet."

An old horse-drawn milk wagon was parked on the lawn of the Waterton Cooperative Dairy on Commercial Street, beyond the main downtown area. Wood rotting and metal wheel rims rusting, the thing had been there for years, a reminder of times gone by. "Imagine having to haul milk with that thing," Will said as they passed the dairy.

"My dad used to do it. Hitched up the horses every morning at five and delivered milk to everyone on his route before ten." He turned south onto Eleventh Street and then east onto Washington. "In the summer he had to buy fifty pounds of ice a day from the ice company to keep the milk cold. Paid for it out of his own pocket."

"I thought he was at the cream separators over on Mulligan."

"He is now, but back then he was a milkman."

"Luka says my dad was a cabbie at Kline's. That's how he met my mother."

"Old George, hero of the Great War, drove a *coach*? That's no job for a white man. Bet it didn't go over well with Margaret."

"Nope," Will said. "She didn't like him working there, and she doesn't like me working at Bob's. 'Common labor,' she calls it."

"Shit, I had your money, I wouldn't work, either."

"You *don't* work," Will said. "Least, no harder than you have to."

"Remind me again why we're friends." They were nearly out of town before Jack spotted a Red Crown station that still had its lights on. Unlike Bob, the owner here had a modern rectangular pump without the visible register tank on top. An obviously displeased attendant shuffled out, fastening a parka over his uniform. He looked to be about Will's age. A halo of frozen breath encircled his head as he delivered pretty much the same stock greeting Bob made his employees say.

"Welcome to Red Crown, sir. My name is Tim. How may I serve you tonight?"

Jack told him to fill the Star with gas and oil, don't bother with the windshield or tires. "Happy now?" he said to Will.

"It's about time," Will said. Out this far the streetlamps were fewer and farther between, so there were long gaps of darkness on the streets where neither moonlight nor electricity could penetrate the leafless branches of elms. Half-moon silver limned the treetops. The stars always seemed so much brighter in the winter sky, but also more remote and unfriendly.

Tim lifted the hood and poured in two quarts of oil. "You were flat out," he said to Jack through chattering teeth. "Ain't so good for the engine."

"So I hear," Jack said, nudging Will with his elbow. When the gas tank was full Tim replaced the nozzle and trudged to the driver's window. The bill came to $3.10. Jack handed him a five.

"Keep the change?" Tim asked hopefully.

"Hell, no, you can't keep the change! They pay you a wage here, don't they?"

"Jesus," the kid said, and went back into the station.

"You are one cheap son-of-a-bitch," Will said to Jack. "Give him a break, why don't you. It must be a hundred below zero out there."

"I don't live in a fancy house on Gloire de Matin," Jack said.

"Like I see any of that money," Will said.

Tim returned and shoved two ones through the window at Jack. "You got a dime? We're about to close. The owner locked up most of the cash. We don't have ninety cents in change."

Jack snatched the ones, then pulled a quarter from his shirt pocket. "*That* change you can keep," he said.

"Thank you for allowing me to serve you," Tim said, his expression stone cold. "At Red Crown the customer always comes first." As he walked away Will was sure he heard the kid mutter, "Asshole."

Jack pulled back onto Washington, but this time headed west. "Boy, I sure am thirsty," he said. "The Garden ought to be hopping by now. They got the best beer in town."

Will watched the houses go by, lights in the windows, smoke rippling out of the chimneys. Plowed snow lay hard-packed in rounded drifts on both sides of the road. Jack stepped on the gas in his hurry to get to the roadhouse. Will didn't say anything for several minutes, but god *damn*, this was not a good idea, not a good idea at all. Luka would have a fit. "Hear about those gangsters who got gunned down in Chicago on Valentine's Day?" he said as they approached Hansbro Avenue. A Ford Model T was waiting at the stop sign there.

"Bunch of guys in a warehouse?" Jack said.

"Yeah. Luka and Red were talking about it the other night. They said Capone ordered it."

"Who's Capone?" Jack sped north onto Hansbro, nearly clipping the Ford.

Will's heart was pounding. He looked back. The driver of the Ford had opened his door and was shaking a fist at them. He didn't blame the man. "You've never heard of Al Capone?" he said, trying to sound unafraid.

"Should I have?" The car hit a patch of ice and spun dangerously close to the ditch. "Whoo-ee!" Jack said, cranking the steering wheel in the opposite direction of the spin. Eventually he got control, and they fishtailed up the street. Luckily, the northbound traffic was well ahead of them and there was nothing southbound along this stretch. Jack pulled to a stop behind six other cars waiting to turn at the T-intersection where Hansbro ended at Prism.

"Jesus, Jack, you are insane."

"Now, Nancy, what did I tell you?"

"Don't call me that," Will said.

The lights of Electrical Park blazed several blocks to the east. Curtis's Garden was across the street from the Park's fairgrounds. A few miles to the west old Indian burial mounds used to line the street, back when Prism was still called the North Waterton-Cedar Crossing Road. Bulldozers had long since plowed the mounds over in the name of urban improvement.

"You ready?" Jack said, creeping to the stop sign after the cars ahead of him had finally turned right. There was usually a dance at Electrical

Park's ballroom on Saturday nights, but Will guessed most of those cars were heading to the Garden.

"No," he said, "but we're going anyway, so let's get to it."

"That's the spirit," Jack said.

LUKA

Luka and Red Fisher were having a drink in a back room of the Garden when the ringer from the front desk buzzed. That usually meant some kind of trouble. "Shit," Luka said, but as he got up from the table the door swung open and Arlen Kelper strode in, followed by two policemen.

"Maybe you're outside Waterton's jurisdiction here," Kelper said, "but these are Red Hawk County deputies. You can't hide from them. Officers, you'll note that these men are drinking alcohol. If you'll check the basement you'll find kegs of the stuff, imported from Chicago."

Kelper had a smug smile that made Luka want to punch him. He didn't, though. This wasn't the first time his place had been raided, and it wouldn't be the last. The worst punishment he'd ever suffered was a $200 fine for possession. Cal Morton, the local D.A., had hassled him a couple of times, but most of his arrests were publicity stunts designed to mollify the Bible thumpers who voted for him. The feds had even tried once to get Luka on an income tax rap. That one never even made it to the grand jury.

Luka was not likely to be intimidated by a couple of county clods. Besides, he knew these coppers. Benson and Yarborough. They'd been on his payroll for years.

"Do your job, officers," Kelper said.

"I'll wait outside," Red said, winking at Luka.

When Fisher left Benson came over to the table and sat down. "Nice place you got here, Mr. Curtis," he said. It *was* a nice place, padded leather upholstery on the chairs, oak table, reproductions of famous paintings on paneled walls, a low-hanging glass chandelier that tossed just enough light to set a cozy mood, and a room not quite sound-proof to allow the orchestra's jazz to seep in beneath the crack of the door.

"Thanks," Luka said. "I only buy the best."

Benson eyed his glass. "You got illegal hooch in there?"

"I'm a law-abiding citizen."

"Then you won't mind if he tests it," Kelper said.

"Be my guest. It's just Dr. Pepper."

Benson raised the glass and sniffed its contents.

"Well?" Kelper said.

"Smells like Dr. Pepper to me," Benson said.

"Let me try that!" Kelper said, but the second deputy, Yarborough, barred his way.

"I think you've caused Mr. Curtis enough trouble tonight," he said.

"What the hell?" Kelper said, and then suddenly he understood. "Oh, I see," he said. "Have we all had a good laugh at my expense?"

"Don't take it too hard," Yarborough said. "I'm sure Mr. Curtis won't press charges for invading his privacy."

"Press charges?" The veins stood out on Kelper's neck, and even in the low lighting Luka could see his face turn red. "You son-of-a-bitch—"

"Naw," Luka laughed, "we're all friends here, Seaweed. Have a Dr. Pepper on me on your way out."

"I can't wait until the city annexes this filthy little cesspit."

"Well, it's the same old song, isn't it? You've been singing that one for years."

"It's coming," Kelper said. "If nothing else, Landon's will need to expand into that area someday. Since they won't want their property spanning two sets of ordinances, they'll pay any price to have it all in one place. *Any* price. Waterton won't be able to ignore hard cash, no matter what tricks you try."

"Tell me, Arlen," Luka said, "do you really think this threat hasn't been used before? What's the point of your little demonstration?"

"Go to hell," Kelper said. He stormed out the door, slamming it shut behind him.

Luka shrugged and toasted his absence. "Have a drink with me, boys?" he said to the deputies.

"We're on duty," Yarborough said. "But, uh, you know, it's Saturday night, and—"

"Pick up your envelopes at the front desk," Luka said. He leaned back in his chair and lit up a cigar as he watched them go.

Red Fisher came back in a few minutes later. "They didn't arrest you."

Luka shook his head. "Arlen Kelper is a jackass."

Red sat down across the table from Luka. Cigar hung in the air between them. "Don't shoot the messenger," he said, coughing and waving the smoke away, "but I just saw your kid come in with another boy."

"Will, in here? I'll be damned." Luka's face lit up. He reached in his pocket, then flipped a dollar coin to Red. "Go buy him a beer, will you?"

YOUNG WILL
Waterton, Iowa
October 28, 1929

Jack's friendship got Will into the game but couldn't get him into the backfield. School had just let out for the day, and a group of West Side High boys had gathered at Sloane field for a friendly football contest. It was Monday, a cold, raw day with low-hanging clouds that threatened to produce the first snowflakes of the season. The turf was mostly mud, pocked with depressions, filled with puddles, topped with thin crusts of ice.

Only nine players showed up. Because of his disability, Will was chosen to be the snapper for both sides, meaning he didn't get to do much of anything. Four boys on offense, four on defense, and Will in the middle hiking the ball to the spinback, then scooting out of the way while the others ran or passed or caught or tackled.

"Let me play end once," Will said. "I can see okay, long as I line up left."

"You dumb shit," Jack said, "your eye ain't the problem. Your problem is you couldn't catch the ball if I handed it to you."

"Could, too."

Jack tossed him a soft underhanded lob.

Will dropped the ball.

The other boys laughed.

"How 'bout if I just snap it?" Will said.

"Now there's an idea."

The rules were simple: knock down whoever had the ball, by any means. Grabbing, tripping, holding, pushing, gouging, punching, and piling on were not only legal but encouraged. There was no punting, no kicking of any kind. Each team had four downs to score. A touchdown counted one point.

The high school football season had just ended. Jack was a starter both ways. Amateurs like the boys playing defense today had little chance against him, especially on a slippery field. Will snapped the ball to him, and Jack just bulled his way toward the goal line, ice crackling under his feet, mud flying. Sometimes the defense tackled him. More often they just bounced off him until he scored.

It wasn't fair the other way, either. When Jack was on defense he was fast enough to reach the ball carrier before the poor guy could even think about running or passing. The only way the other team scored was on an interception return and a fluke end around when Jack's feet slipped out from underneath him.

Dusk came early in October. By sunset Jack's team was ahead 17-2, and they called it a game. Eight of the boys were slathered in mud and wet turf, dripping and sloppy and freezing. Will was pristine, save for muddy shoes and dirty hands. But he was cold.

The others trudged out of the stadium, leaving Will and Jack alone on the field.

"You're too clean," Jack said, and tackled him.

"Hey!"

Will got up and Jack tackled him again. "There. Now you look like a football player."

Will was suitably grimy from head to toe. "You bastard," he said, laughing. "You're the one who made me the snapper. My Grandma's gonna kill me."

"Okay, first thing: football players don't whine about their Grandma."

"What's the second thing?"

"Football players get dirty." Jack pushed him down again.

"All right, knock it off!" Will cried. Grabbing a handful of mud, he got to his feet, then with calm deliberation plastered Jack's face with it. Jack stood there and let him do it. "You look like Al Jolson," Will said.

"*Mammy*," Jack said, wiping mud from his eyes. He clapped Will on the back. "Come on, you knucklehead. I'll drive you home to your precious granny."

The trip to Gloire de Matin Island took twenty minutes.

"You coming in?" Will said as they pulled into his driveway.

"Looking like this? In *that* house? I don't think so."

"Chicken."

"It's okay for football players to whine about their *friend's* Grandma."

Will got out. The clouds were spitting the snow they'd been promising all afternoon, although the flakes melted on contact with the ground. "See you in first hour tomorrow."

He went around to the back of the house. With luck Margaret would be in her bedroom and he could sneak in without being seen. Birgitta would probably still be scuttling about. Since she did the laundry, she'd squawk about his filthy clothes, but she wouldn't rat him out. And who knew where Luka might be? Wheeling, dealing, gambling, scheming, schmoozing? Chasing skirts down at the Garden, if rumors could be believed? Or he could be in the library with a fire in the hearth, smoking a cigar and listening to his Philco. He wouldn't object to Will's appearance, though, as long as Will explained he'd gotten dirty playing football. Football was a man's game, of which Luka approved mightily.

The door creaked as he opened it—it never creaked except when he was trying to enter quietly—and again when he closed it. He crept up the stairs to the kitchen.

He heard voices in the dining room. Lots of voices. Lots of angry, upset voices: Luka's, Arlen Kelper's, someone Will didn't recognize, and his grandmother's. She was crying. Jesus, what was going on?

Forgetting his filthy clothing, he peered into the dining room. They were all seated around the table. The stranger turned out to be one of Margaret's accountants. Will had seen him before, but couldn't recall his name. Margaret had her head down on the table. Luka was massaging her back, comforting her. Comforting her? *Luka*?

Will stepped into the room. They all looked up at him. If they noticed how ghastly he was, none of them said anything. "What's wrong?" Will said. "What happened?"

"The stock market's down again," Luka said. "*Way* down."

Last Thursday, October 24th, the market had fallen dramatically, sending Margaret into a frenzy. It was already being called "Black Thursday" by Wall Street analysts. But prices had rallied somewhat on Friday. "I thought it got better," Will said.

"It did," the accountant said, "but it didn't last. And it's not done. It crashed again today, but tomorrow's going to be worse. There's no way to stop it. The bottom's going to fall out. Tomorrow's going to be the blackest of the black."

"I don't understand."

The accountant exhaled slowly. "Any significant decline in the value of stocks starts a wave of panic selling and trading, which makes the stocks virtually worthless. People who own the stocks are losing millions."

The man might as well be speaking Swahili. "And we own stock?" Will said.

"Your Grandfather has little to fear," Kelper said with disgust, "since his income comes from 'other' sources. But your Grandmother..."

Margaret lifted her head. Mascara trickled down her face, giving her the appearance of some hideous harlequin. "I'll be ruined," she said.

MARGARET
Hammon Falls, Iowa
December 1929

It was a thoroughly miserable day. Layers of clouds rolled low through the sky, spewing needles of drizzle that weren't quite cold enough to freeze on the street, but soaked through clothes and made the temperature seem much colder than it really was. The trees on Gloire de Matin Island were bleak and black, their skeletal branches covered in ice that was starting to melt and drip with the drizzle.

It had been less than six weeks since the stock market's crash. Since then Margaret's net worth had halved, and halved again. She was far from destitute, but she hadn't felt this desperate since the cyclone destroyed Pomeroy in 1893.

She was a passenger in a car driven by her attorney Arlen Kelper. Kelper was giving her a tour of the trailer park Orville had set up north of Gloire de Matin Island, which housed Electrical Park's workers, mostly immigrants from Mexico and northern Europe. The trailers were ugly ramshackle affairs, uniformly gray, some with boarded-up windows, leaking roofs, and outside doors secured by only one hinge. The muddy roads between the structures were rutted and pocked with pools of ice and snow runoff.

"This is what your husband has created," Kelper said. "Look at this place. It's a disgrace. Trailer parks aren't allowed in Waterton, and this is why. The people are here illegally. They live in poverty while Curtis grows fat on their labor. Open your eyes, Margaret."

"And see what, Mr. Kelper? These hovels are dreadful. I accept your word that Orville is responsible. I'm not as naïve as you think, but whatever your opinion of him, he still has legal custody of William." Kelper's car hit a pothole, causing Margaret to jerk forward and nearly hit her head on the dash. "You might consider driving a little slower," she said, taking her compact mirror from her purse and rearranging her mussed hair. She was so gray! "Please, I want to go home," she said. "You've made your point."

The frustration in Kelper's voice was obvious. "Will is going to be sixteen in three months. If you and Curtis were to divorce, the court would almost certainly allow him to decide who he wants to live with. I'd advocate for you again."

"You know how well that worked out the first time."

"Hauken is dead. A new judge will be more sympathetic." He pulled into what passed for a driveway for one of the trailers and turned the car around.

"Orville is a decent father to William," Margaret said. "And he didn't lose his money in the Crash. I'm not ready for the poorhouse."

Kelper turned onto a paved county road and headed south. "You're not broke, Margaret. Even a quarter of your net worth is still a fortune. Why do you think Curtis stayed with you?"

"For my name. It's his turn to pay the bills now—"

"His money is dirty! You don't want any part of that. The reason the Crash didn't affect him is because he's a *gangster*. I'm sure you're aware of the alcohol and gambling but, pardon my language, he also runs whores out of the upstairs rooms of his roadhouse. What kind of father is that for Will?"

Windshield wipers clacked as snowflakes mixed with the drizzle. To the east dead cornstalks limped in the cold breeze, stalks powdered by old snow. Rows made by fall harvesters seemed to stretch into infinity. Iowa was such a dreary place in the winter. Margaret sighed. She'd heard all of these arguments before. Yes, Orville was a criminal, she'd admitted that to herself, but it wasn't like he was harming anyone. He was just giving people what they wanted. Nobody got hurt, nobody died. He was popular in the community, not only for the entertainments he provided but for his social skills, skills Margaret lacked.

None of that mattered to Kelper. He was obsessed with sending Orville to prison, and nothing would deter him. "Do you realize," she said, "that I've been married to Orville more than twice as long as I was married to G.W.? Like it or not, Mr. Kelper, I'm a Curtis."

Kelper pulled over to let another car pass. He took her hand in his and looked into her eyes. "Do you love him, Margaret? Can you honestly tell me you do?"

Margaret turned away. Her breath fogged the window. The drizzle was all snow now. "You are too presumptuous, sir. You're my lawyer, not my minister or my confidant. I'm comfortable, and what woman could ask for more than that?"

And then, for reasons that had nothing to do with their conversation, for no reason at all, she was weeping. Seemed like she'd done nothing but weep for weeks, for months, for years. For her entire life. Lord, what a train wreck she was.

Kelper guided the car back onto the road. "I'm sorry," he said, probably without knowing what he was apologizing for. He just didn't understand, or maybe he did.

GEORGE
Saint-Germain-des-Prés, Paris, France
January 1932

When George returned to his flat after work on a cold night in January 1932, Suzanne was gone.

The shock was not that this day had come, but that it had taken so long to get here. She'd packed her clothes, her makeup, her brushes, her toiletries, her writings, her doodles, everything that was hers. Apparently she'd even swept and cleaned, because not a hair was left behind, not a nail clipping, not a whiff of perfume, nothing.

Except a note, typed and unsigned.

***

Tommy is a grown man. If you haven't found him by now, you never will.
Write to your mother. You owe her that much.
Stop drinking.
I went home.
Be well.

***

George sat at the kitchen table and stared around the flat for a long time. He tried to convince himself he'd never loved her anyway, not like he had Cora, that he didn't need her, wouldn't miss her, didn't care.

He poured himself a drink.

When he awoke it was two days later. Suzanne was still gone.

He didn't know where she'd gotten the money to go back to the States. She hadn't touched their savings. This was good, because his latest drunken binge had finally tested his employer's patience once too often.

"Where the hell have you been?" Paul said on the morning George returned to work.

"I was sick."

"I can still smell the 'sickness' on you."

"I'm sorry. Suzanne left me."

Paul clapped him on the shoulder. "Then I'm sorry, too. But you have a telephone, no?"

"Yes."

"How many times has this happened, George?"

"Suzanne has never left me before."

"You always have an excuse. This time it's Suzanne."

"Please, Paul…"

"I'm sorry about Suzanne, George, but this can't go on. I've got a business to run. There's a Depression. Plenty of people looking for work."

"You can't do this," George said. For Christ's sake, he was practically *begging*.

"I have to. Good luck to you, George."

With that George was unemployed like millions of others throughout the world. Feeling despondent but oddly free, he returned to his flat. There was nothing he wanted or needed there, other than his remaining two bottles of wine and Mick's Celtic cross—and some luck *that* had been.

He locked the door, walked down the stairs, and left the building for the final time. After sleeping off one more drunk by the Seine, he emptied the bank account, sold his car, and used his French passport to book passage to Ireland.

MARGARET
Hammon Falls, Iowa
December 1932

"It will be difficult managing the house without you, Birgitta," Margaret said. She sat on the davenport in her parlor, disinterestedly flipping through one of Will's *Popular Science* magazines. How very tiresome science was.

Birgitta dragged three suitcases down the stairs and set them next to the door. Now sixty-two, she was making her first visit to Finland since she was a girl. Apparently she had an elderly aunt and uncle living there. "You just do not want to do the chores yourself," she said, breathing hard from the exertion. Her face was red.

Margaret glared at the maid. She admired her sharp tongue when used against Orville, but would not tolerate insolence directed at her. "We don't have to give you time off," she said.

Birgitta shrugged. "I have been with Mr. Curtis thirty years. I have never taken a holiday. I will go. It will be only three months. You will survive."

William came bounding down the stairs, schoolbooks in hand. "Hello, goodbye," he said as opened the door. He noticed the magazine Margaret was reading. "That issue's got a great article on distributor caps. Gotta run."

"You will eat first?" Birgitta said.

"No time," William said. "Big test today. Have a great time in Finland, Birgy."

"It is wrong to waste food," Birgitta called to his back. She smiled enigmatically at Margaret and said, "I will eat it, then. The taxi will arrive in thirty minutes."

She left the parlor via the dining room.

Margaret lay the magazine on the end table and turned on her radio. It was a vulgar device. Orville had had one for years. She hated the crackly sound radios made. The music was tinny as a bad phonograph recording, the news announcers brayed like mules, and there was too much sports. But it was noise, something to fill the nothing, and she'd asked Orville for one on her last birthday. When the radio played, Margaret almost felt as if she were in the company of other humans, without actually having to endure their presence.

This morning the Chicago Philharmonic was performing *Jesu Joy of Man's Desiring*, complete with chorus. Even through the imperfect medium of radio, it was a majestic piece.

Bach was followed by Debussy, Ravel, and Gershwin. Margaret didn't approve of jazz, but *Rhapsody in Blue* was a guilty pleasure. The song had just segued into the slower orchestral theme when she heard a horn honk outside. And honk. And honk again.

"Birgitta!" she called. Was the woman deaf?

Margaret stirred from the davenport and looked out the door. The taxi was in the drive, last night's heavy snowfall still on its roof.

"Birgitta!"

Margaret went through the dining room and into the kitchen. Birgitta lay slumped across the table, her face in a plate of eggs, her fork on the floor. She was not breathing.

The poor woman was leaving for Finland this morning. Only now she wasn't, at least not in the manner she'd envisioned.

The taxi continued to honk. *Rhapsody in Blue* was ending.

Margaret steadied her hand as she walked to the telephone. Orville and William were not home, so she'd have to call for the ambulance herself.

LUKA
Waterton, Iowa
April 1933

"I got a $20 bill says you don't pick it up," Red Fisher said.

Luka eyed the pins. He had a two-eight split, could be tricky for a novice, maybe, but Luka was no novice. Bowling didn't bring him the satisfaction boxing had, but it was a nice physical outlet for his frustrations. "You're on," he said.

The Bowl-In was dark except for the two lanes Luka and Red were using. The building was closed, but the manager, Marvin, often opened a couple of lanes when Luka wanted to bowl after hours. Marvin was sitting at the desk at the other end of the bowling alley, reading a girlie magazine. He knew better than to get close enough to overhear Luka's conversations.

Luka approached the line and released the ball. It hugged the right gutter for three quarters of the way, then curved perfectly to graze the two pin on the left side, propelling it into the eight. The sound of the pins echoed in the empty alley. "That'll be twenty bucks," he said.

Red shook his head. "Last curveball I saw like that, Hack Wilson swatted it out of the park." He handed Luka a bill, who put it in his wallet and sat down.

"Today's lesson," Luka said, "is never make bets that aren't already in the bag."

Red retrieved his ball and stepped up to the lane. The ball started down the middle, but then angled left and only knocked down three pins off the back of the rack. "Shit," he said.

"What'd I tell you about aiming for the middle arrow? You got a hook, so you got to aim right. That way the ball breaks between the one and two and bam! you got a strike."

"Every time I try that, my ball straightens out, I miss the head pin and get four."

"Yeah, well, you only got three doing it your way." Luka loved ribbing Red, who was still cocky ten years after his boxing victory. "And use a heavier ball, maybe sixteen pounds. That'll slow it down and get more pin action."

"Thanks for the tips." Red sipped his Coca-Cola while he waited for the ball to return. "I hear Will's running his own place."

"Yeah, he wanted to stay at Bob's, but he's too good to be working for someone else. Bob wouldn't sell, so I let Will manage my Standard station on East Fourth. It's still mine, but Will does the day-to-day stuff. I'm teaching him how to keep the books."

"Cook them, you mean." Red threw his second ball, aiming at the third arrow. The ball tailed to the right and clipped one pin off the other corner. "Great advice. See, I got four anyway. You got lipstick on your shirt." Red grinned. "How'd that get there, eh?"

The stain was just above the belt line. Luka had tried to hide it, but the shirt kept coming untucked when he threw the ball. "Haven't been able to find a housekeeper to replace Birgitta," he said. "Maggie's fired every one I've brought in."

"That's why you still have the stain. I asked how it got there."

"Shut up."

"I make no judgments," Red said, laughing.

They finished the game, which Luka won 237 to 113. LUKA was engraved in a flourish of curlicues on his ball, which he put into its personal carrier bag. Red returned his to the rack. "So," Luka said, "now that's settled, what did you need to see me about?"

They sat down.

"You heard what that son-of-a-bitch Roosevelt did?" Red said.

"The beer bill?" The amendment to the Volstead Act made the transportation and sale of beer legal again, despite general Prohibition. "Yeah, so? I'll just go back to distributing."

"Chicago's nervous. This bill's just the start. You know the whole damn thing's gonna be repealed? By the end of the year, there won't *be* any Prohibition. No hooch, no profits."

"Those guys in danger of starving? They still got slots, numbers, whores, protection, heroin, reefer, you name it. It's all jake. Tell them to invest in legit businesses, like I'm doing."

Marvin approached from the other end of the building. "You gentlemen done here? Mind if I turn off the lanes?"

"Go ahead," Luka said. Marvin waved a thanks and went back to his desk.

"Legit, like Will's filling station?" Red said.

"Why not?"

"Chicago still wants their cut."

"I got no problem with that."

The lights over the bowling pins went off, leaving only the ceiling light above their lanes. The alley looked like a tomb in the dark. "Long as we're clear," Fisher said.

Luka stood up and put his jacket on. It was a cold April night. At his age he felt the chill more every season. "Been a pleasure," he said. "Marvin'll lock up."

"One more thing," Red said, lighting a cigarette. "I had a disagreement with a guy over on the east side. Happened in your territory."

"Anyone I know?"

Red shrugged. "Joey Mara? Won't be any more trouble from him."

"Never heard of him." Luka pulled his cap over his ears. He did know Joey. He was an asshole, but harmless. He didn't deserve to die. Goddamn it, Red was too much of a loose cannon.

Something would have to be done about him.

YOUNG WILL
Waterton, Iowa
March 1934

Will had the job of his dreams. He'd just turned twenty years old and was already the manager of a filling station. He owed his position to Luka, but once he'd gotten the hang of bookkeeping, it was his hard work and mechanical skills, not Luka's, that had made the station a success. And his name on the marquee, Will's Standard, had a nice ring to it.

Jack Reece followed him over from Bob's. Unlike Will, he had aspirations of college, but when the sports scholarships didn't come through, he was stuck in Waterton. Truth was, Jack would never be mistaken for an intellectual, but he was okay with engines and the best paint man in town, bar none. His customer service skills were top notch, when he wasn't hung over.

Will had just replaced the head on a '32 Ford. He smiled as he tightened the head nuts and saw the gasket hold. God, he loved machines! Outside a car turned in off East Fourth. Jack took care of the drive-up customers, but when a black Caddy bumped over the bell hose and came to a stop by the gas pump, Will hollered to Jack that he'd take care of it. He knew that car well, and what a beauty it was. It belonged to Red Fisher. Red was a fanatic for maintenance and cleanliness. Will had just serviced the Caddy last week.

He lowered the hood on the Ford, wiped his hands on a rag, and went out to the pump.

"Doing the grunt work today, Will?" Red said. He was wearing a stylish three-piece suit with matching necktie. A smudge of mud marred the right toe of his shiny black shoes.

"Like to stay involved with the day-to-day stuff, sir," he said. Snowflakes melted to tiny drops on the good lens of his glasses.

"Good man." Red flashed a roll of bills, peeled off two hundreds, and stuffed them into Will's pocket.

"What's that for?"

"I noticed on the receipt you didn't charge me for the tune-up last week."

"All it needed was a lube and oil filter. Everything else was fine."

"Took you time to check, didn't it? You're gonna manage a business, Will, you can't give your time away. People'll take advantage of you."

"A full tune-up's only twenty or thirty bucks, depending."

"Don't worry about it. I just scored a big business deal today. On my way to meet my new partners now. How d'you like the duds?"

"You look great, sir, except—"

"For Christ's sake, call me Red, will you? We're pals, aren't we?"

"Sure, Red." Will handed him a rag. "You got mud on your right shoe."

Red looked down. "I'll be damned. You see better with one eye than I do with two. Much obliged." He spit on the rag and buffed the shoe to match the rest of the shine, then tossed the rag back to Will. "Gotta go," he said. "People to see, and all that."

"Good luck with your new partners," Will said.

Red put the Caddy in gear, pulled out onto East Fourth, and headed into downtown Waterton. Will didn't know if he'd really stopped in to pay for the nonexistent tune-up or if he just wanted to show off. Probably both.

GEORGE
Dublin, Ireland
March 1934

George's savings from Paris didn't last long. Third-class fare from Cherbourg to Dublin was reasonable, but lodging in Ireland wasn't. The first flat he rented, near the Dublin harbor, was much more expensive than the one he'd had in Paris. Because Ireland's electrical systems differed from those on the continent, his Électricité de France certification didn't mean much. None of the Dublin firms would take him on, so for several months his only income came from occasional temporary employment on the docks.

Eventually George set himself up as an "independent contractor," using the last of his savings to buy a beat-up 1926 Daimler Dropland Coupé. The car became his lifeline. Mastering Irish electronics was a snap, but to compete with the firms he needed his own transportation, as he often accepted jobs after hours when no public transit was available.

Work was sporadic. He seldom had enough to cover his living expenses. Instead of selling his car, he changed lodgings. In just over two years he'd moved three times, sinking deeper into the slums with each successive address.

On an unusually warm and sunny March day he checked a flat on Amiens Street, in Dublin's North Inner City. The building was a dirty old brownstone overlooking other dirty old brownstones. The second-story flat was a two-room affair that stank of urine and mold.

"Used to call this part of town the Monto," the superintendent told him. She introduced herself as Mrs. Dunleavy, a widow. She was a woman of about fifty, plump, with two teeth missing from her lower jaw, which made her cheek cave in on the left side when she spoke. "Weren't no itch couldn't be scratched in Monto. The Royal Barracks was here then, and all them Brit soldiers was a lusty lot, dying to spend their coin on ladies and drink and gambling and, well, you name it. You probably heard the song." She sang a tuneless melody:
"*Well, if you've got a wing-o,*
 Take her up to Ring-o
 Where the waxies sing-o all the day—"
"Don't know that one," George said.
"No?" Mrs. Dunleavy shrugged. "Ever been to Amsterdam?"
George shook his head. This flat was appalling. The living room, bedroom and kitchen were the same room, with a separate toilet the size of a closet. The paint, what was left of it, was chipped. The ceiling tiles were water-stained from rain leaking in, or worse, from faulty pipes

above. A bucket in the corner was half full of recent seepage. The mattress was so bowed in the middle it looked like a horse had slept in it. The porcelain on the toilet bowl was cracked and yellow, the inside nearly black. In the summer the flies must be atrocious.

"Well," Mrs. Dunleavy said, straightening the blankets on the bed, "in Amsterdam there's a whorehouse on every corner. In Monto there was a whorehouse in every *house*. I used to run one. 'Mrs. Dunleavy's Boutique,' I called it. Did real good in those days. But next thing you know Michael Collins comes along and boots the Brits out, then the Bible-thumpers shut down the whorehouses. What's left over is the shit of the slums and none of the money to show for it."

"Boutique?" George said, amused. If this was a boutique, his Daimler was an airplane.

"Thought it sounded classy, you know? 'Course, a big, good-looking lad like yourself wouldn't have no need of whores anyway, but them Brits… Say, you got people in England? 'Cause I meant no offense."

"American," George said, "by way of France."

"Could tell you was foreign. So. You want the place or not?"

This cesspit was all George could afford. "How could I refuse?" he said.

"That'll be five s, seven per week, in advance," she said. When she smiled she looked like a bleached and bloated raisin. "Will it just be you? A lady, maybe? 'Cause it's extra for two. And we don't serve breakfast. Tobacconist down the street sells coffee and day-old pastries cheap."

"It's just me," George said. He handed her a five-pound note from his wallet. "This far enough in advance?"

Mrs. Dunleavy peeked into his wallet to see how much more money was there. George snapped it shut. "Not that whores can't still be had," she said helpfully. "Only you got to look for them a little harder now."

"Is there a telephone?"

"Down the hall, five d for three minutes."

"Telephone directory?"

"You can borrow mine, you ask me sweet." She fluttered her eyelids at him. "Did I mention I'm a widow?"

Jesus Christ.

"I'll get my bags from the car," he said.

She dropped the key into his hand, then sang as she descended the stairs ahead of him.

"If you've had your fill of porter, And you can't go any further
Give your man the order: 'Back to the Quay!'
And take her up to Monto, Monto, Monto
Take her up to Monto, lan-ge-roo,
To you!"

LUKA
Waterton, Iowa
March 1934

These things took time, time to cover tracks, time to deflect suspicion, time to arrange alibis so the Chicago people wouldn't come sniffing around afterward. Luka hated this aspect of the business, but what had to be done had to be done. In the past year Red Fisher had become more and more unstable. The man had ambition and he liked killing. That didn't bode well for Luka. Waterton must look like a tempting plum to someone who had no chance of rising any further in the Chicago ranks.

Luka stared grimly up East Fourth from inside the door of the National Bank. Ruts cut through the slush on the road. Light snow was falling, melting on the pavement but sticking like powdered sugar to the tops of parked automobiles. A crisp breeze had come up. Two policemen sat in a squad car across the street, waiting. When the black Cadillac approached, Luka backed farther into the bank. He shouldn't have come at all—Red would be suspicious if he noticed his old boss hanging around—but Luka had to see for himself that this ended the way the police chief had said it would.

Red thought he was meeting with new business associates. He had an appointment, all right, but not the kind he was expecting.

Luka stepped outside as the Cadillac passed. At that moment the cops spun out from the curb into Red's path, blocking the street. As Red slammed on his brakes, two more patrol cars arrived to surround him. He jumped out of the Caddy and fled down a dead-end alley with six armed officers in pursuit.

Luka was parked a block away, on East Fifth. When he heard the gunshots he walked with practiced nonchalance to his new Chevrolet, his feet sloshing through the muck of winter's final weeks. The key was in the ignition. He got in and fired up the engine. There was no need to stay now. Both the law and Luka had rid themselves of a public menace.

Jack thought the sounds were the backfire of a car.

"Backfire, my ass," Will said. He knew a backfire when he heard one, and this wasn't it. "Those are gunshots."

They rushed outside, looking in the direction of downtown Waterton, where the sounds had come from. From the station they couldn't see much, but after a few moments they heard sirens, the intermittent blasts of the police and the high wail of an ambulance.

"Something big's going on," Jack said. "Come on, let's go."

Will grabbed his cap and locked the station door. As soon as they got to the end of the block they saw dozens of people coming out of buildings and running toward an alley off East Fourth. One woman who'd been walking her dog slipped in the slush, fell, and was almost trampled. The dog was barking its little head off.

Will and Jack followed the crowd. There were three squad cars parked outside the alley, one in the middle of the road, and three more racing to the scene. The ambulance pulled in right behind the police. Red's Caddy was straddling both sides of East Fourth, as if he'd skidded to a stop and just abandoned it there. Which he might have done, since he wasn't in it.

"What's happening?" Will said to a middle-aged man with a bald head.

"Someone's been shot," the man said.

Will elbowed his way through the people, losing his cap in the process. Jack may or may not have followed, Will didn't care. He stood at the entry to a blind alley, and the snow fell on his hair and ears and neck. The breeze was cold as hell against his wet skin.

Six policemen were gathered in a circle at the back of the alley. One of them, a young guy probably not much older than Will, was throwing up in a corner. "I had to do it. He would've killed somebody."

An older cop with sergeant stripes and an unlit cigar patted the young officer's shoulder. "I know, kid, you done the right thing. Ain't no other way with scum like this."

Two medics rushed past Will. As the policemen parted to let them through, Will caught his first glimpse of the body.

Oh, no.

He knew who it had to be, but it was still a shock. Red Fisher, in his fancy three-piece suit, lay face up on the pavement, blood oozing from multiple holes in his chest. His eyes were wide open. There was a gun in his right hand.

"Jesus Christ," Jack said, coming up behind Will, "that's Red!"

Two more cops arrived and flashed their batons at the crowd. "Anyone who's got no business here, get lost."

Will gazed numbly at Jack, then back at Red. Slush was soaking into the material of the dead man's clothes. He would have hated to die dirty like that.

One of the cops shoved Will back. "Go on, scram," he said.

"I can't find my cap," Will said.

GEORGE
Outside Dún Laoghaire, Ireland
September 1935

The young woman was playing a violin by a river that flowed out of the Dublin hills, through an oak forest, and to the sea. Her hair and gown were black. The sun was low in the west, skimming through the tops of the trees. Grass seemed to glow in the early evening light, its velvety green dappled by the shadows of leaves.

George had just come from the woman's cottage at the base of the hills. She didn't react to his approach. The melody she played was a beautiful and sad Vivaldi piece he'd heard many times but whose title he could never recall.

He stepped on a twig, and the snap made her lower the violin.

"You must be George Hammon," she said, still facing the river. The lilt in her voice was magical. George had been in Ireland since '32, but he never tired of the accent. It was lovely, and it reminded him of Mick.

"I telephoned," he said.

"I know," she said. She turned to him, squinting against the sun. Her eyes were dark as her hair. "I'm Aubrey. You spoke to Mother. She doesn't like telephones."

"You play very well," George said.

She smiled. "Doesn't put bread on the table." A cool breeze blew off the hills. Although the sky was nearly clear, the air smelled of rain.

"Keep playing," he said.

Aubrey raised the violin and began slow, plaintive strokes with her bow. Her arm barely moved, but her music was rich and deep. George watched her as she watched the river. She seemed transfixed on the sun's last ribbons of light on the current. She had tears in her eyes as she finished the melody. "The world is joined by water, George Hammon," she said. "All waters flow together."

"Why are you crying?"

The sun dropped beneath the horizon, and the shadow of the hills and forest engulfed them. "You're too late," Aubrey said. "My husband died at sea a year ago. I pray that the river will carry my music to him and bring him comfort."

George was moved that she would reach out to her love this way. But...Tommy was *dead*? Two decades of searching had been for nothing? It had taken him three years in Dublin just to come upon this lead. Mick's cross hung like an anvil around his neck. "I'm sorry. Your mother just said that you handle Tommy's business. She didn't tell me he was—"

"No," Aubrey said, "she wouldn't."

"What happened? If I may ask."

She pulled her gown tight. "I'm cold. We should go inside, have some tea."

"I don't want to impose—"

"You've come a long way, George Hammon. You've known pain, too. It's in your face. You're welcome here. Walk with me."

She took his arm and they turned onto the path that led to her cottage. The sky was completely dark now, clouds overtaking the stars. Lights in the cottage windows beckoned with a promise of warmth but, perhaps, not cheer.

Aubrey's mother greeted them at the door. Unlike her daughter, she had the typical red hair of the Irish, and not a streak of gray. But her face was wrinkled beyond her years, and her eyes were so obscured with blue cataracts that George didn't know how she could see at all. "*Dia dhuit*," she said. "*Conas atá tú?*"

George had never heard such a language before. The old woman had spoken English on the telephone.

"Her name is Siobhan Shannon," Aubrey said, pronouncing the first name *shuh-VAHN*. She led George to a sofa with a well-used wooden coffee table in front of it. The circular white imprints of countless cups pocked its surface. "You don't speak Gaelic."

"'Fraid not," George said.

"She said, 'Hello, how are you.'"

"Fine, thanks," George said. He didn't know if it was proper to offer to shake her hand, so he just sat down. "Nice to meet you. You have a beautiful name."

The old woman smiled and blushed. "*Tú ta George Hammon?*"

That was easy enough to figure out. "Yes," he said.

"Speak English for our guest," Aubrey said.

"*An bhfuil tu posta?*" Mrs. Shannon said to George, ignoring her daughter. Her damaged blue eyes twinkled merrily.

"*Máthair, bi samhach,*" Aubrey said. "*Sinn mhaith liom cupan tae, le do thoil.*" She gently nudged her mother toward what must be the kitchen, judging by the luscious aromas wafting from the doorway.

"What was that all about?" he said when Aubrey returned.

"She said she's a foolish old woman on her way to make us some tea."

"Really?"

"No." Aubrey didn't elaborate.

***

"I never met Mick O'Leary," Aubrey said. "More's the pity." She held the Celtic cross in her left hand, absently stroking it with her right. A fire burned in the hearth, casting everything in orange light and shadow. "He died at the Battle of the Somme, in France."

George nodded. "I was with him."

"I was only six then. Tommy would have been eight. We didn't meet for another fifteen years. He didn't remember his father well, but he pretended he did and probably believed he did. He spoke proudly of him, whether or not he remembered."

George thought about G.W. George had been two when the Spanish American War claimed his father. Try as he might, he could conjure absolutely no authentic memories of the man. All he had were photographs and the stories his mother had told, stories of an ordinary life filtered through the mind of a loving wife and embellished into sainthood. He said nothing about this to Aubrey. Tommy might well have been doing the same with Mick.

Mrs. Shannon came in and set two cups of tea on the table, placing them down carefully, as if moving more from memory than vision. She coughed fiercely, then hobbled from the room, saying, "I'll leave you to your privacy."

George smiled at Aubrey, who smiled back. Maybe the old woman wasn't implying anything, but she had that matchmaker aura about her.

"She doesn't look well," George said.

"The earth is calling her back," Aubrey said. Her voice seemed tinged with both sorrow and joy. A log popped in the hearth. "Tell me about yourself, George Hammon."

"You don't want to know me. I hurt everyone I touch."

"You haven't hurt me."

"Give me time."

"Yet you've tried for twenty years to return this cross to a man you never met. That is a wonderful thing."

"In between being noble, I'm a real shit."

Aubrey smiled and sipped her tea. "You've had lovers, of course."

"Only one who mattered."

"And where is she?"

George folded his hands together and stared at his feet. He wasn't comfortable talking about Cora. Never had been, not with Mick, not with Suzanne, not with anyone except his old friend Lewis. Lewis would probably be dead by now, he realized, and the thought saddened him. "Let's just say I've had some bad luck."

"There is no luck. There is no chance. We're all clay of the earth, and the earth moves in its circles."

George loved listening to her brogue, even if her mysticism was nonsense. "We were talking about Tommy," he said.

She stirred the fire with a poker. "He planned to open a tailor shop in New York. Already had a place rented on the East Side. He sailed on the *Megan Marie* last year. He was to send for me and Mum when he'd saved enough back. But the ship went down off the Irish coast. You probably heard about it?"

"Boiler explosion, wasn't it?" She'd said *Megan Marie,* and he did recall that, but what he thought of was the *Titanic,* all those years ago. That was around the time he'd first met Cora. "Some of the passengers survived."

"Not Tommy. Odd thing is, his name wasn't on the manifest. It was a mistake, though, because we motored to the dock together. He *was* onboard. I've not heard from him since."

George had a sudden urge to flee, but to what or whom, he didn't know. He stood up. "I made a promise," he said, "that I would give Mick's cross to Tommy. It's been in his family for centuries. I guess you should have it now."

Aubrey handed it back to him. She had tears in her eyes. "Thank you, but this doesn't have the same meaning for me as it must have for Mick."

George was at a loss. He was at journey's end, but there was no ending. She nodded as if to say, *Go on,* and he put the cross in his shirt pocket. "Mick had a wife and four other kids. Maybe one of them—"

"Mary died of pneumonia years ten ago and the children are scattered to the winds. I don't know where they are. One's in America, I think. We weren't close. You're a good man, George Hammon, a true friend who has journeyed long. Keep the cross."

"It's not mine to keep."

"It is now."

He glanced at the cups on the table and realized that neither of them had touched their tea. Mrs. Shannon would probably think them rude.

WILL
Waterton, Iowa
September 2008

"You picked one hell of a day for your car to break down," Will said, raising the hood on Charlie's Austin Healy. Rain was pummeling the roof of the garage, leaking through in a corner where squirrels or mice had chewed their way through the shingles. After the torrential downbursts of June, July and August had been relatively normal, but, at least on this day in September, the monsoon had returned.

"I don't think it's anything serious, Grandpa," Charlie said. He had only been at law school in Iowa City for three weeks, but already he'd come home for two of the weekends. Who knew, maybe he had a girl up here, although he never talked about that kind of thing with Will. Or it could be that Iowa City was still such a mess from the floods that there was nothing much to do there. "It chugs instead of purrs," he said.

Will looked at the boy. Charlie sure was a handsome youth. Still needed a haircut, though. "Ever get those plugs re-gapped?"

"No time."

No one ever had the time. Will examined the carburetor. In 1986 he'd rebuilt the Healy from an old junker into a work of art, if he did say so himself. But a car still needed maintenance. Charlie, like most everybody else these days, didn't understand this simple fact. Even the best automobile was just a machine, and no machine ran forever. You had to love it and pamper it like a child. If you waited for it to break down, it might be too late—and you could damn betcha it'd cost more to fix then.

Unless you had a Grandpa who knew his way around an engine.

"Carburetor's all gunked up," Will said. "You have to *clean* this once in a while, Charlie. Hand me a screwdriver, will you? I'll show you how to take it out."

The wind was rising, rattling the limbs of Will's favorite black maple against the window on the garage's west side. The storm was right on top of them now, the lightning and thunder occurring almost simultaneously. Each thunderclap was followed by a burst of heavier rain. Rain always seemed to come harder after the thunder.

Charlie slid a bucket under the leak in the corner. "Well, you should probably re-shingle the garage, too," he said.

"I ever tell you I was my own Dad's boss?" Will said, smiling at Charlie's teasing, and then a sharp pain ripped through his left temple. His right arm went numb and his whole body felt wobbly. Suddenly he wasn't looking down at the engine anymore, but up at the old planks of wood stored in the rafters beneath the ceiling of the garage. Will blinked. Huh?

He could still hear the rain, the thunder, a voice, but it was indistinct, dreamlike. "Grandpa!" Hands cradled his head. Couldn't feel anything else. "Are you okay? Talk to me!" Then tap tap tap, tapping that wasn't rain, tapping. "I need an ambulance right away, my grandfather has fallen!"

Darkness alternated with light, silence with sound, but he had no other awareness of time. The voice came and went, soon joined by several voices. A sensation of rising, wet, settling, dry. Something hard covered his nose and mouth, but he breathed easily.

A pinpoint pricked the crook of his left elbow, followed by forward motion, very fast. A siren pierced his throbbing head.

Will closed his eye, and he was in the clearing of some woods near the bank of a river. It was a hot day. The river was wide, its current undulating toward the sea. Dogwood trees lined both banks. The smells of honeysuckle, magnolias, and chickweed filled the air. Insects whirred and chittered. An old man slumped in a wheelchair with a fishing pole, his line bobbing in the water. At least the man seemed old, weathered face, hair streaked with gray, bitter eyes sunken into a morass of wrinkles.

Will approached, using a well-rutted path. The ruts were exactly the same width as the chair's wheels.

The man, Will's father George, took off his straw hat and looked up. *I'll be damned,* he said, *you came anyway. I told you not to bother.*

I wanted to see you, Will said.

After all this time? Well, have a seat.

Will remained standing. *It's pretty here,* he said.

The world is joined by water, George said. He looked back at the river and said no more.

Uh, Dad, Will said awkwardly.

George tested the line but had no bites. *Dad? A little late for that, isn't it?*

There's something I need to talk to you about.

Ah, he said, *so this is business after all—*

A sudden cessation of motion pulled Will away from the conversation at the river. The siren stopped. He rose and descended in rain, moved and settled in dry. Electric lights above.

Dad, he thought.

A young female face appeared over him. "You're going to be fine, Mr. Hammon. You hang in there now, okay? Can you wiggle your fingers for me?"

Will couldn't feel his right hand. He made a fist with his left.

"You're at Salk Hospital, Mr. Hammon. A doctor will see you right away. Your grandson called your daughter. They'll be here in a few minutes."

I'm trying to help you, Will wanted to say, but his tongue was thick and the words sounded like grunts.

"Don't talk," the woman said. "I'm giving you something to make you sleep."

GEORGE
Outside Dún Leoghaire, Ireland
December 1935

George visited Aubrey frequently now. After twelve years in Paris and three in Dublin, he was sick of big cities. Work kept him busy in Dublin much of the time. But he yearned for a simpler life, and when Aubrey invited him to return after their first meeting in September, he'd eagerly accepted. Soon he was coming four or five nights a week. When he didn't have a job in the morning he stayed over, albeit in a separate room.

Aubrey's cottage in the woods below the Dublin hills was right out of a fairy tale—enchanting, beautiful, and maybe a little haunted, much like Aubrey herself.

Irish winter came not with snow, but with wind, low-hanging clouds, and rain. George and Aubrey sat on the sofa in front of her hearth, a fire dispelling the season's dreariness. He treasured these times, although Siobhan's health had taken a turn for the worse, which demanded much of Aubrey's attention. The old woman was bedridden most of the time with a terrible lung infection. She'd lost a staggering amount of weight in the three months that George had known her. Her skin flapped on her bones like tattered canvas, and her face looked like a death mask of itself. She wheezed and coughed incessantly.

"What was Mick like?" Aubrey said. Firelight was on her face and in her eyes. Her black hair was tied back. She was clad in a black housecoat. She called it her "cloak of the night."

The wind and rain had let up, allowing the lulling sounds of the river to creep in.

George smiled at the thought of Mick. "He was the most unhateful guy I've ever met, except my friend Lewis. You couldn't get mad at him."

"Tommy was like that. Oh, he was a blustery bull of a man, but underneath he was kind and caring. He drank too much, but what do you expect, he was Irish." She chuckled to herself at the memory, then playfully touched George's hand. "What's your excuse? That's why Suzanne moved out, isn't it? The wine?"

"Suzanne moved out because she couldn't stand our middle-class life. I worked hard to support her, but she never got past her liberal ideas. She was restless."

Siobhan coughed loudly in her room. George could almost hear the phlegm gumming up her chest. Aubrey poured a cup of tea and rose from the sofa. "Shame on you, George Hammon," she said. "It's easy enough to blame someone who isn't here to defend herself. What would she say if I asked *her* why she left?"

"She'd say I was a boring drunk who never writes to his mother."

"Well, I don't know about boring," Aubrey said. "But as to the rest…." She winked and took the tea into Siobhan's room. The coughing stopped but Aubrey didn't return. After almost a quarter of an hour, George got up and peered into the old woman's room.

Siobhan had a towel across her forehead. Aubrey was stroking her hair.

"*Ta me ar strae,*" the old woman said.

"*Na beagan sin, Máthair,*" Aubrey said.

Aubrey had tried to teach George a few Gaelic words, but the only one he remembered was *máthair*, mother. He didn't need to know the language, though, to recognize the love in his new friend's voice.

George felt a trembling in his chest, something he hadn't experienced in years. He admired Aubrey for her compassion, but goddamn it, he couldn't help but think of his own mother, Margaret. He had *abandoned* her, run away like a common criminal. She'd lost so much in her life—her siblings, her childhood home, her parents, her husband, her stepmother.

And then her only son had fled, leaving her to forever wonder if he was alive or dead.

"*Codladh samh,*" Aubrey said.

Sobhan smiled and closed her eyes. "*A ghrá mo chroí,*" she said.

George turned away before Aubrey could catch him in the doorway. Maybe his mother was sick, too. Maybe she was dead. However she was, he wasn't there for her.

"Jesus Christ," he said.

"That's powerful magic," Aubrey said, touching his shoulder and startling him.

"Magic?" he said.

"Calling on Jesus Christ," she said. She led him back to the sofa. The fire had dwindled in the hearth. She added another log, then sat next to him. "My mother is dying. She will be in the earth, and her body will nourish the plants, and when they sprout she will be *of* the earth. It's a glorious cycle."

The wind had come up again, wailing in the chimney. Rain thrummed on the roof. Aubrey leaned her head against George's shoulder. "Tommy was Catholic," she said. Her fingers massaged George's chest. "You've probably figured out I'm not. We married in his church. That was difficult. I allow for Jesus but Jesus doesn't allow for me."

"I'm not religious," George said.

Siobhan coughed again. Her bed creaked.

"You need to write your mother," Aubrey said. "She may go to heaven when she dies, or she may be reborn in the earth. She could be all around you, but without some kind of faith you won't see her. Now is all you have."

"It's been over twenty years," George said. "She'd be furious with me."

"And why shouldn't she? Take what you've got coming, George Hammon."

WILL
Waterton, Iowa
September 2008

Tubes jutted out of Will's nose and his arms and, judging from the discomfort there, even his pecker. Although in and out of consciousness, he was vaguely aware of people around him. There was a constant stream of nurses and doctors. Katie sat in a chair to his right.

His right hand tingled, but at least he was feeling *something*. Some machine was pinging. He turned his head. Katie was reading a magazine but looked up when she saw movement.

"Hi, Dad," she said. "How you feeling?"

"Tubular," he said, recalling a term Charlie used as a kid. Wasn't sure what it meant then, but it fit now. He plucked at his groin with his left hand. Hell, there *was* a tube in his pecker.

"Don't touch that, Dad. It's a catheter. You need it."

"It hurts."

"I know," she said, gently pulling his hand away.

Will's eye was open but his brain was foggy. He could see Katie and the white room he was in, yet there was also the image of a long-ago roadhouse superimposed on top of the scene, like a movie playing in midair. He saw plush chairs, paneled walls, thick carpeting. He smelled cigar smoke and heard women's laughter. A jazz band was playing. Old Red bought him a beer—him and, who was it, Jack?—after pretending to be angry and threatening to tell Luka. Will laughed as he replayed that night. *It only has one eye, too.*

"What's funny?" Katie said.

"Remember Jack?" he said. No, she couldn't. Jack died in a Japanese prison in '43.

Katie set her magazine on the rolling table that held Will's food. "Talk slower, Dad. Your speech is still slurred."

His tongue did feel heavy. "I had a stroke?" he said, enunciating each syllable.

"A minor one. Thank God Charlie called the ambulance in time. Doctor says you should make a full recovery. It's a wonder you didn't break anything when you fell."

"Where is Charlie?"

"Back in Iowa City for the day. He had a test." She squeezed Will's right hand, and he could feel the pressure of her fingers. "I was so scared of losing you, Dad."

Curtis's Garden faded away as her face, and his mind, came into focus. "What're you scared of? I'm ninety-four, I've had my life. No tragedy in an old man dying. I'm ready."

"I'm not," she said. "Feels like I hardly know you."

Will didn't want to have this conversation now. "How's the construction?"

Katie looked relieved. Maybe she didn't want this conversation, either. "You know how shitty the weather's been. And now with the economy in the tank…We've had delay after delay."

A nurse entered and poked a thermometer into Will's ear. "Visiting hours are over," she said, writing on her clipboard. She checked numbers on the pinging machine that monitored his heart rate and blood oxygen level. "Looking good tonight, Mr. Hammon."

"Maybe next month will be better," Will said to Katie, but he was fogging up again. His daughter's face receded behind another see-through vision. A crowd gathered in a back alley in Waterton. He pushed through them. The snow came down, and police lights flashed, and a man lay on the pavement with blood on his chest. *Where's my cap?* Will thought. Here was a dead man in front of him, and he was worried about his damn cap.

"If not, we could be held up 'til next spring," Katie said.

"I might not be around then," he said. He raised his left hand to his head. "I can't find my cap," he said.

GEORGE
Dún Laoghaire, Ireland
January 1936

The closest Aubrey ever got to George's flat in Amiens Street was a movie house in Dún Laoghaire. "I know all about Monto," she said as George parked the Daimler outside the theatre.

"They cleaned it up in '25," George said.

She smiled slyly. Her mischievous eyes indicated that she suspected George of partaking in some of the fleshly pleasures there, her smile that she did not judge him for it.

George loved her for that. He *had* partaken on occasion.

The movie was *Mutiny on the Bounty*. Released in the States the year before, it was just coming to Ireland. There was a large crowd, and George and Aubrey had to sit at the front.

At one point when Clark Gable was shouting at Charles Laughton, Aubrey said, "He doesn't sound English. If he's playing a Brit, the least he could do is sound like one."

George shrugged. He'd never heard of Clark Gable, but there were times he felt like the actor in this film: out of place. His own accent was probably more French than American now. "Last time I saw one of these, they were silent, Fatty Arbuckle was a big star, and we were still calling them 'flickers.'"

"Shhh!" someone behind them said.

"With Cora?" Aubrey whispered. The projector clacked in a booth at the back.

George patted her hand. "Shhh," he said.

Gable set Laughton adrift in a small boat before sailing the *Bounty* to a little island called Pitcairn. Laughton made it safely to port, there was a naval trial in England, and the movie ended.

In the car on the way home, Aubrey said, "The girls were dressed all wrong."

Winter in Ireland was rainy and miserable, pretty much like summer in Ireland, only colder.

"What girls?" George said.

"The Tahitian girls. They would not have been wearing anything on top."

"Well, they could hardly show *that*, could they?"

"As if breasts are obscene," Aubrey said. "I did not like that movie, George. It was violent and vulgar."

"I'm still amazed by the idea of sound in moving pictures." The movie was okay, but he'd been more interested in the newsreel that played before the feature. A bombastic little man was stirring up trouble in Germany. George had no love for Germans, not since the Great War. The Treaty of Versailles had crippled their military, and yet this man babbled as if they were a world power. The number of people enthralled by him at his rallies was impressive. "What do you think about that Hitler fellow?" he said.

"He looks like Charlie Chaplin," Aubrey said.

George had heard of Chaplin, and had even seen photographs of him in Suzanne's French magazines. There was a resemblance.

After that they rode in silence. She was unsettled, and so was George. Maybe she was anxious about being away from her mother for a few hours, even though they'd arranged for a friend to look after Siobhan for the evening.

For George watching the film brought back memories of Cora. Here he was, two months short of forty years old, in the company of a beautiful woman, and what was he dwelling on? A girl more than two decades dead. It was pathetic, but damn it, he'd never stopped missing her, *never*, despite war and illness, despite time and distance, despite all the whores and all the wine, despite Suzanne and despite Aubrey. Cora. Cora Curtis Hammon, his wife, his love, his life. They were married for what, all of five months?

He hadn't bought her a ring. He hadn't even been in the hospital room as she and their son died in blood and infection. He'd only had that one glimpse of her, that one brief glimpse. Naked, bloody, her face turned toward his, Cora had looked so very very incredibly *dead*.

And, of course, she was.

Aubrey honored Tommy with her music. It was a beautiful gesture. After twenty-two years, how could George honor his wife and child in any way that could possibly matter?

The only sounds were the Daimler's engine, the rain on the roof, the tires spinning. Where paved, the roads were slick and black, where unpaved rough and muddy. Outside the city there were no streetlamps. Streaks of rain knifed across the headlights. After four years in Ireland, George still hadn't gotten accustomed to driving on the left side.

The forest thickened and the rolling terrain tilted upward as they approached the Dublin hills. Soon he heard the rush of the river. "You've given up on Tommy, then?" he said, not sure why he asked.

"There's still a grief," she said, her head turned away, seemingly focused on the countryside outside, though the night was black and there was little to see but the outline of trees. "I don't care what the manifest says. Tommy was on the *Megan Marie*. The only reason he wouldn't contact me is if he couldn't. He went down with that ship, George."

George turned into the lane that led to her cottage. The dim red glow of a dying fire flickered in the windows.

"Stay the night?" she said. "We're both sad."

"I shouldn't," he said, although he had no jobs lined up in the morning.

"Why not?"

"Because we're both sad."

"I forgive you for the movie," she said, trying to sound cheerful. When he didn't respond, she said, "There is a grace about you, George Hammon. You loved your Cora, and there is no greater power in all the world. Come in and be with me, and teach me to love her, too."

***

Siobhan's friend Máire had sat with her in Aubrey's absence. "*Tá sí maith tinneus,*" the woman said on her way out the door. She refused a ride home, as she just lived up the hill.

Aubrey squeezed her hand. "*Go raibh maith agat, Máire. Slán agus beannacht leat.*"

"What was that all about?" George said after Máire had gone.

"She said my mother is very ill. I thanked her for her kindness and wished her peace."

"It's freezing in here. That can't be good for her."

"She likes the cold," Aubrey said, but she put three more logs on the fire. Then she took George's arm and pulled him into Siobhan's bedroom. They both had rain in their hair and on their coats. George stood behind Aubrey as she leaned over her mother and felt her forehead. Siobhan was wheezing, her breath scraping in her chest. "*Ta ainm eadie fliuch,*" she said, her voice barely audible.

Aubrey smiled. "We were out in the rain," she explained.

"*Cad rinn imigh tú?*" Siobhan said.

"We went to Dún Laoghaire. I'm sorry I left you."

"*Ta me tuirseach.*"

"I'm tired, too. Speak English, Mother, George is right here."

Siobhan looked confused, as if she couldn't see him. The wrinkles on her face seemed to expand before his eyes, writhing and gouging into skin almost translucent with age. Even her hair had lost its luster, spreading out around her head like a red halo gone black in the dim light. She lifted her hand weakly and gestured for George to step forward. He did, kneeling next to her. "Here I am," he said.

"Are you good for my daughter?" she said.

George glanced helplessly at Aubrey, who only nodded. "We're friends," he said.

"Well, then," Siobhan said, as if that confirmed her deepest suspicions. Slowly her eyes drifted back toward Aubrey. "*Anam cara*?" she said hopefully.

Aubrey wept. "I don't know," she said.

"*Bainfidh mé codlagh fóill.*"

"Okay," Aubrey said, her voice tight with emotion. She tucked in her mother's blankets and kissed her on the cheek.

Siobhan stared long at George before smiling and closing her eyes. Her weathered old face appeared almost beatific. She was not afraid of her illness. George experienced a moment of clarity as he gazed at her serenity, a moment, for lack of a better word, of holiness. He'd seen too much death—Clara, Cora, Mick, and all the young men on the battlefields of Europe—yet until now he'd never sensed the presence of anything beyond. Maybe his empathy for Aubrey's impending grief was playing on his imagination, but he felt as if he had tapped into some powerful *otherness*. The revelation passed quickly, though, and he was jarred back into one woman's mundane struggle in an ordinary Irish bedroom. Suddenly uneasy, either by the touch of the divine or by its withdrawal, he squeezed Siobhan's hand. "Sleep well," he said.

Aubrey helped him to his feet. "You sensed it, didn't you?"

He didn't answer. They went to the front room. Rain pelted the window, but the logs popping in the fire dispelled the chill. They sat on the sofa, as they did most nights. Aubrey leaned her head into his shoulder and continued to sob softly. He brushed her tears away with his thumb. "What did she ask you?"

Aubrey drew in a deep breath to calm herself. "She asked if you were my 'soul friend.'"

The notion struck George as quaint. "Is she trying to marry us off?"

"*Anam cara* is deeper than marriage, George Hammon. Do not make light of it, do not speak its name without reverence. It is a mystical union of two human souls, merging with each other and with the ethereal world. Cora was yours. I'm still waiting for mine."

"What about Tommy?"

"I loved Tommy," she said, and after a long pause, "but he was not the one."

George put his arm around her. "Why did you marry him?"

"We are none of us guaranteed such a person in our life. Tommy O'Leary was a fine man, a kind man, and worthy of love. He was not my soul friend, but he was my husband. And he brought you to me."

Most days George wasn't sure he *had* a soul. The look of expectation in Siobhan's eyes, and now in Aubrey's, frightened him. He couldn't handle another Suzanne, and there would never be another Cora. "Christ," he said. "I need a drink."

Aubrey's body stiffened. She pushed his arm away and stood up. "Have one, then," she said angrily. Her black hair accentuated the redness of her lips. "You know where it's kept. I'm going to bed."

She strode into Siobhan's room, not looking back. Of late she'd been sleeping on blankets on the floor, next to her mother's bed.

George hadn't meant to hurt her feelings. She'd just taken him by surprise, that's all. He went to the liquor cabinet, found his favorite French wine, and drank straight from the bottle.

He returned to the sofa, put his feet up. Somehow this whole night with Aubrey had gone wrong, but now he was alone and the wine was good. Wine was always good for whatever ailed him. Wine made him forget.

The fire in the hearth had burnt itself out, rain was still buffeting the cottage, and he was stinking drunk when Aubrey came out sometime in the night to announce that Siobhan had died.

George couldn't even stand up to receive the news. He tried but fell off the sofa.

Crumpled on the floor, he blubbered something that might have been condolences. If he had truly experienced the divine earlier tonight, it was far away now.

"George Hammon," Aubrey sighed, and there were no tears, only resignation, "you must help me prepare her body. I will telephone the priestess."

***

The service was a simple Celtic mass performed around a bonfire at the edge of the forest behind Aubrey's house. Eight figures clothed in black held candles while a woman chanted a pagan lament, and then a pagan celebration. Siobhan's body lay on a raised pyre, draped in a beautiful white robe. A store-bought leafy wreath encircled her head. Her red hair was radiant in the firelight.

Although George had been invited to participate, he chose instead to watch from the back porch of the cottage. The night was cold but clear. There was no moon, only brilliant stars blazing through and around the narrow belt of the Milky Way. Orion perched above the Dublin Hills. The recent rain had frozen on the limbs of trees, encasing them in a gleaming, transparent beauty.

Only a few dozen yards separated George from the ceremony, yet it seemed like a vast dark gulf—a gulf of oceans and time rather than dirt and grass. Siobhan had died, but it was Margaret who occupied his mind. If she was dead, who had mourned at her funeral? Who placed flowers on her grave? Who remembered her on lonely winter nights?

Aubrey and her revelers were laughing, sharing the joy of Siobhan's life. Soon the priestess would touch a torch to the pyre, and Siobhan's ashes would rise into the sky, float on currents of wind, and finally settle back to earth where, so Aubrey believed, she would be reborn in the plants and creatures of the world.

It was a lovely idea.

George couldn't watch any more. What if Margaret were alive? He stood up and went inside to the kitchen. He switched on a small lamp on the table. Aubrey kept a pencil and notepad next to the telephone. She had scribbled an obituary for the local newspapers. He read her loving tribute, and then he knew.

"Goddamn it, Hammon, it's time," he said. Yes, Margaret and Luka had concocted the scheme that had driven Cora and George to New York, that had chased George all the way to the battlefields of Europe, but that was a long time ago. After more than twenty years, Margaret may not yet, or ever, deserve forgiveness, but she did deserve to know what had become of her son.

Sitting down, he removed the top sheet from the pad and began to write his own note.

MARGARET
Hammon Falls, Iowa
February 1936

Snow drifted against the marble monument marking the grave that held the remains of G.W. Hammon. Next to that a much smaller granite marker adorned the final resting place of nobody whomsoever. Carved on its surface, though now obscured by snow, were the words GEORGE P HAMMON, BELOVED SON, WHO LOST HIS LIFE IN THE GREAT WAR, MARCH 23 1896-JULY 1 1916. The letters had been cut in block script, with no flourishes or embellishment.

Margaret used to visit the graves every couple of months, bringing flowers on Sunday afternoons after church. Since she refused to learn to drive, Birgitta would chauffer her. As the '20's passed into the '30's she stopped by less and less frequently, and she hadn't come at all since Birgitta's aneurism four Christmases ago.

A taxi waited at the gate of the cemetery, its motor running. Exhaust rose over the fence and dissipated into a brilliant blue sky. Sunshine blazed through the tops of the black maples interspersed among the graves, but a strong north wind made the morning bitterly cold. Snow devils rose up and broke against the tombstones. These little whirlwinds were harmless, but any swirl of wind brought back memories of Pomeroy.

Dressed in her warmest winter attire, Margaret sat in the folding chair she'd brought along for the purpose. She huddled in front of George's non-grave, her shadow stretched out ahead and to her left. Even on level ground the snow was as deep as her ankles. Maples on either side of the Hammon markers shook in the breeze. Ice that coated the branches broke off and rained down like pellets of sleet, despite the clear sky.

Margaret leaned forward and with her right hand brushed away the snow covering George's marker. BELOVED SON appeared in the bare space. She clutched an envelope in her left hand. It was addressed to Margaret Hammon at her home on Gloire de Matin Island — Margaret *Hammon*, not Curtis. The postmark read Dublin, Ireland, dated January 11, 1936.

Back in the 'aughts and 'teens, if the cemetery was deserted when she came to G.W.'s grave, she used to talk to the monument, imagining her late husband's spirit to be present, listening with silent sympathy to her laments of loneliness. Nothing wrong with that, surely many bereaved spouses did it. It was a way to keep hold of the dead. Rumors of this eccentric behavior reached Waterton's upper crust, though, and she became the target of gossip and laughter. Spiritualism was rampant in those days, but her social peers thought it a crass and ridiculous diversion to amuse the lower classes and swindle the desperate. Speaking to the dead simply wasn't done. Margaret hadn't said a word to G.W. since.

But today she wasn't facing G.W.'s grave, she was facing George's. There were no moldy and splintered remains interred here, no spectre to hear her words.

At first she thought the letter was a cruel hoax, the product of a diseased mind, but the more she reread it, she more she realized the details could only have come from George. When she compared the handwriting to some of the schoolboy scribbles she'd saved, it was a perfect match, right down to the large loop at the top of his G. There was no doubt. George was alive. Her son was alive.

He'd been gone for twenty-two years. *Twenty-two years.* For twenty of them he'd let her think he had fallen on the battlefields of France. Maybe he didn't know about the letter from the British government declaring him missing and presumed dead. Even so, he'd made no attempt to contact her, none. Not one peep.

Until now.

Margaret hadn't told anybody, least of all Orville.

A gust of wind came up from the north, spraying snow mist against her face and skewing her hat.

The skeletal maples creaked and bent, their limbs reaching down toward her like vampiric fingers. She rose from her chair, took off her gloves, and carefully removed the letter from the envelope. The entire marker was visible now. GEORGE P HAMMON, BELOVED SON, WHO LOST HIS LIFE IN THE GREAT WAR, MARCH 23 1896-JULY 1 1916.

Good God, the things she had *done* for him, and for William, the son he had abandoned!

With a fury two decades in the making, Margaret shredded the letter with her bare hands and heaved the pieces to the wind. "You son-of-a-*bitch*!" she cried, stomping on the marker as if leather could shatter granite.

When she had screamed herself hoarse, when her anger had cooled, she calmly folded her chair and returned to the waiting taxi.

Margaret smiled apologetically at the driver as she opened the back door of the cab and got in, setting the chair next to her. Her toes were frozen, and she might have taken a chill in her chest. She couldn't wait to get to Gloire de Matin. "Please hurry," she said to the cabbie, her voice scratchy and raw. Now that the screaming was over and she was herself again, there was much to do in the next few months—decorators to call, new furniture to buy, housecleaners to hire, the list was endless.

George was alive.
And he was coming home.

GEORGE AND CORA

CORA
Waterton, Iowa
July 1913

Cora leaned over the edge of her bed and puked into a bucket while Birgitta patted her shoulder and tut-tutted. "You have been ill too long," the housemaid said. "Your father is very worried. I am worried, too."

"I'll be okay," Cora said when she'd finished retching. "It's just the flu."

"Yes, perhaps." Birgitta hoisted the bucket and headed for the bathroom. If she was disgusted by the bucket's contents she didn't show it. Cora watched the woman's stout form as she left the bedroom, walking as she always did with a sense of deliberate urgency, her patterned full-length dress dragging on the floor behind her.

Cora lay back on the bed, her guts gurgling inside her. The room was sweltering. Even closed curtains couldn't keep out the heat of the July sun. Worse, the air was rancid with the stink of her own sickness. The muscles in her sides ached from vomiting. Sweat made her nightgown cling in the most uncomfortable places. Her pillow was wet, and her hair felt as if it had been drenched in oil. What a fright she was.

Birgitta returned and set the bucket on the floor next to the headboard. She wasn't concerned about the room's foul smell or Cora's appearance. She just wanted her young mistress to get well. "I will make you my special soup," she said, "to calm your stomach."

"I'm not hungry."

"Hunger has nothing to do with it. You must eat."

Cora turned to stare at her yellow wallpaper, letting her eyes go out of focus as the paper's black patterns transformed themselves into the tiny faces of women. Today the women were frowning. Some days they laughed. "Birgitta," she said, but nothing more.

The maid felt Cora's forehead, then sat on the edge of the bed next to her and held her hand. "Child," she said, drawing a deep slow breath, "how long has it been since you have had your courses?"

Cora had missed two months, but how would Birgitta even know to ask? "Maybe May. Why?"

Birgitta's mouth got small the way it did when she was sad or angry. "Your father will be disappointed," she said.

"I don't understand."

"I will explain."

And she did.

There was no point in denying it, not to Birgitta. "You can't tell Daddy!" Cora sobbed, and as the panic built her cries grew into screams.

"Foolish, beautiful girl," Birgitta said, kissing Cora's brow, her lips just brushing the skin.

GEORGE
Waterton, Iowa
August 1913

Lover's Island, the timbered speck of land in the Oak River, was always crowded with teenagers this time of year. Mostly kids swam, held hands, or threw rocks at frogs just to watch them jump. The braver ones might kiss, but there simply wasn't the room or privacy necessary for the kind of canoodling George and Cora had grown accustomed to.

For that they had to go elsewhere. Luka's stable was nice if they could get away at night, but it was suffocating on summer days when the sun beat down on the roof and the air inside was hot and still and thick with hay dust. Luckily, George's friend Jack lived on an acreage in a greenbelt area west of Waterton. Red Hawk Creek flowed through the northern half of the property, shaded on both sides by elm, silver maple, and a few cottonwood. At one point the creek looped to pinch off a small U-shaped peninsula from the rest of the greenbelt, creating a secluded cove where the banks had calved off right up to the tree line. There was no beach save for a few yards of sandbar on the inner curve of the loop. To get there from Jack's house required a fifteen-minute walk through the woods, but it was worth the trek since nobody but George, Cora, and Jack's family knew about the spot.

From Cora's home on Middlesex to the acreage was a good eight miles, no small distance for teenagers who didn't drive motors cars. George had concocted a number of strategies for wheedling a horse and wagon from his mother's stable. She was probably wise to all of them, but this morning she had simply sighed at his story and waved her hand as if to say, *I know you're lying but I'm too tired to argue.* Margaret was too tired to do much of anything.

After a pleasant ride through the rolling terrain outside of town, George and Cora left the rig at Jack's house and hiked to their private sandbar. Cora had been complaining of nausea for weeks, but seemed better today. It was early afternoon when they arrived. Insects whirred and buzzed, a breeze shushed through the tree tops. The sky was unmarred even by the usual puffy white clouds of summer. The air smelled of greenery, fresh soil, and water. A few dandelions had found purchase in the side of the bank, adding splotches of yellow and white to the greens and browns and blacks. A toppled cottonwood arced into the creek from a rise on the shore. The section of log just above the water line was a favorite perch for painted turtles to enjoy the sun. They splashed into the creek as George and Cora disrobed.

Cora wanted to swim before getting to the "main event," and that was fine with George. He loved watching her glide under the water graceful as a mermaid. When she surfaced, sunbeams rippled around her head, and when she emerged from the water, she rose like a goddess from the sea, droplets beading on her breasts, glistening in the hairs of her pubic mound.

You're a romantic idiot, he thought. *Well, so what?* He hopped up onto the cottonwood and looked her over. He'd often seen her naked in the past several months, but every time seemed like the first. His physical reaction was immediate and obvious.

Cora smiled slyly. "Think the little fella can hold out for a few more minutes?"

"What do you mean, little?"

She leaned against the fallen tree. Suddenly her expression was sad. She took his hand in hers and guided his fingers over her flat stomach. "Feel anything different?" she said.

"Different from what?"

"Before."

"What's the matter?"

She pulled him off the log and motioned him onto his knees, then cradled his head against her abdomen. "Listen," she said. "What do you hear?"

"Gurgling."

Cora caressed his cheek and turned away. She sat down on the sandbar and drew her knees to her chin. In the creek a small fish snatched a bug that had dipped too close to the surface, causing a little bloop of sound. "I just wanted to know," she said.

George joined her, draping an arm over her shoulder. He extended his feet into the water. It seemed unusually cool, despite the hot day. "Tell me what's wrong."

"There's something inside me."

On another occasion he might have thought she was being naughty. He might have said, *No, but there's about to be.* But she wasn't being naughty, not this time. "Are you sick?" he said.

Cora started to cry.

"Oh, Jesus," George said, "you *are* sick. Why didn't you say something?"

After a while she sniffled and wiped her nose with the back of her hand. "I'm not sick," she said quietly. "I'm going to have a baby."

George pushed away from her, feeling as if the oxygen had been stomped from his lungs. He was seventeen, he didn't know what to do or what to say or how to say it, and so he said the first thing that came into his mind, the worst possible thing. "Is it mine?"

He knew the answer. She'd taken him by surprise, that's all. He was just scared. Cora lowered her head and wept into her hands. When he touched her shoulder, intending somehow to take back his thoughtless words, she whirled on him and slapped him hard across the face. But there was already forgiveness in her eyes, and he realized she was scared, too.

"I love you so much," she said.

CORA
Waterton, Iowa
September 1913

Cora watched from her bedroom window as George helped Luka cut the grass around the stable. Both were pushing hand mowers, which she knew from experience were cumbersome, but their rotating blades made the job quicker than scythes. She wondered what they talked about when they took breaks to sip Birgitta's lemonade. Sometimes they laughed, sometimes they looked thoughtful, and once her father even clapped George on the back. Maybe he'd just told a dirty joke. She'd never been around men when they could speak freely to each other and so had no idea what they might say.

She knew what they were *not* talking about.

It was early evening. The sun was still up, but a fast-moving line of thunderstorms in the west was about to overrun it. Lightning backlit the clouds, although there was no thunder yet.

Cora lay back on her bed and gazed at the plastered ceiling, painted yellow to match her wallpaper. Birgitta estimated that she was three months along, meaning the baby would be born in March. George was born in March. Wouldn't it be funny if they had the same birthday?

She wasn't showing yet but soon would be. Her father didn't know, George's mother didn't know. Nobody knew but her and George and Birgitta. Not even her best friends Millie, Lizzie, and Jean knew. She wouldn't be able to hide her condition much longer. She dreaded Luka's reaction when he found out, but she dreaded Margaret's more. Margaret Hammon was a complete mystery to her, and therefore more terrifying. George said she was probably a mystery to herself, too, whatever that meant. She was just not a happy person, and Cora's news would not improve her disposition, not one bit.

Cora heard the front door open. The men were done mowing. It was a school night, so George wouldn't be able to stay much longer. She got out of bed and hurried down to say goodbye. Birgitta was admonishing George and Luka to take their shoes off, as she wouldn't tolerate grass clippings all over her clean floor.

Her father never ceased to be amused by the maid's insolence, but he did as instructed. Cora reached the bottom of the stairs, all aflutter as she always was when George came in the house. Luka looked at her, looked at George, and smiled. He nodded toward the pantry, giving her permission to sit and talk with George for a few minutes. "You kept supper warm?" he said to Birgitta, and the two of them disappeared into the kitchen.

George was sweating. He smelled of hard work, which was not unpleasant, but he would stink when the sweat dried. Some grass clippings that had escaped Birgitta's notice spilled from the cuff of his rolled-up trouser legs and onto his bare feet. He wiggled his toes, and the grass fell on the rug. "Oops," he said with a grin.

"I'll sweep after you leave," she said. She heard thunder.

They sat next to each other on the sofa. Cora felt strangely awkward and sensed that George did, too.

"Were you sick again this morning?" he said.

"Not as bad as some days."

She wished he would put his arm around her. Instead, he folded his hands together and twiddled his thumbs, watching the movement as if it were the most fascinating thing in the world. "I didn't know your Dad had a brother."

"Carlin? He died in a fire when I was little. I don't remember him much. He had a cleft in his chin, that's about all. And blonde hair." Rain plinked against the roof, slowly at first, with gaps between the drops. "And he used to give me gumballs when he came to visit."

"Luka said they played stickball in Chicago. That's like baseball. What happened?"

"No one knows for sure. They think his dog Hannah knocked over a kerosene lamp in the night. Hannah jumped out a window and ran to a neighbor's, but Carlin never woke up. Daddy says the smoke got him before the fire did. At least he hopes so."

"I'll bet Luka shot that dog. I would've."

Cora shook her head. "We kept her 'til Momma got sick, then Daddy gave her to a farm family. He cried when he did that. I never saw him cry like that, even after Momma died."

She recalled a time Hannah, a fat and mottled blue heeler mix, had come bouncing into the house with a bewildered chipmunk in her mouth. She hadn't hurt the little creature, just wanted to play. This was maybe '01, '02. Her mother was terrified of mice or anything that looked like mice, even if they had cheek pouches and stripes. The chipmunk had gotten loose, of course, all slimy with Hannah's spit. What a time Luka had trying to chase it down! Hannah barking, Momma screaming, Cora clapping and giggling each time it changed direction and skittered under a chair or a table or into Hannah's food bowl. This was before Birgitta had come to work for them. In the end it had simply dashed out the front door when Luka went to get the butterfly net from the stable. Cora didn't think about Uncle Carlin often, but when she did it was almost always in the context of Hannah.

The rain was falling harder now, tapping a steady rhythm. Larger drops that collected on the eave dripped onto the awning, creating a louder, irregular beat. Behind the rain was the wind in the trees, and behind that, the thunder. Cora found the layers of sound soothing.

Behind the rain was the wind in the trees, and behind that the thunder. It was kind of soothing.

"My mother will be going crazy," George said. He'd stopped twiddling his thumbs, but his hands were still clasped. He looked like he was praying. "She hates storms, even little ones like this. She lost her house in a cyclone back in the '90s."

"When are we going to tell her?" Cora whispered. "When are we going to tell Daddy?"

George stood up and slid his hands into his pockets. "I'd better go," he said.

"When?" she said.

"I don't know," he said.

"If we wait much longer we won't have to tell."

"I know." He stooped to kiss her. "I probably stink," he said, then walked out to the entryway, put his shoes on, and left. She heard the front door close and the stable door open. It would be a long ride home for him in the rain.

Meantime, she needed to sweep those grass clippings or face Birgitta's wrath.

***

Her father was astonishingly restrained. Maybe Birgitta had tipped him off in advance, but when he spoke to Cora it was in low, reasonable tones rather than the tirade she expected. She sat on the edge of her bed while Luka loomed over her. Despite his demeanor, she could tell he was simply *vibrating* with anger. His forehead was dotted with sweat, his cheeks were flushed, and the little cords on his neck stood out. His hands shook so much he had to hide them behind him. He was more terrifying this way than if he'd been shouting at her. She was prepared for shouting. She wasn't prepared for this.

"I know a doctor," Luka said.

"No," Cora said. When her friend Lizzie had talked about her experience with boys, she'd mentioned these back-street "doctors" who could fix problems that came up for unwed girls. Lizzie had never needed to visit one herself, of course, but she'd heard stories of wires and blood and lots of pain. *Even after they etherize you,* Lizzie claimed, *you can hear the baby screaming.* Cora didn't believe that, but she wasn't about to have George's child cut out of her body, no matter how they did it.

"Did you just tell me no?" Luka said, his little mustache trembling.

"Daddy, I'm not going to one of those people. I'll drop out of school, I'll go away. I'll do anything. But I want my baby."

"I invited him into my home," Luka said. "I broke bread with him. And he *raped* my little girl." He turned his back and slammed his palm against the wall as he said 'raped.' He was crying and trying not to show it.

"That's not true," Cora said in as quiet voice as she could muster. This had to be difficult for him, accepting that she wasn't innocent anymore, that she had willingly given her virginity away. Yes, Luka had his whores, and they were all somebody's daughter, too, but this was different. Cora was *his* daughter. "Daddy, I love him."

Luka whirled toward her, a look of fury on his face. In her entire life he had never lifted a hand to her, not once, but his fists were clenched, and she was sure he was going to beat her. Instead, he blew out a deep breath, ran his fingers through his hair, and visibly calmed himself. When the worst of his anger had passed what remained could only be called disgust. "Don't talk to me about love," he said, his pitch rising on the last word as if the sentence weren't finished.

Cora finished it for him in her mind. *You little tramp.* She flopped back on the bed and rolled away from him, staring at the wallpaper.

"Look at me," he said.

"I can't."

"Look at me."

She peered over her shoulder. She wished she could throw up or something, anything to end this conversation. If she got sick Birgitta would come in and chase Luka away, as she always did. "You wanted him to court me," she said.

"I didn't want *this*."

"Well, this is what you got, isn't it?"

"Watch your mouth, young lady. I could force you to see a doctor."

Big as her father was, brutal as he was in the boxing ring, he was a weak man, she decided. A bully. She buried her head under a pillow. "Then kill me, too."

She heard him sigh. He sat down next to her and pulled the pillow away, then squeezed her shoulder. "Cora, I know you think I'm only worried about my reputation. But what about yours? Waterton isn't a big town like Chicago. People talk. They'll say cruel things, they'll go out of their way to make your life hell. Is that what you want?"

"I want my baby," she said, "and George. That's all. I don't care about anything else."

"I'm not going to send you away. You won't get an abortion. What's left?"

Cora rolled over and gazed up at him. She saw something in his eyes she'd never seen there before: fear. "I'll be seventeen next month," she said. "We could get married."

"Shit," her father said.

GEORGE
Waterton and Hammon Falls, Iowa
September 1913

"They know what causes that now," Lewis said, working Bucktooth over with a hard-bristled brush. It was ten o'clock on a Saturday night, and he was finishing up before closing Kline's for the evening. "Ain't science grand?"

"Wonderful," George said. He'd walked all the way to the stable to ask his friend's advice about Cora. The manure was more pungent than he recalled, but the straw and hay smelled sweet as ever. The stable was dark, even with kerosene lamps burning and the bright rays of a full moon streaming in through the windows. Bucktooth's oiled pelt gleamed in the lamp light.

"You and your gal been playing peek-a-boo with the little fella," Lewis said. "Being a man of the Lord, I ought to tell you what the Good Book say 'bout fornication. But I got a boy your age. Hell, I remember *being* a boy your age. I know how it be." He stopped brushing Bucktooth and rested his elbow on the horse's rump. Bucktooth flicked his tail as if a fly had landed there. "See, my blood's cooled a spell, so I don't feel them needs like I used to. But a young man, he get hisself in a state, and he don't know what to do 'bout it, 'cept what he *want* to do."

Bucktooth whinnied to remind Lewis of the task at hand.

"What about now?" George said. "What do I do now?"

"Now?" Lewis pulled the brush through Bucktooth's mane, scattering flecks of leaves and straw. "Now you got to do what right, son. You gonna use your pecker like a growed-up man, you got to act like a growed-up man."

"How does a grown man act?"

"He do the right thing."

"That doesn't exactly narrow things down for me, Lewis. The right thing for who? Me and Cora? Mother? Luka? The child? What *is* the right thing?"

Lewis smiled his big yellow smile. "Well, that what you got to figure out, ain't it?"

***

Arlen Kelper sat across the dining room table from George while Margaret spoke in hushed tones to Luka on the telephone. Arlen was a young man not far removed from law school. He'd inherited his position as the Hammon family lawyer from his late father, who had worked for

G.W., and then Margaret, for more than three decades. Although Arlen was not yet thirty, most people referred to him as "old man Kelper" or, behind his back as Luka did, "old Seaweed." Apparently when his father died Arlen not only assumed his clients and his accounts but his advanced years as well. He didn't seem to mind, since being thought of as old conveyed a status and respectability that most people had to actually age to achieve. Still, some wrinkles and a few well-placed gray hairs would add legitimacy to his face.

Estella had made oatmeal cookies, which Ed brought out on china plates and set in front of them. He approached Margaret, but she waved him away, and he retreated into the kitchen.

"What's going to happen?" George said. It was a Sunday afternoon, the day after he'd spoken with Lewis. The sun was shining, the autumn leaves were turning, and he'd rather be anywhere than here, doing anything but this.

"The best thing is to deny paternity," Kelper said. "There's no way to prove it, and if we can produce another boy she's had relations with—"

"*She hasn't been with anyone else!*" George said, his voice sounding shrill even to himself. "*I'm* the father."

"I hope you're never foolish enough to say that in public. As your lawyer, I advise—"

"I don't care what you advise! You're Mother's lawyer, not mine."

Kelper straightened his spectacles and cleared his throat, just like his old man did when he was making a point. George had seen that pose many times. It made the father seem grave and wise. The son only looked silly, a cheap imitation. "George," Kelper said. "If we don't deny paternity and Curtis sues, he'll win."

"I'll pay him. I could go back to work for Kline."

"What did you earn, a nickel an hour? A dime?"

"I don't care," George said. "I love her."

"If I may be so bold, George, you're thinking with the wrong head. You're a minor. Curtis can't sue you, so who do you suppose is going to have to pay child support?" Kelper nodded toward Margaret, who was gesturing wildly to the telephone as if Luka could see her.

"She can afford it. Anyway, Luka's got plenty of money, why would he sue?"

"Because he can." Margaret raised her voice on the phone, saying *No!*, then realized she could be heard and went back to a whisper. Kelper looked at George. "Why should she have to pay for your irresponsibility? And think of her reputation. Hasn't she been through enough?"

George folded his arms on the table and put his head down. "I don't want to cause anybody trouble," he said.

"Goodbye!" Margaret spat into the receiver, throwing it against the wall.

"And yet here we are," Kelper said to George.

Margaret marched over to the table, grabbed George's collar, and jerked his head up. She glared into his eyes with an icy fury he'd never seen before, except maybe when Clara had died. "You are *not* marrying that little Curtis whore," she said.

CORA
Waterton, Iowa
September 1913

In the spring of 1902 Cora's parents re-papered her bedroom. She remembered it clearly, even though she wasn't yet six years old then. A terrible storm raged outside while their dog Hannah ran around in circles barking at her tail because thunder frightened her.

After dragging Cora's furniture into the hallway, Luka and Momma scraped off the old wallpaper. It had an awful pink pattern that had faded over the years to a pastel that defied description. Obviously some previous owner had installed it back in the '70's for a less discriminating little girl. Cora didn't like yellow much better than pink, but at least it was clean and cheerful.

Luka sanded the rough edges of the plaster while Momma mixed paste in a bowl. The work had gone fine until then. The difficulties began when they unrolled the long strips of the new paper and spread them out on the floor. First they slopped paste all over themselves when they tried to brush it onto the back of the strips. They were barefoot, she remembered. Their feet stuck to the floor and their fingers stuck to the brush handle. After that they had difficulty smoothing the paper. Regardless how many times Luka pulled a yardstick down the wall to make the strips lie flat, there always seemed to be a bulge somewhere.

There was a lot of shouting and, on Luka's part, cursing. To make matters worse, the rain was coming down hard and sideways, so they couldn't open the bedroom window as they worked. The fumes of the paste nearly did them in.

For years afterward Luka joked that he and Emma nearly got divorced hanging that damned wallpaper.

But the room eventually got papered and the marriage survived until the cancer took Momma, and Cora had been staring at these same yellow walls for eleven years. There was little else to do now, as Luka had pulled her out of school after arranging an in-home tutor, refused to allow her visitors, and never, never let her leave the house alone. Either he or Birgitta accompanied her every time she set foot outside.

She hadn't seen George since revealing her condition to her father. Oh, Luka assured her, it was only temporary while he and Margaret Hammon discussed the details of the "settlement," but she didn't believe a word of it. Luka hated George, and never used his name anymore. It was always "the bastard," or something worse. From her room Cora overheard him rail to Birgitta almost every day. He knew she was listening. Why else would he raise his voice every time her footsteps caused a floorboard to creak? Because he knew she was awake, that was why.

As she lay on her bed, she wondered how life might have been if her parents *had* divorced. Momma would have been the one to move out, no doubt about that. Even then Luka always got what he wanted. While he might give up his wife, he'd never give up his house or money. Not in a divorce. He would have turned it into a contest, and winning was too important to him.

Momma didn't need his house or money anyway. She'd probably go back to Evanston to live with Grandpa and Grandma Jensen until she got back on her feet. Cora, naturally, would go with her. When Momma died, Cora would stay in Illinois, finish high school, and maybe attend college or learn the proper way to cut ladies' hair. She always did like bobbing her friends' hair. Why not get paid for it? Once she had her own salon, she probably would meet a boy, get married, and have babies. And she would never tell Luka about her salon or her husband or her children. Any man who would throw out his own wife and daughter over some stupid wallpaper didn't deserve to see his grandchildren.

Then again, if all that had happened, she wouldn't have met George—and what a terrible thought that was! She couldn't imagine living without him. She *wouldn't* live without him, no matter what Luka did. But suppose she *had* moved to Illinois in 1902 and grown up and fallen in love with somebody else? George would have been just another person in the world she'd never heard of, and she wouldn't be missing him now. Trouble was, she *liked* missing him.

She liked seeing him more.

Cora opened her chest of drawers. She still had the imitation pearl necklace her mother had given her a week before she died. She'd placed it around Cora's neck like a bishop crowning a queen. "Remember me," her mother had said, kissing her cheek, "on your wedding day." Momma could have afforded real pearls, of course, but this was the necklace Grandma Jensen had passed down to her, back when everyone was poor. It probably wasn't worth a dime, but it had belonged to Momma, and that made it priceless.

Cora put the necklace on and stood in front of the mirror attached to the top of her dresser, visualizing herself in a white gown with a long beautiful train. *I'll wear this next to my heart when I get married*, she thought. *To George. When I get married to George. And since Daddy won't give me away, well, then, maybe George's servant Ed will, or even his Negro friend Lewis. Wouldn't* that *cause a sensation?*

GEORGE
Waterton, Iowa
September 1913

George and Lewis smoked cigarettes in the doorway that opened into the alley behind Kline's. It was a warm, summerlike night. The skies had opened up with a rainstorm, flooding the streets and transforming the gravel alley into a big mud hole.

The sole source of light was an electric lamp at the end of the block, across the street and behind the row of buildings. It illuminated the entrance to the alley and nothing else. The backlit rain looked like slanting streaks of silver, but the lamp threw only shadows where George and Lewis stood. There was no traffic here, but occasional motor cars and horse-drawn vehicles passed on Jefferson Street.

George drew in a small puff of smoke and blew it out quickly. The red glow at the tip of the cigarette flared slightly as he inhaled. "The problem is Luka," he said. "My mother can't stop me from seeing Cora, but he can. He hardly lets her out of the house, and when he does there's always someone with her."

Lewis' cigarette was down to a stub. He tossed it into the rain, causing its little flame to sizzle and go out. "See it like they do, Georgie. I mean like your Momma and Curtis. Nobody think too much, some single poor girl get herself with child. But a rich girl? It be all over the papers just like that, and soon other high-and-mighty so-ci-e-ty folk get to talking unkindly. Only thing mean more to rich people than they money is they reputation."

"Maybe I'll just go over there and take her away."

"What you talking 'bout, *take her away*? Curtis beat the hell outta you, son, and he won't even break sweat doing it. I told you don't mess with that man."

"I'm not afraid of Luka."

"Then you dumber than you look."

Rain finally overwhelmed the eave spout on the roof of the building across the alley. Water gushed down in a torrent, spattering them both. "This keeps up, Gloire de Matin's going to flood," George said.

Lewis took his cap off and stuck his head out from the doorway. He seemed to enjoy the feel of rain on his face. "Shit, son," he said, "you don't know flooding. Back in Mississippi a bunch of us colored folk, we live right on the river. Our houses wasn't much, but they all we had. We built them up on ten-foot foundations to stop them floating away when the river come up."

Lewis smiled, as if recalling a pleasant memory. His yellow teeth reminded George of the cat in *Alice in Wonderland* or *Through the Looking Glass*. He could never remember which was which.

"'Course," Lewis went on, "we ain't never had none of your fancy plumbing and porcelain flush bowls to do our business in, just regular outhouses. When I was a boy, we had this little cocker dog we call Fleabite. Now, you got to realize in Mississippi the fleas is so big they got *dogs*. Anyway, Fleabite gets to sniffing round the outhouse, and sure enough, she fall in. Well, she barking and whining and carrying on—and why not, stuck in a lake of shit? Daddy go out to rescue her but thing is, the hole ain't big enough for him to reach down and pull her out. So he decide to un-anchor the outhouse and tip it over. After that he able to grab hold of Fleabite. Let me tell you, that one stinking dog. Daddy throw her into the river, and when she swim back, he throw her in again. Keep doing that 'til she clean."

"Poor Fleabite."

"Fleabite, hell. You know what really funny?" Lewis said. He stepped completely into the rat-a-tat of raindrops and let the cascade from the clogged eave drench his clothes. "What funny is, he set up the outhouse again but forget to anchor it. When the flood come next spring the water carry it right down the river. Me and him got to go fetch it in a rowboat. We tie it to the house 'til the water go down. And you know what Daddy say about it? He say, 'Well, at least she got one good flush this year!'"

George laughed. "See, you did have a flush toilet."

"Yeah, once. You know what the Fleabite story mean, don't you?"

"Don't let your dog near the outhouse?"

"It mean shit wash off, Georgie. Might take a while, but the shit wash off."

"I don't know," George said, "there's a lot of shit right now."

"Then come out in the rain and get yourself clean." Lewis grabbed George's arm and yanked him out of the doorway. "Now we both wet," he said, and they giggled like kids.

Inside they warmed their hands over the kerosene lantern. Smoke smells mixed with manure and hay while rain pounded the roof and the horses made whinnying sounds in their stalls.

Lewis stripped down to nothing. His black skin looked sleek in the lamp light. His hands were strong and scarred and calloused, the most beautiful things about the man. He wore a wedding ring, probably bronze, and just as precious as the brightest diamond. "I brought me a change of clothes," Lewis said. "Bet you didn't."

"I've got to ride home in the rain anyway."

Lewis pulled on a pair of bib overalls. "Sleep here if you want. I do all the time."

"Can't, it's a school night," George said. "Do you think he'll send her away?"

"Curtis? Maybe. Who knows what that mean sumbitch'll do?"

"I'd marry her," George said. He was glad of the rain, rain to disguise the tears.

Lewis stood up and squeezed his shoulder, "I know you would, son."

CORA
Waterton, Iowa
September 1913

Cora dangled her legs from the swing that hung from the old elm behind the stable. She bit into a piece of bread topped with strawberry preserves. The sun reflected off puddles of standing water from the recent rainstorm, and the grass was as dewy as on a cool spring morning, although the day was warm. The weather vane was still. Autumn was here, winter approaching. Several sparrows, little pests that never flew south, hopped on the ground in front of the swing, scooping up any crumb of bread that fell. A squirrel chattered furiously in the elm, scolding Cora for her presence. Or perhaps it was upset with Birgitta, who was pretending to tend the flower garden by the house. The woman truly did love her flowers, all coordinated by type and color—petunias, zinnias, marigolds, snapdragons, salvia, and geraniums—but the first hard freeze could come at any time to wither them on their stems. Not much could be done for flowers this late in the season, so the reason Birgitta had really come out was to make sure George wasn't lurking in the bushes.

What a situation Cora was in, what a life. She was pregnant, four months on now, if the calculations were right. She wasn't showing much yet, maybe the tiniest of bulges in her tummy, but soon her condition would be obvious to the world.

She refused to have an abortion, and going away wouldn't ease the stigma for Luka, because everyone would know why she left. And since he was adamant that no daughter of his would have a child out of wedlock, there was only one solution left. He had reluctantly agreed to let her marry George.

The difficulty was Margaret Hammon. She would not hear any talk of marriage, period.

"No," she'd said to Luka. "Absolutely not. No. No. No. You're already a laughing stock, and I've been one before. I'll pay for an abortion. I'll pay whatever it takes. Name a number to make this problem go away. My son will not marry your daughter. He will *not*. This is not negotiable."

Cora finished all but the last bite of her bread, which she ground into crumbs to toss to the sparrows. They cheeped and jostled each other to get at the tasty morsels. Nasty little creatures when it came to food, the black-headed males shooing away the drabber females. Males always got what they wanted, even if they were birds.

A breeze had come up from the northeast, promising cooler weather but bringing the stench of the Roth Packing Plant's hog kill operation. The weather vane creaked. *This is not negotiable.*

Of course, Margaret had spoken through her lawyer, Mr. Kelper. He was threatening to claim somebody other than George was the father. He'd even hinted that for the right price a boy could be found who would say he had been with her. "Any number of poor, desperate boys out there," he'd said. "Boys who have no reputation to lose."

Luka's lawyer, Mr. Weinshank, had called the threat "subornation of perjury," a serious criminal offense. He said he was disappointed that Kelper had stooped to such low tactics, but if that's the way it was going to be, by God, two could play that game.

And the scheme Weinshank had come up with....

Cora hoped George would forgive her, but she'd had to sign the papers. It was the only way. The worst part was she couldn't warn him. Neither Luka nor Margaret would let them speak on the telephone, and both parents screened incoming mail. This was going to test George's trust.

She hopped down from the swing. The sparrows scattered. Birgitta looked up from her garden. The sod was still spongy, despite sunshine all day. Her feet squished as she walked to the house. Birgitta fell in step behind her.

Cora waited for her to catch up. Why did it have to be like this? She wished George would just come galloping in on a big white stallion and sweep her into his arms. She wouldn't care where they went, as long as they were together. They didn't need schemes or complications or lawyers or even money. This didn't have to be difficult, it could be easy. Love should be easy.

But Margaret Hammon's horses were hardly white stallions—those old nags could barely walk, let alone gallop—and she doubted if George could even afford Kline's at the moment.

No knight in shining armor for her this time, she was afraid.

Cora sighed as Birgitta arrived at her side. "What is wrong, child?" the woman said.

"You know what," Cora said.

"Yes, I know. Are you certain you want to go through with this?"

"No."

"Then what other way?"

Cora had no answer.

At least the squirrel had stopped chattering.

GEORGE
Waterton, Iowa
September 1913

Before going to school George liked to stop at a greasy little cafe called Corken's Diner and have a green river to wake himself up. Located on the east side not too far from Smoky Row, the cafe was out of his way, but it was near a trolley line that eventually took him to West Side High School on Sixth and Washington. Lewis had recommended the diner to him. The food was dreadful, but the owner was friendly and it was the only place in town that was open twenty-four hours. Isaac Corken—Corky—figured he could make a profit by selling cheap meals to drunks who staggered in after the taverns closed. Unlike many restaurants, Corky was happy to serve anybody, black, white, red, or polka dotted. "Money's all the same color," he said. One sign above the counter read, DON'T LAUGH AT OUR COFFEE. YOU'LL BE OLD AND WEAK SOME DAY, TOO. Another said, DON'T TIP THE WAITER. IT UPSETS HIM.

The diner always reeked of lard and burnt eggs. In full view of the customers – there were only two – Corky cracked two raw eggs into a vat of vile brown cooking oil, where they floated on the surface like a pair of eyes. George usually sat at a table by the window to avoid looking at those bulging yellow monstrosities, but he was running late today, so he went straight to the counter. His throat felt a little scratchy—he'd taken a chill cavorting in the rain with Lewis—so the green river went down smooth.

The other customer was a weathered old sot named Philo, who wore his white hair long, hadn't shaved in weeks, and smelled as if he'd bathed in an outhouse. At the moment the man was nodding over a bowl of chili, sound asleep. Apparently he'd been out quite some time, because his hair had hung down into the bowl long enough for the chili to have congealed into an orange and brown mass around it. A circular white crust of grease lined the outer circumference of the chili.

Corky, a middle-aged offspring of German immigrants, looked at George and winked. *Watch this*, he mouthed. George sensed what was coming and moved away from the counter. Corky leaned right down next to Philo's ear and shouted, "Hey, Philo, fire!"

The old drunk reacted predictably, snapping his head back and pulling the congealed chili up with his hair. The bowl went clattering to the floor while the remaining liquid content sprayed up in a messy arc over the counter, the floor, and, of course, over Corky.

George put his hand in front of his mouth and faked a cough to disguise his laughter. Corky wasn't fooled, but took no offense. "Go ahead and have your giggle," he said, a jot of beef dangling from his nose. "Hell, George, I'm up to my armpits in grease anyway."

"The chili adds color," George said.

"Funny," Corky said.

"Am I on fire?" Philo said, and threw up on the counter.

"Okay," Corky said, "now *that* pisses me off."

George set his empty glass and a nickel on the counter next to the cash register. His head was starting to feel stuffy, and he had a small headache behind his eyes. "I heard," he said, "you have to swallow a toad every morning if you expect nothing worse to happen the rest of the day."

Corky retrieved a rag, a dustbin, and a bag of sawdust from behind the counter. He poured the sawdust onto the vomit. Philo was not the first sick drunk he'd had. "Who said that?"

"Some German philosopher," George said.

Philo, unconcerned, moved two chairs down and fell asleep again.

"*Scheißkopf,*" Corky said.

George knew *scheißkopf* was German for "shit head." What he didn't know was whether Corky was referring to him, to Philo, or to the philosopher. Probably all three. "Guess you swallowed the toad today, huh?" he said, coughing for real now. "All downhill from here."

"Get out of here before I put you to work," Corky said. "Go to school, maybe learn something for a change."

***

The sun was shining and, except for smoke from the factories on Westland Avenue, the sky was clear. Rain earlier in the week had not brought cooler temperatures, although in September this time of morning was always chilly. The leaves were turning orange, red, and yellow with the season, and the dew on the grass was pretty, too. Roth's pollution was in the air, but George's plugged-up nose filtered most of the stink.

A lot of kids rode the trolley to school. In this part of town most of them got off at East Side High, but once the trolley crossed the river more of the West-Siders boarded. George was friendly with some of them. Today a group of his fellow seniors wanted to know why Cora hadn't been in class lately. She was feeling poorly, he said, which was true enough, although that explanation wasn't going to hold much longer.

Luckily, George's own illness rescued him from further discussion. He went on a sneezing jag, covering his mouth with a handkerchief, and soon his friends stopped trying to talk to him. By the time he changed to the Galloway line that went directly to West Side High, his eyes were watering, and his headache hand grown from dull pressure to a pounding throb. He spent the rest of the journey wrapped in silent misery. *Looks like I'll be swallowing toads all day*, he thought.

After exiting the trolley car he stood coughing and sneezing in front of the school's façade of brick and stone, debating whether or not he should just go home. He'd never missed classes because of a simple cold before, but the prospect of returning to his warm bed was tempting.

A motor car sped down Washington Street, splashing through a puddle left over from the rain. Two students, both girls, got splattered. They cursed the motorist, using indelicate language that even made George cringe. More and more girls seemed to be talking like that these days.

George shook his head. He couldn't go home. He had a test in Algebra this afternoon.

***

Solve:

$$x^2 - 6x + 1 = + \left(\frac{3x + 5}{2} \right)$$

George put his pencil to the paper, but nothing came to him. This should be an easy problem. He'd done dozens like it before. His cold was ruining his concentration. This test wasn't essential to his grade—it was still early in the year, and he could make up the points later—but he always liked to do his best. Truth was, he had a friendly competition going with his friend Cale, the class "brain." Loser had to carry the winner's books until the next test came along.

He was on the second floor of West Side High School, near a window overlooking Sixth Street. The noon church bells had just chimed. His teacher, Miss DeVilbiss, sat at the front of the classroom reading a magazine. Her light brown hair was long, tied in a bun at the back. For such a young woman, she was certainly set in her ways. She already had her pocket watch out on the desk, although the test had just begun. She'd given the class precisely forty-five minutes to finish. George hated timed tests. He always got done, but it was the principle. What difference did it make if it took one minute or ten, as long as the answer was correct?

Something small struck the back of his neck. He glanced behind him. Cale was smiling and holding a pea shooter. George touched his neck and came away with ink on his finger. The bastard had not only shot a spit wad, but he'd loaded it up with ink first.

George sneezed, covering his nose and mouth with his hand. The girl next to him giggled. "What?" George said.

"You got ink on your nose," she whispered.

"*Children*," Miss DeVilbiss warned just as George was about to retaliate against Cale.

At the same time he heard a commotion outside on the street below. Some of the kids hurried to the window. "It's the police," one girl said.

"Everybody sit down," the teacher said. "That doesn't concern you."

But it did concern George. Moments later the classroom door burst open and two Waterton officers came in, guns drawn, followed by a Red Hawk County sheriff's deputy.

"May I help you gentlemen?" Miss DeVilbiss said in a squeaky voice that belied her outward calmness.

"We're looking for George P. Hammon," one of the Waterton cops said.

There was a gasp, and then a hush fell over the room.

"Me?" George said, his voice about an octave higher than the teacher's.

"Come with us, Hammon."

"Has something happened to my mother?"

"Shut up. Don't make a scene." The city officers looked almost sympathetic, but the deputy glared at him contemptuously.

George chose that moment to suffer a coughing fit that seemed would never end. *It's just the cold*, he thought, *not nerve*s. He didn't want to appear terrified to the class.

But he was. He had no idea what this was about.

He stood up. A cop put handcuffs on George's wrists. All three officers led him out of the room. Cale's mouth gaped open as they passed.

Outside a police wagon waited. Reporters from the *Waterton Record* and other small-town papers had gathered at the school steps. One of them had a camera. The flash pan ignited, causing George a few seconds of blindness. His mind raced as he tried to blink away the yellow spots in front of his eyes. The only coherent thought he could manage was, *Jesus, they took a picture of me with ink on my nose.*

"What's the scoop?" a reporter asked the cops. "We got a tip to come here."

The county deputy stepped forward as if giving a press conference. "We have an arrest warrant for George P. Hammon. The charge is felonious assault."

"Of *the* Hammons?"

"The same. Son of Margaret and the late G.W. Hammon."

"Who'd you beat up, George?" another reporter said.

"I didn't—"

"Not *that* kind of assault," the deputy said, pausing to allow the implication to sink in. "The complaint was filed by Miss Cora Curtis of Waterton."

CORA
Waterton, Iowa
October 1913

The story ran in the *Record* for days, front page, top half of the fold. Although public decency forbade use of the terms "sexual assault" or "rape" in a family newspaper, anyone with half a brain could read between the lines. Poor George. He only spent an hour or two in jail before Mr. Kelper came to post bond, but he must have been frantic with fear and anger and confusion. If the situation were reversed, Cora would hate him.

Please don't let him hate me, she thought. She'd done it all for him, for them, for the greater good in the long run. In time he would understand that, but that time was not now. Now all he knew was that she had pressed charges and publicly humiliated him. Well, her father had arranged the humiliation, from the arrest at school to the presence of newsmen, claiming it was necessary for the plan to succeed. George would still blame her. Cora yearned to sneak a message to him, to explain and beg his forgiveness, but it was impossible. George was under virtual house arrest, and she might as well be.

She sat barefoot and alone in the parlor, staring absently out the window. A bright October sun slanted in and heated the room. At first the warmth felt good on her face, but after an hour the house had become too hot. It was late afternoon, the day after her seventeenth birthday. Nothing much was happening outside, no weather to speak of, no clouds, no wind, not even the chittering of birds. The leaves were pretty. Cora's mouth was dry. She could feel her mother's fake-pearl necklace next to her heart. She wore a simple blue dress that Birgitta had let out at the waist to accommodate her growing tummy. Her neck was sweating, discoloring the delicate white lace that trimmed her dress, and yet she made no move to get out of the direct sunlight.

She shifted her attention to her feet. Watching her toes wiggle reminded her of a newborn, tiny legs sticking straight up in the air. Would their child be a boy or a girl? Which did George want? Cora secretly hoped for a girl, but he would probably prefer a son.

The telephone bell rang in the kitchen. She heard Birgitta's lilting voice answer, although she couldn't make out the words. Her father wasn't here. He and Mr. Weinshank had arranged a conference with Margaret Hammon and Mr. Kelper to discuss the situation.

Cora cupped her hands over the little bulge in her stomach. The baby kicked, or, more likely, she imagined it had.

Sweet Jesus, what had they *done*?

Birgitta entered the parlor. "You are to meet with your father, Mrs. Hammon, the lawyers, and the judge at the courthouse," she said curtly. "The Hammon boy is there as well." Birgitta didn't approve of George, but she cared very much about Cora's happiness.

Cora felt her heart surge. Her love was waiting for her at last! "There's been a decision?"

"Put on your shoes and a nice dress, girl. And fix your hair. I have telephoned for an automobile to take you to downtown."

A motor car? Cora had never ridden in one before. "Are you coming with me?"

"It is not my place."

Cora pulled on her stockings and shoes and stood up. Her neck was still sweating and her hair was probably a fright. The sun cast her shadow across the floor to the opposite wall. She turned sideways to see her silhouette in profile. Her pregnancy was projected by sunlight to the very spot where the floor met the wall, the angle of their joining distorting the dark lump that would become her child.

GEORGE
Waterton, Iowa
October 1913

George sat at a long table inside Judge Harold Cralin's chambers on the first floor of the Courthouse. His mother Margaret and Arlen Kelper flanked him. Facing them across the table were Luka Curtis and his lawyer Weinshank, whose first name George never bothered to remember. Judge Cralin presided at the head of the table, shuffling some papers. In chambers he didn't wear his robe. Dressed in a suit and tie, he looked like an ordinary grandfather, with spectacles, a neatly clipped mustache, and a bald spot in the middle of his gray hair. The man was hardly an imposing figure. Yet, robe or not, he spoke with the voice and authority of the law.

Thick ceiling-to-floor drapes covered the windows on both sides of the room. The sunshine outside couldn't penetrate them. This meeting was apparently so secret no one was even allowed to peek in the windows. Well, the reporters *had* been a nuisance.

Cora was on her way. Cora, his heart's desire, the mother of his unborn child. Cora, who'd professed her love—and then filed a rape charge against him. George was able to hold his emotions in check here, but in the week since his arrest he'd run the gamut from tears to rage. Jesus, how could she do that to him? Rape? *Rape?* She'd been as willing as he. Once they got the mechanics figured out she'd even been the instigator sometimes.

Why, Cora?

He should hate her, but some part of him strained to believe there was more to this than met the eye, that somehow she was as much a victim as he. Perhaps she, too, was being manipulated by the adults in this room.

For the moment everybody was hush-mouthed. A few days ago Kelper had said, or implied, or allowed George to believe, that the purpose of this meeting was to reach some kind of plea agreement that would allow him to serve less time. George had already forbidden Kelper to accuse another boy, or to do anything that might further damage Cora's reputation. "You are a romantic idiot," Kelper had said. "You're tying my hands. The penalty for first-degree rape is life in prison. *Life*, George. Are you willing to throw away everything for that little slut?"

"Don't call her that," George said.

"I've found three other boys she's been with."

"You're lying."

"Grow up, George. She's not worth it."

"How would you know? No woman's ever loved you."

"This is love? Accusing you of rape? You know as well as I do that she and her father are just after your mother's money. That's why she seduced you."

"Shut up, or I'll plead guilty right now."

Kelper had thrown up his hands in disgust. That same night, according to Margaret, he and Weinshank had spent hours negotiating on the telephone. Luka and Margaret had also spoken at length. Whatever settlement they'd agreed upon would be revealed today.

As soon as Cora arrived.

Everybody in the room had tense, drawn faces. George could smell their sweat. Judge Cralin checked his pocket watch continuously. Finally, after a half hour that seemed like a week, he said, "Gentlemen? Mrs. Hammon?"

"My daughter's condition is delicate," Luka said, "as you can well imagine. She's only seventeen. My maid telephoned for an automobile. She should be here any minute."

"I can't stand it," Margaret said. Her voice vibrated with emotion, suppressed fury or utter dejection, George couldn't tell which. "Judge Cralin, may I have the documents?"

"Margaret," Kelper said, "are you sure?"

"I don't know why I agreed to come. I don't want to meet that girl. I have never wanted to meet her. Just give me the papers, I'll sign them."

"Mother?" George said.

She glared at him as Cralin passed the documents to Kelper, who slid them to her. "Don't speak to me, George Hammon. Don't you dare. Your father would have been so ashamed."

Kelper handed her a fountain pen. She scraped her signature in several places and stood up. "Finish our business here, Mr. Kelper. I'm going home."

"You don't have a ride," George said.

She turned slowly to him. Her hatred for her dead stepmother Clara was nothing compared to the loathing in her eyes now. "Why, I'll call Kline's," she said bitterly. "I'll ask for your colored friend."

George looked away. "I'm sorry, Mother."

"Not sorry enough." Then she jabbed a finger at Luka. "And *you*," she said. George had no idea what she meant by that. Weinshank shrugged. Luka just smiled.

With as much dignity as possible, Margaret stormed out of the room. As she left George caught a glimpse of the police officers guarding the door.

"Well," Luka said, "that was interesting."

Cora arrived a few minutes later accompanied by a bailiff, who Judge Cralin thanked and dismissed. She wouldn't look at George, but he could see she was in distress. Her tears were flowing, her nose was running, and she was hugging herself as if to hold her insides in. She made little whimpering sounds, although she bit her lip to keep from sobbing out loud.

"Sit down, Miss Curtis," the Judge said. When she approached George's side of the table, Cralin motioned her to the other side. "With your father and Mr. Weinshank, please."

She took a seat next to Luka, keeping her eyes down.

"Hi, sweetie," Luka said. "This won't take long."

George felt the same kind of anxiety he'd experienced on the night of their first successful coupling in Luka's stable back in April. He'd almost puked then, and he was afraid he might now. Worse, he had a sudden, overpowering urge to pee. *Damn* it, he hadn't expected that seeing her would be so hard. He rose from his chair, his knees wobbling. "I need to, uh…," he sputtered, almost grabbing his crotch in front of everyone, for God's sake.

"By all means, Mr. Hammon," Cralin said. "An officer will escort you. You might have taken care of this earlier."

Cora gazed up at him then, and when she did he saw such adoration in her face that he knew, he *knew*, everything was going to be all right. She hadn't betrayed him, of *course* she hadn't. How could he have ever doubted her?

I love you, she mouthed. *This was the only way. Trust me.*

And he did, although he couldn't imagine how an accusation of rape could possibly help them. He nodded and smiled. He didn't have to tell her he forgave her. She would see it in his smile. As if a monstrous weight had been lifted from her, she put her head down on her arms and wept. This time, he was sure, they were tears of happiness.

Feeling more light-hearted than he had since learning of her pregnancy in August, George fairly skipped from the room. One of the police officers outside followed him to the Courthouse's public toilet and stood right outside the stall as he relieved his bladder. When he returned Cralin's documents were spread out on the table in front of his chair.

"Sign these," Kelper said.

Weinshank frowned contemptuously at him, but Cora was beaming. Luka was strangely neutral, difficult to read.

"What are they?" George said. He recognized Cora's signature on the first page.

"A marriage license," Kelper said, "and a dismissal of charges."

George nearly fainted. He steadied himself by leaning on the back of his chair, then slowly lowered himself into his seat. "What?" he said stupidly. Dismissal of charges? A *marriage license*?

"You're off the hook, asshole," Weinshank said.

"Watch your language, Mr. Weinshank," Cralin said.

"Go ahead, George," Luka said. "It's true."

"I don't understand ...." Those were the only words George could enunciate without lapsing into babbling nonsense. He couldn't believe this was happening.

It was happening.

Kelper drew in a long breath. "Under Iowa law, a wife cannot file or prosecute a sexual assault complaint against her husband. The only way Curtis would agree to have the charges dropped was if you married his daughter."

"B-b-but—"

"Your mother opposed the marriage under any circumstances," Kelper said. He obviously despised what he was saying. His mouth moved as if he were chewing on bile. "Unfortunately, neither she nor I foresaw this...ploy. Curtis didn't want his daughter giving birth out of wedlock, so he and Weinshank devised this scheme to blackmail Margaret."

"Careful with your terminology," Weinshank said.

"I agree, counselor," Cralin said.

Kelper shot the Judge an angry glare. "Either you be allowed to marry this little bitch—"

"Mr. Kelper!"

"Sorry, Your Honor. Either you be allowed to marry this *young woman*, or they go through with the prosecution and send you to prison for the rest of your life. The D.A. couldn't wait to get his hands on you. Even I was tempted to let you rot. But furious as Margaret was, she couldn't allow that." Kelper thrust the fountain pen at George. "Do you have any idea how much your mother loves you?"

George could barely hold the pen, he was shaking so badly. "And all I have to do is sign?"

"Three copies of each," Kelper said. "Margaret and Curtis have already signed. Weinshank and I will add our names as witnesses."

Somehow George managed to form the letters of his name. When he was done he gave the pen back to Kelper and looked at Cora. She reached across the table and took both of his hands in hers, squeezing his fingers gently. "I love you," she said, still crying.

"Congratulations," Kelper said, perusing the documents. He scribbled his signatures and handed the papers to Weinshank. "You're a free man."

"Not quite," Weinshank said. "It's not official until after the wedding."

Judge Cralin rose, retrieved his black robe from a coat rack by the door, and put it on.

"When's that going to be?" George said.

"Now," Luka said.

"We'll reconvene in the courtroom in fifteen minutes," the Judge said.

**

The fifteen minutes was to allow George and Cora time to freshen up. They did it in ten, then met briefly at the back of the courtroom before the proceedings began. Luka, Weinshank, and Kelper were waiting at the front, with Judge Cralin behind the podium.

"You look ill," Cora said.

"I had a cold," George said, "but I'm okay now. I'd be okay even if I wasn't okay."

"Would is be scandalous if I kissed you?"

"Worse if you didn't."

She wrapped her arms around him and gave him a long, sensuous kiss. No matter how hard she hugged him she couldn't seem to get close enough. Her breasts pressed against his chest, her little bulging tummy against his ribs. God, it felt good to hold her again! George could sense the men watching them disapprovingly, but he didn't care. In a few minutes it would all be legal anyway.

She broke away and tried to explain everything at once. "I've missed you so much. I couldn't get a message to you. I hoped you would trust me. I didn't want to do it, but Daddy and Mr. Weinshank said—"

George touched a finger to her lips. "Shhh," he said. "I never doubted you." It wasn't true, but why spoil the moment?

"Mr. Hammon?" the Judge called. "Miss Curtis?"

"We'll be together forever now," Cora said.

They walked down the aisle hand in hand. "I understand why you had to do that to get my mother to sign," George said, "but I thought your father hated me. Why'd he agree to it?"

"He was pretty mad," she said. "And I know he's worried about his reputation, but I truly think that more than anything he wants me to be happy."

George looked around the courtroom, with its plain white walls and long rows of wooden benches. A ceiling fan circulated dry, stuffy air. "I wanted to give you a church wedding," he said, "with a minister and bridesmaids and organ music and rice. This isn't what I had in mind for us."

"Maybe our first anniversary," she said. "All I want is to be with you and have our baby. Thought of any names yet?"

They arrived at the front and stood before the Judge. Luka and Weinshank were seated in the first row on the left, Kelper on the right.

Cralin adjusted his spectacles and opened a book. "Mr. Curtis is here to represent the bride's family. Apparently Mr. Kelper will serve in Mrs. Hammon's stead for the groom." He peered down at George and Cora, and George thought he looked awfully grave. "This will be a civil ceremony, but it is legal and binding in all forty-eight states. Did anybody bring a ring?"

Luka stood up and handed George a gold ring with a single diamond setting.

"Oh, Daddy," Cora said.

"Thank you, sir," George said. "For everything."

"It belonged to Emma," Luka said, and returned to the bench.

"Shall we get started?" Cralin said. He read in a monotone voice from the book, which was evidently some legal how-to-marry-people text. The service consisted of the usual stock phrases spoken in most religious weddings, minus God: "Love, honor, and obey, for better, for worse, in sickness or in health, 'til death do you part," and so on.

"Do you take this woman to be your lawfully wedded wife?" he said. "Do you take this man?"

George did, and Cora did, and George slipped the ring onto her finger. In a ceremony lasting less than three minutes Judge Harold Cralin, by the power vested in him by the state of Iowa, pronounced them man and wife. He told George to kiss the bride.

"We're married," Cora said, and the tears came anew.

"I don't believe it," George said.

Judge Cralin rose from the bench. "Best wishes to you both," he said before quickly exiting to his chambers. No one else came to congratulate them.

"I've hired a coach for you," Luka said. "It should be here by now."

George and Cora led the way up the aisle, with the three men following, Luka and Weinshank together, Kelper lagging behind.

A brougham was parked on Mulberry Street, just outside the Courthouse door. It was one of Kline's, but Lewis wasn't the driver. Pity. How perfect would that have been? The sun was low in the sky, as it always was on late afternoons in October. A narrow row of yellow flowers adorned the front of the Courthouse, end to end. The leaves of the trees lining Mulberry were nearing the peak of their autumnal colors. Many had fallen and collected at the curbs. A group of mallards flew silently by overhead.

What a glorious day.

The officers who had been standing guard outside Cralin's chambers had come out as well. They were chatting with Weinshank.

Cora kissed George again. "I'm so happy," she said.

"What should we do for our honeymoon?" George said, almost giddy. "And where will we live? I don't have any money."

"We don't need any," Cora said.

"That's right, you don't," Luka said, coming up behind them. He squeezed Cora's shoulder lovingly, then raised her hand to examine the ring. "May I?"

She nodded, and he slid the ring off her finger. "It's so beautiful," she said.

"Your mother was a beautiful woman," he said, and his eyes were misty. He turned to smile at George.

George felt certain his new father-in-law was about to offer him a job or even some kind of bridal dowry. "I can't thank you enough," he said.

"Don't thank me," Luka said, stuffing the ring in his vest pocket. His smile was gone. "If you think you're going to spend one more minute with my little girl, you piece of shit, you are sadly mistaken."

"I beg your pardon?" George said, stunned, not quite believing what he heard.

"Mr. Weinshank," Luka said, "take Cora to the coach."

"Daddy!" Cora cried.

Weinshank grabbed her arm and jerked her away from George. George lunged at him, but the lawyer just shook his head in amusement. "Try it. Please."

"George, don't," Cora said, and he backed off. "Daddy, you promised!"

"Get her out of here," Luka said, and in full view of the police officers Weinshank forced her into the coach. He climbed in next to her. Cora screamed George's name as the brougham pulled into traffic and clattered down the street.

George started after her, but the coach quickly outdistanced him. He stopped running halfway down the block.

"Give it up," Luka called. The police officers were laughing. Kelper had joined them. He seemed mighty pleased, too.

George wanted to cry, but he was too enraged. He bull rushed up the sidewalk toward Luka. "You son-of-a-bitch!" he said.

Luka knocked him flat with a quick jab to the chin. "I've wanted to do that for a long time."

George got to his feet, fists clenched and ready. "That didn't hurt."

"Could you be any dumber?" Kelper said. "He's a *boxer*, for Christ's sake."

"You're lucky I don't beat you to death right now," Luka said.

It was useless. George couldn't take him, and he knew it. Even if he could, the police officers, who had done nothing while his wife was being kidnapped, would intervene on Luka's behalf. They must be on his payroll. "*Why*?" George said, and now he was crying.

"My grandchild will not be born a bastard," Luka said. "I made a deal with the devil."

"*You're* the devil," George said, wiping his nose on his sleeve.

"Not me, kid."

Kelper walked over next to him. "He made a deal with your mother, George. She consented to the marriage on the condition that you be allowed no further contact with Curtis's daughter afterward."

"She can't do that," George said. "We're married."

"She did, and you signed your name to it. You both did."

"Jesus Christ," George said. "You people are monsters."

"Surprise," Luka said, and he walked away.

REUNIONS AND DEPARTURES

WILL
Waterton, Iowa
September 2008

Will lay on his back on a table while a young woman bent and straightened his right leg. All around him people were running on treadmills, riding exercise bikes, lifting weights attached to machines by pulleys. Most were wearing T-shirts or sweatshirts with moisture stains at the armpits and stomach and spine. The room was painted light pink and smelled of sweat.

An IV poked out of the back of his hand, held in place by clear tape, although nothing was hooked up to it. Just a precaution, he was told, should they have to administer medicine quickly.

The young woman's name tag said KRISTIN S, PHYSICAL THERAPIST. She had dark hair and a pretty smile. Her teeth were very white. Will remembered when he had real teeth. "You're doing well, Mr. Hammon," Kristin said, "but can you help me out? When I bend your knee, push your leg to straighten it, will you?" She used her palm to apply light pressure on the bottom of his right foot. Will strained against her hand but had little strength. "Good, Mr. Hammon. Excellent."

This was humiliating. He was ninety-four years old, yet he had to be taught to walk again like an infant. All of his life, all his experiences, his work, his family, everything he'd ever done or known had come to this, a girl just out of college exercising body parts for him because he couldn't do it himself. The catheter was out now, but a nurse still had to accompany him to the toilet. She made him leave the stall door open while he did his business, and then wrote down what she saw before allowing him to flush.

Ninety-four years reduced to this single point of degradation, where the only point remaining *was* the degradation.

Jesus, Charlie, you should've just let me go. Just let me go. Will closed his eye, and he was in his filling station with grease on his young strong hands. A brand new '37 Roadster pulled in next to the pump. There were two young men and a girl, the girl alone in the back seat. They were laughing and carrying on. The driver was a good-looking Irish fellow. *Fill 'er up,* he said. *Don't worry about the windows or oil.*

Will inserted the nozzle into the gas tank. *Nice day, huh?* he said.

The girl hooked her elbow over the side of the car. *How come your left lens is frosted?* she said. *You lose an eye or something?*

Just fell out of my head one morning, Will said. *It was the damnedest thing.*

The girl giggled. *This is Francis and Tony,* she says. *My name is—*

"Elaine," Will said.

"It's Kristin," Kristin said. "I need you to stay with me, Mr. Hammon."

Will pushed against the therapist's hand and his leg straightened. Good. He didn't know Francis at the time, but interspersed with that scene in 1937 was the memory that a few years later Francis became one of several brothers to die on the same ship in the Second World War.

Hey, give her a call, Francis said to Will. *She's* real *lonely.*

Elaine punched him playfully. *You're such a creep,* she said, and they were so young and happy, nobody aware then of the watery doom awaiting Francis or, half a century on, the emphysema that would claim Elaine.

Three bucks even, Will said.

Francis handed him a five. *Keep it,* he said. *I'm serious, call her. She's worse than a kid sister, always hanging around. Cramps my style.*

Like you got girls lining up for you, Elaine said.

They were still laughing as they drove off. In a week Will called her. In a year they were married.

"I think you've had enough for the day," Kristin said. "I'll take you back to your room."

GEORGE
Waterton and Hammon Falls, Iowa
October 1936

George's hands shook so badly he could hardly grip the wheel as he and Aubrey entered the eastern city limits of Waterton. With Aubrey's help he'd sworn off drinking after Siobhan's death. Today, as many days, he wished he hadn't.

Crossing the Atlantic had been peaceful, but from the moment they reached port in July it had been one ordeal after another. New York immediately dredged up memories of Cora, although the two of them had been in Buffalo, nowhere near New York City. George couldn't imagine how his pain could still be so intense, but that one glimpse of Cora's bloody body was as vivid now as it had been twenty-two years ago.

Aubrey sensed his grief, and left him alone about it. She had her own. After passing through immigration, they'd spent two months in a claptrap apartment while they searched public library telephone and business directories for her husband Tommy. For George it was a welcome diversion, for Aubrey a mixture of hope and dread. She wanted Tommy to be alive, but although he was her husband he was not her *anam cara*, her soul friend. If he *was* alive, she'd be obligated to return to him, and she had no particular desire to do that. She was with George now.

"Then why look for him?" George had asked. He still wore Mick's Celtic cross beneath his shirt every day.

"I need to know."

"Why? You don't love him."

"He loved me."

"Then he would have sent for you."

"I need to *know*."

It didn't matter. Her search for Tommy proved as fruitless as George's had, and they finally gave up. They had money from the sale of Aubrey's home in Ireland and George's Dropland Coupé. With it they bought a used Chevrolet, loaded the few belongings they'd brought with them, and headed west.

Driving through Pennsylvania, Ohio, and Indiana, George's anguish over Cora intensified. They'd passed through all these states on the train ride east, back in 1914. None of the terrain was familiar—the train had taken a more northern route—but just knowing he was near to where she had been, to the last few places he'd seen her alive, was agonizing.

By the middle of Illinois another kind of foreboding had entered his thoughts, and once they had crossed the Mississippi onto Iowa soil at Dubuque, he'd convinced himself he was crazy for thinking he could ever go home. Cora was dead, and no one else would welcome him back. Even his mother seemed unsure when he'd telephoned her from New York.

What a conversation that had been.

How do I know you're George Hammon? she said. *This could be a cruel trick.*

It's no trick, Mother. You got my letter, you wrote back.

You don't sound like my son.

You haven't heard my voice in over twenty years. I was a teenager then. I'm forty years old now. I've lived in Europe since I was eighteen. My friend Aubrey says I have a French accent.

Tell me something George would know.

You lived in Pomeroy until a twister destroyed the town in 1893. Your father was Bill Morrissey, your husband G.W. Hammon. Our servants' names were Ed and Estella. My birthday is March 23rd. I got a job at Kline's when I was sixteen, against your wishes. Lewis and I picked up the body of your stepmother Clara from the Presbyterian Hospital and took it to Gindt's. I married Cora Curtis but couldn't live with her because of some scheme you and Luka cooked up. That's why we ran away. It's me, Mother. It's George.

She'd wept then. *My God, how can it be? Oh, George, you should have stayed dead. You don't know the things I've done.*

It's all right, Mother. I've done things, too.

Don't come home, she'd said, followed immediately by, *Please come home.*

George slapped the steering wheel in frustration as he replayed her words, trying to read nuances into them, hints, explanations. The things *she'd* done? He downshifted, stepped on the brake, and pulled into a Texaco station off Highway 20. The engine rattled and pinged. It was mid-afternoon, the sun already low in the sky, filtering through the yellow-brown smoke of factories. He didn't recall October ever being this hot in Iowa. "Jesus Christ," he said, taking the car out of gear.

"Calm down," Aubrey said. She placed her hand over his. "You're home."

"I need a drink."

"You're done with that."

"One to steady myself, that's all."

"You've been a long while away. Anybody would be nervous. Take a deep breath, and finish the journey. Tell me about this town that has your name."

"It's my father's name. He died in the Spanish-American War. They made him a hero."

"He wasn't?"

"Who cares."

Aubrey sighed. "The land must have been beautiful, like Ireland."

George looked at a row of run-down houses to the north, smokestacks to the west. The pollution didn't just come from Westland Avenue anymore. "Used to be," he said. "Rolling green hills, pure water, fields of corn, forests. When I was a kid there were even Indian burial mounds west on the Waterton-Cedar Crossing Road. Those are probably all gone now. Waterton's always been an industrial town, but nothing like this."

"Indians," Aubrey said, as if the notion were charming.

The station attendant approached the driver's side of the car. "How may I serve you, sir?" he said, tipping his cap. He was a blonde kid in a crisp Texaco uniform, maybe fifteen years old.

George checked the fuel gauge. He'd just filled up in Manchester, forty-five miles back. "Just getting my bearings."

"Need directions?"

"I remember a fairgrounds called Electrical Park, had a roller coaster and Ferris wheel and this airplane ride that swung you around in a circle on metal cables. Is it still there?"

The kid looked confused. "Well, Electrical Park's over on West Caladonia. Don't know nothing about rides, though. Its ballroom burnt down earlier this year, but they built a new one. Took my gal dancing there last Saturday night. The Walter Korte Orchestra played."

"We'll dance, too," Aubrey said to George, her eyes bright and hopeful.

"I remember Walter Korte," George said. "Maybe he needs a violinist."

The kid pointed west on Highway 20, toward town, and said, "Anyway, just go straight—"

"I know the way, thanks." George mopped his forehead with a handkerchief. "It was never this hot this late in the year when I lived here."

"Shoot," the kid said, "you think this is hot? Should've seen this summer. Over a hundred most of July and August, and a hundred and twelve one day. A hundred and twelve! Keokuk hit one-nineteen. No rain, neither. People thought the world was ending."

"Glad it didn't," George said.

"Me, too," the kid said. "You used to live here? You sound, I don't know, foreign?"

"I am foreign now, I guess."

"Did you know my Dad, Jake Hutchinson? He's a switchman at the Illinois Central."

"Don't recall the name. Maybe if I saw his face."

"Who're you again? I'll ask him."

"I doubt he'd remember me," George said. "Thanks for the information."

"Do take your sweetheart dancing again," Aubrey said.

"I will," the kid said.

George shifted into first and pulled back onto the highway. "Can't believe how much the place has changed," he said.

***

George had gotten little for his Daimler, but Aubrey had managed a decent price for her home, considering the Depression. They'd spent some of it on their ship fare across the Atlantic and more on the apartment in New York, where neither of them had had an income for two months. Then of course there was the Chevrolet, the gasoline and oil, a new tire in Pennsylvania when a nail blew out the old one, the food and inns along the way, the miscellaneous expenses that didn't amount to much individually but added up. By the time they arrived in Waterton they had little money left. It wasn't enough for a house, even one repossessed by the banks and offered for dimes on the dollar.

Instead, after a few nights in a cheap hotel, they met a real estate agent who pointed them toward a trailer park in Hammon Falls, north of Electrical Park. The trailers were shabby and housed mostly immigrants—and what were George and Aubrey, if not immigrants?—but they were insulated and priced right. Aubrey could pay cash, free and clear, with enough left over for chairs, a table, a writing desk, and a bed from a used furniture store.

She did most of the work in getting them settled. George wasn't of much use. He was too overwhelmed by the sense of *home*, by the overhanging aura of Cora's ghost and the heartbreaking absence of Cora. He wasn't ready to face his mother yet, and didn't want her to hear through the grapevine he was back, so he insisted on putting the deed in Aubrey's name. It was unlikely anyone living in a trailer park would recognize him now, even on the off chance that they'd known him as a kid. Margaret had waited over twenty years. She could wait a few more days.

Like most of the trailers here, theirs was rounded at the top of both ends and sided with metal the color of tin foil. Plopped onto its soggy lot, the thing resembled a giant baked potato. Its roof was flat and had been patched in several places. Shades of Monto. The inside was narrow and utilitarian, but did have nice carpeting in the hallway between the kitchen and the bedroom.

George sloshed through potholes on the gravel driveway, carrying in their belongings, while Aubrey stashed them in what little cupboard space they had.

"It's paradise," he said sardonically.

"It will do," Aubrey said.

He had never been one who cared about status. Certainly after leaving home he'd known humble accommodations throughout his stay in France and Ireland. But he couldn't deny the irony of settling into such modest conditions, here, where if he looked to the south he could see the forested terrain of Gloire de Matin Island and, at least in his mind's eye, the gabled roof of his childhood mansion.

MARGARET
Hammon Falls, Iowa
October 1936

"The delivery truck has arrived, Madam," said the new servant, Ellen. Nearly four years after Birgitta's death, Margaret had finally found an acceptable replacement. Orville didn't care for her, but that was okay. Ellen was a third-generation American of German ancestry. Although not yet thirty, she was a mature, no-nonsense woman who suited Margaret's sensibilities perfectly. She was strictly professional, lacking Ed and Estella's parental doting and Birgitta's sharp tongue and set ways. Also, being third generation, she spoke without a trace of an accent. One thing Margaret had disliked most, and missed least, about Birgitta was her cloying Finnish accent. It had made her sound so *foreign*. Not so with Ellen. She had the comfortingly flat tones of a Midwesterner.

The woman had done a masterful job in preparing the house. She had repainted all the interior walls herself, arranged the donation of the old furniture to the poor, overseen the installation of new carpeting, and ensured every room was immaculate. Neither she nor Luka knew the reason for the changes.

The delivery truck was bringing thousands of dollars worth of new furniture. The only rooms Margaret had left alone were the library and three of the bedrooms, George's, Will's, and Orville's. Orville had put his foot down on that one.

The doorbell rang. "You know how I want everything," Margaret said. "I'm going to talk to Orville. Make sure the men wipe their feet. Don't let them drag dirt all over your clean floors."

"Yes, Madam," and there was a hint of a prideful smile.

With Margaret's fortune slashed by the Depression to a quarter of its original value and Orville's business interests less lucrative since the repeal of Prohibition, they couldn't justify the expenses. But Orville had been surprisingly acquiescent about the whole business. Which usually meant he wanted something.

Margaret had to break the news sometime. She went into the library, where Orville was at his mahogany desk, bent over some account books. Well, she wasn't the only one who'd grown old. His lean boxer's body had gone to seed, as the farmers would say. His arms had grown soft and rubbery, and he had an undeniable paunch around his middle. He still wore his hair slicked back, and it was still black, although the gray showed at the roots if he went more than a few days between dye jobs. He'd tired of trying to color the mustache, so he finally shaved it off. While he wasn't as vain about his appearance anymore, he still cared about status. He continued to display, on a shelf above his desk, the photograph of him with William Jennings Bryan at Chautauqua Park in 1903. The long-deceased Bryan might gaze Godlike from the picture, but Orville had been twenty-eight then, and he was sixty-one now, and neither Bryan nor God nor all the angels of heaven could change that.

"The new furniture is here," she said.

He looked up. The wrinkles on his face made the black hair ridiculous. Margaret had allowed hers to go gray gracefully. "And?" he said.

And the way he looked up at her with such disdain, she couldn't find the courage to say what she'd come to tell him. "I thought you might want to see it," she said.

"Why would I?"

"You could help the delivery men bring it in."

"Aren't we paying them to do that?"

"Of course."

"Well, then."

Orville dismissed her the way he did everybody: he simply stopped speaking. Margaret didn't like being dismissed. At some point she'd have to tell him about George, but not now, not when he was already being unpleasant. "What are you doing?" she said.

"Trying to find the money to pay for all this."

"I've still got a trust fund—"

"No." He glanced back at his books. "Jesus, Prohibition was better. These liquor tariffs are ruining me. That's your fault, you and your goddamn teetotalers." Prohibition had been a victory for the temperance movement, its repeal a boon for the drunkards. But when it ended, the State of Iowa couldn't afford to alienate the teetotalers entirely, so it enacted laws that strictly regulated the distribution of alcohol. "Still cheaper to smuggle the shit in from Chicago," he said.

"I don't want to know about that," Margaret said. Her husband was a criminal, a fact she'd long since stopped denying. And such a crude mouth! In nearly twenty years of marriage, she had never gotten used to his blasphemous language. "Maybe we could sell your roadhouse, if we need the money that badly."

Orville glared at Margaret as if she were the stupidest person on the planet. "Or we could fire Ellen. How much is she costing me? I hate that woman."

"That puts her in an exclusive club, then," Margaret said. Orville's wandering eye was well known throughout Waterton. From what people said, there were few adult females he didn't lust after—Margaret and the dearly departed Birgitta perhaps being the only two. She assumed children were safe from his desires, although one never knew. The rumors were humiliating, but the practical benefit of Orville's philandering was that he left her alone.

Ellen was attractive enough in her way, so his abhorrence of her must be the result of a failed seduction. He'd probably plied his charm and, when that didn't work, gone for his preferred approach of frontal assault, pinching, groping, caressing....

Margaret hoped he'd gotten a knee to the groin for his efforts. Ellen might be the kind to do it.

"Are you accusing me of something, my love?" Orville said, and he bared his teeth in a smile that would turn Satan's head.

"Good heavens, what could anybody accuse *you* of?" she said with sweet acidity, and walked away. She certainly couldn't talk to him about George now.

"By the way," Orville said to her back, "tell old Seaweed to lay off me. I don't like him poking around in my business."

If Orville hated Ellen, he positively loathed Arlen. For years Arlen had been pushing for Waterton to annex Hammon Falls in the hope that the city's tougher ordinances would put a stop to Orville's illegal activities. If the citizens of Hammon Falls didn't vote to incorporate it into an official town, Waterton could absorb it. The vote could happen as early as next year.

She wondered what Orville was scheming now.

"If you want to threaten Mr. Kelper," Margaret said, "do it yourself."

Orville waved her away imperiously. She heard him mutter, "Bitch."

***

Margaret sat on her bed in the dark and looked out the window at the harvest moon. The sky was beautiful tonight, so clear and peaceful. Yet she was not at peace. Truth was, she was frantic about George's return. The man who had written the letter and later spoken to her on the telephone had convinced her he was really her son. He simply knew too much about her to be anybody else. Yes, his voice was deeper now than she remembered, but he was forty years old, not a teenager. And that strange accent...but then, he had lived in Europe for twenty years.

A "V" of Canadian geese winged across the face of the moon, their honking muffled through the glass.

George's letter had come in February, when he was still in Ireland. In it he'd written only that he'd be home "sometime." Their telephone conversation had occurred at the beginning of September. He'd still been vague about his arrival, saying it could be toward the end of the year, perhaps later. He and his new lady friend had things to take care of in New York first.

Margaret lay back on her bed, pulling the shade down over the window. The darkness settled heavily upon her. Orville would be beyond furious. He'd orchestrated the marriage between George and that whore-daughter of his, but that was only to protect the girl's precious reputation. In reality, he'd wanted George dead and relished the news that he was missing and presumed killed in the Great War. She couldn't imagine what would happen when he found out George was alive after all.

But Orville wasn't her main concern. How would the city's people react to their dead second-generation war hero, now miraculously restored to life and returned home? Would they welcome him back or brand him a coward, a fraud?

Would they even care?

More importantly, how would *she* confront this boy, this man, who had abandoned her so long ago? What could they possibly have to say to each other now? Oh, Lord, she'd have to re-introduce herself to him as *Mrs. Orville Curtis.*

Surely George would view her marriage as the ultimate betrayal, of himself and of G.W. If it had been any other man, but Orville Curtis? He'd accuse her of consorting with monsters.

And she was.

Margaret rolled to her side. Her stomach felt queasy. Her choice of spouse wasn't the biggest surprise awaiting poor George. It was true, she'd sold her soul to the devil, but if only he knew *why. Why* was the mitigating circumstance, the justification, the redemptive act that might yet achieve her salvation. She'd never told him about William, by letter or telephone. She'd intended to save up that tidbit of information, to hurt him with it, to devastate him, to punish him. William was George's son. The child he didn't know he had. The child he believed to have been stillborn. The child who knew his father only as a name, a soldierboy gunned down on the fields of France. The child for whom Margaret had bartered away her happiness in order to keep him in his rightful home. What a shock it would be for both of them, two men meeting for the first time, not as spirits in heaven but as living flesh here on earth.

Maybe it would have been better if George *had* been buried in some anonymous grave in Europe. Margaret closed her eyes, but couldn't quench the tears. Her nose ran, her heart ached. That a mother could even *think* such a thing....

The final faint honking of geese faded into the night as the birds passed out of her awareness.

GEORGE
Hammon Falls and Waterton, Iowa
October 1936

George sat on the metal steps outside his trailer, alone, bundled in his flimsy black coat. It was a cold morning, overcast but dry. The sun blazed at the horizon in the gap between earth and clouds. Striated with shades of orange and purple, the clouds rippled like waves on the sea. Aubrey was asleep, and would be for a couple more hours. George liked this time of day. He liked the slow pace of the world's first stirrings, when he could reflect and plan.

The trailer park stretched out for a few blocks in either direction, gravel roads pocked with holes, perpetually muddy, cluttered on both sides with trailers in various states of disrepair. The spaces between them were uneven, with no attempt at straight lines or symmetry. The trailers, baked potatoes all, didn't even set on their lots in the same direction, some oriented north-south, some on the diagonal. Some were right on the road, others well back. Stovepipe chimneys spewed smoke that rose and moored to the clouds. So close to the beautiful forest and spacious homes of Gloire de Matin Island, the park was an eyesore and a slum. Take away the modern trappings, the cars in the yard, the telephone lines, the propane tanks, and the trailer park could be a medieval village like some George saw in France.

Most of the people living here were poor immigrants, a hodgepodge of Germans, Scandinavians, and Mexicans thrown together in an often volatile mix. Some worked in the factories of Westland Avenue and some for the railroads, but many were employed as janitors and groundskeepers at Electrical Park. George had applied for a job there and been turned away.

A few doors down a Mexican family emerged from their trailer: a father, mother, and three children. Every morning the parents walked their kids to the school bus stop at the south end of the park. George found it rather charming. He didn't know the family's name, but he saw them often enough to say hello as they passed. The children were well behaved, always marching in a neat, single-file row. The mother was shy and tended to keep her eyes on the ground, while the father, a small man with a little mustache, was more outgoing. He smiled and waved at George. "*Buenos dias, señor,*" he said.

"*Buenos dias,*" George said.

Other doors opened, and other children came out. The trailer park wasn't much, but it was all these people had. Rumor had it that Waterton was planning to annex Hammon Falls. Trailers themselves were not illegal in Waterton, but trailer parks were. If Hammon Falls were absorbed into the city, everybody here would be turned out of their homes. Although they could move their trailers onto residential lots, how many could afford that? If they had that kind of money, they wouldn't be living in a trailer park in the first place. And what "proper" Waterton neighborhood would welcome an immigrant family anyway?

A cold breeze rose in the north and funneled down the street, bringing with it a promise of rain or snow. George watched the little ones trundle toward the buses and thought briefly about Cora and the child they never had.

***

Inside, he telephoned Memorial Cemetery. Yes, the caretaker said, they had a girl named Cora buried next to Emma Curtis. But it was Cora *Curtis*, not Cora Hammon. Goddamn it, of course Luka would do something like that, the son-of-a-bitch. Cora had died in Buffalo, New York, but George had a feeling she'd find her way back to Waterton, back to her mother. And she did.

Aubrey insisted on coming with him.

They stood before her marker, a simple marble plaque, white with wisps of pink running through the stone. There were fresh daisies on the grave. CORA CURTIS, 1896-1914, ANGEL OF LIGHT.

Angel of Light. Well, Luka had gotten that right.

George had been nervous all the way over. He vowed he'd face this like a man. What a load of shit. It had been so many years in coming, and he was terrified.

Aubrey took his hand in hers and leaned her head against his shoulder. "Isn't her stone lovely?" she said.

George felt as if his legs could no longer bear his weight. He hadn't been this close to Cora in twenty-two years. Here she was, beneath his feet. Beneath his feet. "The world is joined by water," he said, his voice cracking. "You told me that."

"I remember."

"Will you play for her? Like you did for Tommy?"

The clouds were breaking up. Patches of sun and shadow mottled the cemetery. "Of course I will," Aubrey said.

George tried to thank her, but the words wouldn't come. The tears did, though, the raw, primal howl of loss. He dropped to his knees and pounded the ground with his fists. "Oh, Jesus," he wept, "Cora."

Aubrey squeezed his shoulder as he spent his anguish. When he looked up at her he was exhausted. His body ached as if he'd been beaten with hammers. Aubrey smiled. The sun was on her face, setting aglow her white teeth and dark eyes. "There's another shore," she said, "on the other side. You will see her again, George Hammon."

YOUNG WILL
Waterton, Iowa
October 1936

Outside the filling station the first snow of the season was falling, the miserable, sloppy kind, when the temperature was just below freezing and flakes big and wet as raindrops were blown nearly horizontal by a northwest wind.

The snow splatted on the tin roof of the station's unheated garage. Will and the new kid, C.J., ignored the weather. They were busy under the hood of a '31 Lincoln. C.J. was about seventeen, a gangly beanpole with a mop of unruly black hair and six thumbs on each hand, or so it seemed. Luka had taken pity on him and asked Will to hire him as an attendant. The boy was probably the son of some politician Luka was schmoozing. He was more interested in working on engines than in pumping gas, but his skill didn't match his eagerness. Will wouldn't have taken him on, despite Luka's request, except that his friend and former assistant, Jack Reece, had gotten patriotic and enlisted in the army. Concerned about developments in Germany, Jack wanted to be ready when the next war came. "That Hitler fellow's going to be trouble," Jack had claimed. "You'll see." With his friend gone, Will needed somebody at the station, and unfortunately, Luka showed up with C.J. at precisely the right, or wrong, time.

"What're we doing here?" C.J. said.

"I took the generator out. I'm totally rebuilding the electrical."

"Uh-huh," C.J. said, as if Will were speaking in Latin.

"It's not hard. Watch. It's a V-8, see? Look here."

"Okay…?" C.J. he said. He might as well be gawking at the intestines of a cat.

"There are two coils of soft wire wrapped over an iron core. When the current goes through, the core gets magnetized, which draws the contact points together." Will tapped at the wires leading to the battery. "That's what keeps the battery charged. Simple, right? Hand me that gapper."

"Gapper?"

"The little round thing."

C.J. reached into the tool box and found the gapper on his first try. "This?"

Will nodded, which seemed to delight the boy. "We'll check the air gap," he said, "the point gap, and the contacts—"

The bell hose rang as a car pulled up to the gas pumps. "You want me to get that?" C.J. said.

"We'll both go. You're doing fine with the pumping, but you're not so hot with the cash register."

Will wiped the grease from his hands onto a rag and stuffed the rag into the back pocket of his overalls. Donning a coat, he pulled a hat on and the ear flaps down, then exited through the narrow door at the front of the garage, through the office, and outside to the pumps. C.J. tagged along casually so as not to look like what he was, a novice. Will smiled at his awkwardness.

A green '29 Chevrolet with New York license plates was parked in slush next to the office. Sleet mixed with the wet snow, thousands of little ice pellets plinking against the car's metal frame. A man got out of the Chevy. He appeared to be about Will's height, perhaps thirty pounds heavier, wearing flimsy gloves and a worn black coat that didn't look nearly warm enough for the conditions. His hair was dark with streaks of gray at the temple. "Damnedest weather," he said to Will. "A few days ago it was hotter than hell, and now this."

"Hell must've frozen over," Will said. "Welcome to Iowa. What can I do for you?"

"I'd like to see the manager."

Will couldn't identify his accent. The man was trying not to stare at the frosted left lens of his glasses. Everyone did that, so Will wasn't offended. "That'd be me," he said.

"Really?" the man said. "Well. I've been in town for a couple of days. I'm looking for work. I was wondering if you had anything."

Will cocked his head toward C.J. "Sorry, I just hired him. Tried Landon's? Winter's not a good time for ag work, but you never know. They can pay a damn sight better than me."

"Been there," the man said. "No luck."

A piece of sleet bounced off Will's hat, under his good lens, and into his eye. He blinked it away. "How well do you know Waterton? The Iowa Cream Separator sometimes uses temporary help. Might get you on your feet 'til something permanent comes along."

"I'm from here, a long time back," the man said. "Been to the creamery. Nope."

"Hmm," Will said.

"The ballroom at Electrical Park?" C.J. said to Will. "Don't your granddad run that?"

Before Will could respond the man said, "I've got experience as an electrician, too, but no dice. They don't even need a janitor. I've been most everywhere else, so now I'm trying the filling stations."

Will scratched his ear through the flap. It didn't really itch, he just wanted to look like he was thinking. "Don't know what to say. Hey, C.J., at least do his windows, will you? No sense making his trip a total waste.

Check your oil, too?" The man shook his head. C.J. sloshed to the pump to get the glass scraper. "Listen," Will whispered, "the kid's not too bright. I hired him as a favor to my grandfather. I'm guessing he might not work out. Stop back in a few days, maybe I'll have something for you then."

The man shook his hand. "Thanks, I appreciate that."

C.J. returned and cleaned the grime from the Chevrolet's windshield. The sleet intensified for a few moments, then stopped altogether, leaving only snow and wind. "You say you're from here?" Will said. "You don't sound local."

"Been out of the country," the man said. "If you don't mind me asking, what happened to your eye?"

"No idea," Will said. "I was born this way. What's your name, sir?"

The man hesitated. "Mick. Mick O'Leary."

C.J. finished with the all the windows and stepped back proudly. Melting snow was already pulling dirt down from the roof of the Chevy and across the windshield.

Will smiled. "Well, Mick, you don't sound Irish, either."

The man clapped him on the shoulder and climbed back into his car. "No, I don't," he said. "Thanks for your help."

WILL
Waterton, Iowa
October 2008

"I mean," Will said to Kristin, "who's the last person in this world you'd ever expect to meet face-to-face than your father who's been dead twenty years?"

"That's true," the pretty therapist said. They were in the hallway of the hospital. She steadied him as he took tiny steps with a walker.

"The only picture I ever saw of George was as a soldier when he was nineteen. He was forty when he came back. That was seventy-some years ago."

Will's coordination was off. He couldn't seem to get his feet to do what he wanted them to. His big toe came down at the wrong angle, and he stubbed it on the flat linoleum floor, which caused him to lose his balance. His glasses flew off his nose, but Kristin caught him before he fell. "Try to walk normally," she said, picking up the glasses. Before putting them back on for Will, she held them up as if trying to see through the frosted lens. "Heel, toe, heel, toe," she said. "I know it's hard."

"Foot's asleep, is all."

"It's not asleep, Mr. Hammon, it's healing. Healing takes time."

"Nuisance," Will said. "Can't even walk anymore."

"You're going to be fine, Mr. Hammon."

If you don't mind me asking, what happened to your eye?

No idea. But the thing that took the eye, whatever it was, had nearly killed him. George believed Will had died. That's why he had fled the country.

Grandma said the doctors told her I was blue when I was born. It was only after trying to save my mother that they noticed I was breathing.

"A man at forty doesn't look much like the boy at nineteen," Will said, returning to that night in the filling station. "How could I have known it was him?"

"Who, Mr. Hammon?" Katie said. Not Katie, Kristin. Kristin.

"George," Will said impatiently. Hadn't she been listening? "My father. He thought I was dead, too. People say I favor my mother, but I remember I was all bundled up in this coat and silly hat with ear flaps. He couldn't have seen any resemblance. Wouldn't've had any reason to look for one. Said his name was Mick O'Leary. Ha ha. Quite a joke, huh? Mick O'Leary."

Will paused, startled, in a near panic. The Celtic cross! Goddamn it, where did he put Mick's cross? He touched his neck where it should be…No, wait. Come to think of it, he'd never worn it, not now and not then.

"Careful," the therapist said.

The cross was at home, still hanging from the photo of George in Ypres. Of course. Will sighed his relief. "That was close," he said.

"Too close. You can't just stop like that. You'll hurt yourself." Kristin smiled reassuringly. She had no idea what Will was talking about. "Your daughter's coming to visit tonight. She left a message."

Will shook his head. "Sometimes she doesn't recognize me any better than George did."

LUKA
Hammon Falls and Waterton, Iowa
November 1936

Weinshank put his feet up on Luka's mahogany desk and bit into a pastrami sandwich he'd picked up on the way over. "You got a broad polishing your equipment under the desk again?" the lawyer said. Like everyone else, he had grown fat and old. Unlike everyone else, he'd always looked fat and old. Still dressed to the nines, though. Gray three-piece suit – tailored, of course – shiny black shoes, black tie, white fedora with a black band. His face was flushed, and he was sweating. He'd let his nose hairs grow too long.

"I'm a married man," Luka said.

"So was Casanova."

"No, he wasn't." Luka yawned and cracked his knuckles. "There a problem?"

The bulb in the floor lamp next to the desk flickered. "It's hot in here, for one."

"Take your coat off. Anything else?"

Weinshank left his suitcoat on. "D.A.'s investigating your business interests," he said. "Wants a look at your books."

"Again?" A cup of Folger's rested on a coaster on the desk. Luka took a sip. The D.A., a man named Cal Morton, was more nuisance than threat. "Got a search warrant this time?"

"Says he can get one. He plans to convene a grand jury and subpoena them."

Luka nudged Weinshank's feet off the desk.

"Just had it stained again, don't need your smudges."

Weinshank shrugged and took another bite of his sandwich. "I think he'll do it this time."

"Never has before," Luka said. "Anyway, what can he say? I'm a legitimate businessman."

"'Cept for the whores and the rackets and the protection and the smuggling."

Luka smiled. "Except for those."

"And the cops you're greasing, and the councilmen, maybe the mayor himself? And, oh yeah, what about Red Fisher?"

"What about him?"

"You set him up."

"Just being a good citizen, doing my part to get the criminal element off our streets."

"They never intended to bring him out of that alley alive. You knew that."

"So? I kill him, it's murder. They do it, it's resisting arrest."

"If Morton starts in on you, he'll probably dig up the police corruption, too. He can make the Fisher thing stink real bad."

"That's the cops' problem. But there won't be an investigation. I got enough people on the payroll, they'll never let it get that far." The bulb in the lamp popped and went dark. The only light in the library was from the fireplace on the other side of the room. "Shit," Luka said. He rang the servant bell.

"That ain't all," Weinshank said. The fireplace was behind him and to his left, leaving most of face in shadow. "I hear the Phillips brothers are planning to buy the old Timmerman building, fix it up, and open their own roadhouse."

"Like hell. Not in my town. Find a law to keep them out."

"Any law that'll keep them out will shut down Curtis's Garden, too."

This conversation was giving Luka a headache. "You'll think of something."

"Another thing. Landon's wants to buy Hammon Falls, make it part of Waterton."

"Kelper's been threatening that for years."

"It's gonna happen."

"I'll sweeten the council's pot."

"You can't sweeten it like Landon's can. And you know they will."

"Jesus Christ. Any more sunshine to blow up my ass?"

Weinshank lifted the top off his sandwich and used his finger to redistribute ketchup evenly over the meat. "Gimme time," he said.

Ellen knocked on the library door, then entered without waiting for Luka's invitation. "Yes, sir?" she said, her voice venomously professional.

"Can't you see we're sitting in the dark? Get another bulb. And a drink for my lawyer."

"Yes, sir."

Luka watched her leave, the firelight pushing her shadow across the book shelves. "I hate that woman."

Weinshank laughed. "Wouldn't come across for you, huh?"

"Shut up."

"That's what I thought." The lawyer lifted the remnants of his sandwich to his mouth. Before he could take the final bite, though, a quizzical expression crossed his face, as if a question had suddenly occurred to him. He frowned, coughed, and dropped the sandwich to the floor. "What the hell?" he said. He slumped forward onto the desk. The brim of his fedora struck the wood, propelling the hat off his head and forward, where it nearly upset Luka's coffee cup.

"Weinshank!"

Luka shot from his chair and raced around the desk. A line of drool dribbled from Weinshank's lips. In the firelight the slime looked smooth and yellow, with flecks of meat and bread clinging to it like decorations. He must have bitten his tongue, too, because black splotches of blood dotted his trousers.

Luka felt for a pulse on the man's wrist, then neck. There was something in the neck, a quiver, a murmur, a wobble, faint but more than nothing. Luka rang the servant bell again, repeatedly and insistently until Ellen returned on the run. Seeing the lawyer's position, she held a hand to her mouth and inhaled sharply.

"Call an ambulance," Luka said.

"Yes, sir."

As she hurried out the door Luka rose and looked down at this man who for two decades had been his lawyer, his advisor, and, yes, his friend.

"Goddamn it, Weinshank," he said.

***

The funeral was held at the Valley Community Church on the corner of Glimeda and Tindal in Waterton. Most people were surprised Weinshank was being buried in a Christian church. They thought he was a Jew. "With a name like that, how could he *not* be?" they said. Truth was, he was born a Jew, but had had some kind of religious conversion after he left Chicago. Luckily, his adopted faith didn't include legal scruples. Luka knew about the conversion, but neither man ever spoke about it. For all Weinshank's bluster and shrewdness, he had been a private person, keeping his politics and religion to himself. He had a wife and several kids, although Luka had never met them until now.

The son-of-a-bitch never invited me to his home, he thought, with more regret than malice. The minister began the service by inviting the congregation to sing from the hymnal located in front of each of them. A pipe organ bellowed a solemn introduction and the people's voices soared, all six verses with the chorus repeated between each. Luka couldn't carry a tune, so he didn't join in.

Margaret, who was not even bothering with a pretense of grief, sat primly in the pew to his left, wearing a shapeless white dress. *White*. At a funeral. She didn't have to like Weinshank, but she could at least show proper respect. Jesus, the man was dead. Wasn't she the one always bitching about protocol?

"Well, I'm not a Wesleyan," she'd said before the service. "Anyway, I thought he was a Jew."

232

What she'd meant was, These people have been ostracizing me for years, so what do I care if I flout their conventions?

Next to her was Arlen Kelper, come to gloat at the death of his better. But at least he went through the motions, singing when requested to sing, praying when requested to pray, receiving communion when it was offered. Luka did none of these things.

Will was on the other side of Kelper. He was wearing the new suit he'd bought with his own money for this occasion. Luka looked over at him as he sang. He'd grown into a handsome young man – too bad about the eye, though – with Cora's pouty lips and fair expression. Twenty-two years after her death, Luka couldn't stop making the comparison. Will hadn't cared much for Weinshank, but came to the funeral out of simple decency. He was a class act, that kid. Class and decency were traits to be admired and, in people other than Will, exploited. Even Will had occasionally served Luka's purposes.

A few judges were scattered throughout the pews, a few councilmen, a number of other lawyers, none of whom would have pissed on Weinshank if he was on fire. Cal Morton crouched in the back. He glared at Luka the entire time, not paying the least attention to the service. The mayor chose not to attend, mostly, Luka thought, because Weinshank was viewed by many as an unsavory character, certainly not the kind of man a politician seeking re-election could admit to knowing. Ironically, the mayor was one of the few people who actually liked Weinshank, and had his secretary send a nice flower arrangement.

Stepping to the lectern next to the altar, the minister, Reverend Somebody, said a prayer, then read Weinshank's obituary word for word as it had appeared in the *Record*. Seemed kind of impersonal, but it's what the wife wanted. Luka was more surprised at the man's age. Born in 1860? That made him seventy-six years old. No wonder his heart gave out.

Paintings, undoubtedly Biblical scenes, adorned the walls of the church, although they didn't mean much to Luka. He wasn't exactly a regular churchgoer. Christian theology was beyond him, and practical religion was best left to wives and children. Sure, bring 'em up right, but leave him out of it.

One of Weinshank's kids approached the front, brushing the casket with his palm in affection or grief. At the lectern the young man read a poem he'd written for his father.

After that, and another hymn, and more prayers, and *another* hymn, the pall bearers came up the aisle to retrieve the coffin. The family followed behind, weeping or trying not to, and then ushers showed up to release the congregation row by row.

So many rituals. If Weinshank had stayed a Jew, Luka wondered, what would that service have been like? Probably the same mumbo-jumbo, only in Hebrew instead of English.

The usher stopped at the end of his row and nodded. Luka rose, followed by Margaret, Kelper, and Will. They stepped out into the aisle. Cal Morton was several rows behind them, awaiting his turn to be dismissed. As they passed him, the D.A. said, "Who's gonna keep your goddamned ass out of jail now, Curtis?"

Luka smiled and touched a finger to his lips. "Language, Cal," he whispered. "It's a church."

GEORGE
Waterton, Iowa
November 1936

Even with an electric chandelier above and a fire in the hearth in the corner, the room was dark. Maybe it was just George's mood. He and Aubrey were seated in the main dining room on the second floor of the Royal-Sampson Hotel. The floor tiles were a mosaic, polished to a shine that reflected the flames and accentuated the pink and white color scheme. Their table was next to a window that overlooked Commercial Street in Waterton. It was almost seven-thirty, and a light snow was falling through the spheres of light from the streetlamps below. A car parked next to the curb in front of the Waterton Building across the street, and a man got out.

George sighed. He flagged down a waiter and ordered a glass of wine.

"George Hammon, you'll not be having wine," Aubrey said. She was wearing a light blue gown. Her long hair was pulled back and tied with a simple bow behind her head. Her eyes were lovely, as always, nearly black yet sparkling in the firelight. "It's poison to you."

The waiter paused. George nodded and waved him away. "You sound like Suzanne," he said to Aubrey. "She was always nagging me about that."

"She was a wise woman, then. You've done so well. You don't need this."

There were only seven or eight other customers in the dining area. Their voices were a low hum that mixed pleasantly with the crackle of the fire.

"It's only one drink," George said.

"When have you *ever* had just one drink?"

George looked at his wristwatch. "She's late. Maybe she's not coming."

"She waited twenty-two years for you," Aubrey said, clasping his hands. "She's coming."

"Christ, what was I thinking? We should have stayed in Ireland."

"And done what?"

"Avoided this evening."

"It was time, and you know it."

George checked his watch again. "Damn it."

The waiter returned with a bottle of French wine and two glasses.

"None for me," Aubrey said.

"Leave the bottle," George said.

"No," Aubrey said. "I'll go right now if you start drinking."

"I need you with me," George said.

The waiter glanced at Aubrey, then shrugged. He set the bottle and one glass on the table in front of George. "Will you be ordering from the menu this evening?"

"We're not all here yet," George said. He popped the cork on the wine. The *plocking* sound reminded him of the gunshots he'd heard in France and Belgium. Those memories didn't cause him any particular distress. In fact, other than Mick's death at the Somme River, nothing much about the war haunted him anymore. That was probably because losing Cora first had already damaged him as much as he could be damaged. "An older lady will be joining us," he said to the waiter. "Come back when she arrives."

The waiter inclined his head slightly, and left.

George filled the wine glass. Aubrey glared at him as he slowly drank it. He filled it again, and emptied it again.

"I'm ashamed of you, George Hammon."

George laughed bitterly. He filled his cup a third time and toasted her. "Here, here."

Aubrey stood up. "I can't do it, George. I can't meet her like this. I shouldn't have to explain you to her."

"I'm not drunk."

"Yet."

"Don't go."

"Don't drink."

"I have to."

"Then I have to go." There was pity in her eyes, but more than that—disgust, perhaps. Anger, certainly. "Where is the man," she said, "who made that promise to a dead friend? Who spenty twenty years trying to fulfill it? Where is that man?"

George lowered his eyes. "He's still here, somewhere."

"Find him," she said. "I'll take a taxi."

"You'll be there when I get home?"

"You know I will." Aubrey stooped and kissed his cheek. "Be gentle, George. You've hurt her. Let her say what she will. *Slán go fóill, anam cara.*"

George watched her cross the room and retrieve her coat from the coat-check counter. Her shadow from the firelight preceded her. Beneath her, her image reflected imperfectly on the polished tiles. She didn't look back.

***

An hour and another bottle of wine later an old woman appeared at the dining room door. Margaret had grown frail, her hair white, her face wrinkled, her gait unsteady. She'd always seemed ancient to George, although when he left she'd been younger than he was now. Sixty-three this year, she looked eighty. She was decked out in a ridiculously formal evening gown, dark green and too loose at the shoulders, with a fur stole around her neck. A huge diamond adorned her left ring finger, its glittery facets noticeable clear across the room. The ring was nothing like G.W.'s, the one she'd worn when George was a child, the one she now wore on her right hand.

Margaret paused at the entrance to gaze at the other customers. George had told her on the telephone he'd be there with a dark-haired woman, so she perused the couples first. He could see the distress building in her—what if she no longer recognized her own son?

Jesus, he didn't want to do this. He rose halfway from his seat and waved. His head was spinning, and he slumped back down.

Margaret visibly took a deep breath, nodded, and approached his table. Despite her apparent feebleness and silly attire, she still retained the aura of dignity George remembered.

With some effort he steadied himself and stood again. He held her chair out for her.

"Mother," he said.

She didn't sit.

Her lower lip quivered. Her eyes moistened. "George?" she said, her voice cracking.

"Fit as a fiddle," he said, "and ready to hang."

She spent a long time studying him, as if trying to reconcile this thick-waisted middle-aged man with the teenager she'd known. His hair was streaked with gray now and thinning on top.

He opened his arms to embrace her. "It's really me," he said. "I've come home."

She backed away a step, then slapped him furiously across the face, the band of G.W.'s ring scratching his cheek. "Damn you," she said.

The other customers looked up, but quickly averted their eyes in awkward embarrassment.

"Too late," George said. He touched a finger to his cheek. He wasn't bleeding.

"You're drunk," she said.

"You're married," he said.

That seemed to defuse her anger. George pushed her chair in for her as she sat down. He sat across from her.

"Well," she said.

"Well." George looked out the window at Commercial Street. The snow had stopped. After a few moments of silence, he tapped on the wine bottle. "I assume you still don't—"

"No."

"Mind if I do?"

"You will whether I mind or not."

George poured the last of the wine into his glass. "Where's your husband?"

"Where's your...whatever she is?"

"She had to leave."

"I'm sorry, I was delayed."

"*Who's* your husband?"

Margaret watched the fire in the hearth. "You sound so foreign."

"I lived in France for sixteen years."

"I didn't know you could speak French."

"I can now."

"You're from Iowa. You were born here. How can you talk like that?"

"I've had a little too much. I'm slurring. It sounds worse than it is."

The waiter approached with menus. "*Now?*"

George accepted the menus from him. "Now."

"I'm not hungry," Margaret said.

The waiter sighed impatiently.

"We'll order," George said. If they were eating, they wouldn't have to talk as much. "Give us a few minutes."

Another interminable period of silence followed. Neither of them looked at the menus. George finished his wine.

"George," Margaret said finally.

"So who's the lucky guy?" he said.

Margaret folded her right hand over the diamond ring, hiding it beneath G.W.'s. "Lucky?" she said. "You'd have to ask him about that."

"*Who?*"

"Where are you staying, George, you and...?"

"Aubrey. She's Irish. We bought a trailer north of Electrical Park."

"Naturally," Margaret said to herself.

"There a problem?"

"Orville owns that property. Nothing but thugs and illegal immigrants live there."

"Orville Curtis? Luka? I haven't thought about that son-of-a-bitch in years. He's still alive, huh? I haven't seen him around the park."

Margaret looked uncomfortable. "So. This Aubrey person. She's your wife?"

"No."

Margaret nodded as if she'd expected that answer. "Well," she said.

"You don't approve."

"I don't care anymore, George. I'm tired."

She really didn't care. George could see it in her face. That stung. He was prepared for moral outrage, not apathy. "Obviously you're still at the house on Gloire de Matin."

"Of course."

"The mystery man's there, too?"

"Don't do that. You know I hate being teased."

"Dammit, Mother, *what is his name?*"

"Not now, George. I don't want to talk about me. We have so many other things to catch up on. Twenty-two years."

"I want to know about you, too," George said. "It's not just me."

"You're the one who left."

"You know why."

Margaret exhaled slowly. "Yes."

Sometime, somehow, George hoped she might apologize for what she and Luka had done. Maybe some night she would. This was not that night. "You can say her name, Mother—"

"They said you were dead. The British military. I got a letter that said you died in Europe somewhere. They sent a photograph of you in uniform."

So that's what happened. His superiors declared him dead. He'd spent all those years worrying that he'd get arrested for desertion, and they weren't even looking for him. "A news correspondent took that photo after Ypres. He said it wasn't suitable, so he gave me the print." George smiled grimly. "The British military was too late, Mother. I was already dead when I got to Europe."

"You've become cynical."

"Imagine that."

Outside a car horn blared. The wind was coming up. Three of the other customers left the dining room.

"Are you working?" Margaret said.

"I'm looking. We have some money saved back."

"Anything promising?"

"There's this one-eyed kid runs a filling station over on the east side. He might have something for me."

Margaret's eyes widened. She brought her hand to her mouth. Then she did the most amazing thing: she laughed. Inexplicably. Uncontrollably. Insanely. She laughed as George had never seen her laugh. She laughed so hard tears rolled down her cheeks. Her nose ran. It was clear she was trying to hold herself back, but the more she tried, the more she laughed.

George offered her his handkerchief. "What's funny?"

Margaret dabbed her eyes, blew her nose. "I'm sorry," she said between giggles. "I can't talk anymore. We'll meet again."

With that she rose and came as close to fleeing the room as a sixty-three-year-old woman could. It was the second time he'd been abandoned in one evening.

George stared at the door his mother had just vacated, wondering what the hell was going on. The waiter came back and collected the menus.

"More wine?" he said.

"More wine."

Will thrashed in his bed in Salk Hospital's ICU. He'd been home less than a month after the stroke when a fever and wracking cough sent him back to the emergency room. Pneumonia, the doctor said. It was dangerous at any age, but more so in the elderly. Will would be ninety-five come March. He'd been coughing so much his ribs ached.

He was hooked up to IV antibiotics, anti-pain medication, muscle relaxants, and who knew what else. Bags of fluid. More needles and tubes. More bedsores. More poking, prodding, and catheters. Christ.

He was aware of people around him.

Katie was here.

Charlie was here.

A nurse was here.

"Am I gonna die tonight?" Will said, without strong feelings about it either way.

"You're awful sick, Dad," Katie said. She was holding his hand.

He looked at her. Everything seemed dark, but he could see she'd been crying.

"Don't," he said.

"You'll be okay, Grandpa," Charlie said.

Will's friend Jack stood behind Charlie with the same cocky, devil-may-care expression he always had. He was still thirty-one, his hair slicked back, his face unshaved. He was wearing an army uniform. *I went to fight the little German prick and got stuck with the Japs instead*, he laughed. *Don't it figure?*

"Jack?" Will said.

It's all a big adventure, Jack said. *Get off your ass and get on with it, will ya? Have a beer for me. Put it on my tab.*

"You don't have a tab," Will said.

The nurse wrote something on a clipboard.

"Dad?" Katie said, but it wasn't Katie. It was Margaret. She was sitting in a white room with white furniture, at least that was how Will remembered it. Her dress was white. Her hair was white. Even her eyes. Sunlight slanted in through an open window and ignited the whiteness. Everything was suffused in white, softened by its glowing aura. There was a pleasant breeze. It was spring. Margaret's face was ghostly and grim.

Shhh, she said. *Just listen. He was told you were stillborn. Your mother had complications. She didn't make it. He thought you were dead, too. That's why he left. He thought you were dead, Will.*

After they contacted me, Estella and I went to the hospital in Buffalo to bring you home. Took the train all the way to New York. It was so uncomfortable. Cold and cramped and the people were rude. The hospital was one of those awful sisters-of-the-poor charity places that's filthy and smells bad. Before the doctor would let me see you, he insisted on explaining the situation. To prepare me for the shock, he said. Wanamaker was his name. He had old-fashioned mutton chops. Oh, I remember that conversation like it was just yesterday!

"The girl was hemorrhaging," he said. "She was feverish and weak and in terrible pain. She was critical when she came to us. The baby was breech. With that and the bleeding, we didn't dare risk natural childbirth. We decided to do a Caesarian section. It was the only way we felt we could save her life. We did everything we could, but the pregnancy was ectopic. The child had attached itself to the aortic root. The poor girl had no chance. The blood loss was too great. She never woke up from the ether."

Margaret paused. "What about the child?" I asked Doctor Wanamaker. "Why did my son abandon him?"

He said, "The baby wasn't breathing when we delivered him. He was blue and had a massive infection covering the left side of his face. He had peritonitis in the left eye socket. It was the worst prenatal infection I'd ever seen. Frankly, we felt there was no hope for him, so we set him aside in order to save the mother. A nurse broke the news to your son—prematurely, it turns out. He tried to force his way into the operating room, but orderlies managed to stop him at the door. I heard him screaming, Mrs. Hammon. I can't imagine his horror at what he saw. There was so much blood. He fled, and who can blame him?

"The child gasped. A little hiccup of air, that's all. We were astonished he could be alive. Even so, we had very little hope for his survival. I've seen less severe infection kill otherwise healthy adults. But he was a strong boy, and he gradually improved. There was nothing we could do about the eye, of course, but the infection cleared up. To be honest, it wasn't anything we did. The boy just wanted to live.

"Your son never told us his name. When he brought his wife in, she was already critical. We had no time for formalities. Afterward, he was gone. We were making preparations for an orphanage when a doctor who'd spoken to him on the train mentioned a nearby boarding house. We contacted the police, who went to their room. Inside they found a novel. The girl had scribbled in pencil over and over, 'Mrs. Cora Hammon,' 'Mrs. Cora Hammon,' 'Mrs. Cora Hammon.' The officer said the handwriting was flowery and delicate, with little hearts drawn in. The 'Mrs.' was underlined. It made him sad. Part of a train ticket was used as a book marker. It listed the point of departure as Waterton, Iowa. That's how we found you."

Margaret sat in the white room, hands folded primly in her lap. She became very quiet. The sun washed over her, the breeze teased her hair. Birds chirped in the trees outside. *He thought you were dead, Will,* she said.

In his hospital bed Will laughed. "I wasn't dead then," he said, "and I'm not dead now."

"Good for you, Dad," Katie said. "Keep on fighting. We'll be right here."

Margaret was gone, but this room was white, too. There were no windows, though, no sunshine, no breeze, no bird sounds. Katie smiled hopefully.

Jack was still standing behind Charlie. He grinned his goofy grin. *You hang in there, buddy,* he said. *You're living for both of us.*

He turned away, fading to nothing as he spun.

"Bye, Jack," Will said over Charlie's shoulder.

"Huh?" Charlie said.

LUKA
Hammon Falls, Iowa
November 1936

When Weinshank first arrived in Waterton in the early 'teens, his Chicago connections set him up on West Fourth in the prestigious law firm of Rogers, Randle, and Baum. That arrangement lasted maybe a year. Annoyed by his bosses' stodgy insistence on protocol—actually, simply *having* bosses annoyed him—Weinshank decided to go solo. He relocated to a cramped shit hole inside a tenement building on South Street that had once housed reefer dens and wire-job abortionists.

Despite his chosen surroundings, he dressed impeccably in public and, more importantly, was always prepared in court. Luka's other lawyers might be smarter and smoother, but what Weinshank lacked in brains and style he made up for with audacity, doggedness, and plain brute force. Nobody worked harder than he did. As a result, he accomplished things better lawyers wouldn't even try. If he wanted to mingle with dope fiends and baby killers in private, then that was his business.

Now that the son-of-a-bitch was dead, Luka was going to have to make do with a lesser and, sadly, more scrupulous attorney named Aaron Whitney.

***

Luka was in the library. He put his head down on his mahogany desk. It was cold in here. The radiator alone didn't put out enough heat for a room this size, and he was too tired to bother with a fire. What a tangle his life had become.

Before Weinshank had so inconsiderately died, he'd circulated a petition among the citizens of Hammon Falls requesting a vote for incorporation, which would slam the door on Landon's expansion plans and keep Waterton's greedy hands and laws off Luka's affairs. More than half of Hammon Falls' residents had signed it, so that was a good sign. A simple majority was all that was needed. Weinshank had just prepared the brief to submit to Iowa's Secretary of State when he kicked the bucket.

Meanwhile, Arlen Kelper had muddied the waters further by tying roadhouse licensing in with the incorporation vote. The Phillips brothers had bought the old Timmerman building, as Weinshank said they would. They recently announced their intention to open another roadhouse in the spring, in direct competition with Curtis's Garden. Kelper had pulled some strings for them. Luka couldn't figure out what the bastard was up to, but Weinshank had known. He'd planned to crush Kelper's scheme and then rub his face in his defeat.

Now all that was up in the air.

A breeze pushed in through the fireplace. Damn her, Ellen must have forgotten to close the flue. Luka stood up. Hanging behind the desk was the photograph of him shaking hands with William Jennings Bryan in Chautauqua Park in 1903. A lifetime ago. He was twenty-eight that year. His boxing career was just starting. He was an up-and-comer in the business world, too, with everything ahead of him. His first wife Emma, his *real* wife, was alive, four years removed from the cancer that would claim her. They still had his brother Carlin's dog then. What was its name? Hannah?

Luka shook his head. He hadn't thought about that mutt since Emma died. He'd never liked the damn thing, but Cora adored it.

Ah, Cora. She would have turned forty on October 8. She *should* have turned forty.

Luka's sentimentality was a weakness he couldn't afford. Yet surely he could be forgiven an occasional lapse, a moment to lament the little girl who never got to grow up.

The telephone rang.

To hell with it. He was going to bed.

The phone rang again.

Where was Ellen? Wasn't he paying the bitch? Why didn't she answer it?

The phone rang again.

Shit. Luka snatched the receiver from its cradle. "What?"

"Grandpa?"

"Will?"

"C.J. stole money from the register."

"Who's C.J.?"

"The kid you asked me to hire."

Luka couldn't place him, but he had more important things on his mind. "So?"

"So he's been stealing."

"How much?"

"Enough."

"Goddamn it, Will, what's the problem? Fire his ass."

"I would have but, I mean, since you wanted him here, I thought—"

"You can't have dishonest employees. That's no way to do business. Fire him. You won't hurt my feelings."

"I was hoping you'd say that. Thanks, Grandpa."

Luka hung up without saying goodbye. Will was a fine young man, but Jesus. Someone steals from you, you get rid of him. How difficult was that?

GEORGE
Waterton, Iowa
November 1936

Aubrey snuggled behind him in bed, her breasts pressed against his back. She draped her arm over his shoulder and caressed his chest with her fingertips. The wind had come up outside, rattling the trailer's frame. "It went badly," she said.

"She started off slapping me and ended up laughing at me and walking out," he said.

"I understand the slap, but why laughter?"

"No idea. I told her I was looking for work at a filling station."

"That's funny?"

"You tell me." George rolled to his back. The ceiling was paneled with cheap plaster squares, the same grayish off-white as the drywall. He could feel the trailer's narrow confines closing in on him. It was smaller than his apartment in Paris and the first two flats in Ireland, though not Monto. The place was a dump, not worth the price they paid for it. And, it turns out, the money had gone directly into Luka Curtis's pocket. George wasn't surprised Curtis had become a slum lord. "I drank too much," he said.

"I know."

"Shouldn't drink at all," he said.

"I know."

"I'm sorry."

"I know." Aubrey rose to her elbow and kissed his forehead. "I still want to meet her. I shouldn't have left you tonight."

"Story of my life."

"You're pouting again."

"I'm drunk."

"Go to sleep."

George folded his arms around her. "I don't deserve you."

Aubrey smiled. Even in the dark she was radiant. "I know," she said.

***

"Mick O'Leary, wasn't it?" the one-eyed kid said. The morning had dawned cold and snowy. By noon the snow had ended and soupy sunshine oozed through breaks in the overcast.

"Good memory," George said, squinting against the weak light. Wine gave him the most horrendous hangovers. "You told me to stop back, maybe you'd have work for me."

"Depends. I had to let one of my boys go. What can you do?"

Other than the missing eye, the kid had surprisingly delicate features, not the kind of rough-and-tumble look you'd expect in a grease monkey. He was clean-shaven, well-groomed, with smooth skin and full lips. Margaret had found something about him hilarious.

"What do you need done?" George said. "I've been an electrician, fisherman, handyman, you name it. I even dug trenches. Then filled them back in."

"You in the war?"

"Yeah."

"On our side, right?"

"The accent is French, not German."

"But you used to live around here?" the kid said.

"Long story."

"Well, Mick, my electricity's fine, and I don't need any trenches dug. Know anything about mechanical work?"

"Fix-up jobs, is all. No formal training, just what I could figure out on my own. I know my way around an engine."

"We'll see about that."

"Then I'm hired?"

"Name's Will," the kid said, shaking George's hand. "Screw up and you're gone."

George nodded. "Fair enough. Thanks, Will. When do I start?"

"Doing anything right now?"

"Nope."

"We'll keep it simple today. Ever pumped gas?"

"I learn by doing."

Will led George to the pumps. "These are Tokheim pumps. We only sell Red and Blue, no Ethyl. Every ding's a gallon. Watch the dial. I don't cheat anybody."

They headed back toward the station, stopping outside the door next to a rack containing various automotive products. "Always check their oil and wash their windows. Oil's right here. Know the right weight to use. Come on in."

George followed him inside. "Nice place," he said. "You keep it clean."

"That'll be one of your jobs, too." Will patted the cash register. "Can you make change?"

"I can add and subtract. How hard can it be?"

"Kid I just fired had a problem. Subtracting from the drawer and adding to his pocket."

"You don't have to worry about me. I only steal from my friends."

Will glanced at him uneasily, and just for an instant his petulant lips looked familiar. George flashed an *I'm joking* smile.

"Hang on to this," Will said. He slid an index card into George's shirt pocket. "It's our current oil and gas price list. Charge our customers fairly and treat them right, got it?"

"Got it, boss."

A refrigerator stood against the wall next to the register. Will took out two bottles of Dr. Pepper. "Want one?" he said, popping the tops off in the opener built into the side of the fridge.

"Wouldn't be my first choice."

"Better be when you're at work."

"In that case, sure, I'll have one." He accepted the bottle but didn't drink.

Will downed half of his in one long guzzle. He sat on edge of the stool behind the register, one foot on the floor and the other propped on the support slat between the stool's legs. There was a bench opposite the fridge, just outside the door that must lead back to the service bays. A table stood next to the bench, cluttered with the year-old issues of *Popular Mechanics* and yesterday's edition of the *Waterton Record*. Will indicated for George to have a seat. "Drink it before it gets warm," he said.

George sat down and took a swig. He didn't mind Dr. Pepper, except that it reminded him of Cora, who loved the stuff. "How is it you've got your own station already, Will? What are you, twenty?"

"Twenty-two," Will said. "My grandfather set me up. I used to work at Bob's, but Grandpa had this place and told me I was ready to run my own business. I've done it, too. Keep the books myself."

"Bob's Standard? Over on Franklin?"

"Yeah, you know him?"

"Hell, Bob was two hundred years old when I was here."

"When was that?"

"1914."

Will drained the last of his soda pop. "That's the year I was born."

"Bob still alive?"

"Like he'll ever die. Cranky old bastard."

George smiled. "Yup, that's Bob." He nodded in the direction of the garage. "What are you working on back there?"

"P-O-S Ford. 1927. Cost more to fix the damn thing than to buy a new one. Owner says it has sentimental value."

"P-O-S?"

"Piece of shit."

"What's wrong with it?"

"Come on, I'll show you." Will stood up. "Better yet, you can show me how smart you really are about cars."

George set his unfinished Dr. Pepper on the table. "Uh oh," he said, "pressure's on."

Will held the door to the garage open for him. There were two bays. A rusted out bucket of bolts occupied one of them. It might have been green once. Corroded chunks of metal flaked off when Will ran his hand over the hood, which stood open. "See what I mean?" he said. "And the engine's worse than the body."

George walked around the car, examining it from all sides. In contrast to the crumbling body, the tires were brand new, which seemed sort of silly. "You'll need more than tools to fix this thing."

"I tried sprinkling magic pixie dust on it."

"Divine intervention'd be more like it. Whose is it?"

"Maybe you know him. Frank Perkins? Lives on Lafayette? About Grandpa's age, sixties or seventies. He's been around since the '80s."

George shook his head. "Doesn't ring a bell, and I knew a lot of people." He blew on his hands. "It's cold back here. Don't you believe in heat?"

"You'll be working so hard you won't notice the cold."

"Something to look forward to."

Will gazed at him curiously. "You left town in 1914?"

"Best of my recollection. Why?"

"You must've heard of my Grandpa. Everyone knew him, even then."

"What's his name?"

"Orville Curtis."

Suddenly the world seemed very, very quiet. The only sound was George's own breathing, his own heartbeat. "I'm sorry," he said, thinking he must have misheard, "*Luka* Curtis?"

"Yeah, he used to be a fighter or something. Short for *palooka*."

"You could say I knew him as well as anyone did. And I know for a fact he didn't have any grandkids."

"You must be thinking of someone else, Mick. I mean, here I am. I grew up in his house."

George gaped at Will, at the one eye, the unblemished skin, the full, pouty lips. "You never told me your last name, Will."

"Hammon," the boy said. "Will Hammon."

YOUNG WILL
Waterton, Iowa
November 1936

"Hammon," Will said. "Will Hammon."

Mick stepped back. He looked a little bewildered and a lot angry. "This is some kind of joke, right?" he said. "I get it, that's why she laughed at dinner the other night. It was a set-up. Her little revenge."

"What the hell are you talking about? My name *is* Will Hammon! My Grandpa *is*—"

"Knock it off, Will. There was only one Hammon family in Waterton then, Margaret and her son George. That's it. Luka only had one daughter, and she died without kids."

Will folded his arms across his chest. "Maybe it's not a good idea for you to work here."

"Look, Will, I don't mean to piss you off, but you've had your fun. Enough, okay? I still need the job. We can get along, just admit it's all a gag, and I won't mention it again."

"Luka's daughter's name was Cora," Will said, reaching into his pocket for his wallet. "She died in Buffalo, New York. This is a picture of her."

All the color drained from Mick's face as he held the photo. Tears filled his eyes, his hands shook. "Why do you have this?" he said, his voice barely audible.

Will took the picture back. "What have I been saying? *She was my mother.*"

Mick staggered forward, then clutched at his stomach. "Jesus fucking Christ," he said, and threw up on the engine block of Frank Perkins' '27 Ford.

Will grabbed him to keep him from falling. "You okay, Mick? Here, sit back."

Mick collapsed against the car's rear left fender. The rusted metal bent under his weight, but didn't buckle. He put his face in his hands. "No," he said. "No. No."

"What is it? What's the matter?"

"Give me a minute," Mick said.

Will went into the back for rags, a mop, and a bucket of water, moving slowly to allow Mick time to compose himself. When he returned the strange man was still sitting against the Ford, head bowed, hands folded as if in prayer.

"Mick?"

"I'll clean it up," he said softly.

"You don't have to do that," Will said. "Go on home. We'll get a proper start tomorrow."

Mick took a few deep breaths and pushed himself up and away from the car's fender. "Thanks, Will. Maybe I will."

"Need me to drive you?"

"I'll be all right," Mick said.

"What happened?" Will said.

"The joke was on me after all," Mick said. "She gets the last laugh." He looked directly into Will's one eye. "Well, not the *last* one."

"I still don't know what you're talking about."

Mick opened the door into the station, passed the register, and stepped out into the cold November afternoon. Will followed him to his Chevy.

Mick climbed behind the wheel. As the engine fired, he said, "That picture of Cora?"

"Yeah?"

"She was your mother?"

"Yeah, she was."

Mick spit a wad of vomit onto the pavement. "Cora was my wife, Will."

And he drove away.

MARGARET
Hammon Falls, Iowa
November 1936

Margaret, Orville, and Will sat tensely at the dining room table as Ellen served them supper. The entrée was a pheasant Luka had shot last weekend on a hunting trip. There was no wind outside, no rain, no sound to rattle the windows or cause the house's secret places to creak.

Will was seething—with fury, confusion, something. Margaret knew what was bothering him. If he'd learned George was alive, his insides must be churning. It would be like the dead coming back to life for both men. Thankfully, Will chose not to speak his mind tonight. Whether or not Will knew about George, Margaret still hadn't found the right time to tell Orville.

Maybe the time would never be right.

At the moment Orville was immersed in some legal document. His feelings were less complicated than Will's or Margaret's. He was concerned about the only thing that *ever* concerned him: money. His new attorney, Mr. Whitney, had presented to the State Attorney General the petition which called for the citizens of Hammon Falls to vote for incorporation. If Hammon Falls became a town unto itself, Orville believed his "business" ventures would be safe. Margaret was beyond caring about anything Orville did.

Ellen cut slices of pheasant and lifted them onto each plate.

"It smells wonderful," Margaret said.

"Thank you, ma'am."

Will glowered.

Orville ignored his food. "Ellen, get Whitney on the phone."

"Yes, sir." Ellen scurried out of the room. She always seemed relieved, Margaret thought, to leave Orville's presence.

Orville glanced up at Will. "What's the matter with you?"

"Nothing."

"You fire that kid?"

"Yeah."

"Good. Can't have that kind of thing." He slid the document into a folder. "Maggie, after I talk to Whitney, I need to head to the trailer park. Goddamn immigrants are too stupid to know what's best for them unless I'm there to explain it to them."

"May I be excused?" Will said to Margaret.

"You haven't eaten anything."

"I'm not hungry."

Ellen poked her head in the door. "Mr. Whitney is on the line, sir."

Orville rose from the table. Neither Margaret nor Will spoke as he left the room. "What's this shit about inheritance?" he said into the telephone, then kicked the door shut.

"Please stay," Margaret said to Will.

He glared at her. After a few moments of uncomfortable silence he said, "Is it true?"

Margaret looked down at her hands. "Yes."

"How long have you known?"

"He wrote me in February."

Will pounded the table with his fist. "My father is alive, and *you didn't think you should tell me*?"

"I had to be sure myself first. It was a shock to me, too."

Will hadn't cried since he was a boy being teased in school. He was crying now, tears from a single eye. "You said he died in the war. A hero, just like your first husband. That soldierboy picture of him has hung in my room forever. Doesn't even look like him. I'm going to take it down."

"You'll do no such thing. He was nineteen then. People change. He did go to war, and until I got his letter, I thought he *had* died."

"He knew about me, and he still ran away?"

"It's not that simple, Will."

"How complicated can it be? Grandma, the son-of-a-bitch *abandoned* me."

Margaret inhaled slowly. "Language, Will. Come with me."

She rose and exited the door opposite Orville's phone conversation. Will followed.

All three meals were untouched. Ellen would be hurt.

Margaret went down the hall to the library. There was no fire in the hearth. The room was cold. She sat in a chair next to the coffee table, away from Orville's mahogany desk. She knew what went on under that desk. Will came in behind her. He switched on the overhead light.

"No," Margaret said. "Leave it off. Sit down."

Will sat across from her. The only light was what seeped in under the library's two doors. It was just enough to limn Will's face in pale ochre and paint his skin in tones of black and gray. She could only imagine how she looked to him, in her black dress, in a black room, with her black mood. Like a black widow spider, perhaps, slowly drawing her prey in.

"Grandma?"

"Shhh," she said. "Just listen." In almost complete darkness she told him a story. With winter coming, in a chilly room with closed windows and silence from the outside world, no bird sounds, no wind, no warmth, no movement, Margaret told him the story of his mother, of his birth, and of his father's flight.

When she was done she folded her hands in her lap. "He thought you were dead, Will."

GEORGE
Hammon Falls, Iowa
November 1936

The Oak River was calm, reflections of city lights barely rippling on its black surface. The air was cold, but the sky was clear and the stars crisp and bright. This time of year Orion rose early. Orion the Hunter. It had always been George's favorite constellation, although not for any symbolic reasons he was aware of. He just liked its shape.

A lifetime ago he used to walk this way, coming home from Kline's at night, stopping by the river to enjoy the sights and sounds and, when the wind carried away the pollution of the Westland factories, the smells. Most everything in Waterton was different now, but this little spot remained unspoiled.

"Like a night in Ireland," Aubrey said, squeezing his arm affectionately.

Several large crows alit close by and pecked at something under a bench. They flew off as George and Aubrey approached.

"The nurse told me he was dead," George said. "What's the kid trying to pull? I don't have a son."

"It's a terrible joke," Aubrey said, "if that's what it is."

"She was a nurse. She would know. Wouldn't she know?"

"She should," Aubrey said.

"'The baby wasn't breathing,' the nurse said. 'It was blue, with a massive infection over its left eye. Peritonitis. The doctors set it aside to try to save the mother,' she said."

The crows swung around for another helping of whatever they'd been eating, cawing at each other over the best bits. "Why don't you fly south?" George said, lunging at the birds and scattering them again.

"So the child was stillborn," Aubrey said. "That's what she told you?"

"She said *not breathing* and *blue* and *infection*. What else could that mean? If it wasn't breathing, it was dead, right?"

"I assume so, yes."

George jerked his arm away from her. "You *assume* so? Are you saying I ran out on my own son? Is that what you're saying?"

"No. I just meant you were under stress. And this boy at the station is missing his left eye. Maybe she didn't actually *say—*"

George raised his hand as if to strike her. She recoiled. He pulled back. "Do you think I'm the kind of man who would do that?" he shouted. "Am I that much of a coward?"

Aubrey lowered her eyes. She didn't respond, but George could see it in her body language. *You did run away, George. You felt sorry for yourself and you ran away from your home and your mother and your wife, and then you ran away from the war, too. You* did *run away. It's what you do.*

Did you just threaten to hit me?

George sank to his knees in slushy mud. "Goddamn it, Aubrey, she said he was *dead*! That kid can't be my son."

Aubrey didn't offer to help him up. "But what if he is?" she said.

YOUNG WILL
North of Cedar Crossing, Iowa
November 1936

"One thing's for sure," Will said, "I'll never call him Dad."

"No one will expect you to," Margaret said. "Least of all George." She rode next to him in the passenger side of his '34 Chrysler. The windows were up. A new storm was moving in with snow, sleet, and wind. Thanksgiving was in two days, and they were driving to the turkey farm north of town to choose the guest of honor. Birgitta had had this task until her death four years ago. When Luka and Margaret were having so much trouble finding her replacement, Will volunteered. They had Ellen now, but she had pleaded squeamishness, so Will offered to do it one last time. To his surprise Margaret came too. They still had plenty to talk about—and plenty of time to talk about it, as they were stuck behind a line of cars heading to the same place.

"Will he be coming to dinner?" Will said.

"I didn't invite him. Your grandfather doesn't know he's back."

"Why not just tell him?"

"Orville didn't like your father."

"You didn't like my mother."

Margaret sighed. "It was a trying time for all of us. Nobody much liked anybody."

"Except my mother and George. They liked each other, didn't they?"

"Oh, yes. Yes, they did." She looked out the window. Will followed her gaze. A powder of white dusted the fallow rows of farm fields.

"He's calling himself Mick O'Leary. Where'd he come up with a name like that? He doesn't even sound Irish."

He turned left onto a side road. The pavement was getting slick, and he had to spin the wheel to maintain control of the car.

Usually Margaret would be criticizing his driving and yelling at him to be careful. Now she said only, "Mick O'Leary. Well. I believe his new woman friend is Irish. Maybe that has something to do with it."

"So he's not even faithful to my mother."

"Your mother died over twenty years ago, Will. You can't expect a man to—"

"To what?" Will said. Furious, he slammed his palm repeatedly against the horn. *Honk! Honk! Honk honk honk!* The car in front of him slowed as the driver looked back to see what the problem was. Will waved him on. "I *expected* him to stay dead, Grandma! I *expected* to go through my entire life thinking my father was a brave man."

"Expect whatever you want to," Margaret said. "Accept what you get."

The cars ahead turned into a gravel driveway. Just past an old red barn, rows and rows of flat, chest-high white buildings lined the property, each fenced in with a separate concrete yard. Hundreds, maybe thousands, of turkeys clucked there, unaware of the impending doom awaiting many of them. Some buildings housed only white turkeys, some only black. There was no mixing. Will wondered if they'd get gray turkeys if the two mated. Whatever their color, even through the car window they stank worse than any sewer, worse than a hog lot on a hot summer day. Margaret touched her gloved fingers to her nose.

A farm girl directed traffic onto a vacant grass lot next to the house. "First come, first served," she said. "But there's plenty of good ones for everybody."

Will pulled in next to a Ford pickup, put the Chrysler in park, and shut off the engine. "You've never visited my mother's grave, have you? Not even once."

"No," she said, "not even once."

"Grandpa puts daisies on her marker."

"Does he," Margaret said. It wasn't a question.

"Someone does." Several turkey shoppers filed past Will's car. One of them bumped his side mirror, knocking it askew. "Shit," he said, lowering his window and straightening it.

"Language," Margaret said. She sounded weary. "It isn't Orville. I don't doubt he loved your mother, inasmuch as that man *can* love, but he hasn't been to her grave in years. He'd see that as a sign of weakness. If there are flowers, someone else is putting them there."

"Well, it isn't George. They were there before he came back to Iowa." Will opened his door and hopped out. "You sure you want to see this? They butcher it right here."

"Barbaric."

"Do you think the ones you buy at the store are born plucked and gutted?"

"Good heavens," Margaret said. "The smell is atrocious. How do these people stand it? I can't breathe. Close the door. I'll wait here. We'll talk more on the way home. No need for a large one, it's just us and Ellen."

Will pushed the car door shut and went to stand behind people in parkas and farmer boots. Others followed behind him. Most were women who, unlike Ellen and Margaret, weren't squeamish. They laughed and gossiped and didn't seem to notice the stench.

Will stuffed his hands into his pockets. He hadn't decided what to do about George. He had, after all, given the man a job. He could hardly go back on his word, unless like C.J. George took to stealing. Besides, there was some kind of wicked justice in being able to boss around the man who'd left his own son for dead. The so-called father who hid behind his cowardice by calling it grief.

Yeah, there might be some justice in that.

But, Christ, it would be awkward. What would they say to each other? Maybe George would solve the problem by not coming back.

The precipitation kept changing from snow to sleet to a snow/sleet mix. At the moment sleet was dominating, little pinpricks of ice pinging against Will's glasses and sliding down under his collar. The neck of his undershirt was soaked. He was freezing.

He wondered what Luka would do when he found out. It was strange that he didn't know already. He knew everything before anyone else did. Maybe without Weinshank weaseling about town, Luka's main source of information was gone.

A boy of ten greeted Will at the gate. Will had been here before, but he didn't recognize this kid. He was wearing a hat three sizes too big for him. Probably his father's Sunday-go-to-meetin' hat. It looked silly but kept the sleet off his head. "A white one or a black one?" he said.

"White taste different than black?" Will said.

"Nope. Can't tell once they're plucked anyhow."

"Surprise me," Will said.

The kid nodded his head to the left.

Will went left. People were scattered around the turkey houses, inspecting the goods under the watchful eyes of the farmer's family.

"Hey," the kid said, "what happened to your eye?"

"Turkey pecked it out."

"Gettin' even?" the boy said, grinning and drawing a line across his neck with his finger.

Will stood next to a fence not much higher than his knee. A couple dozen white turkeys scuttled about in the paved yard, tapping the concrete for bits of dried corn kernels. The flaps of skin hanging down from their beaks made them astonishingly ugly. The smell was enough to turn Will's stomach.

We *eat* these things? he thought.

A customer came out of the nearby barn carrying a large paper sack stained red. The farmer followed behind her. Thanking her, he turned to Will. "Howdy, son," he said. "Good to have you back. What can I do you for?"

"Not too big. How about that one?" Will pointed to a half-grown turkey in the corner, knowing that by this signal he was sentencing the thing to death. The thought didn't bother him.

The farmer stepped over the fence and snatched the unfortunate creature by one of its legs. Panicked, the others clucked and stampeded about in circles. Apparently turkeys couldn't fly. "Stupidest goddamn birds in the world," the farmer said. "You know they can drown looking up into the rain? Water gets into their nostrils and they're too stupid to look down. They'd be worthless, they didn't taste so good. Come on."

He led Will into the barn while the bird squawked and flapped its wings uselessly. The place of execution was a large metal funnel nailed to a support column, its narrow end pointed toward the floor. The straw beneath it was red with fresh blood, black with congealed blood. The farmer plopped the turkey into the funnel upside down, its tail feathers and legs protruding ungracefully into the air. He reached into the narrow end and gently pulled the bird's head through the small opening. Then, ignoring its protests, he placed the blades of garden shears around its neck and snipped its head off. The legs continued to kick while the blood drained.

Will paid the man.

"Much obliged," the farmer said. "Take it to my wife behind the barn and she'll pluck and gut it for you. Hope you and yours have a nice Thanksgivin'."

He handed the dead bird feet first to Will, who took it around back. The wife was sitting on a stool at a small table protected by a wooden chopping block. There were piles of feathers and piles of guts and piles of severed feet. Blood pooled everywhere, staining every square inch of the woman's clothes and gloves.

She smiled at him. "You know these things can drown looking up in the rain?"

"That's what I hear," Will said.

She lay it on its back on the block. The remnants of its neck hung obscenely from the table, ending in a neat, circular cut where the head used to be. Blood still oozed out.

"Miserable day, ain't it?" she said as she yanked out the first clump of feathers with pliers. "You wanna keep the gizzards?"

***

Will plopped the sack onto the floor in the back seat. Margaret wouldn't look at it.

She said they'd talk on the way home, but they didn't. Must not be anything left to say after all. They rode in silence, Margaret thinking whatever thoughts Margaret thought, Will thinking about George and Cora and wondering who, if not Luka, was placing flowers on his mother's grave.

The drive back to Hammon Falls was interminable. The weather had worsened and the traffic crawled. The tension between Will and Margaret was maddening.

And even dead, plucked, gutted, and washed, the turkey retained some of its stench. Its naked, pasty skin and still-warm muscles gave off a slight but unmistakable odor that cloyed in Will's throat. Ellen would wash the corpse again, flour it, brush it with spices, fill it with stuffing, and baste it for hours in the oven, and when she took it out it would be golden brown, with no hint that, only two days before, this savory treat had been a living creature.

WILL
Waterton, Iowa
December 2008

Between rounds of darkness and silence, the damn machines had been dinging again, like angry little birds. *Cheep cheep cheep cheep cheep.* The sun was in the window. Then there was nothing for a while, but Will didn't know if that was because there really was nothing, or because he'd been napping so much lately. When he opened his eye, the window had gone gray and people were running around like crazy, blurs of white.

Someone was crying.

"Mrs. Rosen, you'll have to step out of the room. Please. Let us do our work."

Cheep cheep cheep cheep cheep, but the crying stopped. There were strange sensations in Will's chest, sensations of both aching and numbness. He couldn't find his breath. Hands tugged at his gown. Something cold and metallic and slimy touched his skin, followed by "Clear!" and a tremendous jolt. It hurt but brought with it a calm and timeless darkness.

At some point Will said, "I won't call you Dad."

"Don't talk, Mr. Hammon. You're going to be fine."

That's good, because I'm not your father.

"I don't like it any better than you do."

Whatever stunt you and my mother are trying to pull, it won't work.

"It's no stunt, George. Or do you still want me to call you Mick?"

"My name is Doctor Hosier. Please, just rest."

Maybe I should find work somewhere else.

"Yeah, go ahead, run away. You're good at that."

"I'm not going anywhere, Mr. Hammon."

I beg your pardon?

"You heard me."

You want me to stay? Because I can take it if you can.

"Tell you the truth, George, I don't give a shit. But I keep *my* word. Just don't screw up, or I'll fire your ass quicker than you can blink."

"Would you like something to help you sleep?"

Fine. What do you want me to do first, boss?

"Stop calling me boss, for once. My name is Will. Will *Hammon.*"

"Nurse."

Will opened his eye. A young woman was injecting something into a tube. The tube led into Will's arm. "Who are you?" he said.

"Hollie, sir. We've met before. I'm your nurse. This will make you feel better."

Hollie had a beautiful smile, like Elaine's. "I'm all right," Will said, "but—"

Sure thing, boss.

"What is it, Mr. Hammon?"

"Don't call me boss."

***

Voices.

His eyelid had a yellowish hue, meaning the lights were on. Must be daytime, then, because they turned the lights off at night.

"So what's wrong?" A woman's voice, his daughter Katie.

"Some kind of dementia, Mrs. Rosen. I don't know if it's from the stroke or old age."

"Will he get better?" That one was male. Charlie? "I mean, will he always talk to himself?"

"Again, I don't know. They got him here in plenty of time when he had his stroke. We should have been able to reverse the effects at that stage, but with his age, his pneumonia...."

"Doctor, is it Alzheimer's?" Katie said. "Just tell us."

"Could be. Or something related. Or some combination of that and the stroke. We could do an MRI of his brain, but to be honest—"

"Maybe he's just confused," Charlie said. "He's been through a lot lately."

Will opened his eye. "Why don't you just ask me?" he said.

Katie, Charlie, the doctor, and pretty nurse Hollie gaped at him in surprise.

"Oh, Dad," Katie said. She was still wearing the shirt with the patch on the chest that said ROSEN and name of her construction company. "We thought you were asleep."

"I was, 'til you all started hollering like a bunch of baboons. Can't a man get some peace?"

"Hi, Grandpa," Charlie said. "You sound better today." His face was so young, so concerned. He still needed a haircut.

Will was seeing a river beyond the white room, or maybe superimposed over it. Shelves of dark ice overhung the shoreline and a swift current flowed below. He could feel the chilly spring air, smell the musty dampness of a world struggling back toward warmth and life. Margaret came to him. Her feet were wet, the ice shelf cracked like an egg shell behind her.

I'm sorry, she said.

"Confused, my ass," Will said. "When do I get to go home?"

The doctor checked readings on the machine. He shook his head.

Katie took his hand. "Not for a while yet, Dad."

MARGARET
Hammon Falls, Iowa
December 1936

In all the years Orville had managed the trailer park, Margaret had never set foot on its grounds, although Arlen had driven her through it once nine years ago. The dwellings were filthy and rundown, with drab gray siding, chipping paint on the doors, and sagging roofs. The park positively crawled with immigrants, many of whom were probably illegal, and one of whom was her own son, George. He was here, after all, on a French passport. *French*. Her son.

Technically, the property belonged to both Orville and Margaret, but she refused to have anything to do with it. She avoided all of Orville's business ventures, yet her lack of complicity had not prevented a further stain on the Hammon name. And she wasn't even a Hammon anymore. G.W., dead nearly four decades now, would roll over in his grave if he knew how far Margaret had fallen from grace, how she had allowed all his good works to be destroyed or perverted.

Ellen dropped her off at George's address, a glorified tin can that looked like every other trailer in the park.

"Wait here," Margaret said. "Leave the car running. I won't be long."

"Yes, ma'am."

Margaret opened the passenger door and stepped out into a blast of snow and arctic wind. Pomeroy was a lifetime ago, and yet wind still set her on edge. She looked up and down the muddy path that served as a street in this dreary cesspit. Despite the cold and snow, little foreign kids were outside chasing each other, making noise, throwing snowballs, and generally being a nuisance. How could these people allow their children outside on a day like this? Just went to show how irresponsible their kind was.

The sidewalk was slushy and unshoveled. Her expensive leather boots would be ruined.

Tiptoeing in a most undignified manner, she made her way to the cheap metal steps leading up the trailer. A pretty, dark-haired woman opened the door for her.

"Come in, Mrs. Hammon," she said with an accent thick as glue. Irish, George had told her. Irish, French, Mexican, it didn't matter. She was foreign.

"I'm not a Hammon anymore," Margaret said, brushing past her into the dark and squalid hovel her son called home. The worst part was, everything looked to be clean and neatly arranged, so the woman had obviously spent a great deal of time preparing for Margaret's visit. Something aromatic was baking in the oven.

"Yes, I'd heard you had remarried," the woman said. "My name is Aubrey."

"I know."

George was seated in a worn rocker, reading the *Waterton Record* next to a window with crooked blinds. He didn't stand when she entered. "Mother," he said, nodding toward a straight-back wooden chair at what must have been their kitchen table. "I see you left the car running. Sit down if you can find the time."

Margaret ignored his rudeness. "The weather is frightful," she said.

George closed and folded the newspaper. "Great, let's talk about the weather. Do you expect it to be sunny tomorrow? And how *do* you protect those tulip bulbs in the winter?"

Good Lord, the hatred in his voice, in his eyes!

"George," Aubrey warned, but she sounded patient and kind. Could he have chosen a nice woman this time? Of course, there had probably been many women between Orville's whore-daughter and this one. But pleasant or not, Aubrey could hardly be considered decent. Neither of them could. They were not married and yet lived together without shame in this dreadful black pit of a home. Aubrey smiled and touched Margaret's shoulder. "May I get you anything, Mrs.—?"

"Yes, Mother, Mrs. *what*?" George said.

"Margaret will do for now. No, thank you, I'm fine. As George noted, I won't be staying."

"I fixed dinner," Aubrey said, "a pork roast." She looked so hopeful Margaret almost felt sorry for her. At least she was making an effort.

Margaret removed her coat. "Would you mind taking this, dear?" she said, lowering herself onto the kitchen chair. Aubrey took the coat to a room down the hall, where Margaret assumed she tossed it on the bed. People in this part of town had probably never heard of clothes hangers. And why would they? The trailers were too small to have proper closets.

George went to the refrigerator. "I need another beer," he said. There were already several bottles on the table next to him.

"No, you don't," Aubrey said from the doorway of the bedroom.

George took a bottle from the refrigerator. He twisted off its cap with his bare hand. "Believe I'll have one anyway."

Aubrey looked at Margaret. "I'm sorry," she said, and Margaret could see the woman was angry. She was also embarrassed for George. Good for her.

"Did you bring it?" George said, sitting back in his rocker. He drank half the bottle in one long swallow.

"That's why I came," Margaret said. She removed a folded piece of paper from her purse, carefully opened it, and handed it to George.

He accepted it, but finished his beer before looking at it. Aubrey stood behind him, reading over his shoulder.

"Well," she said. "That settles it, then. Doesn't it, George?"

George glanced down. "Shit," he said. "You could have had this made at any party gift shop. Great gag, Mother. Ha ha. I'm laughing."

"It's notarized," Aubrey and Margaret said at the same time.

"What's that prove? If you can fake the document, you can fake the notary. It's easy. I knew people in France who could forge passports. *Passports*. How hard can a birth certificate be?"

"George," Aubrey said.

"Was your wife's name Cora?" Margaret said distastefully, as if even now saying *wife* and *Cora* in the same sentence stuck in her throat. "Was that where you stayed in Buffalo?"

"Maybe, but—"

"Was that where you stayed?"

"I don't know the address, goddamn it! I wasn't there long enough."

Donning mitts, Aubrey opened the oven door and removed a roasting pan.

"How could I have known you were in Buffalo," Margaret said to George, "since you never bothered to write me?"

"You're rich, maybe you hired a Pinkerton's."

George was beginning to look desperate, Margaret thought. "I did," she said. "He couldn't find you."

"And look here," he said, jabbing the paper with his middle finger. "The kid doesn't have a first name. *Baby Boy Hammon*."

"He didn't have one until I brought him home. I named him after my father."

Aubrey carved the meat. The roast smelled wonderful. "Will your driver dine with us?" she said.

"We can't," Margaret said.

"Your father?" George said. "You mean the coward who curled up and died because a little wind ruined his day? Nice choice."

"There *is* redemption in names," Aubrey said.

"Shut up," George said.

"Who are you to call another man a coward?" Margaret said.

"Damn you," George said. "My name's not here, either."

Margaret allowed herself a small smile. "You ran away before they could ask you, George. They only found hers because it was written in a novel. She was using a train ticket as a bookmark. The ticket was issued in Waterton, which is how they found me."

"George," Aubrey said calmly, "if she were making a fake birth certificate, don't you think she would have put your name on it, just to make it look authentic?"

"So if it looks fake, it must be real? There's Irish logic for you."

Aubrey turned her face away. Margaret thought she might be crying.

"Leave her alone," Margaret said. "She's right. William Hammon is your son. He's alive and, I understand, now he's your boss." Margaret rose from the chair. "May I have my coat? I'm sure your dinner is lovely, but I must go."

Without a word Aubrey went into the bedroom.

"You've made her cry," George said.

"Despite everything," Margaret said, "I had hoped for more from you. I had hoped—"

"That what? We'd hug and kiss and I'd be seventeen again? You never did that when I *was* seventeen. You've always been a cold bitch with a load of starch up your ass."

Aubrey returned with the coat. "I'm sorry, Margaret. I'm so sorry."

In an unprecedented act of familiarity, Margaret patted Aubrey's cheek. "You're very sweet,
dear."

"Don't apologize for me!" George said to Aubrey. He lurched out of the chair and yanked open the door. "Your car's waiting," he said to Margaret. "You can go to hell."

"George Hammon!" Aubrey said. "She is your *mother*!"

"Is she? You like her so well, why don't you go to hell with her?"

Aubrey looked as if she'd been punched in the stomach. She fled the room in tears.

"She didn't deserve that," Margaret said. "You don't deserve her."

"What's that got to do with anything? Get out."

Margaret nodded as she put her coat on. "By the way," she said softly and cruelly, "my last name is Curtis now. Mrs. Orville Curtis. Mrs. *Luka* Curtis."

With that she exited the trailer and descended the metal stairs. As she slid into the car next to Ellen, she heard something crash and shatter against an inside wall. George's beer bottle, she presumed, or perhaps a plate of delicious pork roast.

LUKA
Hammon Falls, Iowa
December 1936

The temperature was seventeen below zero, a frigid wind howled out of the northwest, and the waning moon cut a silver crescent into the night sky.

The Timmerman building was on fire. Flames billowed upward like glowing hands, shooting smoke and sparks from their fingertips. The intense heat quickly dissipated in the frigid arctic air. Fire departments from Waterton, Cedar Crossing, and Andale fought the blaze. Wherever they managed to douse the flames, the water immediately froze into stalactites of twisted ice. Wind reddened and cracked the cheeks of the firemen. Their breath crystallized around their mouths and noses, giving them a frothy, rabid look.

It was useless. Despite heroic efforts, the Timmerman building was going down. Curtis's Garden just lost its competition, a situation Luka found satisfactory.

He watched the brilliant yellow and orange flames for several pleasant minutes from his car. The fire must be lighting up the sky for miles. To the west, people in Cedar Crossing were probably marveling at an unusually early and lovely dawn.

One of Luka's business associates, a respectable-looking man named Etzel, walked calmly up the sidewalk, looked around, then got into the back seat. "Jesus, it's cold," he said. "Ready?"

"Anybody connect us with it?"

"You know better than that. Cops already got suspects." Etzel smiled and adjusted the brim of his fedora. "I mentioned a couple little nigger kids I saw running away. They got right on it."

"It's a beautiful thing," Luka said. He put the car in gear and the two of them drove off, the Timmerman building an arc of flames behind them.

***

Two days later the weather had warmed to near freezing. The sun was the color of brown tea, but at least there was a sun. Luka had just driven by the site of the fire, reveling in the charred remains, black against the snow. He was in a bleak mood, and the sight cheered him. If only all problems were so easy to solve.

He turned right off Caladonia onto Franklin.

The incorporation vote was scheduled for the first Tuesday in February. Two months wasn't much time to prepare.

Arlen Kelper had been sending out flyers to all residents of Hammon Falls, extolling the benefits of becoming a part of Waterton. He even aimed his propaganda at the immigrants in the trailer park, which amused Luka no end, since most of the stupid bastards couldn't read and weren't eligible to vote anyway – although that had ever stopped them. And if they did vote, why in hell would they choose to be annexed? All they'd be doing was voting themselves off their lots. At the wages they made, how many could afford to relocate?

Not that Luka cared. All the immigrants were to him was cheap labor for Electrical Park. Since the ballroom was all that was left, he didn't need as many employees to run the place anyway. His concern about annexation had always been the fear of falling under Waterton's ordinances. That would definitely be bad for business. He had plenty of officials in his hip pocket, but with the Landon factory's expansion plans, he faced a rival he couldn't outbid.

Luka stopped for a red light at East Fourth. A woman and two kids crossed in front of him, carefully stepping over the remnants of the old trolley tracks.

Landon's wasn't the only problem. Cal Morton and Arlen Kelper were complicating his life with their crusade of righteousness. Luka hadn't found a way to buy them off. Until now they'd only been a nuisance, but if Waterton got its hands on Hammon Falls, Morton and Kelper might acquire real power, not only to put him out of business but to put him in jail. Luka would *not* go to jail. Something would have to be done if they became too much of a threat.

He'd rather not think about that possibility yet.

Luka turned right onto Fourth and right again into Will's filling station. Pulling in next to the pump, he killed the engine and got out of the car. A middle-aged man came out of the office. Although it wasn't that cold today, he wore a hat with flaps over his ears.

"Fill it up, Mr. Curtis?" the man said stiffly. His accent sounded French. He kept his eyes focused on the ground. He seemed almost angry, as if doing his job were an inconvenience. "Your associates are waiting for you in the service bay."

Christ, didn't this guy ever hear about service with a smile? What kind of people was Will hiring these days? Luka would have to speak to him about that. But not now. His mind was on other things.

"Give me the works," he said, and went into the station.

Will must be off today. "Bent Nose" and "Cauliflower," Luka's old friends from the Torrio and Capone days in Chicago, were still delivering the goods, and Luka still didn't remember their real names. With Capone a guest of the feds, Nitti was technically running Chicago now, but everybody knew that Ricci was the real boss. Probably didn't matter much to Bent Nose and Cauliflower. Cauliflower was stupid as a bag of wet cement, and Bent Nose, while smarter and more articulate, apparently had no ambition. Both must be in their sixties, and were still content to drive trucks for someone else.

"We unloaded over at the Garden," Bent Nose said, his New York accent thick as ever, though now peppered with Chicagoisms. "Etzel counted us down. Twenty cases whiskey, twenty rum, eighty-five beer. Need a receipt?"

"Always," Luka said. He paid the men. "Ever miss the old days? Prohibition was the best thing ever happened to this country."

"You're still running whores and numbers out of the Garden, right?" Bent Nose said.

Luka nodded. "Goddamn depression's been cutting down on the clientele. Man can't put food on the table for his family, he won't spend it on gambling and snatch. Hard to make an honest living anymore."

"Heard the new roadhouse burnt down," Cauliflower said. "Real shame 'bout that."

"Yeah, bad luck," Luka said.

Bent Nose handed him a receipt. "What's this annexation shit about?"

"Way for the city to get its hands on my profits," Luka said, "what's left of them."

"Pay 'em off."

"They got a higher bidder."

"Want us to send in some muscle?" Cauliflower said. Luka looked at him. If someone had shaved an ape and stuffed it into a three-piece suit, Cauliflower would be the result. The man could scratch his knees without bending over.

"I got my own," Luka said, "if it comes to that."

"Well, you know who to call, you need help," Cauliflower said. He and Bent Nose left through the rear door of the station.

Luka folded the receipt and put it in his billfold. He watched the men pull their truck into the alley behind the station, then turn onto East Fourth.

The French guy was sitting behind the cash register in the office.

"What do I owe you?" Luka said.

"Didn't think you'd have to pay here, Mr. Curtis. You own the place, don't you?"

"Will runs it. I pay my bills."

"Your grandson," the man said. Something about him was familiar. His face, the tone of his voice, something.

"Yeah, so?"

"So nothing. Fill up, quart of oil, new wiper blade, seven-fifty."

"Do I know you?" Luka said.

The man smiled grimly. "I'm just someone who asked for a job," he said.

"Want to keep it, get some customer service skills," Luka said, giving him a ten.

"Thanks for the advice." The cash register dinged as he rang up the transaction.

The guy was getting on Luka nerves. Dammit, who *was* he? "What's your name?"

Setting $2.50 in change on the counter, he said, "Mick O'Leary."

Bullshit. Whatever his real name was, it wasn't O'Leary. Luka would bet on that. He scooped up the money and put it in his pocket. "I'll be having words with Will about you," he said as he walked toward the door.

"You do that, Luka," Mick said.

Luka stopped, started to turn, thought better of it. He was going to find out who this joker was, and when he did, there'd be hell to pay. "We'll talk again," he said over his shoulder.

***

Aaron Whitney had a corner office at Rogers, Randle, and Baum. It was what Weinshank's office should have been, expansive and luxurious, with oak paneling, leather cushioned chairs, and Venetian blinds on the windows. A ceiling fan hung motionless above.

Luka leaned back in his chair across the desk from Whitney. He noticed a cobweb strung between the blades of the fan, an oversight that pleased him in the otherwise immaculate office. "You got the Garden grandfathered?" he said.

"Kelper never had much of a case in that regard," Whitney said. "The Garden will be safe no matter how the vote goes. Let's talk about incorporation—"

"Let's talk about Maggie."

"Listen, Mr. Curtis. Landon and Company has made an offer," Whitney said, "a legitimate business proposition."

"Screw Landon's. What did you find out about my wife?"

"The only way is if she puts you in her will," Whitney said. His teeth were perfect. Luka wondered if the rumors about his homosexuality were true. Didn't matter much to him. The man could sleep with goats as long as he did what Luka told him.

"Why would she do that if I divorce her?"

"Well, obviously she wouldn't. But under Iowa law, you are not entitled to any property she brought with her into the marriage, which is everything she inherited from her first husband. That would include the house and land on Gloire de Matin, and all the stocks, bonds, or investments that were in his name. Any investments or property purchased together after your marriage would be subject to division by the court, but if she owned it before you married her, it's hers, and there's nothing we can do about it."

"I'm not paying you for 'nothing we can do.'"

"That's small change compared to Landon. All you have to do is quit pushing for incorporation. In essence, do nothing."

"Why would I do that?"

"Because you're greedy, and they're offering outrageous money. The trailer park north of Gloire de Matin? They'll pay three times its value—"

"Goddamn you, I told you I'm not interested in Landon's!" Luka jabbed a finger at the young lawyer, but he thought, *Three times*? "I want a loophole in the divorce law!"

Whitney crossed his legs effeminately. Maybe he really was a pantywaist. "We do everything humanly possible to help our clients within the constraints of legality, but we will not step over the line. Landon's offer is genuine, straightforward, and almost entirely legal."

Within the constraints of legality? Luka tried to remember the last time Weinshank had used language like that. That was easy: never. "You don't get it, Whitney. *Find a way*. There are always other ways. I need that house and I need those investments."

Whitney folded his arms across his chest. "Then don't divorce her."

"Weinshank got things done. He told me once you were a fine litigator. All I see is a limp-wristed fairy boy afraid of his own shadow. I will have that house if I have to kill her for it."

"Wouldn't do you any good. If she dies intestate, you might get half, but only after years of probate, and then only if you're not on death row for murdering her. But Kelper would insist on a will. In that case, her effects will go to her designated heirs, which are her son and grandson."

"George died in the war."

Whitney smiled his perfect white-teeth smile. "Then he's back from the grave, Mr. Curtis. You should pay more attention to your real estate. He lives in your trailer park with a woman named Aubrey O'Leary."

Aubrey *O'Leary*. Christ Almighty, *Mick* O'Leary.

That's where he'd seen the son-of-a-bitch before.

WILL
Waterton, Iowa
December 2008

It was sometime between when George found out Grandma and Luka were married, Will thought, or said, or thought and said, and the Kelper business.

The room was dark, but his door was ajar as always, and light from the hallway tumbled in through the crack. A nurse was checking the machine, or maybe it was Katie. Or maybe it was a shadow and nobody was here at all. That was okay. Shadows were as easy to talk to as people, and they didn't talk back.

He was in the hospital room but he was also in the service bay of Will's Standard. It was the end of 2008 and the beginning of 1937. He and George still didn't like each other much. George was in a terrible mood after learning about Luka.

The hood was folded back on the driver's side of a green '30 Chevy. Will's head was stuffed underneath the hood like an ostrich.

Darkness moved across his line of vision. "Hello?" he said, but it was just a figure in the hallway passing by his hospital door in 2008. Somewhere a bell dinged.

"Did you get that?" he said in both years.

Yeah, George said in 1937. *The guy just needs a quart of thirty-weight. How much we charge for that now?*

Look it up. George turned away, muttering under his breath. Probably didn't have his rate card on him like he was supposed to. When he returned, he hovered behind Will, trying to see into the engine compartment.

Will hated people looking over his shoulder. *Give me a three-eighths box wrench.*

George handed him the tool. *Got it figured out?*

The coil was leaking wax, Will said.

So you replaced it?

Yeah, but now the engine's misfiring.

Sure you needed to replace the coil?

Will exhaled slowly before replying. Why did station attendants always think they were smarter than they were? *It was running weak.*

George used his finger to trace the wiring in the engine compartment. The generator wire to the battery was loose. *The coil was probably overloading*, he said. *The loose wire spiked the voltage in the generator.*

Will stopped what he was doing. *Really? And how'd you know that?*

Ever hear of the law of induction? George said, smiling in self-satisfiction.

"Hey, this is my job," Will said, annoyed. *I just wondered how you knew.*

I told you I was an electrician. Try shunting the wire-set to check for high resistance. Replace any bad ones. "She'll run good as new."

"What's your job, Mr. Hammon? Who'll run good as new?" a nurse said, pulling him right out of 1937. Will didn't see her come in, unless she'd been here the whole time. She stuck a thermometer in his ear. "No temp, that's good. Can I get you something to sleep?"

"I'm okay," Will said. He concentrated, making sure he was saying out loud what was in his head. "George was in a real pissy mood, 'til he thought he could teach me something. Then he got downright smug. But damn it, he was right."

The nurse smiled indulgently. "George?" she says. She injected something into a tube. "Have I met him?"

"I still didn't like the man," Will said, "but I felt bad for him, because, you know, it had to be a shock. Luka and his mother, married? Things were starting to heat up, so I say to him, kind of out of the blue, 'You know how in medieval times the Spanish sailed over to Mexico?' And George says, 'What the hell are you talking about?' and I say, 'Well, they used to load the natives onto their ships and send them back to Spain as slaves. You know what the Spanish king said? He said, 'How many Mayas to the galleon do you get?' Get it?"

George laughed and said, *Jesus Christ,* and the nurse laughed and said, "That's very clever, Mr. Hammon, where did you hear that one?"

"My friend Jack Reece told it to me. He was always the joker." Will chuckled. "He died in a Japanese prison camp in '43."

"Long time ago, Mr. Hammon. You should sleep now."

"George took me out and bought me a beer after that. Funny thing is, he still didn't like me, either, but we talked a long time. Listen," Will said. "To this day I think that night was why he ended up doing what he did."

"What did he do, Mr. Hammon?"

"He saved me. I mean, literally. He took the fall."

GEORGE
Hammon Falls, Iowa
December 1936

"Oh, how the ghost of you clings
These foolish things remind me of you…"

Aubrey pressed her face against George's shoulder as they danced. It was Saturday night. The Walter Korte Orchestra was playing in the Electrical Park Ballroom. The tune, *These Foolish Things*, was one of George's favorites. The singer was no Bing Crosby, although by the way he crooned the lyrics, he obviously thought he was. George rested his palms on the slender curves of Aubrey's waist, inhaled her perfume, felt her breasts rise and fall, and thought about Cora. Electrical Park, cotton candy, hot dogs and Dr. Pepper, the carnies, the children, trolleys, the Spiral Terror, the Aero-Thrill ride swooping down over the placid waters of the Oak River...

Oh, how the ghost of you clings.

None of that was left here now, just the ballroom. Even that was new, the old one having burned to the ground earlier in the year.

The wooden dance floor, sprinkled with sawdust for easier sliding, was framed by pillars, booths, and thickly draped windows. A dozen couples embraced, swaying in time to the wistful music and cooing to each other. George could hear their whispers between the notes.

The singer paused, and a rich horn instrumental reverberated through the hall. The lights were down low for the slow number. The scent of beer tinged the air pleasantly, although tonight George had not been drinking.

"This is nice," Aubrey said.

It was nice. After all the revelations of late, he was exhausted. A quiet night was just what he needed. Aubrey was so beautiful, with her dark eyes and dark hair and dark dress.

"I'm sorry for how I've been behaving," he said, recalling that April night so long ago when he and Cora had first made love. They were so young then, so young.

Their child had *lived*.

"Yes, I know," Aubrey said.

"I'll make it up to you."

"There will be a time for that." Aubrey backed a step and focused her dark eyes on his. "You talked with Will last night?"

"Yeah. The kid's not half bad."

The instrumental ended with a swish of the high-hat. The singer resumed his mournful lament. George hugged Aubrey to his chest, and for a few moments, a few notes, a few lines of verse, he was here in Electrical Park, at the end of 1936, dancing with his Irish love, and everything was all right.

After the song ended Walter Korte announced a ten-minute break for his orchestra. George took Aubrey's hand and turned toward the booths surrounding the dance floor.

"Wait," she said.

Korte was still at the microphone. "Got a surprise tonight," he said. "While the boys are limbering up their lips with a few cold ones, a lovely lass all the way from Dublin, Ireland, will entertain you with her violin. Ladies and gentlemen, please welcome Miss Aubrey O'Leary."

"What's going on?" George said.

Aubrey lifted her hand away from his. "You'll see," she said.

The other couples applauded politely as they returned to their seats in the booths. George stood awkwardly on the edge of the dance floor. Aubrey climbed the steps to the platform, went backstage briefly, and returned with her violin. She approached the microphone stand. The lights dimmed to black, and a single spot shone down on her from above. With her dark hair and clothing she looked like a shadow in a sphere of light, the soft whiteness of her face and arms almost supernatural.

She looked out toward George, squinting against the spotlight. Although she had trained professionally, it had been a long while since she played before an audience, and she appeared uneasy. "A river flows by outside," she said, her Irish lilt beautiful. "The world is joined by water. If we believe enough, the river will carry our music to all our loves, living and lost. This song is for Cora, and for George."

Aubrey raised her violin. The first notes were low and sultry but tentative. The audience, unimpressed by Celtic mysticism, chatted among themselves. As Aubrey gained confidence, though, the music gained clarity and passion. The low, sultry tones rose in pitch and power, expanding to fill the ballroom. For George the single melody felt deeper and more resonant than strings alone could produce. The sound evoked images of summer days, the sun on Red Hawk Creek, a hot breeze pungent with the scents of flower gardens and freshly cut grass.

George's hands trembled, his breath caught in his throat. It was as if, through her music, she were reading his soul. The audience felt something, too. They became still, enraptured by her solitary figure. George wondered if she was tapping into their memories and emotions as well.

Aubrey's body was rigid. The only motion was the bowing strokes of her right hand and the graceful fingering of her left, coaxing magic from catgut strings and a wooden box. As her arm moved back and forth it left an afterglow of white in its wake.

Slowly the music changed from a bright major key to a slow minor one. It grew so soft it might have been inaudible but for the utter silence in the hall. Winter had arrived in the notes, winter and a bitter, frightening train ride, winter and illness, winter and blood, winter and despair in a strange city. Winter, and spring would never come again.

My God, George thought, how does she know? How does she *know*? He'd never told her the full story, not in any way that could explain this music. Someone in the audience sniffled, and someone else, and someone else. Aubrey was breaking their hearts, too.

George leaned against a wooden pillar, lowered himself to his knees. He couldn't stop his tears. Modulating once more to major, the music now suggested that out of desolation hope might yet grow, that peace might yet be found. But by then George was shattered, spent. Aubrey had given him the gift of Cora, and taken her away again.

When she finished playing, there was no sound at all, no reaction from the audience save awed silence. Not until the spotlight faded to black did the applause begin, and when it did it went on for many minutes. Everyone rose and called for an encore.

The house lights came back up with Aubrey still at the microphone, her eyes on the ground, too modest to acknowledge the ovation. She did not play again. Instead, she took her violin backstage, then returned to George.

He was still on his knees by the pillar. He saw vast oceans of love in her eyes, oceans of sadness. She knew Cora would always be the love of his life. The music was for herself, too.

George sensed she had more planned for tonight than just a song. There was something else.

Walter Korte returned to the stage. "How the devil are we supposed to follow *that*?" he said good-naturedly. "Wasn't that lovely? Let's hear another round for Miss O'Leary."

The audience responded enthusiastically.

Aubrey ignored them. "You will see her again, George Hammon," she said. She offered a hand to help him to his feet. "Come on, up with you."

George stood without her help. "You're leaving me, aren't you?" he said.

"Yes," she said.

***

The Oak River was beautiful in the moonlight. The stars, always brightest in the winter, were especially striking tonight. There was no breeze, and the temperature hovered just above freezing. Ice melted from tree limbs along the bank, dripping onto the snow with little plunking sounds. Despite the recent cold snap, a black ribbon of water still trickled through the center of the ice on the river. The reflected light of the moon cast blue shadows on the snow, black shadows on the trees.

George leaned against an elm and watched the water flow through its frozen channel. His breath twinkled briefly and disappeared. He loved this place more than any other, but it could no longer hold him. If Aubrey was leaving, so was he, this time for good.

"Tommy is dead," she had said. While he stood here by the river, she was home packing. Her mind was made up. "I located one of his brothers. He knows a man who sailed with Tommy. It was just a silly mistake on the ship's manifest. They got his name wrong, O'Loughlin rather than O'Leary. He went down with the *Megan Marie*. Tommy's friend saw his body. He's dead, George. There's no more reason for you to search, or for me to hope. His father's cross is truly yours now. Keep it, or give it to Will."

"You don't have to go," George said. "Stay. Just stay."

"I believe we are soul friends, George Hammon, bound together in eternity, but you do not believe it yet. Although we met in this world for a purpose, for now we have other paths to take."

"What purpose, Aubrey? Tell me my purpose."

She kissed his cheek. "That's not for me to say. I only know I am called away, and need to travel alone. Our separation is temporary."

"I don't understand any of this," George said. "Is it my drinking?"

"It isn't anything you did. It isn't you at all."

"Nothing is calling you away but yourself. I can't watch you leave, I can't."

"I'll be gone when you return, then. Know that I love you. I always will. *Slán go fóill, anam cara.*"

Goodbye for now, soul friend.

Goodbye for now. For *ever*, she meant.

"The world is joined by water," George said from the bank of the Oak. He snapped an icicle from a branch and tossed it toward the open channel in the river. It fell short, landing on the ice sheet and shattering into a hundred glittering pieces.

YOUNG WILL
Waterton, Iowa
January 1937

"Can I buy you a drink?" Kelper said to Will. They were seated at the bar in the Royal-Sampson Hotel on Commercial Street. The place was nearly empty, surprising since it was lunch time. Will could hear the noon hour traffic passing on the street outside.

"I've got to be at work in an hour. What's this about?"

Kelper lit a cigarette and flagged down a waiter. "Bring me a Miller," he said. Then he simply stared at Will for the longest time, as if evaluating him. His silence made Will uncomfortable. He looked angry.

"What?" Will said.

Finally Kelper said, "I'm going to level with you, Will. The feds are onto your grandfather's little smuggling operation. They know he runs Chicago booze through your station, and other places, to avoid paying taxes. They think you're involved."

Will couldn't have been more shocked if Kelper had told him his grandmother was a Stalinist. "What the hell are you talking about? Luka isn't running anything through my station—"

"Will, please." Kelper drew in a mouthful of smoke, which seeped out as he spoke. "The same two hoodlums have been delivering the goods there since Prohibition. Don't tell me you haven't noticed them. They were part of Torrio's outfit, then Capone's, now Nitti's. One big and dumb, the other smaller with a smashed up nose?"

Okay, that had to be the men Luka called Cauliflower and Bent Nose. He'd described them as business associates. Will had never actually met them. Of course, Luka knew when Will worked and what time the station closed. He could have been coming in when Will wasn't around.

Will knew that not all of Luka's enterprises were legal—hell, *everybody* knew—but still, smuggling alcohol through *his* station? He didn't believe it. Luka would never jeopardize his own grandson.

The waiter brought a chilled bottle of beer. Kelper took a sip and waited.

"Mr. Kelper," Will said, "I *swear* I don't know anything about it. I wouldn't allow that."

"I don't work for the D.A.," Kelper said, "but here's what Cal will say: your station, your problem. If you didn't know, you should have. And to be honest, neither he nor the feds will believe you didn't know. Curtis owns the station. That makes you suspect. If they can find even a whiff of a money trail leading to you... And they *can*, Will, even if you're as innocent as you claim. They will. Smuggling is a federal rap. So's failure to pay taxes. You're talking Alcatraz. You do *not* want to get messed up in that."

"Why are you telling me this? What do you want?"

Kelper rubbed out his cigarette in an ashtray. "I want Curtis. He's had the run of this town too long, not to mention he's embezzled your grandmother blind. He's made the Garden into a whorehouse and gambling pit, he's paid off the locals, and now I hear he's taking money from Landon's to oppose incorporation. And what about the fire at the Phillips' new roadhouse? That was a pro job, not two stupid black kids playing with matches. He has to be stopped."

"He's like a father to me," Will said.

"I know that, kid. No one said this was going to be easy."

"What do I have to do?"

"Agree to testify against him."

Jesus Christ. Will stood up and slammed his hand on the bar. "Testify to *what*? I don't know anything!"

Kelper took another swallow of beer. "To whatever they tell you to, Will. The only way you're going to keep Curtis's stink off you is to cooperate with them. They'll help you remember."

***

George was assisting a customer in a '32 Ford when Will pulled into the station and parked next to the office. Will still didn't much care for his father, but he felt bad for him because his lady friend had recently deserted him. He seemed so sad now.

After George finished with the customer, Will motioned him over. The unseasonable warmth at the end of December had continued into the new year. Weak sunshine melted snow and ice from the roof and glinted yellow-brown on the puddles in East Fourth's potholes.

"Yeah?" George said.

"Anything unusual ever happen here when I'm not working?"

"Unusual, how?"

"I don't know, weird. Strange people coming around, meeting with Grandpa."

"You mean the guys in the trucks with Illinois plates?"

"You've seen them?"

George nodded. "Pretty hard to miss. Couple of goons, you ask me. They park back of the garage, usually about closing time, but sometimes during the day."

A breeze was starting to bend out of the west, perhaps presaging the end to the sunshine and pleasant weather. It blew the melt-off from the roof onto the men's clothes. Will went into the office, and George followed.

"You could've said something," Will said.

"About the goons? Didn't know there was anything to say. It's your station."

"What's your opinion of my grandfather?"

"How honest do you want me to be?" George said. He rang up the customer's payment.

"Just say it."

"He's a greedy bastard who wouldn't fart if he couldn't make money on the stink. Ever hear about the dirty stunt he pulled on your mother and me?"

"Bad idea, bringing up my mother."

"I loved her, Will. Whatever you think of me, I loved her more than anything on earth."

"Stop it, I said!" Will checked the register's display window for the amount George just rang up. Five dollars even. "What about Luka?"

"Why do you ask?"

"I had a talk with Grandma's lawyer about a half hour ago."

"Who's doing Mother's dirty work these days?"

"Arlen Kelper."

"He's still around? Mother always liked him better than I did."

"He wants me to testify against Luka."

"Since when does Kelper work that side of the aisle?"

"Claims he was speaking for the D.A."

"He should have asked me. I'd do it."

"You don't even know what Kelper thinks Luka did."

George smiled grimly. "Doesn't matter. I'd swear he sleeps with farm animals if it'd put him away. Which he probably does."

"You hate him that much? Why?"

"You told me not to talk about your mother. What are you going to do about Kelper?"

"They can't make me testify, can they?"

"How would I know? I've lived in Europe for twenty years. But I'll bet judges can still issue subpoenas around here. If they get one, you won't have a choice."

"I'll say I don't know anything, because I don't."

"And they'll say you're protecting old Grandpappy."

"That's what Kelper said, too. Dammit, why'd he have to pick me? Wouldn't hurt my feelings if he keeled over like old Weinshank did."

"Why blame Kelper? He's just the messenger. Luka's the problem."

The bell hose rang as another customer drove in and stopped next to the pump. It was a woman in a '28 Mercedes. George went out to serve her.

Will sat on the stool behind the register. The office was spotless. He had to give George credit, he was a hard worker who kept the place spic and span.

Outside, George must have said something funny, because the woman in the Mercedes laughed and touched his hand the way some ladies do. Good customer service, too.

Will rubbed his temples. What should he do? He couldn't testify against his own grandfather, but he wouldn't go to Alcatraz, either. Maybe Kelper was just trying to scare him.

Well, he'd succeeded. Will was scared, damn scared.

There was a '27 Dodge in the garage that needed attention. Usually working on cars eased Will's mind and brought him a kind of peace he couldn't find any other way. But the owner of the Dodge was out of town and wouldn't be back for it until next week, so he decided to do something he never did: give himself an unscheduled day off. He really needed to talk to his grandmother about Luka.

George came in and rang up $6.23. He put a twenty into the register, counted out $13.77, and stuffed the change into his pocket. He fumbled one of the bills, though, and it drifted to the floor. As he bent to get it an elaborate cross on a chain popped out from beneath his shirt. Noticing Will was watching, he said, "She told me to keep the change. Liked my accent."

"It's not that. Where'd you get the cross? Never figured you for a religious man."

"Took it off a dead guy in the war. I meant to give it to his son, but now he's dead, too. Anyway, it's a Celtic cross, pagan or something."

"Can I see it?" George handed it toWill still attached to the chain around his neck. "Great workmanship," Will said. "How old is it?"

"I don't know, centuries."

"Who was the dead guy?"

George laughed. "Mick O'Leary."

Will gave the cross back. "Very funny."

George tucked it under his shirt. "No, really. He was a friend of mine."

"But he died, so you stole his name."

"Just borrowed it. Aubrey said I should give the cross to you."

"I got no use for it." Will checked his wristwatch. "Can you cover for me this afternoon? I need to take off."

"You're the boss. Let me guess: Kelper?"

"Grandma." Will buttoned his coat. "You live in Hammon Falls. What's your take on incorporation?"

"I'm a French citizen, Will. I can't vote."

"That never stopped anybody."

"Doesn't matter," George said. "I don't care one way or the other."

"Luka thinks incorporation would help his business, yet Kelper says he's taking money to oppose it now."

"Luka's beliefs are tied to his pocket book."

"Back soon," Will said.

***

He had to screw up his courage to face his grandmother, so he drove around for a couple of hours thinking about what he would say and how he would say it. He didn't know how much she knew or had deduced about Luka. Probably the illegal activities wouldn't be a surprise—she couldn't be married to the man for twenty years and not suspect something—but the fact that her own attorney was bringing Will into it would be a shock. Margaret Curtis did not handle shock well, although her life had been full of them.

Will didn't handle shock well, either, and this one was a doozy. After driving as far west as Cedar Crossing and as far east as Andale, he ended up at Memorial Cemetery in Waterton, where his mother Cora was buried. He never met her, yet visiting her grave had always calmed him when he was scared or upset. Today he was both.

He parked the car on the gravel road next to her family plot and sloshed through puddles and melting snow to her marker.

ANGEL OF LIGHT, it said.

The usual daisies were on her grave, dead and withered now. Will didn't know how often cemetery attendants cleared off old flowers. Probably once a week. The mysterious mourner had been here within the week, then, but not in past few days. Will wondered who he, or she, was. Not Luka, according to his grandmother, and the flowers predated George's arrival home.

He stood over the stone and tried to picture a living face from the photograph he carried of Cora, a face of color and three dimensions. He couldn't do it. To him his mother would never be more than a black and white image, silent and pretty, a perpetual teenager with bobbed hair and petulant lips. She would never even be a memory.

I loved her, Will. Whatever you think of me, I loved her more than anything on earth.

Will was older now than she ever got to be. "Hi, Mom," he said.

Her answer was the wind in the trees, *shhhh, shhhh,* coming round now from the north, chilly and wet. The warm spell would not last the night.

Will returned to his car. He got in and sat numbly behind the wheel. He put the key in the ignition but didn't turn it. For a long while he didn't allow himself to think, to feel, to do anything. He just sat. Perhaps dozed. His stomach was unsettled, and a little headache niggled at his left temple, but otherwise he had no awareness of his body or time. Nobody came to the cemetery, nobody even passed it by. Darkness had set in before he snapped out of his stupor. By then clouds had blanketed the sky and pellets of sleet were pinging on the windshield. The falling temperature had chilled his fingers to bluish white. They cramped when he moved them.

Dammit, why was he still here, freezing in his car when he needed to be talking to his grandmother? Hours must have passed. His right cheek was wet. Jesus, had he been *crying*?

He gazed once more at Cora's marker. What if she had lived? he wondered. What if she had lived and George had not run and Will had been born with two good eyes and they had shared a home together as a normal family? Maybe he wouldn't be in this terrible predicament now.

Shhhh, said the wind. *Shhhh.*

He turned the key in the ignition, and the engine rumbled to life.

***

"Arlen Kelper threatened you?" Margaret said.

"Alcatraz sounds like a threat to me."

Margaret fell back against the davenport in the parlor, looking flushed and faint. Her Bible was on the table next to her, although she never read it anymore. She spent most of her time these days either here or in her bedroom, just sitting. She used to enjoy the library, but rarely set foot in it since Luka took it over. She knew what went on in there, she once told Will, without explanation. "Arlen isn't a prosecutor," she said. "He has no business pretending to be one."

Will went to the kitchen to pour himself a glass of milk. "He hates Grandpa," he said.

Margaret sighed. "Yes, I know. But enough to go after him through you? I won't stand for that. I'll talk to him. Perhaps he'll listen to me."

Will returned to the parlor, his glass already half empty. "That sounds like something Grandpa would say."

Margaret glared at him. "I said *talk*, not bribe."

She rang the servant bell. Ellen appeared a few moments later. "Yes, ma'am?"

"Get Mr. Kelper on the telephone for me."

Will finished his milk and handed the glass to the maid.

She took it and said to Margaret, "Right away, ma'am."

When she was gone Will said, "Cal Morton's the one who'll come after me."

"I don't know Mr. Morton very well. It wouldn't be proper for me to talk to him. That would be obstruction of justice. But Arlen should know better. He and his father have represented the Hammons since before the turn of the century. I'd hate to have to find another attorney now, but I will if he doesn't leave you alone."

Will sat on the davenport next to her and put his hand on her shoulder. "Grandma, how will that look to Morton? If you tell Kelper to back off, it'll just make me seem guilty."

Margaret squeezed her hands together, her way of not verbally expressing the anger she was feeling. "What a world," she said. "What a life. Why did you come to me, William? Why say anything if you don't want me to help you?"

Will shrugged.

Margaret rose and stared down at him. "You're going to testify against Orville, then?"

"I don't know what I'd say."

After a long pause, she said, "He's planning to divorce me, you know."

Will's mouth dropped open. "He's *what*?"

"Arlen told me some time ago. Orville's trying to find a way to get his hands on this house and my investments. Right now he can only have them if I will them to him, and he *knows* that isn't going to happen."

Ellen appeared in the doorway. "Mr. Kelper isn't home, ma'am. His wife said he was at the office. I telephoned there, but he was out. I left a message with his service."

"Thank you, Ellen."

She bowed her head curtly and left.

Will stood up. "Grandpa's trying to cheat his own wife? *His own wife*? Are you sure?"

"Does it surprise you so much?"

"The son-of-a-bitch!"

"Language," Margaret said.

"What are you going to do?"

"I'm not a complete fool, William. I've taken steps."

LUKA
Hammon Falls and Waterton, Iowa
January 1937

The incorporation vote was a month away.

The trailerites rallied around Luka's car in snow and sub-freezing temperatures. He didn't come this way often, but when he did, he got a rousing reception. The immigrants knew if the vote failed and Waterton annexed Hammon Falls, they'd be out on the streets. Luka was their savior, the hero come to slay the dragon on their behalf.

"Keep your homes!" Luka called through his open window. "A vote for incorporation is a vote for your families. I will stand with you the whole way! Together we can't fail."

He smiled. Truth was, they couldn't *succeed*. Without him the vote had no chance of passage, and he no longer supported it. Money had wooed him over to the other side. He'd decided to accept Landon & Company's offer to buy the trailer park, at three times its value, as well as the lucrative incentive package it had thrown in to sweeten the pot.

The last impediment had been Waterton's roadhouse licensing ordinances, but Whitney had received assurances from the city which grandfathered the Garden's status, guaranteeing its continued operation regardless how the vote went.

"*Gracias, Señor Curtis,*" one man said, pumping Luka's hand.

"Bless you, suh," an old nigger said.

Their gratitude was pathetic. Incorporation had never been about these vermin anyway. Luka would still need the their cheap labor afterward, so he had to put on a show of support, but for the kind of cash Landon's was dangling, the immigrants could build another Hooverville out of cardboard boxes, for all he cared. He'd fight for them and lose, and they'd love him for it.

"Be sure to vote, first Tuesday in February," he said.

Yeah, vote, you ignorant bastards, he thought. You're illegal. The state's just going to throw your ballots out anyway.

He knew that because he'd already tipped off the election officials.

***

"Landon's can't pay the incentive directly," Whitney said. "Even if it's legal, the D.A.'s going to raise hell and make it look like they're in bed with the devil."

"They're just buying property," Luka said. He loomed over the lawyer's desk, a reminder of exactly who was in control here. "Straight business deal."

Whitney looked up over the top of his glasses. "Maybe they can justify the inflated price because the value will increase when they expand the plant. But the other payments will need to be more circumspect."

"I've got holding companies, offshore accounts, whatever we need."

"I don't like playing on the edge," Whitney said, riffling through papers on his desk.

"Don't be so squeamish," Luka said. "Everybody does it."

"Why do *you* do it? You don't need the money. I know you want to be the big man around town, but there's more to it than that."

"Really?" Luka said scornfully. "Tell me, Aaron. Why *do* I do the things I do?"

Whitney removed his glasses. "I think it's the scheming. You can't see a straight line without wanting to bend it. Money isn't the goal. Neither is power. The allure is the scheming itself. Take that away and there's nothing left of you. You evaporate, leaving behind only hot air and the stench of something rotten."

"Watch it, fairy boy." Luka jabbed a finger against Whitney's desk. "It isn't any of that. It's *winning*. It's about having an opponent and beating him. That's what I do. I *win*."

Whitney wasn't cowed by Luka's vehemence. "Is that what you tell yourself?"

"It's the truth."

"You don't always win, Curtis. You just change the rules. You know you can't beat annexation, so you switch sides and pretend that's what you wanted all along. You can't beat Landon's, so you let them pay you off."

Luka patted his suit coat, looking for a cigar. Must have left them in the car. "And yet, Aaron, I get to run my roadhouse without Waterton's interference, which was my intention all along. I get Landon's to buy property on my terms. *Mine*, asshole. That looks like winning to me."

"There's no need for that kind of language. None of that could have happened without this firm. And you still have Arlen Kelper and Cal Morton to deal with. They're bringing in independent investigators. Bribery, prostitution, gambling, arson, income tax evasion, and probably jaywalking, if they think it will help put you behind bars."

"I've got all that taken care of."

"You can't buy off the feds, Curtis. Ask Capone. If it comes to it, that's a fight you *cannot* win. We'll do everything we can within the law, but—"

"Jesus Christ, this entire firm doesn't have a set of balls between you. Weinshank would've had the feds pissing in their own shoes."

Whitney sat up and straightened his shoulders. "Weinshank was a greasy scum spit out of the Chicago machine because he was too slimy even for them."

Luka smiled. "As I recall, your partners hired him. His office was right down the hall."

"He worked under Colosimo. They let themselves be impressed by that at first, but quickly saw him for what he was. He would've been fired if he hadn't quit."

Luka cracked his knuckles and tut-tutted. "It's so unbecoming of you to speak ill of the dead, Aaron."

"Dying was the only decent thing Weinshank ever did."

"Are we done here?"

"There's the business with your wife's will. The deposition worked. Judge Finch signed the order. The papers will be served tonight."

"Was there ever any doubt?" Luka said. He had to give Whitney credit. Weinshank never thought of that. If he had, Luka would've been rid of her years ago. "I want to be there when it happens."

Whitney took off his glasses, folded them, and slipped them into his shirt pocket. "Then I guess we are done. You are one despicable bastard, Curtis."

Luka laughed all the way to the door. "And your point is?"

***

With clear skies and calm winds, the temperature was dropping like a rock. The *Record* had predicted a near-record low by tomorrow morning. In January that meant *damn* cold, 25 to 30 below zero. Still, the stars were brilliant, and Luka was in a fine mood. After leaving the offices of RR&B on East Fourth, he passed Will's Standard, turned left onto Franklin and, a couple of miles ahead, left again onto Caladonia. Gloire de Matin Island was just across the bridge.

The streetlamps washed the snow in a soft green hue. To the southwest, the Westland Avenue factories ejected streams of smoke, but against the black sky even pollution looked blue-white and fluffy.

What a night this was going to be! He couldn't decide whether to break the news to Maggie himself or just enjoy her expression when the Red Hawk County Sheriff knocked on the door. Whichever way it happened, after more than twodecades of unmitigated hell, he was finally going to be rid of that overbearing bitch.Everything that was hers would now be his, and there wasn't one thing she could do about it.

He crossed the bridge onto Gloire de Matin and turned into his lane. With the snow-covered woodlands in the background, the houselights and chimney vapors made the homes here look pretty as an idyllic little village from a Christmas postcard.

Well, this was certainly going to be like Christmas. Luka whistled "O! Holy Night!"

At the house the porch light was on. A dark, probably green, '29 Chevy was parked in the driveway. It had New York plates. Why would anyone driving that piece of shit have come here? The sheriff, being on official business, would have brought the squad car. Besides, he wasn't due for another hour.

Luka pulled in behind the Chevy, set the brake, and shut off the car. He got out to examine the Chevy. It hadn't been here long, because the engine was still warm and no frost had formed on the windows yet. The doors were locked.

What the hell?

As he stepped onto the sidewalk he heard a loud and angry voice coming from inside, a man. He recognized it immediately, despite having only heard it once since 1914, despite the deeper tone and the French accent.

Jesus Christ, not here, not in this house. George Hammon. Luka didn't care that this was once his home. He relinquished all claims when he kidnapped Cora, put her on that train, and let her die in a strange city. Killed her, more like.

Goddamn him.

Goddamn him.

God*damn* him.

It was about time the two of them met up, face-to-face, man-to-man. What better place than here, in Maggie's presence, to beat that bastard bloody? Luka wasn't the fighter he'd once been, but he could still whip George's ass.

Steadying his hands, he turned the house key in the lock.

"You're always accusing me of being drunk," Hammon said.

They must be in the parlor. Maggie's response was soft and unclear, but she might have answered, "That's because you usually are."

"Well, I'm not now."

"Then why are you behaving this way?"

"Because I'm broke and Aubrey is gone. It's your fault."

Luka paused at the parlor door, listening to the exchange, clenching his fists, letting his fury build.

"I didn't cause your financial problems," Maggie said. "I didn't chase away your Irish woman. And I didn't abandon your son."

Luka heard George slam a fist into a wall or door frame. "I thought he was dead!"

"He wasn't."

Maggie paused.

Oh, sweet Jesus, what an amazing scene this must be, Luka thought. Maybe she finally understood what a complete cipher her son was.

But then she said, "If you'll stay, you won't have to worry about money. I've taken care of you."

"Nothing could make me stay in this town. Do you think that's what I want?"

"I don't know what you want, George. Why did you come here? To tell me you're running away again? To say goodbye? You never did before. Just leave, if you're leaving."

Luka sauntered into the room. Maggie was seated on her davenport, George standing across the room. "Yeah, you worthless shit, why *did* you come here?"

George looked at Luka with a loathing Luka had seen many times in many people. He loved being hated. It was the first step to winning.

"Christ, Luka," George said, without the least surprise, "I can smell your stink a mile away. I was wondering if you'd ever find the guts to face me. I'm not a skinny teenager any more, tough guy, and you got old and fat. Take a swing at me now."

"We'll get to that," Luka said. "Answer her question."

"Before I go I wanted her to know how she's disgraced my father's name." He switched his gaze to Maggie. "G.W. *spits* on you, Mother. Look at yourself. Look at the *thing* you married. For what? Money? You had all you needed. Position? You were already at the top. Why would you defile yourself with this walking cesspit?"

Maggie's skin paled, highlighting her red rouge like circles of infection on her cheeks. Tears dragged the infection down to her chin. "I had to, George," she said, her voice barely a wheeze. "He won custody of William. I would have lost the last piece of you I had."

George started to speak, then stopped, as if he couldn't quite believe what she'd said. "What do you mean, he won custody? Of *my* son?"

"You weren't here," Maggie said. "Cora was dead. That left Orville and me. Judge Hauken, may he rot in hell, chose *him*."

George looked at Luka. "That's impossible," he said. "No judge would do that."

Luka smiled. "It wasn't cheap."

"Not even you," Maggie gasped. "Not even you would bribe a judge. You're just trying to hurt me."

"What do you think, you stupid bitch? The woman always gets custody."

"This is your husband," George said to Maggie. "I hope you're proud."

"Everything has been a lie," she said. Her eyelids fluttered. Funny, Luka thought ladies fluttering their eyelids was a cliché, but Maggie always had been a weakling, a stereotype, a ridiculous caricature of herself. "Twenty years…."

"And this surprises you?" George said. "You whored yourself to keep the *last piece* of me. Well, you've lost me anyway, haven't you?"

"George," she said, "don't."

Luka clapped his hands in mock applause. "Bravo," he said. "What a performance. Both of you. I haven't been this entertained in years. Mother and son, how touching. The frigid dowager and the war hero who didn't have the sense to stay dead. Impressive."

"Let's find out if you still have that right cross," George said.

"Let's." Luka took off his parka and tossed it to the floor. As he rolled up his sleeves, he noted how dry and spotted his skin had become. Purple veins popped out on the undersides of his forearms. Yeah, he had grown old and fat, but he still had enough left in him to handle a drunk like George.

Maggie stirred, managed to push herself upright. "You will not fight in my house like…like animals."

"My house," Luka said.

George crouched with fists clenched, moving warily in a half-arc around the room. Luka stood there, amused, and watched him. How many barrel-chested amateurs had he seen do that in the arena at Electrical Park in the 'teens? Feeling him out as if they had a strategy? Acting confident? In a moment, after pretending to survey the situation, pretending to study Luka, pretending he knew anything at all about boxing, George would come blundering across the parlor in a blind charge. Luka would simply step aside and pop him with an uppercut to the nose. George would crumple unconscious to the floor, bleeding all over Maggie's fancy rugs, and the fight would be over. How anticlimactic.

Instead, the doorbell rang.

The sheriff was early.

"Wait," Luka said. He wanted George to see this, to witness his ultimate victory and Maggie's final humiliation. The knockout punch would have to be postponed a few minutes. George would be even more eager for a fight once the sheriff delivered his news.

"Lost your nerve?" George said.

Luka hated the taunting tone of his voice, but he had to take it for the greater triumph to come. "Business before pleasure," he said.

The doorbell rang again.

"Are you expecting someone?" Maggie said.

"Where's the goddamn maid?" Luka said. "Doesn't she answer doors anymore?"

"I sent her shopping when George arrived," Maggie said.

"I'll get it, then," Luka said. "Don't move. I want you both to hear this."

George sat in a chair opposite Maggie. They looked at each other questioningly.

This was going to be *so* incredible! Luka thought. He went to the front door. Expecting the sheriff, he was surprised to find two uniformed officers from the Waterton police. Maybe the sheriff had asked the city cops to cover for him. Both looked to be in their forties or fifties. Experienced men, then. That made sense.

"Come on in," Luka said.

One was holding an official-looking document in his gloved hand. "Mr. Curtis," he said, but Luka stopped him with a finger to his lips.

"Not yet. My wife is in the parlor."

The policemen followed a few steps behind. George was leaning forward in his chair, watching Maggie. Maggie had her hands folded in her lap. She was staring at both of her wedding rings. Mother and son looked up intently when the policemen entered the room.

"Maggie," Luka said, "I believe these gentlemen have something to read to you."

The cops glanced at each other. "It's not for her, Mr. Curtis."

One handed document to Luka. "We have a warrant for the arrest of William Hammon."

George shot to his feet. Maggie's mouth dropped open stupidly.

Luka felt as if he'd taken a knee to the groin. "Will? Why?" he said. His own voice sounded high and mousy in his ears.

"He's wanted as a material witness in the murder of Arlen Kelper."

"Murder," George said.

"His body was found in an alley off East Fourth, near Will's Standard filling station. He'd been beaten to death with a crowbar or tire iron. William was the last person known to have seen him. Is he home?"

"Arlen is dead?" Maggie said, and threw up.

WILL
Waterton, Iowa
January 2009

After seventy-two years it was all a blur, all the memories, all the deaths, the arrest, George's sacrifice, Elaine's arrival in the back seat of that Roadster... 1937 was an eventful year, but what happened exactly when, and in which order, was a mystery that would never be unraveled. Most of it Will witnessed himself, but some was told to him later, and he'd long since lost the ability to distinguish between the telling and the actual experience.

He was wearing hospital slippers as he shuffled down the tiled hallway, Katie supporting his right elbow, an IV needle secured by tape on the back of his left hand. The wheeled monstrosity from whose arms the medicine bags hung and dripped their poison into his veins went everywhere with him. It even followed him into the toilet. It wasn't heavy, just a nuisance to drag around. He'd started calling the thing "Matilda." When he took his twice-daily exercise he told the nurses he was "waltzing Matilda." They smiled every time, although Will suspected the joke had worn thin for Katie.

"You're doing well, Dad," she said.

Will could fall on his ass every other step and Katie would tell him he was doing well. But at least she was here. Until the stroke, she hadn't paid him this much attention since she was a little girl.

Matilda's wheels squeaked. He'd been out of the ICU for several days now, moved to a skilled nursing unit. The lighting in the hall was the same soft white it always was, night or day. Drove him crazy. "How's my old filling station?" he said.

Katie gave him a pitying look. She'd probably answered this question a thousand times, but he didn't remember. "That's all taken care of, Dad. We got the gas tank removed. We had to pull it out of there in pieces. Weather's been so shitty, though, we probably won't resume construction 'til April at this rate. Storm buried the whole site in four inches of ice, then all the snow on top of that. And with the economy like it's been, I nearly lost my company...."

Seen out of the corner of his eye, Katie bore a resemblance to her great-grandmother Margaret, especially when she was wearing her stern, severe expression. Straight on, she was more like Elaine. Her smile, when she chose to favor him with it, reminded him of, well, himself when he was younger, with the full lips Cora's photograph had.

"Katie," he said, "I ever tell you about the time I got arrested for murder?"

At the end of the hall, Katie gently turned him around to begin the journey back. They were up to three laps around Will's wing as they continued to build his strength after his bout with pneumonia. "Oh, Dad, you were never arrested," she said. "You've never even had a parking ticket."

"Was, too," Will said. "When you was a little girl. I remember because my grandma Margaret was holding you in her arms when the cops came for me."

"Dad," Katie said, "I never met Margaret. She was already dead when I was born. I remember Great-Grandpa Orville, but not Margaret."

Will stopped abruptly, causing Matilda to wobble. 1937. Right, right. He met Elaine in 1937, married her in '38, so Katie couldn't't've been around yet. She came along during the war, when Will was Four-F. "Well, I *was* arrested," he said. "Somebody killed Grandma's lawyer, Kelper. Luka always called him 'Old Seaweed.' *Kelp*er, Seaweed, eh?"

Katie stopped the medicine bags from swinging on Matilda's arms. "That's funny, Dad. You be careful now. You don't want to punch a hole in these things."

"Whoever did it beat him with a tire iron. He was found near my station, and let me tell you, I had plenty of tire irons there. They said I was the last one to see him alive."

"Why would you kill anyone?" Katie said.

"'Cause Kelper was trying to get me to testify against Luka. They said that was my, what-you-call-it, motive."

"I think we should cut your walk short tonight, Dad. It's late, and I've got a big meeting in the morning."

"You just don't want to listen to me any more."

Didn't she know that stories were all he had left? But dammit, his left calf was starting to cramp up. Will tugged on Matilda, and they waltzed down the hall toward his room ahead of his daughter. The nurses were already waiting. Katie rushed to catch up. "Come on, Dad, you know I love to talk to you."

Like hell.

"Okay, Katie, but you ever wonder why you never met your Grandpa George?"

"The way Mom told it, he ran out on you."

"There's more to it than that," Will said, but then they arrived at his room and the nurses fussed over him, lifting him into his bed and hooking him up to the beeping monitor machine.

MARGARET
Hammon Falls, Iowa
January 1937

Orville and George ignored her on the davenport. Margaret lay on her side, nearly unconscious, her own filth drooling from her mouth and nose. She was aware of heated voices, Orville and George shouting, the two policemen answering politely.

"Are you drunk?" Orville screamed. "Will didn't kill anybody!"

"You're sure you have the right guy?" George said.

"Fellas," one of the officers said, "we have a warrant. He's wanted as a material witness, that's all. When do you expect him back?"

"Shouldn't somebody help the lady?" the other officer said.

"Your superiors will be hearing from me," Luka said.

"That may be, but we still have to serve the warrant. Do you know where he is?"

"Why the hell would I? He's a grown man, for Christ's sake. He goes where he pleases."

"Can you account for his whereabouts yesterday?"

I saw him last night, Margaret thought, but she couldn't find the breath to speak.

"Get out of my house," Orville said.

"Ever heard of obstruction of justice?" one of the policemen said.

Orville laughed. "Do you have any idea who you're talking to? Scram."

"We'll be back."

Footsteps receded from the room, a door slammed, a car engine started. Margaret felt a hand on her forehead, a handkerchief wiping her nose and mouth.

"Mother," George said, "sit up. You made a fool of yourself."

***

Orville and George left shortly after Ellen arrived home with groceries. George went looking for Will, Orville to apply a little muscle with the authorities.

Ellen returned from the kitchen. "Are you all right, ma'am?" she said, glancing at the vomit on the floor.

"No," Margaret said. "No."

"I'll clean that up," Ellen said. "Shall I call the doctor?"

"I'll be all right." She would not be all right. Not ever again. "Help me to the chair."

Ellen grasped her elbow and lifted her up. They moved across the parlor. Margaret was dizzy and wobbly. She eased onto the cushion and lay her head back. She closed her eyes to try to stop the spinning, but that only made her nausea worse.

Ellen went to the kitchen for a mop and pail. Margaret drifted in and out of coherence. She was aware of a cool, wet cloth being placed across her brow and the stench of vomit giving way to the pleasant smell of Pine-Sol.

"You're burning up, ma'am," Ellen said at one point. "Sleep now."

Ellen was right. She should go to bed. There was nothing she could do now. She had never slept in a chair, at least not since the bad times after Pomeroy and before G.W.

Some time later—an hour, a minute—the telephone rang. She heard Ellen's voice, then felt hands shaking her. "Sorry, ma'am, but you must take this call. It's Will. He's been arrested."

Margaret pushed herself out of her chair, made her legs bear her weight into the kitchen. She wrapped her fingers around the telephone receiver and raised it to her ear. "William?" she said.

"I'm in jail, Grandma. They say Arlen was killed and I know something about it!"

Margaret couldn't think straight. "Where did they find you?"

"I was at Jack's sister's. They just had a baby."

"A baby? How nice—"

"Grandma! I'm in jail! I need you to put up bail. I'll pay you back somehow. I gotta go. I just have the one call. Please, get me out of here."

This was something Orville should handle. He knew all about this kind of thing.

The line went dead.

"William?"

Margaret looked at Ellen, whose expression was a mix of compassion and panic. "What can I do, ma'am?"

"I don't know. He said something about bail."

"He's been arrested? There are bail bondsmen...."

"Will they take a check?"

Someone knocked on the door.

Good heavens, what now?

Margaret stood in a daze while Ellen answered the door. William was in jail. He was in *jail*. For murder. Of *Arlen*. Margaret steadied herself on the kitchen table.

Ellen returned followed by a man wearing the tan uniform of the Red Hawk County Sheriff's Department. The officer was middle-aged, with a neat black mustache.

"He demanded to speak to you, ma'am."

"Mrs. Curtis?" he said. "I'm Sheriff Metzger."

"Is this about William?" Margaret said.

The sheriff gazed at her, took a deep breath. "This is about you, ma'am. I have a court order here, signed by Judge Finch."

"A court order?" Margaret said.

Metzger opened the document and appeared to study it. "I'm sorry, Mrs. Curtis, I hate to do this. My Daddy knew G.W. back in the '80s. …" Margaret could see him clenching his teeth by the way his jaw pulsed. "Dammit, it's a committal order, ma'am. You're to be removed to the Mental Health Institute at Independence until such time as the doctors see fit to release you. Your husband Orville has been granted power-of-attorney."

"There's nothing wrong with her!" Ellen cried.

Margaret collapsed onto one of the kitchen chairs. *Removed*. To the insane asylum. "I don't understand," she said.

"Ma'am," Ellen said, "it's just another of Curtis's schemes! You can't let him get away with it. The son-of-a-bitch!"

"Language," Margaret said, a stultifying calm settling in on her. This was it, then. God had finally and utterly forsaken her. "Must I go now?"

"That's what the order says." Metzger said. "Mrs. Curtis, call your attorney, fight this."

"My attorney," Margaret said, "is dead."

"There must be someone."

"There's no one," Margaret said. She almost smiled. Damn Orville, he'd *won*. "It's my will. If I am of unsound mind, my will is invalidated. He's outfoxed me again."

"Ma'am," Metzger said, but she cut him off with a wave.

Her attorney was dead, her grandson in jail for his murder. Her son had disowned her. Her husband had declared her crazy. Everyone she loved was gone, by death or circumstance. What remained of her fortune would soon be in Orville's hands. I don't deserve this, Margaret thought. The good didn't deserve damnation nor the bad salvation, but that's how it worked out sometimes. Somewhere God was laughing. She was as lucid as she'd ever been in her life. "Maybe I *am* crazy," she said. "Who wouldn't be? Can you give me time to get my affairs in order, Sheriff?"

Metzger lowered his eyes to the floor. "A couple of hours," he said, "but then I'll have to take you in. It's my job. I'm truly sorry, Mrs. Curtis. Find an attorney. Find someone."

"Call me Hammon," she said.

***

There was nothing to be done, no affairs to put in order. Sheriff Metzger had left, and try as she might, Margaret couldn't think of one thing to do to save herself. She asked Ellen to bring her the checkbook. She signed her name to one and tore it from the book. "Take the car," she said, handing the check to Ellen, "find a bondsman, get William out of jail. I don't care what it costs, just fill in the amount."

"No, ma'am, I won't leave you alone."

Normally Margaret didn't tolerate backtalk from servants, not even Ellen, but tonight she simply smiled grimly. "Thank you, dear, but what *else* could happen to me? I'll be all right. I do have a dreadful headache, though. Is there any aspirin in the house?"

While Ellen was gone, Margaret got up and walked through the first floor of the house: the kitchen, the dining room, the parlor, Will's bedroom, her own bedroom, avoiding only the library. She loved the smells of this old house, not just the spices and foods, but the wood and plaster and rugs and furniture.

She was to be *removed* to the Mental Health Institute in Independence, some twenty-five miles east on Highway 20. It might as well be twenty-five thousand miles, another state, another country, another planet.

Good Lord.

Ellen found her in the parlor. She gave Margaret a glass of water and two aspirin, then bundled up in her winter coat. "Once this is all over, if I may be so bold, you should throw Mr. Curtis out."

Margaret pushed the aspirin to the back of her throat and took a sip of water. That was the only way she'd ever been able to swallow pills. "Thank you," she said.

"I'll be back within an hour," Ellen said. "Then I'll start calling attorneys for you. We'll get through this, ma'am. We'll save Will and prove your husband a liar."

"Of course we will, dear," Margaret said.

Ellen left, the car tires crunching ice as she backed down the driveway.

Well, then.

Margaret went to her bedroom and changed out of her evening clothes. She chose a nice gown—black, naturally—one that was conservative but stylish, then donned black fur-lined boots, her formal winter coat, and an attractive hat that matched the outfit.

The wind had picked up, whistling in the chimney flue, rattling the windows, and causing the whole house to moan. It was going to be astonishingly cold out there, but in Iowa when was January ever anything else?

Margaret left the porch light on for Ellen. She did not lock the door when she stepped outside. The wind blew straight out of the northwest, whipping frigid air down from the plains of Canada. Clouds streaked across the stars, eventually blotting them out completely. Tree limbs crackled and rustled.

Breathing the cold was like drawing fire into her lungs.

Margaret picked her way down the driveway and onto the lane, avoiding clumps of ice and snow. She wasn't accustomed to exercise, so by the time she reached the Gloire de Matin Bridge she was winded. For a few moments she stood on the east foundation, admiring the view. Snow-covered woods lay to the north, framing the homes of the island. In all other directions city lights illuminated the cloud cover, giving the sky an unnatural gray-yellow glow. The Oak River was virtually icebound, blue or black depending upon placement of streetlamps. But somewhere down there was a channel of open water, for she could hear its tumbling even above the rush of the wind.

A little footpath led from the bridge down to the river's edge. In summer the path included a set of concrete stairs, now barely discernable in the snow. Margaret descended to the bank, not slipping once. From here she could see the black thread of water cutting through the ice. At one point the flow curved in on itself, carving a semi-circular shelf.

Margaret stepped out onto the shelf. Below her the water whorled and eddied, spinning up a miniature maelstrom beneath her feet. She watched it with fascination. Swirling, swirling, black against gray, with white froth that froze on contact with the ice. Water, air, it didn't matter. It brought back memories of Pomeroy nearly half a century ago.

She wasn't afraid.

She removed Orville's wedding ring from her left hand and dropped it, with great pleasure, into the frigid water. Then she transferred G.W.'s ring from her right hand back to the left, where it belonged.

Looking up, she made a bet with God that the ice shelf could not long bear her weight.

God, laughing, did not take the bet. Margaret stamped her foot, once, twice, a third time.

Eventually a crack formed behind her and slowly zigzagged across the shelf. Over the rippling of water and wind she could not hear the creaking of the split, but she sensed it. It began as a small scratching sound, a small popping, but grew into a hiss as the crack expanded, into a rumble, into a shriek like a woman's voice.

Margaret did not cry out as the ice snapped. She did not pray. She did not lament her life nor imagine a heavenly reunion with her lost loves. Rather, she envisioned a whirlpool scouring her body, drawing her not up into the funnel and ultimate light but spiraling her down into an abyss of everlasting darkness.

GEORGE
Waterton, Iowa
January 1937

George had rushed out of Margaret's house in a mad fury, but, truth was, he had no idea where to look for Will. He wasn't at home and he wasn't at the station. Although their relationship had improved—*how many Mayas to the galleon*, Jesus—George still didn't know who Will's friends were or what he did for amusement, if he was seeing a girl, or anything at all about his personal life. All he knew was that Will had uncharacteristically taken the afternoon off on the very day Kelper was beaten to death because he'd been agitated *about* Kelper.

Could he have done it? Could his son be a murderer? In the short time George had worked for him, he didn't *seem* like a killer. But then, who did? Luka's Chicago goons, sure, but Will? Who could say what he could do when provoked? In the War, George himself had shot men with whom he had no personal quarrel. But that was war. Killing wasn't called murder then.

He got a beer from the refrigerator, thought better of it, and settled for a Pepsi. The trailer was quiet now that he was alone, although a north wind rattled in the siding. What a dump it was. What a travesty he'd made of himself. Well, he wouldn't be staying in Iowa much longer anyway, although the wretched hull he called George Hammon wasn't so easily escaped.

Material witness. That was a nice term for *suspect*. George's nerves prickled. It wasn't as if he'd formed a paternal bond with the boy, yet Will was the child Cora gave her life to bring into the world. Surely George had some responsibility to him.

Bursting with energy, eager to do something, in the end he did nothing but take an aspirin, finish his Pepsi, and fall asleep in his chair.

***

On his way to work the next day he stopped at a small craft shop on the east side to order a decorative wooden jewelry box, oak with bas relief letters spelling out HAMMON on the lid. It was an expense he couldn't afford, but he wanted a suitable place for Mick's Celtic cross. Leaving a deposit and promising to return for the box later, he drove over roads covered with ice packs as large and gnarled as the roots of trees.

He half expected to find the station locked, but, surprisingly, Will's car was there. George parked next to the office. When he walked inside,

Will was at the register, going over receipts as usual. "Hey," he said without looking up, "you're late."

"Where you been?" George said. "The cops are looking for you."

"They found me. Grandma bailed me out."

"They tell you why they arrested you?"

Will paused to erase a figure, then added the column. "Kelper's dead. They think I know why."

"Do you?"

Will looked up at him. "What, you think *I* killed him?"

"I didn't say that."

"The cops just needed to account for my whereabouts."

"Did they?"

"I was driving around. I went to visit my mother's grave, for one."

"Only been there once. I couldn't stand it." George took a deep breath. "Anybody see you? Driving around's not much of an alibi."

"They let me out, didn't they?" Will double-checked an entry. "Somebody really buy nine dollars worth of gas yesterday?"

"Big truck. So it's over, then?"

"Far as I'm concerned. D.A.'s still got some questions, I guess, but Luka said not to worry. Don't you have something to do?"

Bail proved only that Margaret had the money to spring him. A potential murder rap, that would have cost her. But maybe Luka got involved. If anyone could pull strings, he could. "Sure thing, boss."

***

That night George telephoned the house on Gloire de Matin. He didn't want to talk to either Margaret or Luka, but they were the only ones who might know something. The cops weren't just going to let Will walk away. Not with a high-profile murder case on their hands. Iowa was a hanging state, and the thought of Will dangling from the end of a rope was ghastly.

"Mrs. Curtis?" the maid answered anxiously, not even saying hello.

"It's her son," George said. "She's not home?"

"We haven't seen her since last evening. I don't know what to do, Mr. Hammon."

"She's been gone all night?"

"Her bed hasn't been slept in. Mr. Curtis won't lift a finger to look for her."

Odd. Margaret had never been impulsive. She wouldn't just leave, although Luka was such a conniving asshole, who'd blame her if she did? "Is Curtis there?"

The maid's voice grew cold. "I'll put him on the line."

There was silence for a few moments, then Luka said, "What the hell do you want?"

"What's this about my mother?" George said.

"What's what?" Luka said. "She's not here."

"Where is she?"

"Holed up in the loony bin by now, I hope. Otherwise, I got no idea."

George could hear strain in Luka's voice. "Loony bin," he said.

"Just wishing out loud."

"I'm worried about Will."

"Take a number. I called in every favor I had, and nobody will touch this. Morton wants Will bad, and there's nothing gonna stop him. He's the D.A. The bastard's so clean his ass squeaks when he walks. He called in the feds to investigate me. Murder's not in their jurisdiction, but with them sniffing around, nobody's taking handouts."

"Will said you told him it would be okay."

"Well, it isn't okay. I can't make this go away. I don't know how he got out on bail."

Luka seemed evasive. George said, "Did he do it?"

"Hell, no. That kid? He doesn't even step on spiders."

"Who did, then? Do you know?"

There was a long pause. Luka was breathing heavily. "It wasn't Will."

"Damn it, Luka, if you know, how can you hang your own grandson out to dry? It was you, wasn't it?"

"I was with my lawyer, ironclad. Morton would love to pin Seaweed's death on me, but he can't. I never liked Kelper, but I didn't hate him enough to kill him."

"Then tell the D.A. who did."

"Goddamn it," Luka said, "it's not that simple. You don't just turn these people over to the law. Not if you want to stay alive."

"So you'll let Will swing to save yourself. You gutless piece of shit."

"Don't you know how much Morton is *enjoying* this? He doesn't just want a conviction. He wants to *hurt* me. Ony way to do that is take away the one person I care about."

"Then give him someone you don't care about. Give him the killer."

"Are you deaf? *I can't do that.* They'll not only come after me, they'll come after Will and Margaret and probably you, too, if they know about you. Not that *that* would be any loss. Are you getting this? If I rat them out, Will's dead anyway."

"Why'd they do it?"

"Business."

"Business?"

"Best I can do. Ask them yourself."

"Do something, Luka! Cop a plea, say it was an accident—"

"Eighteen blows to the head from a tire iron?"

"Christ," George said, "I hardly know the kid, and I'd take the fall for him if I could."

There was another pause. George could hear the wheels turning in Luka's mind. Finally Luka said, "Let's talk about that. Weren't you planning to leave town anyway?"

***

They met at George's trailer the next morning. It was a relatively warm Friday. George sat in a kitchen chair, while Luka perched on the edge of the couch. Both men were nervous, angry, uncertain, each determined to be tougher than the other.

"You're sure about this?" Luka said. He was still wearing his coat and gloves. A rucksack rested between his feet.

It had been a surprisingly easy decision. George could never be a real father to Will, could never make amends for abandoning him, but he could do this one good thing for him. This one good and decent thing. "Everything I need's packed in the car."

The letter he'd written for the D.A. lay on the table.

"Where you heading?" Luka said.

"Does it matter?"

"You leave Iowa, that's interstate flight. The feds'll come after you."

"They catch me, I'll hang. So what? I've been dead since Cora anyway."

Luka glared at him. "Don't ever say her name to me again."

"Or what?"

Luka didn't answer. Instead, he opened the rucksack and took out a bloody tire iron, holding it in his gloved hands. "This is the murder weapon. It's clean, no prints." He offered it to George. "Don't touch the dried blood. Prints on top of that, Morton will know you put them there afterward. They'll compare them to ones they take from your trailer."

George handed the letter to Luka, then accepted the tool, thinking, Jesus Christ. Jesus Christ. This is it, this is a murder rap.

Luka perused the letter.

My name is George Hammon, it said. *I am a French citizen. I killed Kelper. You'll find my passport and photo in my trailer in Hammon Falls. The tire iron I used is under the trailer.*

"So much for Hammon war heroes," Luka said.

George gave the tire iron back to Luka. "Who really did it?" he said.

"Man who calls himself Etzel. I don't know his real name. He's long gone."

"You ever going to tell me the real story, now's the time."

"Would you believe me?"

George took the letter from Luka, folded it, and stuffed it in an envelope addressed to Cal Morton, District Attorney. "Will's going to be taken care of?"

"With prints and a confession, they'll have to drop the charges."

"That's not what I mean."

"I've already started a trust fund for him, and when Maggie and I are gone, he gets everything. Good enough for you?"

"You back out on this," George said, "I'll come after you. They can't hang me twice."

"Save the bullshit threats. Will's more of a son to me than he ever was to you. I'll do right by him." Luka removed a roll of bills from his shirt pocket. "There's six hundred and forty-five dollars here. That's enough to get you away from here."

"Six hundred bucks?"

"It's all the cash I had on hand. How'd it look, I make a huge withdrawal just before you disappear? Take it or leave it."

George jammed the money into his pants. It wasn't the first time he'd accepted payment to jump town. "I just sold my life for six hundred dollars."

Luka stood up, grasping the tire iron between his forefinger and his thumb. "You bought Will's," he said. "I'll stash the weapon under the trailer. Get going. The feds'll be after you soon as Morton sees that letter."

"That won't be until Monday," George said. "I'll be a thousand miles away by then."

"Find some different plates. People around here will remember New York plates. And don't talk too much. They'll remember the accent, too."

"Shut up," George said.

Luka smiled mockingly. "One thing you do know how to do is run away."

At the very least, Luka was an accessory after the fact. He might be more deeply involved than that. George shouldn't have to do this. He pictured Luka dropping through a trapdoor and snapping his neck at the end of a rope, arms bound behind him, feet kicking, eyes bulging, face blue from lack of air. It was a pleasant fantasy.

But it was not to be. Saving Will was George's one good act. It was his penance, his redemption. Sometimes to save the saint you had to set the devil free. "Did my mother ever come home?" he said.

"Do you care?"

"Not really," George said. And he didn't.

***

George posted the letter in a mailbox on Sycamore Street on his way to the craft shop.

The jewelry box he ordered was ready. The raised letters HAMMON were highlighted with bronze gilt. It was a beautiful and sobering symbol of the final degradation of his family name. He paid the balance and returned to the car.

Turning left onto East Fourth, he headed toward the station. Will wasn't scheduled to work today, so there'd be no awkward goodbyes. He pulled up to the pump and got out of the Chevy, jewelry box in hand. The new kid Will hired a couple weeks ago scuttled out of the office, all bundled up in a parka and fur-flapped hat. "Hey, George," he said.

"Give me the works, will you?"

George went inside, though the office and into the garage bay. Using a wrench from the tool box, he removed the plates from the '27 Dodge Will had been working on and hid them down the front of his pants, beneath his coat.

Back in the office, he opened the jewelry box and traced his finger over the red velvet lining inside. This was surprisingly difficult.

Mick's Celtic cross, as always, hung around his neck. After more than twenty years, its weight was as familiar to him as his own arms. He slipped it off and wrapped the chain around its elaborate tines. "Sorry, Mick," he said. He set his friend's heirloom inside the box—a perfect fit—closed and latched the lid, and placed the box beside the cash register.

Nothing left to do, it was time to hit the road.

George paid the kid, got into the Chevy, and drove off. Without once looking over his shoulder, he crossed the bridge, followed West Fourth to Highway 212, called Washington Street in this part of town, and turned south.

He was tired of cold weather.

YOUNG WILL
Waterton, Iowa
February 1937

It was pure luck she was found when she was. If a woman's dog hadn't escaped its leash and run down the slope by the Sixth Street Bridge, Margaret's body might not have surfaced until spring, probably many miles downstream. Even then, had a constant flow of water draining from a sewer tunnel not carved a hole in the ice, she might not have been noticed. But the dog escaped, and when the woman went to fetch it, she spotted a human foot protruding grotesquely over the lip of an icy tide pool near Lover's Island.

Despite the frigid water, her skin had bleached and bloated into gelatinous sludge. She was identified by her clothing. Charitably, the coroner ruled her death an accidental drowning.

No one believed a word of it.

Will sat next to Luka in the back seat of the second car in the funeral procession. He sobbed off and on as they wended through the narrow and frozen lanes of the cemetery. Luka was dry-eyed. In fact, he was perusing some parcel that read "Landon & Co." on the letterhead. Now that the Hammon Falls incorporation proposal had been defeated—by a 63 to 37 count, with Luka's help—he was busy helping Waterton officials plan the annexation. He claimed to be burdened with financial headaches Will just couldn't understand.

Will did understand. Those "headaches" included deciding where to invest the legitimate profits he raked in from Landon's for his property and how to hide the less legitimate kickbacks. He couldn't be bothered, even for his wife's funeral, to divert from his purpose.

Will despised him. "Don't you feel anything?" he said.

Luka glanced up. "What do you want me to say, kid? You know we didn't get along. What good is pretending now?"

A light snow was falling, but there was no breeze and the temperature was fairly pleasant, for February. Will looked out the window as they passed row after row of tombstones, nearly all of them white, save for the occasional black marble crypt. Copses of trees were scattered throughout, their limbs frost-covered from last night's freezing fog. The frost was white and twinkled like glitter. The cemetery was beautiful, serene.

Will had been adamant that Margaret be buried with the Hammons. She deserved a final resting place next to her beloved G.W. and George's never-to-be-filled grave, whose marker still listed his death as July 1, 1916.

The Curtis and the Hammon plots were at opposite ends of the "rich Protestant" section. The funeral procession took them past Cora and her mother Emma. A movement there caught Will's eye. He nudged Luka.

An old colored man, leaning on a cane, bowed his head over one of the markers. From where he sat Will couldn't see whose it was, but it was definitely one of the Curtises. The man seemed to be praying. Then with great effort he knelt in the snow and reached inside his coat.

"What's that nigger doing?" Luka said.

Will swallowed hard and felt the tears anew. "He's putting daisies on my mother's grave."

GEORGE AND CORA

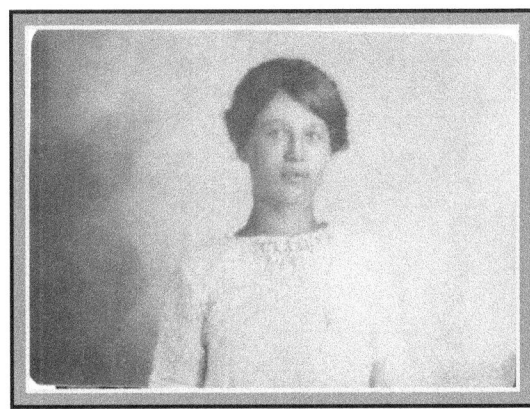

CORA
Waterton, Iowa
March 1914

Naked, Cora stood sideways before the full-length mirror inside her closet door. Her stomach stuck out farther than her breasts now, although those had grown, too. Her nipples had become sensitive, and she was still plagued with occasional blood "down there," but overall she felt good, good and hopeful. She cradled her belly in her hands and imagined holding her living, crying child. The doctor said it was due in March, right around George's birthday on the 23rd. Wouldn't that be something?

She prayed for a girl, although she knew George wanted a boy.

Pacing in front of the mirror, Cora waddled like a fat old penguin. Her navel poked out now, rather than in. George would think she looked so silly, if only he could see her. She always fantasized him kissing her tummy and singing to the baby. He was going to be a wonderful daddy. Only two or three more weeks.

She hadn't seen him since their sham wedding. One hundred and forty-eight days, to be exact. Save for church, she was a prisoner in the house. Tutors came in to tend to her schooling. Margaret was probably doing the same to George in Hammon Falls. They were determined their children would never meet again.

But the long separation was going to end tomorrow. Luka's maid Birgitta, Margaret's servant Ed, and George's friend Lewis had been doing some scheming of their own. The unlikely conspiracy began just before Christmas. For the past few weeks, whenever Birgitta went downtown to the dry cleaners, she'd smuggled, one piece at a time, Cora's dresses, underclothing, and toiletries to Ed, who delivered them to Lewis at Kline's. Birgitta had a cousin in Albany, New York. Lewis had connections at the train station.

It was all arranged.

Cora was giddy. *New York*! Nobody would ever think to look for her there. It was practically another country, but it was a safe place where Birgitta's cousin's family would help her through her pregnancy.

Since Christmas her tantrums with Luka had stopped. She no longer cried herself to sleep or refused to come out of her room, no longer spoke of woman's rights or complained of women's work. She'd even started doing her chores again, at least those she could manage in her condition. Her father, always willing to see the worst in everybody, had a blind spot for Cora. When she quit fighting him, he convinced himself that she had accepted the situation.

She had not.

All she had to do was slip away without being caught. That was arranged, too. At church tomorrow she would excuse herself during the service under the pretext of using the toilet. Ed would be waiting in his motor car. He would take her to George at Kline's.

Birgitta knocked on the door, then entered. She frowned at Cora nakedness. "Good heavens, girl, put some clothes on! With your problems, you do not need to catch your death, too."

"My baby is kicking," Cora said.

"Babies do that," Birgitta said.

"You're sure Daddy's not going with us to church?" Cora said.

"He has other business. The colored man has purchased the tickets."

Tomorrow. *Tomorrow*! One more day, and she would be with George forever. She imagined the two of them strolling arm-in-arm along a tree-lined boulevard, pushing a baby carriage. It would be a warm spring afternoon, the sun bright. George would wear a top hat, and maybe smoke a pipe. She'd be bedecked in a colorful Dorelia dress like the fashionable ladies of Paris. Every New Yorker who saw them would envy their style and grace. And all of them would want to kiss her perfect baby.

"Oh, I can't wait! I—"

"Shhh," Birgitta said. She didn't like George, didn't approve of him, but she loved Cora, and was willing to set aside her personal feelings for her. She was risking her job for it. "Your father is downstairs. You have waited this long. Patience, child."

"Patience," Cora said, giving the maid a big hug.

Birgitta pushed her away playfully. "Enough, now. It is not seemly. You are undressed."

Cora took one final glance into the mirror. "A penguin," she said. She put her hands to her sides and touched her heels together, splaying her feet apart, then walked with the funny little steps she'd seen penguins do in the Des Moines zoo.

Birgitta laughed out loud, something she seldom did. "More like a fat monkey, I think. Now on with your bedclothes, silly girl. You will need your rest."

Cora made monkey faces and sounds while the maid laid out her nightgown. "Ooh ooh, I want a banana," she said.

Birgitta laughed harder, and cried some, too. "I will miss you so, little one," she said.

***

Cora rode with Birgitta to church in the carriage. Birgitta handled the reins. If any of her father's spies were following, Cora couldn't see them.

It was a cold, cold day, with a powdery fall of snow. "You do understand what this means, child?" Birgitta said.

Cora squeezed her arm. "That I will be with George."

"Yes," Birgitta said. "You will be with George. But also you will be away from *us*. From your father and me and your friends. You cannot come back. We will never see you again. *I* will never see you."

Cora lifted her head and looked at Birgitta's profile. "We'll come back, you know we will. Daddy'll get over being mad, and anyway, what can he do? We are married, after all. This is just 'til we have the baby and maybe it's a little older. I want her to know her grandpa."

The carriage wheel struck a rut in West Fourth's pavement. The jolt sent a stab of pain through Cora's abdomen. "Do not underestimate your father," Birgitta said. "He will not stop looking for you. He will discharge me if he learns what I have done."

"He won't," Cora said, massaging her bulging stomach. She kissed Birgitta's cheek. "Who will tell? I'll come back, you'll see. You can move in with us."

Birgitta turned right into the lot of the Waterton Church of Christ and tied the horse. Wind dislodged a stray lock of hair from her tight bun. "I am worried for you. In your condition, perhaps this is not the best time."

True, but if she waited until the baby was born, she'd never get away. "I'll be all right," Cora said. At the bottom of the street, where West Fourth intersected Washington, she saw Ed waiting next to the curb in the motor car Margaret had bought for him and Estella. "There he is!"

Birgitta glanced in that direction but said nothing. She helped Cora from the carriage.

Pastor Darland greeted parishioners at the door of the church with "Bless you, sister," or "Bless you, brother." Cora and Birgitta shook his hand and entered, hanging their coats on the pegs inside the door. They took their customary aisle pews toward the back.

Cora scanned the faces of the crowd, looking for Luka's associates. Many acquaintances were there—he seemed to know everybody in town—but she didn't see any of his usual spies.

"My cousin will meet you at the station next Saturday," Birgitta said into her ear. "Her address is in your suitcase. She does not have a telephone. Edward has given George money to last many months. I have altered your dresses. You will have to buy new clothes once the child is born." She sighed. "I did not want this day to come."

The lights were low. Pastor Darland started off with the hymn, *Amazing Grace*, accompanied by the church's big pipe organ. The congregation rose to sing. The second hymn was to be *The Old Rugged Cross*, followed by a sermon from *The Book of Acts*.

Cora had always liked *Amazing Grace*. She sang extra loud to quell her nerves. This was really happening! Where was George? Was he ready? Was he as anxious as she was? As excited? As scared?

***

Amazing grace! How sweet the sound
That sav'd a wretch like me!
I once was lost, but now am found.
Was blind, but now I see.

***

They'd only been here a few minutes. As the voices rose to a beautiful crescendo, Birgitta, tears flowing, nudged Cora with her elbow and whispered, "Now! Go!"

Cora gazed at her, squeezed her hand, and stepped out into the aisle. Pastor Darland seemed to be looking right at her, but the church was so dark, he probably couldn't see her. She grabbed her coat from the peg and ducked out the door.

Ed had pulled the motor car right up next to the church. "Hello, young lady," he said with a friendly smile. "Get in. It's time to go to your husband."

So far this had been surprisingly easy. It wasn't until they were nearly to Kline's that she realized she hadn't said goodbye to Birgitta.

GEORGE
Waterton, Iowa - Chicago, Illinois
March 1914

Lewis handed George two sets of train tickets. "Ain't no record of these," he said. "My friend at the booking window, he tear up the carbons, so when Curtis come looking, can't nobody say you and your gal was on the train."

George looked at the names on the tickets. Mr. George Hammon on one. Mrs. George Hammon on the other. Waterton, Iowa, to Albany, New York, with stopovers in about a million towns in between. They'd have to change trains in Dubuque, Chicago, Elkhart, and Buffalo.

Unbelievable. This was the day of all days.

"Now, listen here," Lewis said. "These the best seats I could get, but they not all first class. And there a separate ticket for each part of your trip. Don't you lose them, or you have to pay all over again at your next stop. Ain't any seats left, then what you do? Be careful."

"I will." George put the tickets in a pocket inside his vest.

"One more thing," Lewis said. "Chicago a different breed of town than you ever see before. 'Til you been there, you can't get it into your head how big it be. Hell, the train station itself 'bout the size of Waterton. Easy to get lost, Georgie. Make sure you ask porters what train to get on there. Others maybe not so bad, but you watch out for Chicago."

George drew in smoke from his cigarette and slowly released it. Old Brownie, the palomino mare, stomped her feet. She never had liked smoke. "I wish we were going to Mississippi to stay with your family," George said.

Lewis rubbed Brownie's nose, fed her a cube of sugar. "They good people, but they don't need no white kids hanging 'round. That just asking for trouble. White folks down South, they don't take kindly to mixing. You better off with the Finnish woman's clan out East. Everybody the same color there."

George checked his pocket watch. It was ticking off seconds like they were hours. He dropped his cigarette and crushed it under his foot. "Church should've started by now."

Lewis smiled his infectious yellow-toothed smile as he hooked Brownie up to a brougham. "Keep it in your trousers, son. She'll be along presently."

The wind whished lightly outside the window of the livery. The horses snorted. "Think we'll ever see each other again, Lewis?" George said.

Lewis reached up with his huge leathery hand and squeezed George's shoulder. "I don't s'pect so, Georgie. But it was good 'til now, wasn't it? It was good. Now come on, time to take the coach out."

George and Cora were traveling light, each bringing only one suitcase of clothes and toiletries smuggled out by their servants. They could buy whatever else they needed on the train. Ed had cobbled together for them a virtual fortune of more than four hundred dollars.

Was this really going to work? George knew Ed could be trusted, but he wasn't sure about Birgitta. The woman had never liked him. If there was a weak link, she was it. But what sane person would risk Luka's wrath? George had never heard of him striking a woman, but that didn't mean he wouldn't.

Lewis got Cora's suitcase from his locker and put it in the back of the brougham. George threw his in on top. They led Brownie out into the powdery snowfall.

***

He must have kissed Cora a thousand times. He couldn't stop, couldn't get close enough to her. "Careful," she said of his tight embrace. George couldn't believe how much her tummy had grown since he'd last seen her in October.

"I love you I love you I love you I love you," he said. She was so beautiful in her prettiest church dress, now altered to accommodate her pregnancy.

"I love you, too," she said. "Can you feel our baby kicking?"

Ed sat in his motor car.

Lewis sat in the driver's seat of the coach.

Brownie nickered.

"You two don't slow down," Lewis said, "you gonna make a new baby right here on the spot 'fore the first one's even borned. Come on, got to go. With you or without, train pull out at twelve-oh-six. You can get all lovey-dovey once you on board."

George helped Cora into the brougham. He smiled at Ed, who tipped his hat. Ed was not a sentimental man, but he was obviously fighting emotion now. George waved and mouthed the word, *Thanks*. Ed nodded, then drove away down Jefferson Street toward Hammon Falls.

George climbed in next to Cora. Lewis made a clicking noise with his tongue. Brownie pulled out into the Sunday morning traffic.

All the way to the Illinois Central Station George and Cora alternated between staring at each other and trying to talk at the same time. Then they'd giggle and kiss and stare and talk and giggle and kiss.

At last, at last, he was with his *wife*. He didn't think about Mississippi anymore, or New York, or anywhere. As long as they were together, they could be flying to the moon.

Lewis pulled into the station around 11:30. There were few travelers on Sundays in March, so few people to note a young couple boarding the train east. Lewis hopped down from the driver's seat and opened the brougham door. George got out, followed by Cora. Lewis set their suitcases on the ground.

They stood gazing at each other for a long while. George felt his eyes welling up.

"None of that," Lewis said, although he was also misty.

"I don't know how to thank you," Cora said.

Lewis opened the compartment in the back of the coach and removed a small bouquet of daisies. "For you, Miss Cora. Got 'em over at the greenhouse last night."

Cora clutched the flowers to her chest. "I didn't know this would be so hard," she said.

Lewis passed a few bills to George as he shook his hand. "I know Mr. Ed give you money," he said, "but every little bit help."

Lewis was a poor man. He couldn't afford to give away his hard-earned salary. "I can't take this," George said.

"Hush now," Lewis said. "Just don't you flash big wads of cash 'round in the city. Thieves be happy to take it off you."

"I'm proud to be your friend," George said.

Lewis stood a good eight inches taller than Cora. She reached up behind his neck and pulled his face down to hers. Then, in broad daylight, in front of the Illinois Central Station, she kissed him on the cheek, a white girl showing affection for a black man.

"Thank you, Lewis," she said. "Thank you."

Great tears rolled off his chin. "Shit, I said I weren't gonna do this." He clasped her tiny hand in his. "God bless you, Miss Cora. My love to you both."

***

Every mile east of Independence was another mile farther from home than George had ever been.

The land here was astonishingly flat. The horizon looked a million miles away in every direction, the monotony broken only by the husks of last fall's crops poking through the snow. A small snow devil rose and dissipated in the field to the south. The sky had cleared, and parentheses of colored light bracketed the sun. Sundogs, George remembered from school, an indication that the air was very, very cold.

Their berth was comfortable, what might almost be first-class on an ocean liner. The bench, cushioned in red felt, was divided by an armrest, creating two separate seats. The walls were paneled in some dark brown wood. Thick red drapes hung over the window. Opposite the bench was a sleeping compartment. The berth had a uniquely *train* smell about it, with a whiff of Cora's daisies to add flavor.

George found the rhythm of movement and clackety-clack of the wheels soothing. By their first stop in Manchester the terrain was more rolling, and by Dubuque wooded bluffs towered over the banks of the Mississippi River. The trees were barren now, but he thought they must be beautiful when in full bloom.

They switched to the Chicago Great Western line in Dubuque. The station was small, and they had no problems. If anything, their berth in this train was more spacious than the last.

"Why don't you change out of your good clothes and get into bed?" George said to Cora. "You can rest for a few hours anyway."

"Okay," she said. She pawed through her suitcase and found an old brown dress that, from its size, style, and numerous stains, must have belonged to Birgitta. After putting it on, she folded the church dress carefully, repacked her bag, and lay down.

She fell asleep quickly, but George remained awake, as the train was due into Chicago by midnight. The sun set in western Illinois, and in less than an hour the sky was completely black.

A previous occupant of the berth had left behind a novel, *The Valiants of Virginia*, by Hallie Ermine Rives. George remembered reading a favorable review of it when it was published last year. He turned on the electric lamp over his seat and opened to the first page.

***

"FAILED!" ejaculated John Valiant blankly, and the hat he held dropped to the claret-colored rug like a huge white splotch of sudden fright.

***

Ejaculated, he thought. Ugh. Mrs. Rives meant "said," he knew, but that's not what he thought of when he read "ejaculated."

Well, maybe Cora would enjoy it. He closed the cover and watched her sleep. She was curled into a ball on her right side, knees drawn up, squeezing George's pillow to her breasts. A little dab of drool moistened the corner of her mouth. Her face was so pretty, so peaceful.

Every now and then, though, he'd see her wince or hear her moan softly. What a thing it must be to have another entire person inside her! It was bound to be painful sometimes, wasn't it, especially when the baby kicked?

He turned off the lamp and rested his head on the back of the seat. It had been a long, exhausting day, and he dozed a bit. He was awakened not by the sounds of Chicago but by the looming *sense* of it—the sense and the smell. Chicago was known for its stockyards, and the stench of cattle manure and blood and guts overwhelmed the sweet aroma of Cora's daisies.

Cora stirred on the bed. "Oh, my God," she muttered, "what is *that*?"

George peered out the curtains. Facing south, he couldn't see the city proper yet, just outlying suburbs and lots of slaughterhouses. The cloying stink reminded him of the Roth's Packing Company back home, multiplied by a thousand times.

"Chicago," he said.

In a few minutes lights rose out of the darkness, thousands of them, earth-bound stars eclipsing their heavenly counterparts in both number and beauty. The lights twinkled and burned and glowed, rose and fell and stretched into forever. *Chicago. A different breed of town than you ever see before.* Not a town, Lewis—a country, an empire, an entire world. How did anybody ever, *ever*, navigate those endless lights?

"Jesus," George said.

"What is it, honey?" Cora said.

"Chicago," he said again.

Cora rose to her elbow. "Chicago?"

George theatrically drew open the drapes. "Chicago."

Cora gasped. "It's pretty, but…Is every light a place? *Every* light?"

"And every place is filled with people," George said. "Jesus."

CORA
Chicago, Illinois - Erie, Pennsylvania
March 1914

The train took forever to get to the station. It slowed and sped up and slowed and stopped, only to lurch forward again. The motion nauseated Cora, and the incessantly clacking wheels drove her to distraction. The whistle announcing its arrival seemed right over her head. At least the stockyard smell had faded. Her face burned, her head pounded, and her insides ached. Not just the baby, but her guts seemed to be swelling, pushing outward, stretching her skin to its limit. She didn't want to alarm George, but her body felt as if it could explode.

At the station someone knocked on their door. George rose and let a porter in. The man urged them to hurry, as other people were waiting to occupy the berth.

Cora sat up on the edge of the bed, letting her feet dangle. In this position her belly hung halfway down her thighs. What a sight she must be, a fat monkey with mussed hair and eyes that must be blood red from sleep.

"We're going to Elkhart," George said to the porter. "Do you know which platform?"

The porter frowned at him scornfully. "The hell? I look like a damn information booth?"

George pulled a dollar coin from his trouser pocket. He looked so handsome in his suit and tie. "Now do you know which platform?" he said.

"Well, shit," the porter said, "why'n't you say so? Lemme see your ticket." George handed it to him, along with the coin. The man glanced at their names, then stared them both up and down. "You ain't old enough to be no Mister and Missus, but by the looks of things, missy, you been *actin'* married...." George took a step forward. The porter shrugged. "Ain't no bid'ness of mine. Looky here, Lake Shore and Michigan Southern Line, platform 27-A."

"Which is where?" George said.

"Over on the other side of the station, up some stairs. Follow the signs. You got plenty of time. Train don't pull out 'til six in the a.m. Hell, that one coming from the Twin Cities, don't even get in 'til five." The porter gave George's ticket back. "Someone to carry your bags?"

"We only have two," George said. "I'll get them."

"Have it your own way," the porter said, and left.

George helped Cora to her feet. He set their bags on the bench next to a book.

"What's that?" she said.

"*The Valiants of Virginia,*" George said.

"By Mrs. Rives?" Cora said. "I've wanted to read it. She wrote an etiquette book, too, which I hated, but I heard her fictional stories are good. Did you buy that for me? How sweet."

George looked like he was about to say something, but didn't. He opened her suitcase and slid the book inside, then peered out the curtains.

In that brief glimpse Cora saw a mass of shoulders and hats pass through the steam and smoke from dozens of trains. "What can all those people be doing out at this time of the night?"

"Travelers just like us," George said. "Come on. Maybe we can find a place to for you to sit until our next train comes."

With one bag under his right arm, the other in his right hand, and his left arm wrapped around Cora, he led them out of the berth, off the train, and into the appalling streams of humanity that clogged the station. People were smoking cigars and cigarettes, and the stench from their body odor and the train exhaust was overwhelming. Although the crowd was surprisingly considerate—many folks noticed her condition and made room—it still crushed in around them like some great fluid beast. The walking seemed endless as they followed the signs along a maze of twisting corridors, going up and down stairs. The final set, at least thirty steps, were brutal.

Cora feared she might give birth right here in the station.

She didn't, but by the time George found her a spot on a public bench near platform 27-A, she was panting and sweating, and her calves were cramping as if pierced by nails.

"How you doing?" George said, kissing her brow. "You're burning up."

They'd left Lewis's daisies behind. Perhaps the next people in that berth would enjoy them.

Cora smiled weakly and said, "I didn't burst."

***

At least five trains pulled in and out of platform 27-A before the Twin Cities train to Elkhart arrived. Cora lost count as she drifted in and out of sleep leaning against George. Once he woke her to get on the wrong one, St. Louis, only to be kicked off by a grumpy conductor checking their tickets. "Can't you read?" he said. "Times and trains are posted on the big board."

The departure and arrival schedule, a sign taller than a house, was not twenty feet away. "Sorry," George said. Cora was too tired to care.

When the Elkhart train finally did come, their berth consisted of a narrow mattress in a compartment separated from the aisle by a thin white curtain. There was no bench, no chairs, and no room to put any. They could barely even sit upright in bed. George let Cora climb in first, then followed after her, using his body as a barricade so a sudden jolt wouldn't dump her into the aisle.

"How long until Elkhart?" Cora asked.

"There's a dining car we could sit in," George said, trying to sound hopeful.

"You need sleep," she said. "I don't suppose there's a bathtub on board?"

George ran his fingers beneath his collar and examined them for dirt. "Do I stink?"

"We both do."

He removed his suit coat and tie. "It's going to be a long trip. Sleep."

Cora rolled to her left side, facing the wall, which was paneled with cheap plywood that held the smells of hundreds of other travelers who'd slept here. The sheets and pillow cases reeked of sweat and hair oil, and probably hadn't been changed for a week. There was no window.

George snuggled up behind her, draping his arm across her breasts and nuzzling her cheek with his chin. He needed a shave.

Cora sighed happily. This was the way things were meant to be, George and Cora, Cora and George, lying together in the same bed as husband and wife.

"I was hoping you'd be wearing our wedding ring," he said.

"That was Momma's," Cora said. She closed her eyes and savored the warmth of his breath on her neck. "Whatever you think of Daddy, her ring belongs to him. It was just temporary anyway, 'til we could afford our own."

"What do you think old Luka's doing now?"

Whistle blaring, the train jerked forward to begin its slow acceleration out of the station.

"I'm sure he's frantic with worry," Cora said. "Poor man."

"We wouldn't be on this train if it wasn't for him."

"That doesn't mean he's not scared, and furious, and sad. He's probably got every policeman in Iowa looking for us."

George stroked her hair. "Your bosoms are getting big."

"Sore, too."

"Wonder why." He cupped her right breast and squeezed gently. "Does this hurt?"

"A little."

He let go. "What can the cops do, do you think? I mean, we're married."

"I don't know. We signed all those papers. Who knows what we agreed to? I didn't read them, did you?"

George rose to an elbow, resting his free hand on her hip. "I'm more worried about Birgitta. She won't tell, will she?"

The train picked up speed, rumbled and swayed, clickety-clack.

"Not if he tortured her," Cora said. "But she's the one who'll have to face him, and *nobody* gets mad like Daddy. What about your mother?"

"She'll claim that God is testing her. Again. She thinks she's so special that every time something goes wrong, it's because God himself has it in for her. Nothing just happens for her. A twister didn't hit Pomeroy, God sent it. My father didn't die of his wound, God killed him. I didn't make you pregnant, God did."

Cora giggled. "I don't think I'm a virgin."

"I can testify to that."

Cora nudged him in the ribs. "You're ornery."

"Anyway, the cops'll tell her the same thing they tell Luka."

"She'll just let us go, then?"

"Will your father?"

"No."

"But they won't find us."

Cora closed her eyes. She was exhausted, and she'd gotten a little sleep tonight, on the Chicago train, on the platform. Poor George had had none. "I'm scared," she said.

"Yeah," George said. "Me, too."

***

The next afternoon they changed to the New York Central line in Elkhart, Indiana. The station was bigger than Waterton's but nothing compared to Chicago's. Their accommodations were no better, but the train wasn't full and George paid to upgrade to second-class.

Three days later they'd only made it as far as Pennsylvania, calling at every little town and hamlet throughout Indiana and Ohio along the way. At one station, Cora got off the train to use the toilet. They had a forty-five minute layover to pick up more passengers and change engineers, so she took the opportunity to stretch her legs. Besides, the toilets on the train were barely big enough to fit inside and still close the door.

Her insides were on fire. The food George bought on board was terrible, and she had a hard time keeping it down. She was constantly excusing herself, claiming the baby was pushing on her bladder, then rushing to the water closet and puking into the foul-smelling bowl. The train toilets flushed, although all that did was spew the vile contents onto the tracks below.

325

Luckily Birgitta had sent mints along with her toiletries. She used their aroma to disguise her breath from George.

The station had no running water. In fact, it had no toilet other than an old-fashioned outhouse in the back, which was in use. While George shopped for snacks at a little general store there, Cora waited patiently for the outhouse's occupant to finish. It was a chilly night, and a light rain was falling. Pockets of snow piled up against buildings and in ditches, but for the most part the terrain was barren, last autumn's wet, brown grass plastered against the ground while living green shoots poked up between the lattice of lifeless blades.

So this was Pennsylvania. A little more rolling, a little more wooded, but not so different from Iowa, really.

The outhouse door opened and a little boy emerged. He smiled mischievously at Cora, then raced into the station. Inside, a kerosene lantern hung from a rafter above, its fumes more odious than the bodily odors they masked. A plain box of toilet tissues, recently opened, rested between the two holes on the bench. Well, that was one advantage of a small town. In a city someone would have stolen the tissues just to steal them.

Cora latched the door, lifted up the old brown dress she was still wearing, and pulled down her underclothing. Almost since the baby was conceived, it seemed, the act of urination burned, but today it was worse than usual. It felt like liquid fire, with a smell rancid as pus. She bit her lip to keep from screaming.

The burning continued for several long seconds after she finished. When she used the toilet tissue she noticed clots of blood on it, black in the lantern light, streaked with yellow mucus. Horrified, she dropped the tissue down the hole.

"Oh, no," she said. Not again.

George would be so disappointed in her.

Although she was pregnant, Birgitta had known she wouldn't be for much longer, and had packed menstrual rags. Those were in her suitcase, however, so Cora stuffed a handful of toilet tissues inside the crotch of her underclothes.

The effort to stand almost caused her to faint. The kerosene emissions were frightful. How could anyone breathe in here? Straightening her dress and composing herself, Cora unlatched the door and stepped out. Two young women were waiting to use the outhouse. They appeared ready to scold her, but one look at her face quelled their anger.

"Go fetch a doctor," one said.

"No," Cora said. She breathed in the misty air. Its cool healing spread through her body, and she felt somewhat revived. Maybe that was all she needed, a little fresh air. "I'm all right," she said. "My husband is just inside the station."

The women looked skeptical, but went into the outhouse together.

Cora found George in the general store, trying to decide on which kind of chocolate bar to buy. "Hersheys or Nestles?" he said.

Cora smiled the brightest smile she could muster. "Both," she said.

***

Some stops were no more than a lone depot building in the country. It took them another two days to reach Erie, by which time Cora's bleeding had slowed but not stopped. She had plenty of menstrual rags but no place to wash the used ones, so she ended up throwing them away in the trash barrel outside her car's onboard toilet.

Cora slept when she could and read *The Valiants of Virginia* when she couldn't. She used the torn half of the Waterton-Chicago train ticket as a bookmark. As George snored peacefully beside her, she wrote her name in pencil inside the front cover. *Mrs. Cora Hammon.* That looked and felt so wonderful, she kept on writing it. *Mrs. Cora Hammon.* *Mrs.* *Cora Hammon.* She drew little hearts around the "Mrs." and the "Hammon." Doodling helped to take her mind off the pain, and soon several pages were decorated with her flowery scribblings.

I am Mrs. Cora Hammon, she thought. I'll be brave for George. Just two more weeks and the child will be born. I can hold up that long.

Between sleeping and reading, she discussed baby names with George in the dining car. They agreed a girl would be Emma after her mother, but they weren't as sure about a boy. Cora wanted George, Jr., but George didn't like the idea. "Who wants another George Hammon running around?" he said, squeezing her a little too tightly.

"How about Orville?" Cora said teasingly, trying to ignore the cramps in her abdomen.

"How about Butt-face McGee?" George said.

"That's not nice."

"Neither is your father."

"Well, then, how about G.W.?" Cora clenched her teeth as a wave of cramping built and dissipated inside her without ever reaching a crescendo. She took a few small pain-free breaths before the next round started. "Does anybody know what the 'G.W.' stood for?"

George shrugged. "G.W., I guess," he said. "I never asked."

By sheer will Cora was able to keep from shrieking when the pain came again. Perhaps because they both reeked of sweat and felt miserable, George didn't notice her agony. Perhaps he was gallantly pretending not to notice. Perhaps Birgitta was right, this was no time for a girl in her condition to be traveling.

But she only had to make it through one more change of trains, in Buffalo. They'd be in Albany by the weekend, then the road would be smooth and Birgitta's cousin would give her all the care she needed.

GEORGE
Erie, Pennsylvania - Buffalo, New York
March 1914

The Erie station was almost as crowded as Chicago's. Unlike the small-town whistle-stop depots, though, it had modern toilet facilities with running water and flush toilets. There were no baths, but both George and Cora were able to wash up in the sinks and change into clean clothes during a long layover.

Cora looked relieved to have clean hair and skin again, and her altered blue gingham dress still had the fresh starchy smell of its most recent laundering. But it wasn't until the grime had been scrubbed away that George realized how pale she was. She had dark circles under her eyes, and her face was alarmingly gaunt, considering the weight she'd gained. She seemed fragile.

"I'm ready to not be pregnant anymore," she said with a weak smile. The strain in her voice was obvious.

George helped her into bed. Why hadn't he noticed her condition before now? "I'll get you whatever you need. Don't you move again until we get to Buffalo."

"I'll *have* to move before then, silly."

George felt his cheeks redden. "Well, except for that."

She was asleep before the train left the station. Their berth had a window, but it faced south, so George didn't get to see the shoreline of Lake Erie. He'd missed Lake Michigan in Chicago because of the darkness, and now he was missing Erie, too. Oh, well, maybe they'd get a glimpse of Niagara Falls when they changed trains in Buffalo. How nice would that be, George and his new bride at Niagara Falls?

Cora gasped. Her face was dotted with a fine layer of sweat, her arms and legs thrashed, and her abdomen positively *gyrated*, although by some force of will she slept through it all.

George found a cloth in her suitcase and mopped her forehead and cheeks.

Jesus, could she be having the baby *now*? He had no idea what was supposed to happen when a woman gave birth, what the signs were. But it wasn't time! According to the doctor in Iowa, she should still have at least two weeks yet, probably more, because first babies, he said, "were always late."

In flailing about Cora's dress tangled around and between her legs. George straightened it, giving her more freedom to move. A streak of blood had seeped through at the crotch.

Even George knew that a woman's monthlies stopped during pregnancy. If she was bleeding there, then something was wrong, something was terribly wrong.

She needed a doctor.

George covered her with a blanket and stepped out into the corridor. He headed toward the dining car, looking for the conductor, the engineer, a porter, any railroad employee who might have access to a passenger list.

Eventually he located the conductor who'd taken the bottom half of their Elkhart-Buffalo tickets. He was coming out of the toilet. George put a hand on his shoulder. "Excuse me, sir, but do you know if there's a doctor onboard?"

"Usually is," the man said, pushing George's hand away. "What's the problem?"

"My wife is ill."

The conductor looked him over. "Your *wife*? How old are you, son?"

"Never mind about me. Is there a doctor?"

"I'll have to check. What berth are you in?"

"31-B."

"What's wrong with her?"

"She's bleeding."

The conductor smirked. "How old did you say you were?"

George grabbed his lapels. "She's pregnant *and* she's bleeding!"

"Okay, calm down." The man took the torn ticket stubs from a pocket under his belt and riffled through them. "First child?"

"We're seventeen!" George said, although he'd be eighteen in less than three weeks. His panicky voice sounded like a little girl's. "*Yes*, it's her first child. Our first."

"Go back to your berth, take care of her. I'm sure I saw a Doctor Somebody on the fares. If he's a medical doctor, I'll send him right down."

"Thank you," George said. "She's eight-and-half months along."

***

No doctor came that night.

Cora woke screaming, and no doctor came. She dripped blood as George practically carried her to the toilet, and no doctor came.

"Why didn't you tell me?" George said as he eased her onto the toilet.

"I'm fine," she said. "Just a few more days and we'll be in Albany."

"You are *not* fine."

"Let's not argue," she said, and she cried out as her urine stream struck the metal bowl. She reached for a tissue. "Close the door, please."

"I'm not leaving you."

"This is private. I don't want you to see. Please?"

George backed into the hall and pushed the door shut. He could hear her weeping. He paced frantically, chasing away a couple of other passengers by snapping, "It's occupied!"

Jesus, Cora. *Cora*!

Goddamn it, *where was the doctor*?

A few moments later the door swung open and Cora staggered out. She paused to drop a bloody rag into the trash barrel. "It's not as bad as it's been some nights," she said. "Just a little trickle. I think I'm getting better. I feel stronger. Take me back to the bed."

George guided her down the corridor. The odor of blood and infection was unmistakable.

She slept through the night, but George didn't get a wink. He cried and worried himself to the point of nausea.

In the morning a doctor came, a middle-aged gentleman and his wife.

"My name is Cavendish," he said in the corridor when George answered the door. He had a medical bag. "I understand there's an ill young woman here?"

"My wife Cora," George said. "What took you so long?"

"What's wrong, dear?" Mrs. Cavendish said.

George started to explain but found he couldn't say the words in front of a lady.

"She's with child?" Cavendish said.

"Yes. We're going to Albany."

"Let me see her."

George admitted them. Cavendish went straight to the bed. George tried to follow, but Mrs. Cavendish took his hand. "No, dear, let him do his work. Sit with me."

They sat on the bench opposite the bed. Cavendish pulled the curtain that separated the sleeping chamber from the rest of the berth. George heard him opening his bag. All he could see was the outline of the doctor's back and arms against the cloth. He could tell when Cavendish bent forward, could imagine as he placed the stethoscope between Cora's breasts, as he lifted her dress, drew down her undergarments. Another man was looking at his wife…down there.

George inhaled sharply.

"Shhh," Mrs. Cavendish said. "It's all right. He's a doctor. This is what he does."

The curtain opened a moment later. "Where did you say you're going?" Cavendish said.

"Albany."

"No, you're not. This girl needs a hospital. *Now*."

"What is it?" Mrs. Cavendish said.

"Breech," he said grimly. "Probably ectopic. Not Fallopian, or she would have lost the baby long before now. Perhaps cervical. Please God let it only be that."

"Oh, my," Mrs. Cavendish said.

"What's that mean?" George said.

"It means you're not going to Albany. Listen to me, son," Cavendish said. "We travel this way often. There's a boarding house next to the train station. Do you have money?"

"Some, yes—"

"Good. Check in the instant this train stops. Do you understand? The *instant*. You cannot wait. Have the proprietor telephone for an ambulance or policeman, even a taxicab. There's a charity hospital nearby. You must get her there immediately."

"Is she in danger?" George said. Cavendish didn't need to answer, his expression said it all.

"George?" Cora moaned from behind the curtain.

"The child is in distress as well," Cavendish said. "Its heartbeat is very faint."

George clasped his hands over his mouth to keep from puking.

Mrs. Cavendish put her arm around his shoulder. "There, there, dear."

CORA
Buffalo, New York
March 1914

"Where are we?" Cora gasped. Everything was spinning, even when she closed her eyes.

"A boarding house in Buffalo," George said.

"We're going to Albany," she said. The ceiling, when it stopped moving, was white plaster. An electric light burned above her, a ceiling fan pushed warm air downward in slow circles. There was a strange man and woman in the room, older, with salt-and-pepper hair. Cora was lying on a mattress. At the moment her insides didn't hurt at all. The baby wasn't kicking.

"Don't talk," the strange man said, although Cora wasn't sure who he was addressing.

"What's wrong?" she said to George.

George was digging through one of the suitcases, which lay open at the foot of the bed. "Where's that address Birgitta left you? I'll write to her cousin, tell her we'll be delayed."

"Delayed? Why?"

"Please," the strange man said, "rest."

"The baby isn't kicking," Cora said.

George glanced up at the man and the woman. He looked so worried, so scared. "I can't find the address," he said.

"Don't worry about the address," the woman said. "It'll turn up."

"Who are you?" Cora said.

"A doctor," the man said.

"Is George sick?"

"No, dear," the woman said.

"Why isn't my baby kicking?" Cora said.

"An ambulance is on its way," George said. His voice squeaked. "I don't remember her cousin's name."

Cora heard bells dinging outside, softly at first but more loudly, more frantically as they approached, accompanied by the clopping of horses and the clatter of wheels.

"It's here," the man said.

A knock, a creaking door, a muffled voice: "She's in the back room." Footsteps, another door. "Hurry," the man said to whoever came in.

Concerned faces, swimming in circles, looked down on her. Young men in white uniforms. White. White. White.

"You're going to be all right," George said, kissing her.

"Please, young fella," someone said, "out of the way."

"Why isn't my baby—?" Cora said. An *ambulance?* "My baby!" she cried. *"Why isn't my baby kicking?"*

She tried to sit up. Hands held her in place. She thrashed, fought them, screaming in her head, or maybe aloud, *My baby! My baby!*

"Calm down, miss!" the doctor said sternly. "This isn't helping. Talk to you wife, son, make her understand. She could kill them both."

George gently grasped her arms. Tears were dripping out of his eyes, snot out of his nose. But his voice was so kind and loving. "Sweetie, you have to be quiet. You're going to be all right. Our baby's going to be all right. But you have to be quiet. We're going to the hospital now. I'll be with you the whole way."

George looked at the men in white. They nodded. "Let's go," they said.

Cora had the sensation of being lifted. The dizziness was making her queasy. Her back came to rest on a coarse material that sagged like a hammock. Her insides suddenly hurt again. Spasming. Cramping. Something seemed to pop. She felt liquid spew out between her legs, soaking her thighs.

"Christ," someone yelled. "Move!"

She jostled back and forth as the ceiling flew by. George had her hand. Someone did. A doorframe, the sound of hinges straining and wood smacking against a wall. A slate sky. Misty raindrops. Her face was on fire, the water soothed her. The smell of horses. A rectangular carriage or wagon. Or hearse. White. White. White. Sliding, her backside against a wooden floor. George's face, then darkness as a door closed. "Hold on, honey," she heard him say. "We'll be there as soon as we can."

Cora lost consciousness as the carriage lurched forward.

***

More white, white, white. The ceiling. The walls. The people. Women in masks. Not masks, habits. Nuns. There were nuns all around. A crucifix went by on a wall. Cora was moving fast. She could hear wheels spinning on a smooth floor. She was still lying on her back. On a rolling bed, apparently. At least four men surrounded her. She didn't see George.

A man's voice, the doctor. "It's breech," he said to somebody. "Vaginal bleeding, probably ectopic. You'll have to do a Caesarian."

"How long has she been in labor?"

"Not long, but you can't wait."

"Where's George?" Cora said, but no one heard her.

Her entire entourage turned a corner.

"Second room on the right," someone said.

They turned again, then came to a sudden stop. White, white, white. Ominous machines. Another crucifix.

Scissors were cutting her clothes away. Cutting?

"Is my baby all right?" Cora said.

This time someone heard. A nurse or nun mopped her head with a wet cloth. "Your baby is fine, sweetie. You're both going to be fine." Something cold touched her nose and mouth. It smelled funny. "Breathe deep," the nurse or nun said. "This will make you sleep."

Her baby was fine.

Her baby was fine.

Her baby was fine.

Cora smiled. "Tell George," she said, lifting her hand to grasp something, anything. Someone pushed it gently back to her side.

"Strap her down," said a man's voice.

"Tell him what, honey?" the nurse or nun said. Fingers caressed Cora's cheek.

"He was so worried, the silly. Tell him we're okay. Tell him I love him."

GEORGE
Buffalo, New York & Beyond
March 1914 - February 1915

George sat on his suitcase on a chair in the waiting room, brow touching his knees, arms curled over his head.

"The baby wasn't breathing," a nurse was saying. "It was blue, with a massive infection over its left eye. Peritonitis. The doctors set it aside to try to save the mother."

George stood up. Without thinking he grabbed the suitcase. "I need to see her," he said. He felt as if a motor car were parked on his chest.

"Sir, you can't. She's…The fetus had affixed itself to the aortic root instead of the uterine wall. That's where it grew. The aorta burst when the doctors removed the child. There was nothing they could do—"

"*I need to see her!*" George shouted. His mind was coming apart.

The nurse tried to hold him, but he pulled away and ran down the hall in the direction from which the nurse had come. "Sir, you can't go in there! Help! Someone, help!"

George shouldered through a metal door. There were several hallways lined with rows of rooms. Operating rooms. People's lives were being saved here. He didn't care. He peered into the round windows of each, the nurse in close pursuit, accompanied now by two orderlies.

He found her in the second hallway, second room on the right.

The doctors were huddled to one side, away from the main operating table, ignoring the table, ignoring *her*. Cora lay there, naked, face turned toward him, lips parted, eyes open. She was looking at him.

She wasn't looking at him.

She didn't see a thing. There was no light in her eyes, none.

Her stomach was gashed like a trout's. Blood was everywhere, in her hair, on her breasts, on her privates, on the table, on the huddled doctors—Jesus, *on the wall*.

Blood.

Cora's blood.

Aortic root.

A man put a hand on his shoulder. "Sir…."

A scream more solid than iron churned inside of him, sharper than knives.

Cora.

Cora!

He couldn't contain it. "Cora!" he wailed, and crashed through the door. He had to be with her.

The doctors looked up in shock. "Get him out of here!" they cried.

The orderlies tackled him, dragged him out of the room. "She's gone, sir," one said with a gentleness that belied his strength.

"Cora!" George cried, and "Cora!" and "Cora."

The men escorted him back to the waiting room.

"I'm sorry," an orderly said, "but we need some information."

"What was her last name?" the nurse said.

George pulled his arms away from the orderlies. He had never let go of his suitcase, although he'd left hers in the boarding house. "I'm all right now," he said.

He wasn't all right. Without another word he fled the hospital, exiting beneath an oversized lacquered crucifix that hung over the entrance.

I am the light of the world.

He ran until he'd left Buffalo behind.

He had money. He ran, by foot, by train, by taxi, always east and north. Margaret and Luka would not welcome him home. There was nothing for him in Iowa.

He ran.

He ran for days, for weeks, for months. He had no plan, no hope, no reason to stop.

He just ran.

He ran to Canada. To Quebec. East and north. To Newfoundland. East and north.

In June an archduke was assassinated in Europe. George ran to the sea, and when hostilities engulfed the Austro-Hungarian Empire, even the great Atlantic couldn't contain him. He ran, by ship, to England.

He joined, he trained, he marched, he learned to shoot a rifle.

In the winter of 1915 his regiment was shipped to the Continent. It was a cold and snowy February morning when they came ashore. They started by digging trenches.

Like his father before him, George Hammon had run off to war.

THE CELTIC CROSS

WILL
Waterton, Iowa
June 2009

The soldierboy stared out of the photograph at Will, his right eye swirling with light, the left shrouded in shadow, echoing the empty socket of the son he didn't know he had.

The Celtic cross hung from the picture frame.

Will was ninety-five years old. He'd survived a stroke and pneumonia. His daughter and his doctor had saddled him with a home care specialist, which was a nuisance, but at least he was *home*, not in the hospital or some "retirement village."

He looked up at his father, man to boy, eye to eye. "Why didn't you just give the cross to me in person?" he said.

You wouldn't have taken it, George said. *And I was in a bit of a hurry, if you recall.*

"I'll take it now," Will said. He rose from his bed and lifted the cross from the frame, placing the chain around his neck. George wore it for more than twenty years in memory of his friend Mick, but this was the first time for Will.

It would be the last.

How's it feel?

"Heavy," Will said.

That it is.

Will had a wheelchair, but he refused to use it unless he was very tired or Katie was visiting. This morning he was visiting her. Charlie would be here to pick him up any time. He dressed in a brown polyester leisure suit that had been out of fashion for thirty years. Will thought he looked pretty snazzy in it, even without the tie.

He felt good. The weakness in his right side was almost completely gone. He still had a nagging cough sometimes, but what the hell, the sun was shining and the birds were singing and a breeze carried the smell of his neighbor's freshly cut grass through the screen door.

Right on schedule Charlie drove up in the 1967 Austin Healy Will bought and restored for him. His grandson always had been a fanatic about being on time. He still needed a haircut, and now he'd taken to wearing a silly beard that never quite filled in. Young people these days.

Will pushed open the screen door.

"Hi, Grandpa," Charlie said. "You ready?"

"Here I am," Will said.

"Listen, Mom'll skin me alive if I don't bring your wheelchair."

"She'll get over it."

Charlie hopped out of the car and helped Will into the passenger seat. "Well, don't blame me if she yells," he said, climbing in behind the wheel. He backed out, drove two blocks on Carlyle, and turned left onto Prism Drive. "Wanna go by the old place?" he said.

Gloire de Matin Island was one of the few spots in Waterton that looked pretty much as it did when Will was growing up. Some of his most precious memories were associated with the island. He and Margaret and Luka and, at one time, George had lived in a beautiful mansion there. So had Ed and Estella and Birgitta and Ellen. He'd heard the new owner had dropped a hundred thousand bucks into salvaging the house after the flood.

"That's okay," Will said. "Just the quickest way."

Most of the rest of Waterton was unrecognizable from his childhood. The old train depot on Washington Street still stood, as did the Waterton and Block's buildings, and the former YMCA. The *Waterton Record* was here, although now it was the *Waterton-Cedar Crossing Record*. The Oak River still churned its way to the Mississippi.

Little else was the same. The covered walkway over the Fourth Street Bridge was nice, and the globed street lights added a touch of class, but Will prefered things the way they were.

Charlie seemed content to enjoy the day quietly. He passed the bank that occupied the space where the Majestic Theatre once stood, crossed Franklin Street, and proceeded northwest past the KWRC Building. The Healy's convertible top was down, and the wind tousled what was left of Will's hair. He hadn't been up this way in decades.

The ceremony was to be a simple one, a ribbon cutting and a speech by the new company's president. Katie wouldn't even be involved. Her part was done. Her construction firm had built the place, now someone else got to gloat. But she wanted Will there to see what she had done, this wonder she had erected on the site of his old filling station, Will's Standard. What she really wanted, Will thought, was for her old man to be proud of her.

And he was.

They'd had their differences and distances through the years, but she'd been rock solid for him since his stroke and illness. Maybe she always had been, and Will just hadn't noticed.

A small crowd had gathered outside an unspectacular structure, three stories tall with a stone façade. Dignitaries stood in a semi-circle in front of a ribbon stretching across the main entrance. Channel Eleven had sent a cameraman. A bored TV reporter checked her notes while she waited for the festivities to begin.

Will couldn't even picture the filling station, there was so much clutter now. But with strategic mental subtraction he could still remember the Tokheim pump out front—it would have been just about here—and hear the dinging of the bell hose as a customer drove up. He could still see a brand new '37 Roadster pull in, a man doomed to watery death at the wheel and Will's future wife Elaine in the back seat.

I'm serious, the man said, *call her. She's worse than a kid sister, always hanging around.*

"It makes bottled water," Charlie said as he pulled into the parking lot and found a space. "They're bringing a hundred and fifty jobs to Waterton. This'll really help people out, with the economy like it is."

Will chuckled.

Bottled water? George said.

"Shhh," Will said. *I can't talk out loud to you. Charlie will think I'm crazy.*

"What, Grandpa?"

"Just think it's funny that people buy water in bottles. What's wrong with the tap?"

"It's big business, Grandpa. You ought to be drinking that instead of pop or beer."

"Otherwise I might die young," Will said.

Katie was sitting on a bench at the north end of the parking lot. When the plant opened, employees would be taking breaks here, eating lunch and smoking cigarettes. Katie was smoking one now, although she snuffed it out when she saw Will. As if at her age she couldn't do what she pleased.

Charlie and Will got out of the Healy. Charlie took Will's arm and escorted him across the lot. Somebody in a suit stepped up to a microphone and introduced somebody else. A company official, apparently.

"Hi, Dad," Katie said, taking his arm from Charlie and leading him to the bench. "The reporter interviewed me for the five o'clock news. Hope I don't get edited out!"

Will gazed at her face, at her obvious satisfaction in her work, at the little crow's feet that so recalled Elaine. *Go on,* George said. *Do it, complete the circle.*

The company official was talking, but his voice was lost on the wind.

"Katie," Will said. He removed the Celtic cross from beneath his undershirt. "I want you to
have this."

Katie looked surprised—surprised and pleased. "Your father gave that to you."

"And I'm giving it to you."

Although the cross wasn't dirty, it was tarnished and clashed with her dress. It was a relic that didn't fit in her modern world. Will expected her to be polite, to thank him, to put it in her pocket or purse. Instead, she lowered her head and allowed him to place it around her neck, as if he were knighting her or blessing her.

Will was doing neither of these things. Here on the site of his youthful dreams fulfilled, where he met his future wife and Katie's mother, he was laying a wreath.

"It's beautiful," Katie said. "Thanks, Dad."

Thanks, Will, George said.

Charlie nodded approvingly. He probably didn't realize it, but one day the cross would come to him.

The dignitaries applauded at some comment the bottled water official made. The TV cameraman moved in for a better angle.

Will smiled at Katie.

"Remind me to tell you the story," he said.

EPILOGUE
ANAM CARA

YOUNG WILL
Pascagoula, Mississippi
June 1961

The trailer was a rundown affair of rotted wood and loose siding set on a sandy lot. The lot was strewn with junked-out car husks, old tires, scraps of wood, rusted nails and tools, and piles of old magazines that had been rained on so often that the pages had melted into one waxen mess. A telephone wire swayed from a connection under the eave to a pole out on the gravel road. Will could see a light in the window, so he knew the place had electricity, but running water was a different story. There was a hand pump in the front yard and an outhouse in back.

Nobody answered the door.

Will went round to the back, but nobody answered there either. Someone should be here because he'd phoned ahead. A river flowed several hundred yards behind the trailer, spanned on both sides by a thick greenbelt of dogwoods. The day was oppressively humid, as he imagined most summer days were in the south, but the verdant scents of honeysuckle, magnolia, and chickweed were deep and lovely and brought the foliage eerily alive. Insects provided a pleasant whir, although their biting was annoying. Well, Mississippi had nothing on Iowa when it came to bugs. Will brushed them away and followed a well-rutted path into the woods.

A man wearing a straw hat sat in a wheelchair in a clearing, a fishing line bobbing in the river. Thick with algae, water greener than the trees lolled lazily toward the sea. A tackle box rested against the right wheel of his chair. On a rise overlooking a sandbar some distance away the remnants of a picnic lunch were spread out on a blanket.

Will approached the man from behind, making sure to snap twigs to avoid startling him. The man, his father George, removed his hat and looked up. "I'll be damned," he said. "You came anyway. I told you not to bother."

George was only sixty-five but appeared much older. He'd gotten heavy in the twenty-four years since Will last saw him, probably a function of being in a wheelchair and having limited exercise. His face was heavily lined, with skin hanging from his jowls and beneath his neck.

"I wanted to see you," Will said.

"After all this time? Well, have a seat."

There was nowhere to sit but on the bank next to his wheelchair. "It's pretty here," Will said, kneeling next to George's chair and resting his arm on the tackle box.

"The world is joined by water," George said. He put his hat back on. A turtle or fish snapped an insect from the surface of the river, causing a plinking sound and a small ripple.

"Uh, Dad...."

George tugged on the line. The bobber floated easily toward him. No bites. *"Dad?"* he said. His accent was now an uneasy blend of Midwestern, French, and Deep South dialects. "A little late for that, isn't it?"

"There's something I need to talk to you about."

"Ah, so this is business after all. I didn't think it was a pleasure visit."

"It's not like that, Dad."

"Stop it. Call me George or Mick, anything but Dad."

"Took me two years to find you."

"Feds never did. What *is* it like?"

"My grandfather died in '59—"

"Luka Curtis is dead? About goddamned time."

"He suffered, if it makes you feel better. Diabetes, bad. He left you money in his will."

"Why the hell would he do that?"

"I don't know. But it's not a small amount."

"Doesn't matter. I don't want it. Don't need it."

"Dad—"

"George."

"George. Look at this place. You could fix it up. Or move somewhere else."

George reeled in his line. "This is my home. I like it fine here."

Will removed a paper from his pocket. "I've got a check made out to George Hammon."

"I haven't been George Hammon for a long time, Will. Maybe I never was." He examined the jig at the end of his line. "Grow big catfish down here. Luka leave me a forty-pounder in his will?"

Will heard movement in the woods behind him. He didn't see anyone. "You can't just walk away from this kind of money."

George laughed. "I can't walk at all."

"You know what I mean. Don't you even want to know how much?"

"Is that all you came her for? To give me his dirty money?"

"I'm trying to help you."

"Really? Then turn your ass around and go back to Iowa."

Will rose from his knees. "I was hoping for something a little more civil."

"Then how about starting out with, 'Hello, George, how you been?'"

Will sighed. "Hello, George, how you been?"

"None of your damn business." Smiling, George rummaged through the tackle box for pliers. Finding some, he snipped the line at the junction of the tines and returned pliers and jig to the box. "Only thing I ever wondered was where did my mother wander off to? That night no one could find her?"

Will nearly told him the truth. Instead, he said, "Just running errands, I guess. She divorced Luka and booted him out of the place on Gloire de Matin."

"Good for her." George spun his chair around to on the path. He wouldn't let Will help him. "Do this every day," he said. "She still alive?"

Will shook his head.

"Well, she'd've been almost ninety," George said.

Will heard the movement in the woods again, and this time a woman stepped into the clearing, carrying a basket full of blackberries. She was slender, with long straight hair that had gone pure white. She wore denim shorts and a flannel shirt with the sleeves cut off at the shoulders. "Hello," she said.

"Light me a cigarette, will you?" George said to her.

The woman put the basket down. She pulled a cigarette from a pack of Camels in her shirt pocket, held it between her lips, and flicked a butane lighter. Coughing, she drew in one puff to make sure the flame took, then handed the cigarette to George.

"The townspeople smashed up your grave marker," Will said, "after your confession."

"Well, I'm not in it anyway." George looked at the woman. "Say hi to Will," he said to her.

"Pleased to meet you at last," she said liltingly. Even with wrinkled and leathery skin, her smile was radiant. She offered Will a blackberry. "They're fresh, I just picked them."

George inhaled a mouthful of smoke. "Will, this is my wife Aubrey."

Authors' Notes and Acknowledgments

Underlying many works of fiction is a grain of truth. In *Hammon Falls* that truth is a sad moment in time unnoticed by the outside world: nearly a century ago a girl named Cora Hileman died in childbirth. She was not yet seventeen years old. All that remains of her is tucked away in an old family album: a few grainy photographs, some newspaper clippings, and a letter she wrote two days before she died. The events leading up to her death became the starting and ending points for *Hammon Falls*. Of all the characters and storylines in the novel, Cora's is nearest to the truth. There was no fevered escape by train to the East Coast, and perhaps no love story, but there was the pregnancy, the arrest, the courthouse marriage, the parting at the door, Cora's untimely death, and the improbable survival of her infant son, who was born infected, disfigured, and not breathing. It took only 33 words, half a sentence, to explain the real story. The other 113,000 words in *Hammon Falls* were the parts we made up.

While we're speaking of fiction, let us make it clear that Waterton, Iowa, does not exist. It borrows its history and geography, extensively but not exactly, from the very real city of Waterloo, Iowa. Historically, many of the events we portray in Waterton also happened in Waterloo. Some happened, but at different times, and some didn't happen at all. For instance, in Waterton a fictional gangster named Red Fisher is gunned down by police in an alley in March of 1934. In Waterloo, the real gangster Tommy Carroll, an associate of John Dillinger, died in the same manner, but three months later, in June of 1934. Also, in our story the fictional village of Hammon Falls votes whether or not to incorporate in 1937. In real life, the township of Rainbow did the same in 1939. A few of Waterloo's place names were retained for Waterton, but most were changed. Some of the businesses existed when and where we say they did (albeit with different names), while others did not. And so on. In short, Waterton is based on Waterloo, but it is not intended to *be* Waterloo. Where Waterloo suited our needs, we used it. Where it didn't, we didn't.

Now for the fun part. The authors would like to acknowledge the following kind people whose comments and suggestions provided much needed guidance: Carol Kean, Bob Schott, Jim Jetter, Kevin McKelvie, Barb Lewis, Bill Tate, and Brad Allen. Also, several of our friends graciously allowed us to use their first and/or last names for some of our minor characters: Whitney Erin DeVilbiss, Kristin Soliah, Hollie Hutt, Katherine Volmensky Gannett, Elyce Josephson, Paige Metzger, Ashley Ellen Etzel Grandstaff, Kathy and Jack Williams, Laura Carlin and her son Landon, Wayne Clayton, Dave Wanamaker, Robin Darland, Chuck

Hosier, and Paul Finch, who is also responsible for the "galleon" pun joke. Thanks, Paul…we think ☺. And, of course, we owe a special debt of gratitude to Phil and Deb Harris of All Things That Matter Press for their trust in publishing *Hammon Falls* and all their hard work in bringing it to fruition.

Finally, we'd like to thank co-author Roger Hileman's extended family, Hilemans all, people who are no longer with us but whose lives inspired us to write this novel: Lester and Celia, G.W. and Hannah, Bob and Elaine, and especially Cora Felton Hileman.

That said, all but one of the characters of *Hammon Falls* are inventions of the authors. Even then, while we borrowed some of the facts of Cora Hileman's life, the character of Cora Hammon is almost entirely speculation on our part. Otherwise, resemblance to real people is coincidental and unintentional. The historical personages who appear in *Hammon Falls* are used fictitiously.

About the Authors

Dave Hoing has been gainfully employed at the University of Northern Iowa's Rod Library for a very long time. Although he is a member of Science Fiction and Fantasy Writers of America with numerous short story publications, *Hammon Falls* is his first published novel. He has two stepchildren, Jon and Jovan Hampton, and lives in Waterloo, Iowa, with his wife Joni, a dog named Tree, and a cat named Toro.

Roger Hileman is a Test Development Associate for ACT, Inc. After spending many years as a local musician and playwright, he decided to make the transition to writing fiction. Hammon Falls is his first published novel. He has three daughters, Andrea, Rachel, and Carlye, and lives in Iowa City, Iowa, with his wife Lu.

ALL THINGS THAT MATTER PRESS ™

FOR MORE INFORMATION ON TITLES AVAILABLE FROM
ALL THINGS THAT MATTER PRESS, GO TO
http://allthingsthatmatterpress.com
or contact us at
allthingsthatmatterpress@gmail.com